MIAMI
HEAT

JEROME SANFORD

MIAMI

HEAT

ST. MARTIN'S PRESS ▬ NEW YORK

To Jeanie, Tracy, and David—
for believing in me.

MIAMI HEAT. Copyright © 1991 by Jerome Sanford. All rights reserved. Printed in the United States of America. No part of this book may be used or reproduced in any manner whatsoever without written permission except in the case of brief quotations embodied in critical articles or reviews. For information, address St. Martin's Press, 175 Fifth Avenue, New York, N.Y. 10010.

Production Editor: David Stanford Burr

Design by Judith Stagnitto

Library of Congress Cataloging-in-Publication Data

Sanford, Jerome.
    Miami heat / Jerome Sanford.
        p.   cm.
    "A Thomas Dunne book."
    ISBN 0-312-05469-6
    I. Title.
PS3569.A52625M5   1991
813'.54—dc20   90-20271
                                     CIP

First Edition: February 1991

10 9 8 7 6 5 4 3 2 1

MIAMI

HEAT

PROLOGUE

May 13, 1984
Islamorada, The Florida Keys

"It's not Estevez!"

"Who is it? Where's Roger?" David Knight fired the words into the ear of the man who had just dropped a frozen daiquiri in his lap.

Shouldering closer to the bar, the man reached for a stack of cocktail napkins and began wiping the bottom of Knight's soaked shirt. His face registered apology, but his lips barely moved when he whispered to Knight.

"I don't know. He says he's a DGI colonel. That's heavy, David. I don't like it; something's wrong," Miguel Torres said, then turned quickly and pushed his way back through the crowded room.

"Asshole!" Knight called drunkenly at Torres's back. He did not watch his informant wade farther into the noisy, jostling sun-tanned bodies replenishing themselves with rum and beer. He knew Torres, only a few inches over five feet, would soon disappear in the mélange of boisterous divers, boaters, and fishermen at this Sunday-afternoon drink fest.

That was precisely why Knight had chosen The Rum Barrel, however. Not only was it less than a two-hour drive from his FBI office in Miami; every Sunday afternoon from April through October, men and women addicted to water sports and the opposite sex jammed the sprawling, thatched-roof drinking landmark. The pulsing, inebriated shoulder-to-breast throng was a secure atmosphere for the meeting between two spies. Here, Knight had no need for constant visual surveillance; the sheer number of people disposed of any concern for his informant's safety. And this meet was not a drug deal with potentially violent traffickers; it was a meticulously arranged sit-down for Miguel and Roger Estevez. . . .

Dammit! Miguel had said Roger didn't show, that his contact is a colonel from the Cuban intelligence service. What the hell happened to Roger? I better check this guy out before Miguel gets in too deep, Knight thought, rubbing the four-day stubble on his cheek that he had grown for his own cover today.

Knight tilted his ragged straw hat lower so that its brim leveled with his sunglasses. He slid off the bar stool, staggered a few steps, then eased toward the direction Miguel had gone. As he neared the windows closest to the marina, he spotted the two men at a small table against the wall. Knight saw the Cuban colonel's profile, his jaw working furiously at Miguel, who sat with an obsequious look on his face. The din of voices and rock music obliterated any opportunity for Knight to overhear the conversation.

Knight shuffled to his right and took off his sunglasses, trying to get behind the colonel and catch Miguel's eye. Suddenly, the man shoved his chair back and stood up, glaring at Miguel. When he wheeled around abruptly and began to walk away,

Knight saw that he was easily six feet tall, with powerful shoulders and thickly muscled arms. A poorly healed scar seemed to circle his left forearm.

Knight stood in the colonel's path to the door, and he did not move away. He dropped his chin, keeping his eyes on the man moving swiftly toward him, then deliberately stumbled.

"*Estúpido!*" the colonel growled. He grabbed Knight's shoulders to shove him aside.

For an instant, they stared at each other. Knight had never seen eyes so black. They were feral and piercing, and Knight felt a shaft of fear reach into his stomach. But when the colonel strode toward the door, the feeling vanished.

Knight took a deep breath and walked back to the bar, abandoning Miguel. They would leave in separate cars and meet in Coral Gables two hours later if they were not followed. Knight hoped Miguel would have an answer about the missing Roger Estevez.

It had been two years since Knight had turned over Estevez, one of his best informants, to the CIA. But he knew he was way out of bounds today because he hadn't cleared the proposed Estevez meeting with the Agency. If the station chief of the CIA's Miami covert office found out about even this failed attempt to see Estevez, he would eat Knight for breakfast, lunch, and dinner.

Maybe it's better that Roger didn't show up, Knight thought. I'll just send Miguel back into Cuba to talk to him in Havana. The station chief won't have to know; it wouldn't be the first time I made an end run around the Agency without prior knowledge and permission. Anyway, that's just part of the game.

ONE *December 15, 1989*
Cuba

The simultaneous crack of five AK-47s sent five 7.62 mm bullets spinning through the slender Cuban's body, splintering his sternum and tumbling him into the shallow pit behind. One of the four enlisted men standing by moved the spotlight that had illuminated the man to shine on his twisted body. Three others then joined him and shoveled eighty pounds of lye into the hole, tromping in heavy, caked boots as they filled the makeshift grave with black clay from the fringe of the Zapata Swamp.

Colonel Eladio Ruiz, dressed warmly in the cold-weather uniform of the Cuban Revolutionary Armed Forces, listened to the clay splat into the hole. While the shovelers placed bits of shrubbery on top, he stepped forward and addressed each man of the firing squad with a salute and a handshake. An eerie glow from the spotlight gave their somber faces a ghostlike color of paste. Though they stood at attention, one shuddered as the wind wailed through the swamp.

Ruiz turned and squished through knee-high saw grass to his Russian Gaz, latched his seat belt, and nodded to his driver, Captain Rafael Herrera. As the four-wheel-drive vehicle bounced toward the highway that would take them to Cienfuegos, he looked at the luminous hands on his watch. They brightened when the December moon poked through the drifting cloud cover. It was 8:30.

He shivered and switched on the car's rarely used heater, then jammed his hands into the pockets of his olive serge greatcoat. Its musty smell annoyed him; it had been packed for over two years, and he had not worn it since he had returned from his post as senior military attaché of the Cuban embassy in Moscow.

The Gaz jerked and spun its wheels, kicking up gravel, when the driver reached the asphalt access road two miles from the main highway. Scanning the dark, desolate marsh on both sides, Ruiz muttered, "*Apúrate!*" "Faster!" to his aide. He was anxious to know whether the contact had been made in Miami tonight. A sudden gust rocked the Gaz, and Ruiz wondered whether his agent in Miami felt the same bitter chill piercing his bones.

MIAMI

Raul did not like the Ruger Mark II bulging inside the waistband of his grease-stained jeans. He always thought .22-caliber pistols were for *niños*, babies, not for action men like himself. A Colt .45 was his favorite: He loved its glistening chrome, its heft in his hand, and the nearly half-inch hole the bullet made when it buried into human tissue.

Two days ago, however, El Aura told him he had to take the Ruger with a five-inch silencer. Raul pleaded for permission to bring his .45, but El Aura was adamant and dismissed him with a backhanded wave.

Tears in his eyes, Raul cursed and kicked at stones on the hot, dusty road as he walked the mile back to his quarters. And his lovely .45 had stayed in Mexico.

Now, he shifted the Ruger. The cold steel silencer felt like an icicle rubbing against the flesh of his right buttock, sending a shiver into his body. The insides of his thighs were beginning to numb after two hours in the chill night air, and he suppressed the urge to urinate for a third time. A blast of cold wind from Biscayne Bay, a hundred yards east, caught him flush in the face. His ears stung, as if a boxer had pounded them with left and right hooks. He cupped his hands over both sides of his head, shielding his ears.

Coño, he thought, this is Miami, not Union City. Why is it so cold? It must be forty degrees by now! How much longer do we have to wait? *Mierda!* Shit! When is that *maricón* going to come out of his office?

He squinted at the roof of Mercy Hospital. Against dense and shapeless clouds, Raul spotted El Aura's form, night-vision binoculars to his eyes, outlined near the parapet of the northeast corner of the building. Raul ached for the sign—three rapid flashlight blips—that signaled the doctor had left his fifth-floor office in the Professional Building that rose tall into the black night, seventy yards across from the hospital. He slammed his right fist into the palm of his left hand when he saw a dim glow coming from the window high above.

Raul turned back to look under the upraised hood of the car parked in the shadows of giant ficus trees. He was not a mechanic, but the grease on his jacket and pants told an observer Raul had spent a long day working on automobiles. A dirty, crumpled New York Yankees cap perched on his head. His superior on the last three operations, Colonel Jorge Posada, sat in the cab of the tow truck stolen six hours earlier from a Plantation service station twenty-two miles north of Miami. With a false license plate and repainted signs on its doors, it would not be discovered for days, certainly not tonight.

The tow truck was backed up to the car Raul was looking into, a five-hundred-dollar junker bought from an ad in *The Miami Herald*, cash, no questions asked. Since they had arrived at the Professional Building's parking lot and found the DOCTOR'S ONLY section at eight o'clock, Jorge, sixteen years senior to Raul, had stayed inside the truck. That was not part of the plan; it was simply Jorge's use of authority that kept him warm while Raul stomped and cursed and held his bladder.

Raul walked to the other side of the truck, away from the wind and the Professional Building. He leaned against the wheel well, folded his arms tightly across his chest, and, for the shortest of moments, closed his eyes to think of the warm sun and the tanned bikini bodies at Varadero Beach. But even that brief reverie was too long.

"*Estúpido!* What are you doing?" Jorge said with a gravelly whisper, standing next to Raul. "He signaled two times! Are you crazy? *Vamos!*" Jorge grabbed Raul by the arm and spun him around the truck.

Raul caught his balance and looked at Jorge with a frown of embarrassment. He turned without speaking, and both walked to the entrance of the doctor's building. Each took a position in the shadows on both sides of the electronic sliding doors, out of view from the lobby. Raul's neck suddenly broke out in a sweat. His pulse began to race, and he felt his lips smack from saliva spilling into his mouth. As he pressed his shoulders against the wall, he took the Ruger out of his belt and held it tightly to the back of his thigh. He saw Jorge's dark profile begin to move.

Two footsteps sounded on the rubber-covered pressure plate on the floor of the lobby. The hydraulic motor engaged with a click, and the glass doors hissed as they parted on rubber tracks. The man who stepped out paused and set his briefcase on the ground. He pulled up the collar on his raincoat, picked up his briefcase, and began to walk with his head tucked away from the blustering wind.

Before Dr. Victor Milian took his fourth step, Jorge was in a crouch behind his back. Raul moved toward them. With a blurring motion, Jorge's left arm drew back as his right arm shot forward. The brass knuckles on his fist drove into the doctor's right kidney. As Milian's body buckled, Raul grabbed his right arm to hold him upright. Jorge threw another karate punch at the left kidney, then held the man's left elbow to keep him from lurching forward. The blows made no sound, and the two groans from the doctor were muffled and lost in the stiff breeze.

The punches had more effect than the men desired, though. Milian fell to his knees and almost passed out. Instead of hustling him quickly into his car, they had to lift and drag him. The toes of the doctor's shoes scraped loudly on the asphalt. *"Apúrate! Apúrate!"* Jorge whispered loudly in his victim's ear. Milian began to take staggered steps as Jorge and Raul forced him to move faster.

They slammed him into the side of his 1982 Chrysler New Yorker. The man was flabby, no match for the senior agent's strength. At forty-five, Jorge had the lean, muscular build of a man fifteen years younger. *"Las llaves! Dónde está las llaves?"* "Where are the keys?" he asked, squeezing the doctor's fleshy bicep.

Jorge had read Milian's description in the surveillance reports, but now, for the first time, he looked at the face of his target. The gray bushy eyebrows could not hide the terror in the man's wide eyes. His face had a bluish pallor under the parking lot arc lights, but it was not from the weather—it was fear. When he tried to answer Jorge, the words stuck in his tightened larynx. He began to gag.

Raul pushed the silencer tube hard into Milian's right kidney. Breathless, the doctor pointed to his left coat pocket. Jorge let go of the man's arm, slid his hand into the pocket, and pulled out the car keys.

He opened the door and tossed the keys to Raul, who ran to the passenger's side and got in. With a vicious shove, Jorge pushed the doctor behind the steering wheel, shut the door carefully, and went back to the tow truck.

Milian's mouth twisted from the pain in his back. He looked at Raul, who motioned to the ignition with his pistol. The doctor's hands shook as he missed the key slot twice. The car whined loudly when it finally started, and crept forward toward the parking lot's entrance. Raul sneered through his crooked teeth, even more yellow in the glow of the dashboard lights, and reached across to turn off the headlights. He motioned with his arm and the doctor turned left, heading east. The tow truck, parking lights on, pulled in behind the car.

They were on the perimeter service road of the hospital, traveling away from the Bayshore Drive entrance and the arc lamps that illuminated the front of the building like the Orange Bowl during a night football game. But the perimeter road that circled behind the hospital, following the Biscayne Bay shoreline, was shrouded in darkness. Although it had two lanes of concrete, there was no visible separation between the road and the ten-yard grassy strip that divided black water from black land. As the car and truck curved to the south, the lights disappeared and the shadows of the hospital enveloped the vehicles.

Raul jabbed the silencer into the doctor's shoulder and ordered him to drive onto the grass, then to stop short of the eight-inch seawall. On the other side of that abutment, bay water lapped gently against the cement, three feet below. It was high tide. The water was at least seven feet deep.

Milian struggled for breath with loud gasps, his mouth wide open, dragging in oxygen. The windows of the car fogged quickly, and his view of the outside world was cut off. His hands clenched the steering wheel so hard, the veins on his wrists stood out. His forearms shook with uncontrollable spasms.

Raul set the pistol in his lap and opened the doctor's briefcase on top of it. With a penlight, he rustled through medical and laboratory reports. He flipped the pages of Milian's daily diary, then held it up and shook it. He turned every document over, looking at the reverse side. Sweat was beading on his forehead.

"*Mierda!*" Raul said, still looking in the briefcase. He threw it on the floor and opened the glove compartment. Maps, pencils, parking receipts, and tissue. The skinny agent scraped them out in a frenzy.

He glared at Milian. His jaw was set forward and his lips stretched thinly across his face. Grabbing the pistol, he turned his body and placed the silencer on the doctor's cheekbone. The small hole in the barrel pointed at Milian's right eye. The doctor shrank back, pushing his body against the door.

Raul slid toward the doctor, pressing the cold silencer harder. Then he lowered the barrel, inching it down Milian's chest until it reached his heart. "Don't move. I'm coming back," he said, shoving the pistol into the doctor's soft flesh. He grabbed the keys from the ignition and left the car.

Raul stood next to Jorge's open window, teeth chattering angrily as the wind chilled his sweating body. "It is not there! I looked at every damn piece of paper in the damn briefcase. I told you he would not have it with him. Why didn't you listen to me? It has to be in his office. The *mierdas* must have missed it when they searched!"

"You are the *mierda*," Jorge said in a low voice. "And stop shouting. You will wake the cripples, and then we will both be *mierda*—and worse. They did not miss it in the search. You are certain you looked everywhere? Yes, of course you are. Perhaps he already got rid of it. But we do not have time to wonder, or to talk. We must finish this, now."

His teeth began chattering again, but this time Raul was afraid. Afraid of the consequences of failure and the report Jorge would write about this mission. "Yes, yes, you are right," he whispered, looking at the black sky. "We must finish it, yes."

Jorge handed him a flashlight through the window. "Give El Aura the signal, Raul. And give me the pistol."

Raul held the Ruger by the grip. His forefinger curled next to the trigger. Then he handed the gun to Jorge, butt first. He stepped to the hood of the truck and scanned the roofline of the hospital. When he saw the dark figure, he pointed the flashlight at El Aura. Two longs, one short. Repeat. Two longs, one short. After the response of one long beam, the figure disappeared. Raul thought he felt El Aura's disgust in that ray of light. He gave the flashlight back to Jorge, and turned to walk to the car.

"Raul. Wait. I will go with you." Jorge was out of the truck, striding to catch up. He put his hand gently on the back of Raul's neck. "My friend, let me talk to him."

Jorge eased the car door open, and the dome light came on. Milian fell heavily sideways, his head and shoulders hanging down through the open door. Jorge caught the man's coat collar and pushed him back upright while Raul got in on the other side. As Raul sat down and shut the door, Jorge saw Milian's sweat-drenched shirt and the wet crotch of his pants. The stench of fear entered Jorge's nostrils, but it did not make him sick. After twenty-four years, he was used to it.

"Doctor, I presume you know what we are looking for. You know we are not delinquents. We are doing our job, just as you do yours. If you tell us where it is, I assure you your death will be more pleasant." Jorge saw Milian's eyes widen. He put his hand over the doctor's quivering mouth as it opened. "Please, let me finish. You did not think we would allow you to live, did you? No, of course not. And as a doctor, you know some deaths are more pleasant than others, no? There are many ways to die." His black eyes stared without blinking into Milian's face. "So, my friend, do you have an answer for us?" He took his hand away and wiped the spittle on Milian's lapel.

Milian put his chin on his chest and cleared his throat. Raul's breath was hot, panting on the doctor's neck and right ear. Looking up, Milian squirmed on the seat and turned his head toward Jorge. His lower jaw still quivered as the words came out.

"Yes, I know of death. I have seen many deaths, more than I care to think of, and too many from the hands of people like you." Milian's voice was hoarse and raspy from his dry throat. He took a deep breath and swallowed. "I know what you want, but I do not have it. I knew your people were watching me, and I knew that someone like you would come, and probably try to kill me. I do not deny that I am frightened, frightened by the thought of my death. But I am not frightened of you."

"*Maricón!*" Raul yelled, and slapped Milian's right ear with his open hand. As he began to strike it again, Jorge grabbed his wrist and glared at Raul.

Milian put his hand to the right side of his face. His eyes were closed, but his body was no longer shaking.

"As you wish. Unfortunately, Doctor, we have no choice. We cannot waste any more time. We will find it eventually, and you will be dead." Jorge waited for a reaction, and thought for a moment about Milian's last words. But he saw that the fear had left the doctor's eyes, and knew there would be no response. He opened the door and pressed the doorjamb spring button so the interior lights would not flash on. A strong gust swept into the car, catching the side of Jorge's face, and his eyes began to tear. The wind muffled his voice when he said, "Good-bye, Doctor."

Just before he closed the door, he gave a curt command to Raul: "Do it." Then he pushed his weight against the door until it clicked shut.

Raul took his eyes off of Milian to watch Jorge's image through the fogged windows. It was like an apparition, eerily fading into the darkness. Raul, who secretly practiced Santeria, the Cuban religious cult with rituals similar to Haitian voodoo, believed Jorge had the gift of magic. He had seen it before, and now he had seen it again.

It is his eyes, Raul thought, he has it in his eyes. Even I cannot look into them without having to look away. It is as if he reads my mind with his eyes. And *coño*, look what he did with this *mierde* doctor. After I scare the piss out of him, Jorge tells him he is going to die, that we are going to kill him. And what happens? The doctor is no longer afraid! I am going to kill him, right now, yet he has the look of a man who has just lit up a delicious Monte Cristo.

The rumble of the tow truck's engine jolted Raul away from his thoughts. But he did not grin or sneer as he usually did before he killed. His movements were deliberate, as if in slow motion. He gripped Milian's right wrist to force him against the steering wheel and felt his pulse beating steadily but not rapidly. Raul did not have to push; Milian complied. When he put his hand on the back of the doctor's head to press it on the steering wheel, there was no resistance.

Raul began to feel nervous and afraid. He could not understand how Milian had been so terrified before, but when death was seconds away, he was calm and even compliant. Raul liked his victims to fight back: He knew they could not win, and he received immense pleasure from their screams and useless efforts. This was the first time Jorge had ever talked to one, and it made the act of killing very confusing to Raul.

He knew he would carry it out, though, even though he did not like the plan. The death had to appear like an automobile accident, so there could be none of the violence on which he thrived. But as he focused on the plan and his disappointment, his thoughts of Jorge left. He would get his satisfaction. He began to salivate as he took out the twelve-inch pipe with ten ounces of extra steel fused, knoblike, at one end. Raul held it by the tacky rubber grip on the other end.

He wrapped a chamois cloth around the weighted end and secured it with a heavy rubber band. Testing its heft, he saw that Milian's eyes were closed. Raul fixed his eyes on a point two inches in front of the doctor's right ear, as if he was about to drive a nail into a plank. With his mind empty of any thought, he raised the pipe and, with all his strength, clubbed Milian's skull. He had been told only to render him unconscious, but he did not pull back on the blow as Jorge had instructed him. His heart beat rapidly as he felt the rush of adrenaline.

The doctor's head slid off the steering wheel and rested against the door. Raul reached across the seat to feel for a pulse in the carotid artery. There was none. He pulled the body away from the door, sat it up, and placed the hands in its lap. He put the keys into the ignition and shifted the transmission lever into neutral.

Raul left the car, making sure the interior lights did not come on. He walked around the rear and gave a hand signal to Jorge. Then he carefully opened the driver's door, lowered the power window, and closed the door. He waved to Jorge, who eased the tow truck forward until its large rubber bumper made contact with the rear of the Chrysler. Raul reached into the Chrysler with both hands and began to turn the steering wheel, angling it toward the seawall, as the truck pushed the car forward. When it was within eight feet of the abutment, he raised one hand to Jorge, telling him to stop. Raul was sweating heavily, and his Yankees cap had blown away. But the car was positioned perfectly.

He turned the ignition on and put the other power windows down two inches from the top. With both arms up, he waved Jorge forward. Raul heard the truck's engine rev up in neutral. When Jorge engaged first gear, the truck's rear wheels spun, caught the grass, and accelerated into the rear of the Chrysler. The luxury car lurched forward and skimmed over the abutment as if it were picked up and thrown. Like a killer whale rolling, it turned over slowly in the air and entered the water with its grill pointed down. Raul saw Milian's body bounce upward and sideways inside the car.

The top hit the water with a loud splash, spraying saltwater into Raul's eyes. He rubbed them with his dirty cuffs in time to see the wheels, transmission shaft, and muffler sink below the black water. Small waves bumped against the seawall. Raul could not see the air bubbles breaking the surface, but he heard the gurgling and then a muffled scraping sound as metal crunched on coral rock. He squinted, trying to see whether any object floated out of the car. Nothing. The water was calm. And the night air was still. Raul got into the truck and Jorge drove back to the paved road.

Neither man saw nor heard the small inflatable raft and the two men in black wet suits paddling slowly to the spot where the

Chrysler submerged. The taillights of the tow truck were barely visible when the divers slipped into the water.

As Jorge steered the truck out the service exit of the hospital, Raul's heart still pounded from the adrenaline pumping through his veins. He wanted to let loose with a joyous yell to show Jorge the ecstasy he was feeling. But Jorge looked through the windshield with unblinking eyes, as if Raul were not even in the truck.

Tomorrow I will celebrate, Raul thought. I will not have to see or think about Jorge in Mexico. I will grab a whore and get drunk for two days. Fuck Jorge. No, fuck the whore. He laughed to himself. Then I will talk to El Aura about Jorge, and tell him it was Jorge's fault. El Aura will know what to do, and I will have a new partner.

He closed his eyes, tilted his head back, and remembered the baseball cap. Shit! That will go into Jorge's report also. Coño, so what? It was a piece of shit, anyway. I will write my own report this time, Jorge, you shit! I will think up a good story tomorrow. Right now, I want to think about fucking the whore.

Jorge steered the truck north on Seventeenth Avenue. He pulled off in front of the 7-Eleven convenience store across Dixie Highway, avoiding the bright lights in the parking lot. He saw two men standing by the outdoor telephone near the entrance. Each was holding a small brown paper bag with a can inside. When they brought the cans to their lips at the same time, Jorge looked at Raul.

"They are here. Get out and walk north. They will pick you up at Twenty-third Street, one block before Coral Way. Move. Now."

Jorge was driving away by the time Raul had both feet on the ground. There was no need to look back; he would never see Raul again.

He is no better than a Mariel delinquent and has no business working for the Cuban intelligence service, he thought. I will make certain he receives the usual disciplinary punishment. Anyway, I have always operated better by myself. There is too much at stake to rely on such incompetents. This mission must be accomplished according to my methods.

Still, Jorge was angry because they failed to find the message Victor Milian was said to be carrying. If the doctor had already delivered it, the plan could be in severe jeopardy. Jorge would have to use any means necessary to find that letter, or whoever had it.

And if other deaths are required, I shall be the sole executioner, he thought, allowing himself a thin smile. In fact, that would be excellent preparation for the final act.

TWO
December 16
Miami

David Knight walked toward the seven-foot double doors that held the bold brass letters LAW OFFICES OF PAUL S. SINGER. No light shone beneath the space at the bottom. Fishing through the change in his pocket, he took out the gold handcuff key chain Kathy had given him and opened the door.

He flipped on the light and picked up the weekend mail strewn on the floor. When he dumped it on Maria's desk, he saw Paul's yellow stick-up note on the secretary's telephone: "David—Maria quit Friday. I've got a part-timer coming in. Talk to you around ten on Monday." Knight crumpled the note and browsed through the mail. He picked out one computer-addressed letter and recognized the pink paper in the window envelope. It was a notice for the sentencing of an armed robber, a court-appointed case Paul had given him.

Tossing his blue blazer on the chair next to his desk, Knight leaned against the narrow table in front of the tenth-floor window. His crewneck sweater felt bulky on his lean frame, but he was glad he wore it in the early-morning chill.

He watched the rush-hour traffic streaming north into downtown Miami along Brickell Avenue, a chrome and glass canyon penetrated by long slivers of sunlight angling through tall office buildings. Scurrying tenants, mostly lawyers and bank employees, hurried past the front fountain and spun through the revolving doors he had entered minutes earlier. A hot-dog vendor steamed his wares under a broad umbrella on the corner, hoping to catch a hungry worker who had skipped breakfast.

The bustling activity on the ground held little interest for Knight, however. His eyes followed the street running west from the intersection below, stretching farther than he could see, deep into the Everglades and on up the west coast of Florida. Early settlers had called it the Tamiami Trail, until it became U.S. Highway 41. On the City of Miami map, it is S.W. 8th Street. But for the last twelve years, Knight knew the four-mile section from Miami Avenue to Lejeune Road as Calle Ocho, the throbbing heartbeat of Little Havana and the embodiment of everything bad and good he had done as a special agent of the Federal Bureau of Investigation. Two months ago, at forty-four, a new career as a criminal defense attorney had put him into this office in a luxury building.

Calle Ocho was more than a landmark street that displayed the phenomenal success stories of Cuban immigrants fleeing the tyranny of Fidel Castro. Knight knew it held more secrets than Houdini had taken to his grave; and when it came to illusions, that master magician had had no more than a foil-gum wrapper in his bag of tricks compared to the halls of mirrors and multiple images created in the bodegas and safe houses of Little Havana.

"David! *Qué pasa?* Work, work, you're a lawyer now. You gotta think dollar signs, buddy. No more of that spook stuff or public servant crap." Paul Singer bobbed his head into the doorway. His suit coat hung on a finger over his shoulder and a tie, unknotted, draped around his shirt collar. He held a duffel bag in his other hand.

Knight smiled, trying to pull his thoughts away from the past before he answered. He saw that Singer had been to the health club early this morning.

Singer took a few steps in and fingered three ceramic figurines on the desk. "My God, look at your desk. You still don't have one goddamn piece of paper on it, just these half-assed monkeys. It doesn't even look like a lawyer's desk. You gotta have piles of papers; you need shit all over it if you want to impress clients. Tonight I'm gonna empty my wastebasket on your desk so you know what I mean. Listen to me, David, I know what I'm talking about. You need to at least look like you're busy."

"Sorry, Paul. It's habit. I always clear my desk and lock the drawers. I guess it's just a hard one to break."

"Jesus, what is this? You got the plans for the next invasion of Cuba stuck away in there? Maybe an atom bomb that fits in a stapler? C'mon, David, I want to make you some money. It isn't that hard, believe me. And if that won't change your habits, I don't know what will."

Twisting to look at the walls, Singer shook his head in mock dismay. "When the hell are you going to hang something up in here? Where's your degree? Don't you even have a picture of Jesus or something? This room looks like a goddamn jail cell."

Singer didn't wait for a response. "Hey, where's the new girl? Goddamn Maria, two years I treated her like a queen and she dumps on me. I don't believe it; now I gotta train someone all over." His voice trailed his steps as he walked away from Knight to his own office.

Knight was used to Paul Singer's abruptness. They had been friends for more than twenty years, since both were law students at Northwestern in Chicago. In early 1968, the first year they met, the competition for law review was fierce, almost ruthless. The selection process narrowed down to Knight and Singer for the last slot. With identical grade point averages, the dean decided to choose one from a joint interview.

Knight was at an immediate disadvantage. In the classroom, he dreaded any question from a professor. When he stood to answer, his knees became rubber bands. The bright fluorescent ceiling bulbs made him blink foolishly. When he tried to speak, his saliva turned to cotton. It was always a painful experience that no amount of mental fortification could overcome.

However, everyone in the law school knew that Singer's goal was to become a trial lawyer. He had the tenacity and abrasive personality of a tough cross-examiner, and his acerbic tongue had intimidated even two of the younger instructors.

The interview went badly for Knight. He had the legal knowledge to answer the dean's questions, but his stammering replies twisted the meaning into what seemed like faulty reasoning. Singer, less versed in the intricacies of the law, used a seasoned trial lawyer's technique: If you don't have the law, argue the facts; if you don't have the facts, argue the law; and if you don't have the law or the facts, argue louder than your adversary. Singer didn't know the facts or the law, but he buried Knight with an onslaught of legalese that sounded as if he knew what he was talking about. And he got the slot.

Their enmity ended the next semester, however, when Knight, quarterbacking the law school's intramural football team, found that the sticky fingers of his favorite receiver belonged to Paul Singer. After combining for twelve touchdowns in the first four games, Knight and Singer were dousing as much beer over each other's head as they were drinking in postgame celebrations. Knight's take-charge leadership ability on the field seemed to contradict the deferential attitude he displayed at the law school. It showed a cool reserve under pressure and an ability to get people to give their best effort for a common cause. It was a side of his personality that Paul Singer liked and encouraged, and their friendship grew stronger because of it.

To many, it seemed like a strange affinity. A close relationship between the brash Jewish kid from Chicago's north side and the soft-spoken Presbyterian from the suburbs should have been a cultural anomaly. In another sense, though, it evidenced a trait

Knight possessed that was not easily detected by others who thought they knew him well. He had an instinctive ability to attract opposites, a sensitive empathy that led someone like Paul Singer to place absolute trust and confidence in him. It was so deeply ingrained in his personality that Knight was not even aware of its existence until years later.

Months before graduation, Knight realized he did not possess the cutthroat, competitive instinct necessary to succeed in the practical side of law—the business of making money. He enjoyed jousting with legal issues, but he lacked any concern or motivation for the end-zone goal of putting dollars in his pockets.

In his senior year, his emotions were transformed by what was happening across, and to, the United States. John F. Kennedy's inauguration address from 1961 still rang loudly in his ears; he wanted—needed—to do something for his country. His friends, other than Paul Singer, were puzzled by this new interest. He never had been stirred to any intellectual passion in his undergraduate days; in fact, no one could recall Knight ever taking a strong, visceral stand on any issue.

In law school, though, he watched the country plunge into a whirlpool of political chaos and social upheaval. His view of the action was not at all distant; he dwelled on vivid and brutal scenes of the riots after Martin Luther King's assassination and the Democratic National Convention in Chicago in 1968. In June, when Bobby Kennedy met death on a hotel floor in Los Angeles, angry sorrow sat like a chip on his shoulder for months afterward.

Knight's thoughts of the nation in crisis burrowed so deeply that his grades declined drastically in his last semester. But in the space of one year, his embryonic idealism crystalized into an absolutist belief in good and evil, of right and wrong, and a compelling need to bring decency and law and order to an imperfect world. The Savior Syndrome clamped to his conscience like a vise.

Six months after graduation, David Knight was at the FBI Academy at Quantico and Paul Singer tried his first murder case as a neophyte criminal defense lawyer in Chicago. And although they rarely saw each other over the next eight years, their friendship stayed strong through correspondence and long-distance calls.

When Singer's parents retired and moved to Fort Lauderdale in 1977, he gave up his lucrative practice in Chicago and moved to be close to them. He took a job as a federal prosecutor with the United States Attorney's Office in Miami to test the legal waters and establish a reputation in south Florida. He also knew he would have a good time in "The Magic City," even if he was starting over: David Knight had been working in the Miami Field Office of the FBI since 1975.

It didn't take long for either to become well known in the legal community, but not because of Elliot Ness-like attacks on crime. When they joined a Justice Department team in a law firm football league, six of the most high-powered firms in Miami were decimated by Knight's arm and Singer's hands.

Surprisingly, though, their work did not bring them into professional contact. Singer was struggling with a mountainous caseload of drug-smuggling conspiracy cases from the Drug Enforcement Administration; but the FBI never came near those back-alley violations of federal law in the late seventies. Old crag-faced J. Edgar Hoover would have risen from his grave to stop his button-down-collared agents from soiling their hands in that trade.

As close as Knight and Singer were socially, David rarely mentioned his work to Paul. If Singer probed, Knight gently deflected and changed the subject. Assistant United States Attorneys were charged with trying the cases that client federal enforcement agencies brought them. Of course, the FBI was one of those clients, but David Knight's squad rarely made official arrests that ended up as public prosecutions. Knight prowled different dark alleys than the enforcement side of the FBI; he was a counterintelligence agent, and had earned a reputation as one of the best in the Bureau by turning spies into double agents.

Now, Knight and Singer were in private practice together. Most observers of the legal scene in Miami thought it was a natural evolution for two good friends. But one had left the government by choice, for the "greenback" pastures of a criminal law practice; the other could not comprehend why he had been forced to leave the job he had loved.

Knight picked up the newspaper Singer had dropped on his desk a few minutes earlier. He pulled out the local section first, another routine of his years as an agent in Miami. Few days passed that he did not recognize a name, an incident, or a location that had a past or future meaning. Even though he was no longer an agent, it was a habit of curiosity he could not break.

Experience had taught him that intelligence was, more than anything else, a laborious fact-gathering process. But the imposing demands of counterintelligence placed no limit on the type of information he collected. He analyzed everything that came before his eyes with the scrutiny of a microbiologist searching for an unknown disease. Most often, that evaluation required a three-dimensional view of the most innocuous-appearing detail, looking for obvious and well-hidden meanings. It was tedious and time-consuming, but always necessary; he could not afford to overlook or take anything for granted. Knight operated under the epistemological axiom adopted by every counterintelligence agent: All things are truly possible. And in Miami, that belief made a counterintelligence agent's task as formidable as in any city of the world.

For David Knight, the Miami newspapers presented nearly as much raw data as the FBI's reftels, airtels, and daily interviews. Miami's reputation as a modern Casablanca was not just a popular catchphrase; the city was a magnet for operatives and conspirators from every continent, hatching every conceivable plot. Its news media was often more adept than government agencies in ferreting out pieces of complex, clandestine puzzles, even if they were never painted with all the colors. Knight always stood ready with a brush and palette to complete the picture.

Today, however, the section was thin; not a murder, not a crime, not even an allegation of corruption against a public official challenged his curiosity. As he folded the newspaper, he saw the photo of a young woman in the obituary notices. That was a section he never read, because of the anxiety even that brief glimpse of the picture evoked. It was an emotion that constricted his throat and forced him to take deep breaths. Knight was shaken by death when it came to someone so young, with so much for which to live. He had shut more intense feelings behind a locked door seven years ago, and had sealed it with the bricks and mortar of psychic numbness. Obituaries of young people always threatened to chip at that defense, so he diverted his eyes to a side column. A short paragraph drew his attention.

CUBAN DOCTOR DROWNING VICTIM
Victor Milian, a Miami internist whose office was in the Mercy Hospital Professional Building, died last night when his auto accidentally ran off the perimeter road behind the hospital. The vehicle was submerged in eight feet of water in Biscayne Bay. A trained scuba diver, Milian was unable to exit the car. Milian came to Miami from Cuba five years ago. He is survived by his wife, Ana.

Knight put the paper on his desk and rubbed his right cheek, curious about the doctor's name. His eyes narrowed, unfocused. Milian, Victor Milian. His mind flipped names and images like a computer screen, and then it came up with a hit. Knight remembered that Ben Warden, another member of the Bureau's counterintelligence squad, handled "listeners," low-level spies of the DGI, the Cuban intelligence service. "Listeners" was the designation the FBI gave to dozens of Cuban operatives in Miami sent by

Fidel to gather gossip, rumors, and intelligence on prominent Cuban exiles. One of those agents handled by Warden, Knight recalled, was named Milian.

Most "listeners" were benign and warranted only occasional spot checks by the surveillance squad. Yet in the violent war against Castro in the seventies, some functioned as an early warning system, monitoring the virulent anti-Castro activists who carried out bombings and assassinations against Fidel's interests, including his foreign diplomats. But that era had passed, and now the "listeners" were more concerned with giving Fidel precise reports on the activities of rising successful exile businessmen and politicians.

Knight wondered whether this Victor Milian was Warden's "listener," and he was bothered by the newspaper's account of the accident. He knew how the perimeter road behind Mercy Hospital ran adjacent to Biscayne Bay; it was a service road, not a route that a doctor or a patient would take to go in or out of the hospital grounds.

His suspicion grew when he recalled that Warden once had told Knight he thought that Milian might also have operated for the FAR, the Cuban army. Knight had seen CIA intelligence reports alleging that some DGI assassins were recruited from the Cuban military special services. He let his mind wander into speculation. If Victor Milian fell into that category, his "accident" could have been a hit. Maybe a retaliation?

But why kill a Cuban agent in Miami now? The exile activists have been dormant for years; are they cranking up again? With communism dying all around the world, maybe they think it's a good time to pull Fidel off his throne. Who else would have the guts and the motive to pull off something like that?

With stark chagrin, Knight halted his futile inquiry. Why the hell should I care if a Cuban agent gets killed here? It's none of my business now . . . and there's not a damn thing I could do about it even if I wanted to.

"David! What about the hearing yesterday? What happened with the motion for bond reduction?" Singer called from his office. "C'mere and tell me what the judge did."

Dammit! The goddamn bond hearing! Paul's shout shunted Knight's musings aside. He got up slowly and walked into Singer's office to confess.

THREE

Singer sat behind a shiny ebony desk with the telephone crooked between his shoulder and right ear. Letters, court pleadings, and split-open books littered the desktop. Four crushed cigarette butts stood in the ashtray, where a fifth sent wafting smoke trails into the air. Case folders, strewn on the floor next to his chair, tried to contain protruding legal papers.

Singer clutched a brown legal file in both hands, ruffling through the clipped pleadings. "Hal, give me a goddamn minute, I've got it in the file. I'm looking for it right now." Holding up a flat palm to Knight, Singer motioned him to sit in a black leather chair.

Knight disregarded the command and stepped to the wall of windows, twenty feet of a panoramic view of Biscayne Bay. The sun was a white beach ball, casting silver sparkles on the choppy water. Even in the cool morning, it was blistering the noses and shoulders of the northern snowbirds who mistakenly thought that six hours of maximum exposure would turn their skins to golden bronze.

To the south, cars and vans coursed over the humpbacked Rickenbacker Bridge, trekking to the beaches at Crandon Park on Key Biscayne. Two sailboats, jibs billowing, tacked in the brisk northeast wind for the open seas past Cape Florida. North, to Knight's left, gleaming cruise ships moored at Dodge Island were filling with Caribbean-bound tourists. Bleached buildings of Miami Beach poked into the eastern sky, spilling out hotel guests trying to outspend each other with tips to the cabana boys for the best chaise lounges by the pools.

These were the images Miami sent to the frigid snowbound cities of the Midwest and Northeast, postcards of a paradise in the warm sun, tropical breezes guaranteed to chase away chills and worries, palm trees and Orange Bowl princesses around every pool. Get out of your overcoat and galoshes, put on a bathing suit and sandals, feel the pulsing beat of Latin rhythms. *No problema, señores y señoritas.* Look in the mirror—it's magic!

But they were not the images of Miami Knight had viewed as an FBI agent in Miami. His had been kaleidoscopic shades of gray, never black and white, and certainly not the pastel promises promoted by the chamber of commerce and the tourist bureau. The members of those organizations had a greater interest in hiding the pictures Knight had in his portfolio. In fact, he knew of some who deliberately did so, for self-interested reasons. But when David Knight looked into Miami's shadows, he saw a seething cesspool of underground pipelines, connecting some of the most deadly and dangerous people and organizations in the world; a volatile, combustible mixture of intrigue, crime, and politics heating in the sun.

He heard Singer winding up the conversation. When he sat in the chair, he felt like a ball in the deep pocket of a baseball glove. The leather aroma surrounded him as he sunk into it. It was a chair he never liked to leave, but he knew it was also Paul's subtle way of ensuring a captive audience.

"So what happened? Did he reduce the bond? Did the guy's family show up?" Paul never asked one question.

Knight took a deep breath. "I forgot about the hearing. I didn't show up." Enough said.

"What? You gotta be kidding. I don't believe it. Jesus, David, what do you mean, you forgot it? How the hell did you forget it?" Singer rocked in his high-backed chair and looked at the ceiling.

"Paul, I'm sorry. I was at the library checking some old news clips, trying to find an article. I got involved and forgot the time. I tried calling the judge's office, but he wouldn't wait. I had it reset for Friday." Knight hated to make excuses. Worse, he hated to let Paul down.

"Listen, I got two grand cash in my pocket for you for that hearing. They already paid me. My God, I'm gonna get a phone call from Manolo and he's gonna ream my ass but good. What the hell am I gonna tell him?" He clasped his hands and clutched his chest.

Knight did not answer the rhetorical question. There was nothing he could say.

Singer leaned forward. He put his elbows on the papers on his desk and ran his fingers through the thin black wisps of hair high on his forehead. His voice was calm.

"The library again. All right, tell me. No, let me tell you. You're looking up shit again. You got another bug up your ass because of that goddamn FBI crap.

"David, I keep telling you: Let it go. *Let it go*. It's over, finished, you gotta get on with your life. How many times do I have to tell you, there's not a damn thing you can do now. You can't do anything. You should know that better than anyone. You had to do it with Kathy; you gotta do it now."

Knight tensed. His eyes widened and he glared at his friend. Kathy's name triggered the painful memory.

It had been eight years ago, that terrible accident, when their car had plunged off a winding North Carolina road into a rain-swollen stream on the last day of their vacation. Knight freed himself from his seat belt and escaped through the window, but the rapids swept the car swiftly downstream, dragging it away from him when he tried to reach Kathy and Jill. He swam after it frantically until he saw the white water rolling it over and over, carrying his wife and daughter farther away. The car finally crashed against two river boulders, upside down, nearly a mile from the point where it had entered the water. Still thrashing in the stream, Knight had floated into it twenty minutes later. He had been the first to find their bodies.

Kathy and Jill had been the only two people he had ever wanted and loved so deeply in his life. Mired in grief after their deaths, he turned to his work as a counterintelligence agent for solace. There, he found he could seal his psychic pain behind a fragile wall of single-minded dedication, devoting himself to one compelling obsession: the pursuit of truth. That his goal always lay at the end of a torturous path in a wilderness of mirrors only served to insulate him further from his devastating loss; but he was smart enough to realize that the denominator for most of his thoughts and actions was a sublimated instinct for self-preservation. By searching for answerable truths, he avoided the painful, unanswerable "Why?" of his personal horror.

Still, guilt and underlying turmoil occasionally surfaced in his unconscious mind during times of extreme stress, striking with harrowing nightmares of vicious ferocity. His placid and passive personality concealed an intense inner struggle against those emotional demons, but in that battle he found a psychological weapon to use on all of his enemies: a fervent belief that by fighting for the truth, he was serving the United States. But since last May, truth had become lies and lies had become truth, plunging him into a labyrinthian maze from which he found no escape.

Now, Singer pushed back from his desk, hands in his lap. His shoulders slumped. "I'm sorry, David. Jesus, I'm sorry I didn't mean to . . ."

"It's all right." Knight's gaze softened. "I know you didn't mean to bring it up. It just slipped out; don't worry about it. You've got a right to be upset with me." He looked out the window when he felt anxiety pulling the ties of a knot in his stomach, but he took a deep breath and it loosened.

Knight pushed himself out of the chair and walked to the rear wall of the office. Four ebony bookcases stood on four ebony cabinets. He reached to one shelf and ran his forefinger around a tarnished football trophy, identical to the one in a box in his apartment. It was another bond between David and Paul, a melancholy symbol of their past that linked them in the present. He picked it up and looked at Singer.

"I locked the memories out, Paul. I've tried to push them so far away, I don't even know where they are. I try not to think about her anymore. And sometimes, even when I want to, I can't. Sometimes I can't even picture her face." He stared at the trophy in his hands. His thought disappeared behind a heavy door slamming shut. "Damn it, you've heard all this before. And I know you're right, but . . ."

"Hey, buddy, you're my best friend. I know how you feel. Maybe not exactly, but I understand. It's been a long, hard eight years. You know you can have my ear anytime you want; that's what I'm here for. That's why I wanted you in this office with me. Hell, sometimes I wish you'd just let go and yell and scream at me. It'd be good for you, but you keep so much inside, you should have three ulcers by now." A smile traced over Singer's lips. "Listen, I know what you need. She's on the fourth floor, a body that won't quit, twenty-three years old, legs so long . . ."

A broad smile came to Knight's face. He walked to the windows, but when he turned, the grin was gone. "I wish it was that easy, but that won't get rid of the self-pity I hang around my neck every day. I just don't know what the hell to do. This business with the Bureau, that's what I'm stuck on now, more than anything else. That's what I just can't let go of. It's still like a bad dream I'm trying to wake up from, hoping it'll go away and everything will be the same again. I still can't believe it. . . . I can't accept it, Paul; it still doesn't make any sense." He leaned on the leather chair, bracing with his arms. His voice had Singer straining to hear.

"Maybe I'm just using it to keep myself down, to keep wallowing in my own damn misery so I won't have to face up to the truth. But I don't even know what that is anymore. I've got to get some answers, from someone, but no one in the government will talk straight to me." He paused. "I wish I could tell you what happened, Paul, honest to God. But I can't even do that. I still have to go by the CFR rules."

"You know, I really don't understand you." Singer's words rained on Knight like a sudden summer storm. "Jesus, the FBI fucked you, David, and you're still so goddamned concerned about the Code of Federal Regulations, holding on to your secrets. Fuck the code! What the hell do you owe those bastards? They broke your lance right over your head and then stuck it in your back. You never told me, but I got a damn good idea of what you were doing. I told you I'd sue the Bureau and graymail the shit out of them, get a lot of money and maybe even get you reinstated. How the hell can you still be so dedicated, so careful about that national security crap when they treated you like that? Where are all your Bureau buddies now? How come I never see one up here? They won't even come close to you, will they? I'll tell you why, because they're all covering their asses and cutting you out like a black sheep! And you know I'm right, goddamn it!"

Singer eased up. "C'mon David, use your head. Let me file the lawsuit. We'll get all the answers. Otherwise, forget it. You're tearing yourself apart, piece by piece. I don't want that to happen to you now. Anyway, you're too good for those assholes. Fuck 'em."

Knight stared at the floor, massaging his temples with both hands. He felt weak, empty, and alone. Everything Paul said was true. But there were so many questions, so few answers, and no solutions. A lawsuit would never get the real truth; the wagons would just circle tighter. He knew there were other methods.

"I can't do it like that. I have to do it my way; I can't get you involved. There's too much, Paul; it goes too deep. Look, there are things you can't know." Knight stopped himself from saying it might be dangerous; Singer would laugh and say he'd been playing James Bond too long. Yet Knight yearned to confide in his best friend, to get Paul's raw perspective, to seek his sound advice. He was certain Paul would know what to do.

He held Singer's eyes for a moment, then looked away, swallowing his clutching desperation. The goddamn CIA, he thought, that's where it all began last May. Why did those bastards set me up with those lies? And why did the Bureau go along with it? I've got to get some answers, somehow, soon, then I can go to Paul.

"Right. I can't know about the *government's* goddamn secrets, but I know everything about my goddamn best friend's private life for the last twenty years. You know, I had a clearance, too." Singer spun his chair sideways to the desk and stared at the open door. His face betrayed an emotion rarely seen by others. Knight recognized it instantly, and knew Paul was hurt. It was a pain that penetrated his otherwise sclerotic skin. And it silenced him.

Knight decided to use Singer's shouting tactic. "What the hell good would it do for you to know? You just got done telling me to leave it alone. How the hell can I do that if I bring you into it? Do you really think that's going to help?" He was surprised at his raised voice, and paused as he sat on the couch in front of the windows. "Anyway, I already told you, it's too complicated. You wouldn't understand."

Singer turned his chair slowly and fixed his cross-examination eyes on Knight. "Try me." He smiled. "And don't give me that 'deep sigh' shit. Just talk to me."

Knight thought for an instant. Maybe I should tell him; not everything, but at least enough to get some of it off my chest. Anyway, it might be better if someone else knew a little about what happened. Who better, and safer, than Paul?

Knight had used verbal feints and dodges before, without lying, to make an explanation sound plausible. On most of those occasions, the atmosphere had been more tense and much less hospitable. Now, the idea of finally talking about the problem made him feel fresh, confident. His mood lifted. He wouldn't lie to Paul, nor would he tell him why it had happened. He couldn't, because he didn't know that himself.

"So?" Singer snapped.

Knight stood in the middle of the room, hands clasped behind his back. "All right, Paul, relax. It isn't that easy. Let me do it my way," he said, taking a deep breath.

"Part of it you know anyway from when you were prosecuting for the feds. Call it interagency rivalry or bureaucratic jealousy, it was always a problem whenever there were jurisdictional fights about what agency should handle a case if they got involved in overlapping crimes. DEA, IRS, ATF, Customs, the Bureau— they'd all get riled when one thought the other was stepping on its toes. Hell, Paul, how many times did you have to settle a dispute even *inside* an agency because one squad used another squad's informant?"

"David, c'mon! Why the hell does it always take you a year to explain something? Tell me something I don't know, dammit."

"Hey! You asked; just listen," Knight said sternly. "I didn't catch it on the law-enforcement side; I got the squeeze from the intelligence community, my own damn counterintelligence people and the CIA." He sighed. There, it's out. Now keep going.

Knight paced, bringing his thoughts together. Singer sat impatiently and lit a cigarette.

"This is history, but you have to know it to understand what I'm talking about. Remember, JM Wave, the Agency's station in Miami, was the largest in the world in the early sixties. But after the Bay of Pigs and Operation Mongoose, around 1965, the CIA began to lose most of their deep-cover agents in Cuba. Fidel picked off a bunch of them, but that was when the government turned its attention to Vietnam and southeast Asia—the late sixties, early seventies. Dozens of agents were pulled out of Cuba to work over there. Even when the Agency got rid of Allende in Chile in seventy-three, its sources in Cuba had dwindled to a handful." Knight walked to the bookcase and lifted a Miami Dolphin autographed football off a shelf. He twirled it in his hands.

"David, look, if I want a history lesson, I'll go to the University of Miami. Will you please get on with it? And stop spinning the goddamn ball!"

Knight smiled at Singer's exasperation, then spoke.

"Okay. The CIA just about wasted itself in Vietnam, and then got hit by Congress: the Pike and Church committees ran the Agency up a greased pole and let it slide down into a pile of shit because of the disclosures about its assassination plots and domestic intelligence activities. If J. Edgar had been alive, I guarantee you would have seen the old bastard laughing for the first time in his life.

"The CIA had to wire its jaws shut, hoping the heat would blow over. And by then, it barely had any sources in Cuba. So the Bureau started recruiting and running Cuban double agents from Miami for counterintelligence operations. That's about the time I came here, and I learned the game fast. We developed our own 'dangle' operations, fine-tuning them to an art, but it wasn't that difficult."

"'Dangle'? What the hell is a 'dangle'?"

"That's one of our sources we'd send to the DGI. He'd offer to spy for Fidel against the Cuban exiles in the United States. We'd 'dangle' one and hope the Cuban intelligence service would snap him up. If they did, then we'd have a double agent inside the DGI."

Singer nodded and picked up a silver letter opener, testing the point on his palm. *"Dangle*—what a goddamn word," he muttered.

"Listen, Paul. In a few years, we had more and better sources in Cuba than the Agency ever dreamed of. We got word they were really upset we were running so many agents there and in some other countries. But when Reagan made Bill Casey the director of the Central Intelligence Agency, Casey found out how source-poor they were in Cuba. So he bullied our director into turning over to the Agency our guys that had stayed in deep-cover in Cuba by saying they were gathering intelligence. Casey told him that was their turf, not ours." Knight tossed the football to Singer. It slipped through his fingers, bounced on the desk, and knocked the ashtray on the floor.

"Shit! Damn you, David." Singer leaned over and picked up the ball, but not the ashtray. "Get to the point, okay? How did you get screwed over?"

Knight returned Paul's glare with a grin. Inside, though, his heart was beating rapidly, anticipating the final disclosure.

"This is what I didn't want to tell you, so keep it between us. I recruited a double—I can't tell you his name—about nine years ago to go deep-cover. He was so smooth, Paul . . . the man operated like a magician, even got the DGI to send him to the Soviet Union for advanced training. He gave us information you wouldn't believe. But in eighty-two, I had to turn him over to a CIA case officer. My source couldn't stand him; he was an old German who should have retired years ago. They never should have let him run Cubans—he was too rigid. But my guy followed orders as long as they came from the United States government.

"The next I heard about him, he's got a job in the Administrative Service Directorate of the Ministry of Foreign Relations, right next door to the minister's office. From what I could learn, he produced reams of high-level, grade A information." Knight spoke faster, knowing he was coming to a crucial but painful memory. He swallowed and felt his mouth drying.

"About a year ago, I got called to headquarters. They told me the CIA sent word that the double was burned out and wanted to come home, but he didn't trust his case officer or anyone else in the Agency. He wanted *me* to bring him in, so they asked me to handle the operation to get him out of Cuba. But to do it, I had to be detached to the CIA and work with their people. I said 'Yes, fine,' and we began planning the operation." He paused. This is where I have to hide the truth from Paul, he thought, choosing his next words carefully.

"So what happened?" Singer said anxiously.

"That's what I don't know, Paul. For some reason, the op was canceled. The Bureau and the CIA got into a real pissing match, but I never found out what happened or why. Or if my source ever got out of Cuba."

"So you decided to resign because of that?" Singer asked, eyebrows raised. "You mean you were *forced* to resign."

"More or less," Knight said, trying to sound nonchalant. "For some reason, the operation got messed up, but I didn't have anything to do with that, believe me. They were on my back for a while, tried to throw some blame on me, to cover their asses. Nothing ever came of it, but I could tell they were setting me up for a blackball. I just got fed up with the pressure, too many unanswered questions, too much goddamn frustration. And I was angry about my source; they used him, wrung him out, and let him dry." Or die? Knight wondered.

"They wouldn't let me go back to CI work, and I didn't want to do anything else. I finally burned out." He turned his back to the desk, hoping Paul didn't see the sweat beading on his forehead. After he wiped it with his cuff, he looked back at Singer. "That's what happened, Paul . . . that's it."

"That's it? Just like that? David, Jesus, there must be more. Are you bein' straight with me?"

"Paul, why would I tell you all this? I don't lie to you, not to my best friend. The only thing left is a lot of questions that I'd like to answer . . . someday." Tomorrow wouldn't be too soon, he thought, avoiding Paul's eyes.

Singer exhaled loudly and furrowed his brow. "Look, pal, I know you. Something doesn't sound right; maybe I'll figure out this spine-tingling bullshit and we'll talk about it again. You're not telling me everything." He shook his head side to side, looked at his watch, and shoved four files into his briefcase.

"Damn, I gotta be at the federal courthouse in ten minutes. You want to play more James Bond, be my guest. But I'm gonna make us both some money." He tossed a roll of bills wrapped with a rubber band to Knight. "Take the two grand. I'll talk to Manolo. But do me a favor: Show up on Friday. I don't know what you have to do to get this outta your system, but do it fast. We got a law practice to run, partner."

Knight caught the small bundle and looked at it. He still found it strange to take cash payments after twenty years of a brown government paycheck. He stuffed the wad into his pocket, uncomfortable with the bulge.

Singer shrugged into his gray suit coat and marched out of his office. Knight followed him to the hallway.

"Hey, I don't know where the new girl is, but tell her to at least take the phones until I get back. You oughta like her, David—she used to be a cop," he called out when he got to the front door, and slammed it shut.

The office was quiet. Knight leaned against the doorjamb of Singer's room, listening to the low hum of the air conditioning. Fatigue from a fitful, draining sleep last night crept into his arms and legs. When his eyes began to droop, he shook himself and rubbed his face with both hands. He went to the small closet kitchen and made a cup of instant coffee, black. The first sip scalded his tongue. He held the mug up and looked at the words of the FBI crest: Fidelity, Bravery, Integrity.

Self-doubt scraped his insides, gnawing on questions he could not answer. I still believe in those ideals. I believed in the Bureau. Why didn't they believe me? The director himself asked me to help the CIA bring in Roger Estevez. But that was before the Agency said I had to take a polygraph. After that, my world turned upside down. That's what I can't tell Paul: the goddamn polygraph. What they said would be just a routine test turned into a setup, I'm sure of it. But why? What the hell really happened last May?

His thoughts shot back to the small green room in Washington, with its room-wide two-way mirror, the long cylindrical microphone hanging from the ceiling, and the black padded straight chair. He remembered the tightness of the pressure cuff around his right bicep and the rubber tubes banding his chest and stomach. Again he heard the shrill voice of the belligerent, condescending CIA polygraph examiner. After six charts had been run, the short rat-faced man battered him with demeaning and degrading allegations, accusing him of lying about his personal life and his loyalty to the United States.

Knight had never been attacked so viciously. He tried to reason calmly with the examiner, but the man stomped on every one of his denials and explanations. Knight was caught completely off guard; he knew he had not given one false answer. When he tried to argue back, he was shouted down each time. The examiner did not believe a word he said. Five hours after the test began, his throat was dry and raspy and dried saliva clung to his lips. When he left the government building that afternoon, he was shaking with rage but overwhelmed with confusion and exhaustion. He immediately called his supervisor in Miami to explain what had happened, seeking sympathy and understanding; the only response he received was an order to report to headquarters at eight o'clock the next morning.

However, the results of the lie-detector test and the transcript of the examiner's questioning went straight to the FBI's Assistant Director for Intelligence that afternoon. Knight's security clearances were pulled before five o'clock.

The next day, two hatchet men from the Bureau's Office of Professional Responsibility interrogated him for seven hours about his "lies" on the polygraph, ripping his reputation to shreds. Knight returned to Miami that night, numb from the ordeal. For the next week, his mind felt empty and blank and his body ached as if he had fought a heavyweight fighter. But somehow the word that he had failed the polygraph leaked from headquarters and spread around the Miami Division Office. Within days, he became a pariah; faces turned away and conversations hushed or ended when he walked down a corridor or into a squad area.

Less than a month later, the chief of OPR recommended a four-month suspension without pay, a demotion to street agent, and a transfer to Omaha. Or a low-profile resignation. He was lucky, the chief told Knight's supervisor, that they didn't go to the Justice Department for a criminal prosecution.

On June 10, three weeks later, Knight handed in his credentials and his service Smith & Wesson model 13. He could not continue working for the FBI when he knew his own agency had gone along with the deliberate setup by the CIA, and it was beyond his comprehension to understand why the polygraph had been rigged against him. He had been thrown into a black hole that destroyed his reputation, and never told why. There was no other choice but to resign. And his unanswerable questions had become a nightmare that had no end.

The shock of the experience put him into a dark depression for three months, until Paul Singer convinced him to take the small office in his suite. Knight wanted to tell everything to Paul, but it wasn't a matter of trust, confidentiality, or national security. If *he* didn't know what happened or why, how could he explain it to anyone else?

The irony of his plight did not escape him, however. He had survived in the nether world of counterintelligence by constantly sharpening the skills of lying and deceiving; now, he was the victim of a contrived deception more devious than any he had conceived as an agent.

Still, his craft and experience in that trade sparked a smoldering desire to find the answers. His emotions were finally simmering, but his logical mind fanned that need into a flaming obsession to search for the truth; he had to find out why the FBI and the CIA had turned on him. All he wanted was a place to start.

FOUR

"Mr. Singer? Are you Mr. Singer?"

The voice at his back startled Knight. His hand jerked and coffee sloshed over the rim of the cup, dripping onto the beige carpet. The brown liquid soaked in two small blotches. One drop splashed the shine off his right shoe.

"I'm sorry, I didn't mean to scare you. I'll get some cold water. Why don't you put the cup down?"

He looked up, to see the back of a head covered with silky brown hair that gently curled three inches below the collar of a white blouse. She was leaning into the closet sink, running water on a paper towel. He barely saw her face as she turned and knelt to the carpet stains. The blouse stretched tightly on her back, outlining taut muscles across her shoulder blades as she rubbed the spots.

Her slate gray skirt was hiked into folds around her knees. A wide black patent leather belt wrapped around a narrow waist. Faint scuff marks showed on the backs of her black high heels.

"Hand me a dry towel." It was an order.

Knight ripped two sheets off the roll and gave them to her. He saw that she had no makeup on her cheek. Her skin was smooth and lightly tanned.

"That should do it. You have to get the spot right away, or else—"

"I know about stains. And you didn't scare me."

When she stood up, smoothing her blouse and skirt, he was instantly sorry he had used a harsh tone. The sweet citrus fragrance of her perfume separated them by less than two feet. He looked into pale green eyes four inches below his and saw only a trace of eyeliner. Her mouth was wide, but she wore no lipstick. He felt a red tinge rising on his face. She was beautiful. For an instant, he could not think of anything to say.

"I'm sorry, I didn't hear you come in. Don't worry about the spill." He hoped the blush in his cheeks was fading away. Relax, damn it. "I'm not Singer. Are you the new secretary?"

She stepped back. Her eyes had tiny black flecks, but Knight sensed something in her face not visible. It wasn't her expression, which was serious, not at all apologetic. He felt a sudden emotional link with her, a shared poignancy that conveyed a silent sadness. His recognition of the feeling surprised him; Knight could not remember the last time the spark of someone else's deep emotion had touched his. Somehow, he knew she masked an underlying hurt, a pain hidden but not lost. There was a hint of something unresolved, unfinished. It made him feel uneasy. Still, he sensed her protective gloss and wondered whether it was as thin as his.

Knight wasn't always aware of this trick his mind played on him. It was an intuitive identification from a distant realm of his unconscious, traveling far before it surfaced. Most of the time, it arrived quickly and unexpectedly. But whenever he felt it around, he knew he was right. It had been tested in more stressful circumstances than this.

"I didn't want to be late, but I've never driven this far downtown in rush hour. I saw the desk out front; I'll just get settled and start taking the phones. Sorry about the coffee." Her voice was abrupt. She dropped the wet towels in the sink. "Oh, are you Mr. Singer's partner?"

"No, I just share space with him. We're friends. My name's David Knight." He held out his hand and she shook it firmly; she was stronger than he expected.

"I'm Jennifer Ferrer." She turned and walked to the reception room.

Knight watched her narrow hips as she glided away. She might have been a cop, but he found it hard to picture her breaking up barroom brawls, chasing burglars over backyard fences, or trying to handcuff a belligerent drunk driver. Maybe a dispatcher or a secretary in administration, he thought, but not on the streets.

He went into Singer's office and took the book on the Omnibus Crime Control Act back to his own. The government prosecutor would be asking for pretrial detention at the bond hearing on Friday, and Knight thought it would wise to prepare for something he had never done. Although he was friendly with the United States Magistrate and knew she would overlook his errors, he had never handled a bond hearing by himself. He did not want to look like a rookie right out of law school in a courtroom packed with defense attorneys who callously scrutinized the tactics of their brethren.

Knight unlocked his desk and took a legal pad and a pen from the center drawer. With the book in his lap, he looked in the index of the thick blue volume and found the heading Bail Reform Act. He riffled through the pages and propped his feet on the corner of the desk. When he moved his heel and accidentally shoved the newspaper to the floor, he remembered the death notice of the Cuban doctor. He put the book facedown on its split-open pages and picked up the paper.

Folding the creases, he reread the article until a ragged memory again traced from Milian, the drowning victim, to Miguel Torres, a walk-in double agent Knight had begun controlling just after the Mariel boat lift in 1980. The association fed his interest. He was certain it wasn't from a Miami case; he wondered whether it tied into one of Torres's operations inside Cuba. Dammit, Miguel, I wish you were here to tell me whether I should know this man.

Knight sighed when he realized four years had passed since the Bureau's Intelligence Division had spirited Torres away from him for an assignment in Europe. Countering past policy, the chief of the ID never told Knight the specifics of that operation, nor did he give a reason for selecting Torres. Withholding such information from Knight, Torres's control agent, was an unusual deviation from standard ID procedure. It had been and remained a mystery to Knight, because he knew too well how strictly the FBI enforced its foreign counterintelligence guidelines.

The primary caveat was quite basic: Do not send a Bureau source overseas without proper authorization. The FBI's jurisdiction did not extend overseas, except in counterintelligence operations. By law, foreign intelligence gathering rested solely in the zealously guarded domain of the Central Intelligence Agency. But to execute its duty to protect the nation from enemy spies, the FBI's CI agents were often required to send their informants into foreign countries. In these murky waters of disputed jurisdiction, both agencies occasionally tried to split hairs with a blunt hatchet rather than a cooperatively honed scalpel. David Knight had his own scars from some of those raging battles.

Now, as he sat at his desk and searched his memory for a Milian-Torres connection in an overseas operation, he remembered the xenophobic jealousy with which the CIA protected its responsibility to conduct foreign intelligence activities. Five of his cases, two with Torres, had to be shut down because they crossed wires with Agency operations. But he had heard horror stories of FBI agents who wound up as "brick" agents, reputations ruined, because they ran afoul of a screaming CIA station chief when they tried to go operational in another country without the CIA's approval. He knew of only one agent rumored to have escaped severe discipline after getting caught in an unauthorized overseas operation. Ironically, that agent had been in the Miami Division Office before Knight arrived.

The problem was not infrequent: Whenever an FBI agent wanted to send a double agent across a border, the FBI director had to request authorization from the director of the CIA. It was a tedious process, requiring reams of written justifications to be pushed through the unwieldy interagency bureaucracy. By the time the DCI granted his approval, it was often too late for the FBI operative to begin, let alone finish, the proposed assignment. This was a particular frustration in Miami, with Cuban exiles who jumped borders on an hour's notice. Yet Knight and other Bureau CI agents knew that the delay usually came from a CIA desk officer who didn't want to see an FBI source on his turf.

But with Miguel Torres, Knight had no reason to blame the CIA; his complaint rested on the doorstep of the FBI's Intelligence Division. With lightning speed, the ID yanked Torres away from him just when the likable stubby Cuban exile was poised to bring Knight irrefutable evidence of a Soviet-trained agent who had penetrated a CIA operation in Central America. It had taken Torres ten months to draw that agent into his confidence. Knight worked closer with Torres than any other double he had controlled, and their relationship had quickly taken on the characteristics of close brothers.

The painstaking planning was done by both as a team, with Torres often overriding Knight's ideas with strong suggestions of his own. It was a grueling effort that drained the emotions of each, but Torres moved closer and closer to his target. In the seventh month, Torres discovered that the penetration agent was deeply into a CIA network that began in Nicaragua. Yet Knight moved cautiously, fearing the slightest mistake might blow Torres. He begged permission from the deputy to the assistant director for the Intelligence Division to keep his reports from crossing the Potomac to the CIA headquarters at Langley until Torres maneuvered the Cuban agent into Knight's trap. Both knew that strategy risked a full-scale confrontation between the two agencies. Yet, given the potential success of the operation, it was a risk Knight accepted—along with sleepless nights.

When the ID grabbed Torres, however, Knight staggered into quicksand. If he gave the real reason for his protest, the directors of the FBI and the CIA would be throwing ashtrays at each other across the National Security Council's mahogany table. The resulting battle would set back even the minimal gains each agency had accomplished in their few cooperative efforts, with Knight taking the blame behind a safe but fictitious reason thought up by the Bureau to prevent bad publicity: "voucher padding," perhaps. In the intelligence community, though, he would have been dubbed a "cowboy" who thought he could run his own operation without proper clearance. Then he would have been blackballed and regarded as untrustworthy by both agencies.

Knight had only one choice; he pulled in his horns and covered his tracks. He never learned the true identity of the penetration agent. And when the CIA net was blown in 1986, Havana broadcast a television series called "Project Forty," a devastating exposé filmed by hidden cameras, showing the CIA agents' activities. The Agency's operations in Cuba were set back at least seven years.

Knight never saw Torres again. Two months after they said good-bye, a television broadcast in Miami told of a bombing in Madrid. A Spanish army general was killed by the Party of God terrorist group when he started his car outside the National Palace. Three bystanders were also killed, the anchorwoman had said. One had been a Cuban exile from Miami named Miguel Torres.

Now, the Milian article stirred Knight's emotions, bringing up painful memories he thought he had buried in a remote black corner of his mind. But his intuition, sharply honed by the regimen of counterintelligence work, told him to logically search for any link that might show a connection. From the first link, he would go to the second, and then to more, until a chain of evidence circled an irrefutable conclusion. The process, almost scientific and certainly not foreign to his intellect, was an ingrained talent and pushed him forward.

Since he had begun working with Paul, he had often been drawn to the hypothesis that Miguel's disappearance was tied to his own problem with the CIA polygraph, if for no other reason than the counterintelligence rule of noncoincidence; a CI agent had to assume the conjunction of possibly related events unless proven otherwise. But he had never found an articulable basis on which to bring those events together—until now. As hidden thoughts crept into his receptive mind, one shadowy recollection nudged Knight into an association between Torres and Milian . . . and the polygraph.

Knight listed the years he was with Torres on a yellow pad, writing brief notes about the operations they had worked. He stared at the paper, trying to recall meetings and conversations with Torres. As he circled 1983 over and over, one session with the double agent that year, like a developing photograph, emerged in focus. Knight pictured the two of them sitting in the living room of Torres's house in Coral Gables.

Torres had been talking about his last trip to Cuba, a week earlier, and said he had run into Roger Estevez, the CIA's deep-cover agent who once had also been Knight's agent. It was a chance meeting, a brush contact in the Miramar section of Havana. Estevez said he had met a Cuban Army colonel who was a confidant of Fidel Castro. The colonel had given Estevez the name of a contact in Miami if Estevez ever needed to reach him. Knight practically had to pry the contact's name from Torres, but Miguel finally told him it was Milian. Miguel didn't remember the man's first name, but he said he was a doctor. At the time, Knight had paid little attention to Torres's information; the CIA was handling Estevez and he saw no reason, nor did he desire, to step into the Agency's operation.

Knight pushed away from the desk and stared out his window, thoughts racing, puzzle pieces falling in disarray. But he caught one piece faceup. He glanced at the article again: Victor Milian was a doctor, the same occupation as Miguel's Milian. That was too close for Knight to accept as a coincidence. He thought for a moment, then decided to run his idea against the other known facts.

All right, for now I'll assume it's the same Milian. That makes Milian a DGI agent. Then Estevez must have given the same information to his CIA control officer; so when the FBI and the CIA "chose" me for the Estevez operation, they must have known about the Estevez-Milian link. So did I, from Miguel. But it never surfaced in the polygraph session or during the day-long interrogation by the men from the OPR. Why didn't someone bring it up?

Knight now thought it curious that neither the examiner nor the OPR men had mentioned Estevez or Milian, because they had bled him of virtually everything he had known and done as a counterintelligence agent. Suddenly, he remembered another strange omission: They never had asked him about Miguel Torres, either; they never even brought up his name. That seemed like more than a curious oversight to Knight. Did the examiner and the OPR men *deliberately* omit those names? If they did, was that part of the polygraph setup?

Knight had never understood why they put him on the lie detector in the first place; he already had the highest security clearances in the government. It didn't make sense to him, but he went along with it when the CIA section chief told him it was just a formality. Then the polygraph devastated him like a force-five hurricane. But now, he wondered whether he had found the missing pieces he needed to reconstruct the disaster that had made every day since a living purgatory.

Maybe this is the connection I've been looking for: Estevez and the rigged polygraph. And maybe Milian, possibly a DGI agent who gets hit in Miami, is part of it, too. But how am I going to test or confirm any theory I come up with? How can I find out more about Milian? Damn, I wish Miguel were alive; I'm sure he knew more than he ever told me.

He slammed the pen on his desk and ripped off the sheet of notes. Tearing the yellow page into little pieces, he stood up and put them in his pocket. The next time he left the office, he would toss them in a garbage can on the street.

Knight read the article again, hoping for some clue, one more word to convince him he was on the right track. He didn't find it, but he knew he had to keep analyzing. Still, he was satisfied that some links hung together and he felt an intense, compelling drive to tighten the chain. If he succeeded, he was confident he would find the true reason he had been destroyed by his own government.

He saw the telephone flashing and faintly heard the chime from Maria's—Jennifer's—desk. The intercom on his phone buzzed a few seconds later, and he picked up the receiver.

"Mr. Knight, there's a Tony Costas calling. Do you want to speak to him?" Her voice was husky on the phone.

"I'll take it." The call reminded Knight of his plans.

"Tony, I didn't forget about today." It was a little lie he knew Costas would not believe.

"Sure, just like the last two times. This time, I'm coming over to drag you out of your office and tie you to a chair. So where do we meet? You want seafood?"

"No, I don't want to eat at your uncle's Greek place again; I want American for a change. How about P.J.'s?"

"Hamburgers at the greasy spoon? Christ, David, you're a helluva gourmet. Okay, so I'll have the runs for the rest of the day. One o'clock?"

"Make it one-thirty. I need to take care of something first." Knight looked down at Milian's name. He decided to take a chance. "Tony, does the name Victor Milian mean anything to you?"

Nearly ten seconds passed before Costas spoke. The lightness was gone from his voice.

"You saw the paper." It was a statement, not a question. "I'll see you at lunch. Remember, you're not on a green phone anymore."

"Right. One-thirty."

Knight heard the phone click. He was glad he asked the question; he knew there was a reason for Tony's cautious response. *If my friend from the CIA won't talk on the phone about Milian's death, I must be headed in the right direction.*

The end of their conversation confirmed what he wanted to do before he met Tony. He pulled off his sweater and grabbed his blazer, then passed through the reception room in a blur, telling Jennifer he'd be back around three. He had to hurry.

FIVE

As Knight turned left from Bayshore Drive to the entrance of Mercy Hospital, he slowed the car. He sighted the Professional Building left of the main building and followed the road past the patients' parking lot. When he reached the walkway between the two buildings, he stopped. The sign for the doctors' parking area was west of the offices. He noticed that the perimeter road was an extension of the pavement he was on, heading east toward Biscayne Bay.

Knight rolled down his window to get a better look from this view. It doesn't make sense, he thought. The most direct route for a doctor parked in his space would be to come out of the lot and turn west, and go straight to Bayshore Drive. Why would he turn left and drive toward the bay?

He drove forward, creeping, craning his neck to see the lights along the roadway. The high arc lamps stopped at the edge of the

Professional Building. The were no light poles on the perimeter road.

The grass between the pavement and the bay was long, six or seven inches high, waving in the breeze that was still wafting in cool air from the northeast. It looked more like weed patches, not the meticulously manicured St. Augustine grass gracing the front of the hospital.

He drove still slower, looking for black smudges on the road that might be skid marks. His head was out the window, eyes tearing from the wind, scanning the uncut growth.

Then he saw something: the indentation marks of a vehicle that had driven off the road onto the grassy area. Knight pulled over on the grass opposite and turned off the engine.

Cleansing salt air filled his nostrils as he took a deep breath and stretched, loosening the cramp in his back. The crushed grass from the tire impressions was beginning to rise up, but the tracks were still clear enough to follow the path. As they angled toward the low cement abutment, the marks became more compressed, as if the car had stayed in one spot for a longer time.

I don't get it, he wondered. If the car drove across the grass and hit the seawall with the force to go over, how could it have stopped? Maybe I'm wrong; maybe it didn't stop.

Knight turned around to look at the tire tracks from the road. About ten yards back from that point, he saw another set of indentations. His eyes followed them, and they converged into the first set. He walked closer and squatted to touch the matted grass. The impressions were deeper and wider. Four feet farther, the grass was broken and shredded, showing dirt, as if two of the larger tires had spun on the grass.

Now he was more puzzled than before. There was no question in his mind that another, bigger vehicle had been at the same location. But was it here at the same time? Was there a collision? I'm no traffic reconstruction expert, but I've got to believe this was no accidental drowning. How could it have been classified as one?

He wanted to follow the tracks to the seawall, to look into the bay water. But suddenly, his heart was pounding and his throat felt constricted. Queasiness roiled his stomach. As he started to walk toward the choppy whitecaps, he felt his neck sweating and he began to shiver. His vision blurred and the ground tilted with each step. The buildings across the bay were spinning, picking up speed. Vertigo spun the ground, sucking oxygen from his lungs and draining the color from his face. He knew a blackout stood a foot away, squeezing his arteries to keep blood from reaching his brain. He stumbled and fell to one knee, holding his head down while he retched and gasped for air.

I can't do it! Dammit! His mind swirled with contorted images and frantic thoughts, a dizzying mélange of psychic terror. He had to get away from this place, from the water. With his head still low, he searched for the car. The panic began to subside when he spotted it. He stood uneasily and walked slowly, shuffling to feel the ground steady under his feet. He leaned against the car door, wiping sweat from his forehead with his hands. Then he got in and turned the air conditioner on, holding his face inches from the vent. The digital dashboard clock flashed one-twenty. He didn't even pay attention to the route as he drove back along the perimeter road to Bayshore Drive.

Anthony Costas sat at a small round table in the rear of P.J.'s tiny bar and grill, two miles north of downtown Miami. It was near, yet out of the way, perfect for a quiet conversation.

When he heard footsteps on the tile floor, he looked up at Knight. He folded *The Miami Herald* sports section and took off his glasses, smoothing his prematurely white hair. The top button of his blue shirt was open beneath the loosened knot of a red and navy tie. He reached for Knight's hand without standing. The frown on his face made Knight uneasy.

"You want the usual?" Costas asked. When Knight nodded,

Costas gave the waitress an order for two cheeseburgers with lettuce and tomatoes and two Diet Cokes.

Costas warmed as they ate. Their conversation jumped from bewailing the Dolphins' dismal season to trading stories about old friends and distant enemies. But Knight sensed a guarded tone from Tony. They had talked on the phone a few times during the last six months, but they had not seen each other since the week after Knight's resignation, when Knight had not been at all communicative. Knight wondered aloud whether Tony had any reservations about the trusting relationship they had shared in the past.

Costas creased his napkin carefully and patted his mouth. "David, this isn't easy. You know I've always been up-front with you. For me, I don't have a problem. But to be honest with you, I shouldn't even be here."

Knight's eyes dropped to his empty plate. He felt as if a two-hundred-pound barbell had settled on his shoulders.

"Look, I'm here," Costas said. "But the crap flowing from the creeps at my headquarters hasn't stopped. They've spread all kinds of rumors about you: You were bought off by dopers; you had people killed; you went over to the other side. I know it's bullshit, but you know how that stuff goes around. And it doesn't matter if it's true or not; as soon as people start talking about it, you're garbage.

"Honest to God, David, I don't know what you can do about it. You can't prove negatives, we both know that." Costas wadded up the napkin and dropped it on the plate, but he kept talking to Knight's glum face.

"I told you right after it happened, I wish you'd have talked to me before you went to get fluttered. I would've warned you. Some of our own guys have been nailed on the lie box real good, for no damn reason. It's the modern version of the medieval torture rack," Costas said, smiling wanly.

Knight nodded, but his words were still stuck in his throat.

Costas continued: "I don't know, maybe it wouldn't have

helped. But if I can help you now, I will. We went through a lot together, and I'm not just saying this because I owe you. We helped each other out of some tough spots. I know you, David, as well as anyone else you've worked with—and I just want you to know that I don't believe what other people have said about you."

The words were soothing to Knight. Tony had an uncanny ability to decipher fact from fiction, a talent that served him well as a covert CIA operative in Miami. Using the cover of a real estate broker, Tony was not required to pay homage to the Miami covert chief of station. He was totally independent, and his autonomy was limited only by orders from Langley head-quarters.

His task for the last eight years had been to recruit and run Cuban exiles for clandestine operations outside the United States. That role put him in touch with a multitude of sources, from high-rolling bankers to curbside dope dealers, who came to him with tidbits of information. There was little that happened in underground Miami of which he was not aware. He had more than a need to know about the activities of pro- and anti-Castro Cuban exiles—and that's how he and Knight had become close friends.

At first, they'd simply shared information, but they quickly developed the kind of a relationship that comes only from deep trust forged in trying, tension-filled situations. Taking risks, sometimes hazardous, the trust they shared was different from that of mere friends: In the shadow world of clandestine intelligence, an agent must make a conscious, deliberate decision to trust someone, and it must be done carefully and not quickly. Once Costas and Knight made that mutual decision, it resulted in a tighter bond than most people ever share.

But now, Knight had to find out whether that bond of trust was still as strong as it had been seven months ago. He was almost afraid to ask.

"I need help, Tony. You may be right about proving negatives, but I've got to find some answers. I'm trying to find a place to start." Knight didn't attempt to hide the sound of desperation in his voice.

Costas looked around the restaurant, now nearly empty of the lunch crowd. A waitress roamed the tables, refilling sugar and salt and pepper holders, while three people waited at the cash register. The only sound came from the intermittent clatter of a busboy collecting dirty dishes in his cart. Tony inched his chair closer and folded his hands on the table.

"Ask me." Tony's voice was low, almost harsh.

A slight smile was the only sign of relief Knight allowed himself to show. He held in the sigh that pressed against his lips.

"Tell me about Milian. Who is he? What's the story with the drowning accident?" Knight didn't want to tell Tony he had been to the scene at the hospital—not yet.

Costas pursed his lips. "I thought about that after we hung up. I don't think it'll help you, David. I don't see a tie-in between Milian and your problem."

"Let me decide. If it doesn't, it doesn't. Tell me what you know, Tony."

Costas polished the lenses of his glasses with his tie. "We think it was a hit, but we're not sure. The city police might do a homicide investigation, but we're waiting for their results." He held the lenses up to the fluorescent lights.

Knight pushed his chair back. "What? Since when do you wait for homicide reports? Then are you going to give them your reports? I didn't know you guys shared everything now," Knight said incredulously, not sorry for his sarcasm.

"You asked, I'm telling. Orders from Langley. Nothing I can do about it." The edge in his voice surprised Knight.

"Tony, you know that doesn't make sense. What about your sources? What are they saying? You must have put your feelers out. What'd you get back?"

"Langley says no feelers until they give the word. I started to, but they said not yet. I have to sit back and wait until I get an order." Exasperation replaced the edge in his voice.

"I know you, Tony. Remember whom you're talking to. Don't bullshit me that you haven't talked to anyone. Give me what you've got, whatever it is." Knight knew he could get it, but he didn't understand Tony's reluctance.

"Listen, your sources are better than mine, David; they always were. You know more about what goes on in this town than anybody in my outfit or yours. Jesus, you had Julio Cruz all to yourself for years. Why don't you reach out, hit up on some of those guys? They're still around. You want something about Milian, maybe they'd talk to you. You might find out before I do." He paused and looked at his hands. "Better yet, why don't you just stay the hell away from it?"

Tony's attitude confused Knight. But he didn't accept the turn-about, and he wouldn't be put off that easily. There was more behind Tony's charade.

"What are you trying to say? You know I've been cut off. I haven't been on the streets in seven months. I don't know what's going on out there now and I don't know if anyone would even talk to me." He leaned his elbows on the table and lowered his voice. "Tony, I don't deserve to be jerked around like this, especially by you. Tell me what the hell is going on," Knight pleaded.

Costas shifted his weight on the small cane chair and looked to the front of the restaurant, avoiding Knight's eyes. He rubbed the back of his neck with one hand, then spoke in a tone just above a whisper.

"You really don't understand, do you? Maybe you can't see it yourself." Costas drilled his eyes in Knight's. "People are afraid of you, David; you have to realize that. I'm your friend, I always will be, but other people . . . you're dangerous to them. You always were, but now more than ever."

Knight was stunned, but his words came out rapidly. "How the hell can I be dangerous to anyone now? My God, I'm out of the government; I couldn't do anything if I wanted to. Tony, that doesn't make sense. I'm just a lawyer now, and I'm not even a good one. Who would be afraid of me? The bad guys? The Cubans? The Soviets?"

"You can't figure that out? Jesus, David, everybody! Don't you see why? You know too much, dammit. Even the Bureau and the Agency are scared of you, and they probably more than anyone else. Why do you think they put out those rumors about you? You had to be discredited and knocked on your ass so you wouldn't be a threat to them," Costas said, softening his gaze.

"Look, when you were an agent, the Bureau had controls on you. There were things you *could* do and things you *couldn't* do. How many times did you have something pulled right out of your hands, just when you thought you were going to wrap it up in a shiny bow? But that can't happen now. You've got so much information—you know who everybody is and how they operate and who does what to whom. You know sources and networks on both sides. That's dangerous to some people, and damn valuable to others. But who's going to trust you? Who can take the chance now?"

Costas was speaking New York-fast, but Knight didn't want to interrupt. As he listened, a few pieces were fitting into his puzzle. But he felt worse, not better.

"You have to get this into your head, David: Your world is upside down now. Before, you were a government agent. Even then, you were a mystery to a lot of people. Now, they don't know what the hell you are. They don't understand why or how you could leave the Bureau when you did. Whatever the rumors are, it doesn't make sense to them. I know, I've talked to some guys who can't figure you out. Nobody knows whose side you're on. You're a damn enigma . . . you don't fit in anywhere." Costas stopped to watch a black Pontiac cruise past the plate-glass window, then he turned back to Knight. His voice was hushed.

"Look at it this way, David. Anybody can come at you from any direction, for any goddamn reason, and you'll never know why. You won't know whom to trust, or whether you're getting set up. You have no protection now, no backup. . . . You're not a part of Uncle Sam's eagle anymore; you're just a feather."

Knight fell silent, brooding, staring at his clenched fists. He didn't want to answer Tony, didn't want to ask, argue, or say another word. Between Paul and Tony, he'd heard too much today. The weight of the barbell was up to five hundred pounds and he didn't have the strength to shove it off his shoulders. He didn't even want to try.

The afternoon sun crept across the floor, slicing their table in half with a bright glare. The whirring ceiling fans had little effect on the rising temperature and humidity in P.J.'s un-air-conditioned confines. It was time to leave.

Costas picked up the check and headed toward the cash register. Still sitting, Knight drained his water glass and slipped two dollars under the mustard jar. He caught up to Tony outside the screen door. Both men squinted, adjusting their eyes to the sunlight, and walked toward the fenced-in parking lot. Costas put on smoke-lensed sunglasses.

"I'm sorry, David, I thought you would have figured most of this out by now. See, you can't go back; you can't try to get all the answers. There's too much against you. Take my advice: Stay away from it. Build up a law practice with Singer; I hear he's really got the touch. You don't need more aggravation. There's not a damn thing you can do about it, believe me. You've got a chance to make more money than you ever did. Go for it; enjoy your life. It's the best thing you can do for yourself."

Knight squeezed the handcuff key ring in his palm. He heard Tony, but he wasn't listening; he had been thinking.

"Maybe you're right. I guess it's about time I started being good to myself and get away from all this crap. I've been thinking about getting out of Miami, maybe Atlanta, and really try to put all this behind me," Knight said, trying to sound sincere.

"Now you're talking sense. It's cheaper up there, too. Get a little piece of property, relax. Practice country law in a small town. I'll bring Sarah up if you promise to learn how to make mint juleps." Tony gave him a soft punch on his shoulder.

"You got it. But Tony, just one favor. Milian. Get me what you can. If I can't run with it, it's over. That's a promise. One last shot, just a small one, that's all I want. You can do that much for me," Knight said, knowing it sounded like a demand.

Costas kicked at a pebble. "You won't quit, will you? You and your damn lance, always poking people to get what you want." He sighed. "All right, I'll see what I can do. But remember, nothing official. There's a Bay of Pigs reunion tonight. I wasn't going to go, but I will. I'll ask a few guys I trust. Someone might know something. But no promises, David, you let me decide if it's something you should know. I'm not going to stay too long. They're giving an award to Harrison Witham, and I don't want to be there for that. The Cubans love him and he eats it up, but I can't stand the guy."

"Witham's in town?" Knight asked, surprised. "I thought he retired. How long has it been since he was here? Five, six years?"

"I couldn't care less. Whenever he's here, he's a pain in the ass. All he ever talks about is how he led the Brigade ashore at Girón, bragging about how he was the first American to hit the beach. You'd think Rip Robertson and Gray Lynch never got off Garcia's boat, to hear him tell the story."

Costas took his jacket off. The cold front had gone through and now he was sweating. He wiped his forehead with a handkerchief, then he looked around to see whether anyone was nearby.

"Here, chew on this, but I don't know if it has anything to do with what you're looking for. We got word there's supposed to be a hit on Fidel. It's coming from a new group, not the old guys from the seventies like Omega or the FLNC. These are young guys, a new breed, more violent, real anti-Fidelistas who see this as the perfect time to take down Fidel. Maybe it's something; I don't know yet."

Knight let a chuckle slip through. "Tony, you can't be serious. Another Fidel plot? Nobody around here's into that nymore, not for the last ten years. The young Cubans in Miami don't want to go back to Cuba; they've got it too good here. Nice try, but don't throw that at me, not if you really want to help."

"You asked for something; that's what I've got. I thought you CI guys never let anything slide by without putting it under a microscope," Costas said, shrugging his shoulder. "Anyway, I'll let you know if I pick up anything on Milian, but don't count on it. Go hit the books; maybe I'll need a lawyer someday." Tony finally smiled when they shook hands.

"Give my love to Sarah and the kids. Hey, you want a ride to your car? It's getting hot," Knight said, returning the smile.

"Naw, it's just a block away. Tradecraft, you remember. Anyway, the walk'll be good for me. I need the exercise," Costas called, strolling from the parking lot.

Knight waved, then got into his car. He was certain Tony was holding back, and he knew there had to be a good reason why Costas was keeping the Milian matter so close to his chest. But he had mentioned a possible anti-Castro plot against Fidel. Knight didn't believe Tony would feed that to him as false information; there was no reason for that.

But if I turn it around, Knight thought, maybe Tony was giving me a hidden message, something he wanted me to know but couldn't say. He wouldn't give me disinformation, just to see what I did with it . . . would he? Dammit, what if the CIA is using Tony to drive another nail into my coffin? No, I can't believe he'd do that.

Knight took a deep breath. He was glad he hadn't told Tony about his trip to the site of Milian's death or his theory about the Estevez-Milian connection. He couldn't help wondering whether Tony trusted him; if Costas had any doubts about Knight, their lunch conversation would end up in a detailed report faxed to Langley. The thought of that possibility sent a tremor of anxiety through his body.

He felt a wave of fatigue sweep over him as he drove away from P.J.'s. Emotional exhaustion left no energy or desire to go back to the office. He pulled over to a pay phone, called Jennifer, and told her he wouldn't be in until tomorrow. She didn't ask why.

With mild relief, he headed up the expressway ramp to I-95. He looked forward to a fifteen-minute swim and then collapsing into bed. But a twinge of fear kept his mind racing when he thought about Costas and the Bay of Pigs veterans' dinner tonight.

Tony, don't fall down on me; you've got to come through. I need your help just to give me a little ray of hope. Just a keyhole of light to shine into this darkness, that's all I want.

SIX *December 17*

━━━━┥ He didn't know how long he had been swimming. Silt and saltwater stung his eyes, and the water was so murky, he couldn't see his hands as he breaststroked under the water. His lungs screamed for oxygen, but he could not keep the air bubbles from popping from his lips and puffed cheeks. Still he swam deeper, searching. Just as he was about to turn back toward the surface, he glimpsed the shadowy outline of a car resting on the bottom. A dark object floated above it. At first, he thought it was a giant manta ray flapping its wings; but as he paddled closer, he saw it was a black billowing shroud hovering over the roof of the car. Chilling panic shivered through his body, but he jackknifed and plunged deeper, trying to grab the cloth before it draped over the submerged vehicle. A dark silhouette appeared in the front seat, pressing against the windshield, eyeing his slow-motion movements. He saw the person's mouth opening, stretching wide.

━━━

Though the pressure pounded like thundering drums, a piercing, mournful "Hellllllp!" came from the car, echoing in his ears. The water turned to thick molasses as he struggled to reach the shroud to pull it away, but it dropped, slipping from his fingers. His lungs were bursting when all strength left his body. He hung motionless, watching the shapeless cloth quickly envelope the car. Suddenly, the shroud rose toward him like gaping black jaws, obliterating his vision and any escape. He stroked and kicked frantically to get away from it, but his body tumbled over and over, rolling and spinning, head over toes. The shroud wrapped around his flailing arms and legs, dragging him deeper under the water into a black void. With his last breath, he screamed a shrill, unintelligible sound. But he knew no one would hear it.

Knight's cry woke him up. The sheets were disheveled and drenched with sweat from his nocturnal thrashing, which also had sailed one of his pillows across the room. He sat up clutching the other against his chest with both arms, trying to stop his body from shaking. The luminous numbers from his Sony digital alarm clock cast a pale green glow into the black room, and he tilted his head to see the time. It was four in the morning. He began to rock back and forth, still holding on to the pillow. The sobbing began slowly, but when it changed to wailing, he stretched on the bed, jerking with convulsive spasms. He pounded the mattress with his right fist and buried his face in the pillow to muffle the animal-like shrieks climbing out of the pit of his stomach and the deepest recesses of his mind. When the sounds stopped, he turned over the side of the pillow wet with tears, pulled the top sheet up to his clammy shoulders, and drifted asleep.

It wasn't until 9:30 A.M., when he pulled into the parking lot of 8 Brickell Plaza, that he remembered he had had a nightmare last night. His mind was blank as to any detail or recollection, but from the stark sense of fear, he knew it had to have been about water again. He forced the thought away, not wanting to remember, and the fear went with it. He hurried into the building, hoping that Tony would be calling soon with news from the Bay of Pigs veterans' dinner.

Knight heard the clicking of the word processor as he opened the office door. Jennifer had the Lanier dictation earphones on, but she looked up when he entered the reception room and then took them off.

"Morning," he mumbled, forcing a small smile.

"Hi." Her face was serious, but her eyes told him to look to the other side of the room.

A woman sat on the edge of a plush burgundy chair, tapping the carpet with the toes of her low-heeled pumps. Her hands twisted a small handkerchief as they rested on a black purse in her lap. The yellow shirtwaist dress she wore was wrinkled, but that color seemed bright compared to the pallor of her face. Her hair looked as if it had not been touched by a brush for days. Red rims circled her brown eyes, narrowing them to slits. She inched forward on the chair as Knight walked to her, then grabbed his outstretched hands to pull herself up.

"David, oh, David! Tony's dead!" Sarah Costas cried, pressing her head to his shoulder and burying her face in the lapel of his suit coat. Knight gasped, then held her shoulders tightly, muffling her sobs.

Her body rocked against his, quivering uncontrollably. He had seen this reaction before from wives of men he had worked with. It was the shocking reality of the dread every government agent's wife lived with and hid from; it was the lightning bolt from the ugly black cloud that hovered over the happy facade of camaraderie at their backyard barbecues, wedding receptions, and retirement parties; it was death in the line of duty. And in its tragic wake, it left children without fathers, widows with shattered dreams, and a soon-forgotten name on a dusty plaque in some agency's headquarters.

As she pressed closer to his chest, Knight felt his own pain growing. This time was different from others; this time, Tony Costas was the dead government agent.

Wives rarely spoke of this omnipresent anxiety to each other or their husbands. But during those lonely sleepless nights when they waited for his familiar footsteps, few did not sink with panic when the telephone rang, fearing it would be the voice of a senior agency official instead of her husband. This stress, more than any other, threw sacred wedding vows onto a path of steady disintegration that led to drugs, alcoholism, and broken marriages. Darwin was right about the nature of this female species: Only the strongest survived.

Knight knew Sarah Costas was one of those women. She was endowed with a tenacious emotional resilience that withstood the intense pressure of living a secret life because of her husband's dedication to his job and country. She also possessed a unique combination of compassion and intelligence that not only allowed her to console Tony and Knight when they voiced their fears and frustrations but frequently to give insights and sound advice about their operational problems and solutions. Sarah was more than a CIA case officer's wife; she was Tony's best friend and closest co-worker. Yet Knight knew her strength was not self-sustaining; it was drawn from the fountain of unselfish love and devotion that flowed for her husband.

Now, as he held Sarah, the realization that Tony was dead made him weak and queasy. Nausea flooded his stomach and crawled up his neck, sticking in his throat. He felt her pain join with his overwhelming bitter anger. His body tensed and he kept his arms around her, as much to control himself as to comfort Sarah. He led her down the hall to Paul's office, holding her thin, trembling shoulders tightly. Guiding her to the couch, he sat down and took her hands in his.

They reached into each other's eyes while Sarah took deep breaths. There was no need for consoling comments. She was as much a professional as any agent, and he knew she would want to go straight to the facts. When the tremors left her hands, Knight spoke.

"How did it happen?" His voice was sympathetic but firm.

"A car, David, a hit-and-run driver, on Calle Ocho near Twenty-fourth Avenue. The police called at one-thirty and said it happened a little before one. They said the car must have been going at least fifty, that Tony was dead before he hit the ground." Tears trickled down her cheeks, but she stayed composed.

"Witnesses?"

"No one, nothing, not even a description of the car or a license number. It was almost right in front of Centro Vasco. His car was right across the street. The police say he smelled of liquor, and probably wasn't even looking when he crossed. It's wrong, David, I know it and you know it. That restaurant doesn't close until three, and it must have been crowded because of the reunion dinner. Someone had to see something; someone had to be outside. People are always coming and going at that time."

"What about the valet parking?"

"That's what I asked the police. One was inside; one was looking for a car in the lot. I guess that's possible, but liquor on his breath? And Tony's car, David. Across the street?" A tinge of anger crept into her soft voice.

"I know, that's what I thought of when you first said it. He always parked at least a block away from any meet, so he could check for surveillance. Even a block was close, and he did that only if he felt secure." Knight leaned back and gazed at Paul's cluttered desk, but he was thinking about the car.

Sarah anticipated his thought. "But this was at night. You know how careful he was. Going to a place like that, he'd park a mile, maybe two, and take a cab. He'd never park across the street from anyplace he went. I can't tell that to the police, but that's how I know." She turned to look out the window and dabbed at her eyes with the handkerchief. "That's why I'm sure he was murdered."

As she confirmed Knight's conclusion, a wave of guilt swept

through his body. Tony had gone to Centro Vasco for him, to help him. Could that have caused someone to kill Tony? Did Sarah know that Tony went to the dinner because he pressed him for information on Milian? Knight could not bring himself to ask those questions now. The nausea returned and he wanted to vomit. But he had to know more.

"What about the Agency? Have they been to see you?" Knight asked.

Sarah took another deep breath. "They came to the hospital about three, two men from the Office of Security. We went to a hotel room at the Omni. Another one was waiting there. I don't even remember their names. They were very nice, not at all a heavy team, and they kept me there until five. They asked the standard questions: Did I notice any strange behavior, any new friends, drugs, drinking problems, another woman, was Tony unhappy about anything, did he say anything bad about the Agency, why did he go to Centro Vasco last night."

Her calm, thorough recitation bothered Knight. But not because he thought it was too concise, direct, or unemotional; he expected that. It was his own inner turmoil, contrasted to her control, that made him uncomfortable while he listened to her.

"It all seemed very routine. They tried to make me comfortable, and I think they were satisfied with my answers. But when I told them about Tony's car across the street, they just said, 'That's interesting.' It was funny, but I almost got the idea that they weren't interested. It was just a feeling I had, but there was something about their attitude I didn't like. Somehow, it almost seemed too routine. Maybe I'm wrong; I don't know. I had all kinds of feelings, but most of the time I was numb. One drove me home in my car and another followed. They said they'd probably get back to me in a few days."

"What about a polygraph?"

"They didn't say. And I didn't volunteer. I don't think it'll go that far."

Knight had to ask the next question, but his stomach churned as he thought about the possible answer.

"Did they ask you anything about me?"

"No." Sarah paused. Her eyes fell to her lap. She raised them slowly, and her voice dropped to a whisper. "But I lied about why Tony went to Centro Vasco."

Knight put surprise on his face. "You lied? Why did you lie about that? What did you tell them?"

"David, I know about yesterday. Tony told me about your meeting at P.J.'s. You know how we felt about you. Tony and I talked about your problem with the Agency polygraph for days, hour after hour. There were some things he said he couldn't tell me, but he did say you were set up. He didn't know why; I really believe that. If he had, he would have told me.

"Before he went to the dinner last night, he said he was worried about you. He was really upset after you asked him about the Milian thing; he said he thought it was too dangerous for you to get involved. I haven't seen him like that in a long time. But I don't know what it was; he said he couldn't tell me. I honestly don't know anything about Milian. He almost didn't go, but he said he had to help you. I told him that if there was anything he could find out that might help you, he should go." She closed her eyes and covered her face with both hands, then folded them in her lap and looked at Knight. "David, don't feel guilty. You would have done the same for Tony; I know that. I can be strong. I can handle this. But I wish I knew more, for both of us."

Knight took her hands again, squeezing them gently. "Sarah, I'm going to find out what happened, and why. Whether it had something to do with Milian or not, I'll get the answer. I won't stop until I do, no matter what the Agency says or does." It was the strongest conviction he had voiced in months. A surge of emotion tried to lift his sadness to angry determination.

She nodded and squeezed his hands. "Oh, I forgot something, but I don't know what it means. Just before Tony left, he said something like 'Torres is the missing link.' I'm not sure, Patrick was crying to be fed and I couldn't hear everything Tony said. I tried to ask him which Torres, but then he walked out. He said he'd be home before twelve. By one o'clock, I was getting worried. You know, it's funny. I was getting ready to call you, to see if you'd heard from Tony. But the phone rang, and it was the police."

Sarah sat back against the couch, folding and unfolding the handkerchief, staring at the opposite wall. There were no tears now, only a vacuous, immobile expression of silent pain. Her stoicism had faded, yielding to the bleak, numbing reality that invaded every cell of her body: Tony was dead.

Knight helped her up from the couch and embraced her. She quivered in his arms for an instant, then backed away, holding his elbows. She sniffled from the watery fullness coming back to her eyes.

"Sarah, listen to me. There's more to this than Tony ever knew; I'm sure of it. I don't know what it is, but I've got to go after it. The Agency will never tell you the truth even if they know; they'll just wrap it up in national security labels and bury it in the basement at Langley. That's why I've got to do it on my own.

"But I can't let the Agency or the Bureau know that I have anything to do with this. I don't trust them and neither should you, especially now. I'll have to do it on my own, but we can't have any open contact with each other. They'll probably be watching you. You'll have to be cooperative, but very careful," he said, as if he were giving advice to a criminal client.

A sigh relieved his tension, but he was sorry he had been so blunt. He wanted to help Sarah and the children through their grief, to be near whenever she needed someone. But he knew it would be impossible to do that and run his investigation as a singleton: a lone operative in the cold, without any allies or support to fall back on.

Tony's murder injected a personal factor into Knight's equation; one of his closest friends had been killed because he tried to help him. Despite Sarah's admonition, guilt penetrated his psychic membrane like a scalpel slicing into his chest. He had to turn the feeling around, redirect his anger, and unleash its fury on those responsible for killing Tony. He could wait no longer for the right time to begin; he had to start now. While she searched her purse for another handkerchief, he sifted through Sarah's account of her last conversation with Tony.

From the remark to Sarah about Torres being "the missing link," Knight assumed Tony meant Miguel Torres. If it was Miguel, then Tony must have known something about him that Knight did not. And Tony had confirmed to her Knight's indelible perception of the CIA polygraph debacle: He had been set up for destruction by unknown and powerful adversaries. If fact and theory fit together, he had another link—but to what?

Miguel was *my* source, he thought. How could Tony have known more about him than I did? If he did, why didn't he tell me?

Knight didn't have time to answer his bewildering questions: Sarah was his consideration now. He walked her silently through the reception room, out to the elevators. There, she hugged his shoulders and kissed his cheek.

A thought suddenly jolted him, but he spoke calmly.

"Sarah, did Tony mention anything to you about a new exile plot against Fidel? Young blood, not the old guard?"

She stared at his chest, then looked up. "No, I don't remember anything like that. Why? Did he say something to you?"

"No . . . it was just a rumor I heard. You know how those things go around in Miami. It's probably nothing."

He didn't want to burden Sarah with more than she had to deal with now. If Tony hadn't told her about an anti-Castro exile plan to assassinate Fidel, the information couldn't have been that credible.

They made arrangements to talk by a coded telephone call to his office if Sarah learned anything, but otherwise they would have no contact. She stepped into the empty elevator and stood at the rear wall. Knight thought she looked as frail and vulnerable as a scarecrow in a hurricane. As the doors shut, he sent a small smile to her. Then she was gone.

His steps back to the office were slow, burdened by the weight of sadness and uncertainty and a confusing mixture of anger and grief. He believed Tony had tried to help him . . . and that he had died because of it. The tragic irony hung in Knight's throat: Tony had told Sarah the Milian issue was too dangerous for Knight; yet his attempt to help his friend, by bringing it up at the dinner last night, turned out to be fatal for Tony.

Knight felt clammy. A cold sweat spotted his collar and forehead as his conscience, shorn of psychological defenses, heaped the responsibility for Tony's death on his shoulders. He found no consolation from the apparent connections between two probable murders and the Estevez message to Torres about Milian, nor did he even want to think about how these events related to the CIA polygraph. For now, no thought could or would enter or leave his mind, not as long as numbing, mournful guilt and sadness permeated his soul.

SEVEN

Jennifer was on the telephone when he entered the office. He waited in front of her desk as she spoke to a judge's secretary, setting a hearing date for a motion on one of Paul's cases. Her profile was stunning, and Knight caught himself staring at her; he wasn't sure what thoughts she evoked in his mind, but they pushed some of his sorrow away. Whatever those feelings were, he had a difficult time keeping them from interfering with his emotions of a few minutes ago. She hung up the phone and turned to him.

"She was here about ten minutes before you came in. I called you as soon as she told me she needed to talk to you, but I guess you were already on your way. I'm sorry, but I overheard. What happened, was her husband killed in an accident?" She hesitated for a moment, avoiding his eyes. "I didn't mean to pry, it's just that I've seen women like that before."

Knight pictured Sarah leaving on the elevator. "Accident? . . . Yes, I guess you could say that. He was a friend, a good friend I'd known for a long time. I just tried to calm her down," Knight said hoarsely. He felt his eyes reddening. I need to be alone, he thought. I can't stand here talking.

"I've got some work to do in my office, so hold my calls. Tell them I'm in court and I'll be back around two. But if Mrs. Costas calls, put her through," he said, hoping she didn't notice his reaction. Then he saw her eyes.

There it is again, just a flash, that silent recognition. She knows something's wrong; my God, I can feel her sympathy. How can she read me like that? Why do I sense it so easily?

It vanished as quickly as it had appeared, however. She picked up the dictation earphones and turned back to the word processor without a comment. Her fingers jumped on the keyboard before Knight took the first step toward his office.

He closed his door quietly and took off his suit coat, draping it over a hanger on the doorknob, and rubbed his eyes. His desk was bare except for a yellow legal pad and the three white ceramic monkeys on the corner. He sat on the edge and picked one up, brooding over their symbolism.

Every client or casual visitor who saw the simians thought they were the classic three monkeys: hear no evil, see no evil, speak no evil. Yet only occasionally did Knight point out the error in that supposition. A closer view revealed one cupping its ears to hear better; another shading its eyes to see better; and the third covering its mouth, to speak without being seen. Their deceiving appearance totally refuted Occam's razor, the scientific and philosophical principle that the best explanation is the simplest, using the fewest assumptions.

More significantly, though, they exemplified the cutting edge of Knight's trade for the last twelve years, characterizing the quintessential ground rules of the counterintelligence game: Everything is deception, nothing is as it appears, illusion is reality, and coincidence is far beyond the out-of-bounds line.

The monkeys had been given to Knight by Julio Cruz, a notorious Cuban exile who had been a master practitioner of the game. Trained by the CIA in the early sixties, his talents had been used by the Israelis in the 1967 and 1972 wars against Egypt. After that he traveled widely, weaving intricate webs of deception and disinformation, addicted to the danger of playing multiple roles for different masters at the same time. Yet when he returned to Miami in 1979, Knight developed a bond of trust and a shared idealism with him that few in the intelligence community counseled or understood; other agents had been burned by Cruz, and thought he was the epitome of betrayal.

However, the continuum of Cruz's vast knowledge gave Knight information of inestimable value. Cruz divulged computerlike data during their clandestine meetings, and often spoke of the motivation that governed his complex machinations. He once summarized it in a single sentence: "David, I never play to win or to lose; I just play to stay in the game." Still, he was adamant in his belief that a network of pro-Castro Cuban exiles had burrowed into the economic and political power structure of Miami, with designs to manipulate their paths to the highest levels of government in Washington. Cruz was certain the plans had been in place since the late sixties. While Knight's other sources never speculated about such a scenario, their bits and pieces of information tended to corroborate Cruz's grand theory.

Crossing from one shadowy side of the underworld to another like a cat in a dark alley, Cruz had collected a mental catalogue of the deepest secrets of those exiles who had risen to false respectability in the business, banking, and political hierarchies of Miami. The plans he had discussed with Knight to surface them, though, never became operational. Cruz finally paid the ultimate price for knowing too much; he was killed in a mysterious boating accident in 1983, but there was little doubt that it was a hit designed to keep him quiet, forever.

The exiles he had named to Knight breathed a collective sigh of relief, believing they were finally safe from compromise when his body disappeared in the depths of the Great Bahama Bank, twenty miles off the northwest coast of Andros Island. A few thought Cruz might have confided his secrets in Knight; and to those miscreants, David Knight had once been a constant threat to the existence of their hidden agendas. But when he had been drummed out of the FBI and discredited by the CIA, the word in underground Miami quickly spread that he was a man without a badge. But ironically, he now saw his diminished stature as a means to reverse to his advantage. If he was not seen as a federal agent, his movements would be under less scrutiny, allowing him more freedom to act than he had when he was an agent.

Now, slowly shedding his guilt about Tony, Knight felt himself drawn back into the game by the events of the last two days. Setting the monkey on his desk, he remembered the meeting at P.J.'s. His thoughts of Cruz sharpened the focus on Tony's comments, and he realized that unknown enemies might have perceived him as an inconvenient obstruction. But if the knowledge he had in the past was enough to put him into that category, how would he be viewed by those people if they knew he was now searching for more? He didn't need an answer for that rhetorical question.

Despite their close relationship, he knew he could not play the game by Cruz's rule; the stakes were too high and already too dangerous. Knight had to win, at any cost. Still, other lessons he had learned from Cruz would serve him well in the wilderness of mirrors he was girding himself to enter.

For now, though, he would begin his first phase with the fundamental purpose of counterintelligence: detection, the identification of the hostile activity and any person or group involved in it. Meticulous investigative planning and methods had to be developed to gather solid evidence. But as he would be operating on his own, Knight would not have the resources he so easily relied upon in the past. What he didn't have, he would create with his ingenuity.

Unwitting cutouts would be required to collect the data he

needed to confirm his suspicions before he moved to the next phase. But they would have to be chosen carefully and manipulated cautiously. He calculated the margin of error factor in the red-line danger zone, and knew there was no latitude for the slightest mistake in this operation. Every move would have to be made with the precision of a brain surgeon performing laser surgery.

He decided to begin with Milian's death, to mount enough evidence to satisfy himself beyond a doubt that it was a murder. At this point, he had a possible motive but no suspect, not even a cause of death that clearly showed foul play. He had never even been involved in a homicide investigation, despite the violent deaths of people to whom he had been close. He had always backed away, removing himself from any association with them; in his work, that had been a mandatory directive.

From his limited knowledge, though, he knew the medical examiner was required to perform autopsies on persons who died from causes not readily classified as natural. That report would have details of the anatomical condition of Milian's body, as well as the precise cause of death. He had to get it as quickly as possible, but caution whispered in his ear.

It wasn't only his need to stay out of the picture that made him hesitate; he didn't even know how to get the autopsy report from the ME's office. There were some police officers he thought he could trust, but then he realized even that was too risky. Sarah was out of the question, and Paul would be too inquisitive. He drew circles on the yellow pad, filling each one with an X when he decided a name was not suitable. He finally concluded that the idea of using a friend or someone he knew was not safe; his assessment of a possible trace back to him underscored the danger of using that tactic.

Frustration nagged at him from this early obstacle. There had to be someone he could use. To accomplish his purpose, total trust was not even a consideration. All he needed was a person who knew how to get the report and didn't need to know why.

He stared at the telephone, hoping a name would jump out of his memory of past sources and contacts. His eyes focused on the intercom line, and then the answer came to him. He picked up the receiver and pushed the button.

"Jennifer, would you come in? I'd like you to do something for me." He hung up, wondering why he didn't think of her from the beginning. With her police background, Jennifer should know exactly what to do; and as his secretary, she would not need to know why. She was the perfect cutout.

He sat back, relieved that he solved the problem. A slight burst of adrenaline charged into his veins, and he felt his heart rate increase. As he recognized the stimulating surge of excitement, he smiled at the three monkeys. It had been a long time since he had experienced this feeling. But he knew what it meant: The game was about to begin.

EIGHT December 17
Cancún, Mexico

The colonel balanced on cement footings with his dusty construction boots, arms akimbo, facing the shimmering Gulf of Mexico. Distant, deep indigo water shaded to cobalt, then creamy emerald, and finally to white ribbons of foam lapping onto the pale yellow Cancún coastline. Closer to Eladio Ruiz, two dormant bulldozers faced each other like abandoned Russian T-42 tanks. An orange film of rust from the constant salt spray ran a jagged outline around their blades and turrets, while mounds of earth thousands of years old waited nearby to be pushed and leveled to fill the foundation of the new Mexican tourist hotel.

Ruiz had selected this site for two reasons: It was fifteen miles south of the crowded hotels, sybaritic beaches, and cheap concession shops flooded by free-spending gringos; and its flat white-sand desolation made it nearly impossible for any surveillance to hide undetected from his trained eyes.

The sun reflected from the water so brightly that his eyes narrowed behind black-rimmed sunglasses, but it had little effect on his leathery face and brown arms. To any observer speeding on the Tulum highway two hundred yards distant, he was a construction engineer surveying the site and planning its next phase. His broad chest stretched the sweat-stained Coors Beer T-shirt when he inhaled the salty air, but the operational phase that made him sigh was five hundred miles away, in Miami.

The man standing at Ruiz's back was at least six inches shorter, with cropped curly hair graying at the fringes of a bald spot on the back of his head. His wiry muscles pressed through the yellow undershirt Ruiz had sent to him this morning. Perspiration oozing from his pores soaked his clothes more than any day he had spent during his nine-month tour in sub-Saharan Africa, where the temperature had never been as comfortable as this morning in Mexico. He stood rigid, almost at attention, waiting for Ruiz to speak.

"I read your report, Captain Herrera. You are to be commended for your detail and efficiency. I am gratified that you carried out your mission with such precision."

Ruiz leaned over to pick up a small rock. He tested its weight, then flung it eighty yards into the Gulf with the fluid motion of a professional outfielder. Thirty-one years ago that had been his only dream, when he had played in the Cuban baseball league. But on the day the New York Yankees scout came to his home in Matanzas with a contract in hand, Ruiz was trekking to the Sierra Maestre to join Fidel Castro and his small band of idealistic revolutionaries. Since that time, Ruiz, now chief of the Directorate of Foreign Relations of the FAR, the Cuban Revolutionary Armed Forces, had been a devout believer in fate.

"Captain, you know you have always had my utmost confidence. I would trust you with the lives of my children if I had to, so do not be concerned that I have any underlying reason for asking this question." Ruiz had a larger rock in his hands and juggled it from one to the other. "Where is the letter? Are you certain your divers were as thorough as you instructed them? I do not have to remind you of the consequences if it has fallen into the wrong hands." He spoke calmly, but he wheeled quickly and his arm shot forward like a driving piston, a violent thrust that made him wince from the sharp pain in his elbow.

The rock shattered the windshield of a bulldozer, sending shards of glass flying into the mounds. Herrera ducked quickly from the explosive sound and the expectation that a sliver might pierce his body. He stared at the construction vehicle and held his breath, trying to recall the scattered thoughts he had planned earlier in order to explain the failure of the divers' mission. The penetrating gaze of the colonel made it impossible to piece them together, but he had to say something.

"Comrade Colonel, the divers were not able to stay at the scene long enough to examine everything in the car. The Miami police came sooner than we expected, shining powerful spotlights on the water." Herrera hesitated, not wanting to make the next statement, but loyalty overcame his reluctance. "One of the divers thinks they may have been seen by the police. My opinion is that they were not: They were not pursued, nor did they hear any voices calling to them. I believe they left the area undetected."

Ruiz took eight paces, counting the steps silently. It was a childish superstition that had followed him into manhood: Eight was his lucky number. When he turned back to Herrera, his eyes were hidden by the dark lenses.

"Captain, that is a reasonable opinion. It is not necessarily faulty, but it is not a fact, don't you agree?" He did not wait for a response. "But it *is* a fact that we did not recover the letter, is it not? Or do you wish to offer another opinion, comrade?"

The words were not harsh, not even sarcastic, but Herrera felt a tightening in his throat. "You are correct, Colonel." He forced the words, and they came out in a whisper.

Ruiz looked at his shoes as he walked toward Herrera. When he stopped, he spoke in a low, soft voice.

"Now, let me give you an opinion. It is very probable that homicide investigators were called into this so-called accident. It is also likely that an autopsy was performed on the body. We may therefore assume that either the police or the medical examiners have the personal effects of Victor Milian—which may include the letter.

"However, we *cannot* assume that it would have no meaning to anyone who might see it. We both know how deeply the Miami Police Department is penetrated, and that some of those agents may, in fact, be looking for the letter. Or may have even found it by now, Captain." He paused and looked at the breaking waves, adjusted his sunglasses, and turned to his companion and confidant of twenty years.

"So, my friend, what do you think we should do now?" Ruiz asked.

Herrera knew it was a rhetorical question, more of a game Ruiz had played with him over the years, using him as a sounding board. Still, he understood the colonel's thought processes and was rarely off the mark when he responded to that familiar question. And if he was wrong, he knew Ruiz would simply correct him without penalty.

"Comrade Colonel, I took the liberty of giving a directive to our people in Miami, but I did not authorize them to act without your approval. They are standing by to take the appropriate measures within the police department and the medical examiner's office. I am certain the letter will be recovered within the next few hours," Herrera said proudly.

Ruiz slapped Herrera's sunburned left shoulder, leaving a momentary white handprint. "*Muy perfecto*, Captain, well done. But you must move quickly now to give that order. You know where to reach me when it has been recovered. I must know instantly. *Vamos*, Captain!"

Herrera's arm raised to salute, but he held it down before Ruiz reached out with his hand. He turned on his heel and jogged to the rented Ford Escort parked two hundred yards away.

Ruiz walked to one of the bulldozers and swung himself up to the tattered vinyl seat. He took off his construction helmet and wiped the sweat from the inner headband with his wrist, staring through the smashed windshield.

He was disturbed at the deception he had played on Herrera, but it had to be done. Herrera did not know Ruiz was more concerned that the divers failed to get close enough to identify Milian's murderer; nor did Herrera know how difficult the operation would be, now that Anthony Costas had been killed. As much as Ruiz trusted Herrera, he could not jeopardize the meticulous planning of this operation by telling him more than the loyal captain needed to know.

His eyes wandered to the nearly indistinguishable horizon where blue sky met blue sea. A hundred miles farther, his communist homeland, once known as "The Jewel of the Caribbean," held Maria and their four niños in a comfort befitting a man whose direct superior was Raul Castro. They had luxuries unknown to his disgruntled countrymen, who envied their friends and relatives and the consumer madness in the United States.

To Eladio Ruiz, however, that materialistic fervor was not only a flaw in his people, the Americans, or any other nationality; he viewed it as a cancer of greed that reached deep inside all humanity, and the failure of his or any other ideological system to solve that problem plagued him painfully.

Ruiz slammed his fist on the construction helmet. This operation must succeed, he vowed. It is finally, and perhaps our last, chance for the beginning of change. We have started and we must go forward. But now, we have no choice but to get David Knight involved, at any cost. Ruiz stared at the rolling waves, marshaling his thoughts. Then he sighed and made his decision: We will use El Leon.

Suddenly, a chiseling sense of fear opened a crack between

hope and reality, wedging into his consciousness like a cold saber. He thought of the next eight crucial days—and the disastrous consequences if the plan failed.

Closing his eyes, he leaned his head forward and performed an act he had kept secret from everyone, even his wife and children, since he first joined Fidel. He prayed.

NINE *December 17*
Miami

Knight turned north on Brickell, deep in thought. A following car swerved closely around his rear when he changed lanes, preventing a collision that would have emptied the nearby buildings of scores of personal-injury lawyers.

Jennifer looked at him with wide-eyed surprise from the passenger's seat, then watched as he missed the yellow and turned quickly onto Seventh Street, running a red light.

"Are you all right? It's only four-fifteen, the medical examiner's office is open 'til five. We'll be there in fifteen minutes."

"What? Sure, plenty of time. Why? What's wrong?" he said, oblivious to the two traffic violations he had committed in less than half a minute.

"Nothing, never mind." She waited for a siren or the flashing red and blue lights of a police cruiser. You're lucky, Knight; I'd have had you in a minute, she thought. Then she fixed her eyes on the vehicles and traffic signs ahead.

Knight was lost in his own thoughts. After he had asked Jennifer to get the Milian autopsy report, Harrison Witham had called. Knight had never met the veteran CIA case officer before, but he recognized the deep, boisterous voice from television interviews and broadcasts of congressional hearings at which Witham had testified.

Witham had called to extend his condolences about Tony's death. He said he had talked to Tony at the reunion dinner, and that they had regaled each other with old CIA war stories. Tony had told him something about a problem Knight had with CIA headquarters, but nothing specific. The ceremonies started around eleven and Witham had been on the dais until after one. The last time he saw Tony, he said, Tony was at a table with some *Brigadistas* during the speeches.

Knight said little to Witham, and nothing about Sarah, even after the CIA man asked whether Knight thought there was anything unusual about Tony's death. If Knight wanted any help or information, Witham said, he still had connections high up in the CIA that he could call on. Just before the conversation ended, Witham said he wanted to talk to Knight in person about something he could not mention on the telephone. Knight had agreed to meet later that night.

The call had puzzled Knight, and he had spent nearly an hour thinking about it before Jennifer buzzed him to ask when he wanted her to go to the medical examiner's office. His need to see the report was now more urgent, and he had told her he would go with her to get it.

Now, half-listening to Jennifer's street directions with one ear, he mulled over the phone conversation. He remembered that Witham had strong associations with the violent anti-Castro exiles of the seventies, but most of them either had turned to drugs and were in jail or had simply retired from the terrorist trade to pursue more mundane activities in Miami as politicians or real estate entrepreneurs.

Witham sounded sincere, but why would he . . . Damn it! Tony told me about a younger group of exiles plotting a Castro assassination. Could Witham be involved? Is that what he wants to talk about? But why me?

"Slow down, it's the beige building on the right," Jennifer said, interrupting his thoughts. "There's a space; you can park right in front."

Knight stopped next to a parking meter and left the motor running. He gave her a five-dollar bill. "That should be enough for the report. I'll be back in ten minutes."

"I thought you were coming with me. You said you wanted to see how to do it." Another quizzical look crossed her face.

"I forgot, I need to drop a file off at the Justice Building. It'll just take a few minutes. I'll be right back." He watched her skirt slide up her thigh as she eased out of the car, then saw her blush when their eyes met. She slammed the door and stalked off to the entrance of the building.

Knight couldn't tell her he was going to drive double-back routes to be sure they weren't under surveillance. If he did, he would have to make more explanations. The thought of going even this far with Jennifer suddenly disturbed him. He didn't know her background or what ties she had, other than that she was Cuban. Am I taking a chance with her? Could this backfire on me now? My God, what if her father or another relative is a *Brigadista*? As he drove away, an uneasy feeling of doubt slid down his throat into his stomach.

Jennifer was leaning on a railing next to the steps, paging through a document, when Knight came by on his third pass. He pulled into a parking space and kept his eyes on her face when she got into the car.

"What took so long? I thought you said ten minutes," she said.

He didn't want to tell her he had passed by the building twice before. But he wondered why *she* had taken so long.

"Got tied up," he lied. "Did you get it?"

She held up the stapled pages and he saw the large printing on top: OFFICE OF THE MEDICAL EXAMINER, DADE COUNTY.

"You said this was a wrongful death case, right? Have you ever read one of these reports?"

Knight shrugged his shoulders. "Not really. See, I'm helping a friend who's going to teach me personal-injury practice. He says there's better money there than criminal defense work." Dammit, I've deceived and lied to the best the KGB and the DGI put in Miami, but I sound like a six-year-old kid when I talk to her.

"Oh, okay." Jennifer nodded, still holding the report. "I ran into Ed Turner, the pathologist who did the autopsy. I know him from when I was with the department. I asked him about the death." She paused and set the report on her lap. "He's not positive it was an accident. He thinks it might be a murder. Did your friend mention that to you?"

Knight thought he heard skepticism in her voice, but he had to keep playing the game. He summoned his most innocent look and hoped it would work.

"You're kidding. Damn, he never said anything about that to me. Why does Turner think it could have been a murder?"

Jennifer showed him a page. "Here, under External Examination, look what he wrote: 'There are areas of wear and tear approximately over both knees, with areas of bloodstaining over both knees. There is an irregular one-quarter-inch laceration over the left knee and a one-inch vertical laceration on the medial aspect of the right knee.'

"And down here"—she pointed—"he says, 'There is a one-half-inch laceration bilaterally seen on the dorsum of the hands, with abrasions on the knuckles.'" Jennifer handed the report to Knight.

"So?" Knight said.

"Turner says these injuries wouldn't have come from a drowning in a car, even if the body had been tossed around from the impact. He thinks they must have happened before the victim got into the car. Maybe from being knocked to the ground.

"But there's more. He says he told all this to homicide and said they should do a more thorough investigation. They came down hard and told him just to classify it as an accidental death by drowning, that they've got more serious murders to investigate. He even tried to get more information from the case file, but they told him it was sealed. He's really upset, 'pissed off' is what he said. When he complained to his boss, he told Turner just to forget it."

Knight started the car and pulled away slowly, but his mind began to race. He didn't need any more confirmation that Victor Milian's death was a premeditated murder. But why was the homicide file sealed, despite the medical examiner's protest, killing any further investigation? That was the investigative report for which Tony Costas had said he was waiting. Christ, Knight thought, now the Miami Police Department is involved in a cover-up of at least one murder. And if that's true, how the hell does Tony fit in?

"Knight, put your lights on. It's dusk, almost dark," Jennifer said. "And I think you better tell me what's going on."

"I told you, I'm just doing this for a friend. I don't know what this means. I'm no homicide expert," Knight said sharply, fighting for time to put the new pieces into place. He drove up the ramp to the Dolphin Expressway and then headed south on I-95 as the high arc lights sputtered on.

"I know that. I'd rather know why we've been followed for the last two miles by that Chevrolet," she said, motioning to the rearview mirror with her head.

Knight's eyes flicked to the mirror and he observed headlights less than a hundred yards behind. He saw the outlines of two figures in the front seat.

"When did you see them?" he said, darting a look at Jennifer. Then he crossed two lanes without a turn signal. The headlights followed and drew closer, narrowing the gap.

"They pulled out a block after we left the ME's office. I wasn't sure, but now I don't think I'm wrong," she said, looking over her shoulder at the car behind.

Dammit! How did I miss it? Who the hell are they?

"I asked you a question." Anger raised her voice. "What's going on? Why is that car tailing us?"

His tone matched hers. "I don't know. I'm trying to figure that out."

"Why don't you try to figure out how to lose it, then find out why? I don't like this, Knight. Whatever you're involved in, I don't want to be a part of it." Her eyes pierced the side of his head.

They crested the slope where I-95 ended and changed into South Dixie Highway, three southbound lanes of creeping rush-hour traffic. Knight's thoughts flashed from Milian to Tony to Witham, but they jumbled together in the glare of the headlights now only a few car lengths behind.

"Turn here!" Jennifer shouted.

Knight spun the wheel sharply to the right and headed north on Third Avenue, but the tail car fell into place, speeding to catch up. Jennifer watched it closely and saw the car begin to pull abreast in the left lane.

"Get over," she motioned, "cut it off. Make a half-left at Five Points, then another quick left. Maybe we can lose them in the Roads or get them jammed in the traffic on Coral Way."

Knight knew what she meant. The Roads section was a confusing area of angled streets that intersected streets and avenues at locations inconsistent with the typical north-south, east-west street layout of the city. But suddenly he saw a stop sign shining at the busy Coral Way intersection.

"Get across and go left! Drive!" Jennifer said, slamming her hand on the dashboard.

He pulled into the onrushing westbound stream of cars. Tires screeched and headlights flashed into the car as he cut across and turned east. The tail car was at the stop sign now, but irate drivers kept moving, preventing it from crossing Coral Way.

Knight drove down a side street to Twenty-sixth Road, made a right and then a quick left to go up the ramp to northbound I-95.

"Get off at Eighth Street," Jennifer directed, "and go into the Wendy's parking lot, on the other side of the building."

A space between a van and a high-wheeled Bronco gave a hidden view from the street and passing cars. Knight shut off the ignition and loosened his tie, staring at the customers in the bright fast-food eating area. His appetite was not stimulated by the hamburgers and french fries on the blue and yellow tables.

"What the hell is going on?" Jennifer grabbed his wrist and pulled his hand from the steering wheel, forcing him to turn and look at the ember specks in her blazing eyes. "If you knew you had a problem, why'd you involve me? Why did you drag me into something dangerous? What would have happened if they'd caught us? What kind of a man are you?" She barely paused for a breath.

"Who are they, Knight, some guys you ripped off on a fee? Friends of a client you guaranteed a walk, but the guy got twenty years instead?" Her hair whipped around her face as she looked away.

"Forget it. I don't want to know. You criminal lawyers think you can have everything. You always play so close to the line, or cross over it, trying to stay in the fast lane with your clients. God, I've seen so much of it in this city . . . and I'm goddamn sick of it."

Knight sat silently, listening to her tirade.

"Dammit, am I stupid. When I saw you with that woman in the office, I thought you might be different. You looked like you cared about something or someone, but I was wrong, dead wrong. You're sleaze, Knight, just like all the others."

Knight knew she was spent, though her chest still heaved with anger. But her outburst solved his immediate problem. He slumped behind the wheel and frowned, hoping his silence and abject demeanor would cement her spoken suspicions. Better to let her think he was dirty than try to explain questions he couldn't answer.

Cut her out, he thought, and minimize the risk. Close off this compartment right now, while you have the chance. Jennifer's too volatile, a little too clever—and maybe too dangerous.

TEN Four blocks from Wendy's, a noisy drizzle spattered the windshield. Knight turned on the wipers and the dry rubber squeaked a metronomic cadence that heightened the tension in the car.

"Go back to Coral Way, up to Nineteenth Avenue, and take a right," Jennifer said softly. "It's my uncle's house. I stay there when I don't go out to my apartment in Kendall."

Knight's emotions rumbled beneath his stone-faced facade, barely visible in the glow from the dashboard lights. Who was in that car? Why were we followed? Who could have known that I was going to the medical examiner's office? His mind came up blank when he sought the answers, and he eyed Jennifer with his peripheral vision.

He could not understand the effect she had on him. Every logical thought told him to be quiet, to concentrate on his questions, but her presence only intensified the strange, uncomfortable feeling that he wanted to tell her what he was doing. It was one of his rare intuitive flashes that made him believe she could help, but he had no idea how or why.

Lightning illuminated the car's interior, followed by a crackling thunder roll from the west that startled him, but the jolt dispelled any thought he had of taking her into his confidence. Not now, Knight, get her out of your mind; focus on what you have to do and stay with it, he thought. The impulse to divulge the truth to her fled like the beading raindrops running off the hood of the car.

"Third house on the right," she directed impassively.

Knight pulled in the driveway, two strips of concrete splitting the front-yard grass of a small bungalow. A globe fixture lit the cement porch, where two web-strapped lawn chairs soaked in the windswept rain. He parked behind a battered Toyota, a car length away from the porch. Reaching into the backseat, he held up a compact umbrella to show Jennifer.

"The least I can do," he said, and stepped into the rain. He walked around and kept the umbrella over the open door as Jennifer put her foot into a pool of water. She muttered a word in Spanish he could not understand.

As Knight collapsed the umbrella under the porch overhang, the front door opened. A slight, narrow-shouldered man stood silhouetted against the inside lights.

"Jennifer! I worried about you, the storm, the rain! I'm glad you're here," the man said, hugging her shoulders. He smiled at Knight. "Thank you, sir, for taking care of my niece."

She glared at Knight, then looked at the man. "Uncle Felix, this is one of the lawyers I work for. He gave me a ride."

Knight reached for the man's outstretched hand, expecting a gentle handshake, but it felt like squeezing a rock.

"It was a pleasure; I'm glad I could help. My name's Knight, David Knight." He watched Jennifer step inside without looking back, but the man still held his hand.

"David Knight?" He pulled Knight closer, bringing him into the glare of the porch light. "FBI?"

Knight's foot caught the door mat and he stumbled into the foyer, but he was thrown off balance more by the man's word of recognition than by his own clumsiness. Caution and curiosity told him not to respond. In the brighter interior, Felix's face was a total blank to Knight's mug-shot memory.

A few inches taller than Jennifer, his facial skin was puckered and wrinkled below his gray crew cut. His shoulders sloped so sharply that his body was almost feminine, but his forearms were muscled like an arm wrestler.

He finally let go of Knight's hand and moved behind him to close the door. Knight's quick estimate put Felix in his early fifties, and he was surprised at the man's dexterity.

"Ah, Mr. Knight, this is a great pleasure. It is an honor to meet you." His eyes brightened with his smile, but he quickly threw his shoulders back when he saw Knight's puzzled look.

"*Permiso*, Mr. Knight, I am sorry. I am Felix Monzon." He said his name politely, formally introducing himself with a nod of his head. There was no hint in his voice that the name would or should have an impact on Knight. Nor did it.

Knight followed him into the small living room, where Monzon offered him an overstuffed chair next to a lamp table. A similar chair was opposite, with an open *Time* magazine sprawled on the seat cushion. Monzon folded it carefully and put it on the table. He looked out the window behind Knight.

"This weather, it's a terrible storm. Please, sit and have coffee with me, Mr. Knight. Perhaps the rain will let up soon."

It was a reasonable invitation, but Knight was still thinking about the surveillance car. He needed time; this might give him a chance to collect his thoughts.

"Fine," Knight said, standing up to take off his damp suit jacket.

Monzon smiled and disappeared into the kitchen.

Knight glanced around the room. A television sat on a movable stand in front of a flowered-fabric couch. Two jammed bookcases stood on the sides of a fake fireplace with a white mantel, and a basket filled with magazines rested on the floor near Monzon's chair. But instead of pictures on the walls, five rectangular boxes hung with no particular design. Knight ambled to one for a closer look.

It was a miniature room, and Knight recognized it instantly—the Oval Room of the White House, detailed to pencils on the President's desk, flags, trophies, the presidential seal on the carpet, and the view of the Washington Monument, the Ellipse, and the East Lawn from the windows. The precision was flawless.

"What do you think of my hobby, Mr. Knight?" David turned quickly and saw Monzon beaming. "I made everything you see in that box, even the box. I am a miniaturist."

"I've never seen anything like it. The detail is remarkable. I've only seen pictures of the Oval Room, but this is even more realistic," Knight said. "How do you do it?"

"I have been crafting miniatures for many years." Monzon's voice was suddenly serious. "I believe in total precision, mastering the most minute detail, creating the perfect replica. It is all a matter of practice and discipline. It has helped me in the past to focus my mind on the most important task at hand. And, Mr. Knight, it is also an illusion; it is true, but it is not real. Like so many things in life, don't you think?"

Monzon did not wait for Knight to answer. "Here's the coffee. Why don't we sit?"

For the first time in the last ten minutes, Knight wondered what Jennifer was doing. He didn't think she had heard Monzon's term of recognition at the door. It was just as well she was not in sight, nor too much in mind; he wanted to concentrate on her uncle's familiarity with his name. Knight was more than curious, but not apprehensive—unless Monzon gave him a reason.

Knight knew that in the underground concentric circles of

Miami in which he had traveled, different lines and avenues of communication had a unique tendency ultimately to overlap or intersect with each other. Names, dates, rumors, conspiracies, and convoluted schemes passed through the denizens of this shadowy world like thousands of telephone wires feeding into the gigantic Southern Bell switchboard. Yet their whispers were always word-of-mouth: hushed voices at a table in a restaurant, cryptic words on a street corner, a one-mile ride in a car to pass information to a cop or a coconspirator.

Like electric impulses radiating from a vast power plant, data and knowledge generated through complex networks that linked spies, terrorists, informants, drug dealers, shady bankers, intelligence services, and law-enforcement agencies. And though secrecy and compartmentalization were paramount, there were always other people who knew what the secret-holders wanted to keep hidden.

However, David Knight was more than just an operative who had stalked the Miami labyrinth for more than fourteen years. He was a gringo federal agent, a law-enforcement officer whose duties, and his own desires, kept him in the darkest corridors of intrigue and intelligence activities. It was in this realm that his name would surface, often as an enemy, sometimes as a friend, frequently respected, mostly feared.

So he didn't find it unusual that Felix Monzon had heard of him. Knight thought Felix might have associates who had mentioned his name. At best, Felix might be a peripheral player in the game. More likely, Knight surmised, Monzon was an insignificant exile who picked up on gossip flowing at the dozens of outdoor Cuban coffee stands in Little Havana. If he was something else, Knight was certain he would have heard of Felix.

A sudden torrent of rain thudded on the thin tile roof as Knight sipped from the cup. "American coffee? I'm surprised, Mr. Monzon."

"I'm sorry, but I don't drink Cuban coffee. Too strong, you

know. I had an ulcer many years ago," Monzon said, patting his stomach.

Knight decided to be direct. He folded his hands and tried to straighten his back against the lumpy cushions.

"I'm a lawyer downtown, Mr. Monzon. You mentioned the FBI. Why did you say that?"

Monzon smiled. "Mr. Knight, please, I didn't mean to surprise you. David Knight of the FBI is not unknown, nor is his face."

Knight sat back. Now he was surprised. He took a deep breath and hoped it wasn't noticeable to Monzon.

"In fact, you are well known, but I had no idea I would ever meet you, especially like this," Monzon said, sweeping his right arm at the room. "In my home, I mean. I am very pleased that you came with Jennifer tonight."

"Well, like I said, I'm trying to be a lawyer now. I'm not with the Bureau anymore. That's all behind me." He turned and put the cup and saucer on the table.

"No, no, no, Mr. Knight, I understand. It's just that I have heard so much about you, that you are a man of honor, a good person, a very fair man. I should not have to tell you that is not said about many men, especially in Miami."

Knight wasn't sure what to make of the flattery, but he had no quarrel with Monzon's last phrase. His mind flashed to the CIA polygraph operator for an instant, then he looked down at his folded hands. He felt tired.

"Thank you, you're very generous. But I really must be leaving. I have to be in court in the morning. Tell Jennifer—"

Monzon interrupted. "Please, Mr. Knight, stay a short while. It's still raining. I'll get you more coffee. Let's talk. Jennifer won't bother us." His voice had an edge of firmness, a slight tone of a command.

Knight didn't argue. The chair's comfortable, the coffee's hot, and my own apartment is as dreary as a damp stable. A sharp jolt of panic cramped the small of his back. My apartment! Dammit! After that chase, whoever was in that car might be waiting for me to show up. I can't go there now! Easy, easy, he told himself. This is as good a safe house as you'll get tonight. Let Monzon talk, and take the time to figure out your next move.

Monzon held the *Time* magazine in his lap, tapping it on his thigh. Knight glanced at the cover and saw the profile of Fidel Castro. He thought of asking whether it was the current issue, but Monzon was already talking.

"*El Máximo Líder*, Mr. Knight, on the front of *Time*. Can you believe it? This cover will be a, how do you call it, a target board . . ."

"A dart board."

Monzon chuckled. "Yes, a dart board, in one hundred thousand homes in Miami this week." His gaze lingered on the picture and his grin faded. He looked up at Knight.

"But he is old and tired, I see it in his eyes. I believe things are not going well for him, from what I read. What do you think, Mr. Knight?"

Knight didn't expect such an abrupt question, so he ventured a bland opinion. There was no need to be specific or provocative.

"He's had some hard times, but not all bad. Thirty years in power shows that he has something the people in Cuba want. That's more than our own Democrats or Republicans can say. He's a survivor, he's proved that, but I've read about some dissatisfaction on the island. Look at Mariel and the raft people that keep leaving Cuba. I guess that means something."

"Ah, yes, the dissatisfaction. Some people say it is much stronger than he or anyone in Cuba will admit. But that is a difficult fact to prove in a closed society. Even though he is old, Fidel is very, very smart. He has played his game well for many years. This business now with the Soviet Union . . . with Gorbachev is very interesting. Glasnost, perestroika, what does that really mean?" he asked rhetorically.

Monzon opened the magazine to a tabbed page. "See, here he admits that the Soviet Union and other communist countries may be going through a stage of modernization and liberalization. But then he says in a speech a week ago, 'Cuba will never adopt methods, styles, philosophies, or idiosyncrasies of capitalism.'" Monzon read the sentence as if he were giving the speech.

"It is curious, don't you think? What do you make of it, Mr. Knight? Is this not confusing?"

Knight sipped his coffee before he answered. He knew the names and the psychological profiles of the three speechwriters for Castro, but that short quote was not enough to identify which one. Even if he could analyze it on the basis of who wrote it, he wouldn't give that type of response to a stranger. Keep it simple, basic, noncommittal—don't get drawn into something when you don't know where it's headed.

"Maybe he's just being stubborn for now, or maybe he doesn't understand the role Gorbachev wants the Russians or the Cubans to take. Most people aren't even certain about that, so maybe Castro's taking a wait-and-see attitude, like everyone else. Sure, he's had problems with the Soviets: before and after the missile crisis in sixty-two, the Tri-Continental Conference in sixty-five, the mess with the invasion of Czechoslovakia in sixty-eight, Guevara in Africa and Bolivia, the Venezuelan episode.

"I don't think this is unusual or so confusing. The Soviets will just pinch his toes when the time is right and he'll fall into line; it worked before, it'll work again. It's not so complicated." That's about one-fiftieth of the iceberg, Knight thought, but there's no reason to go into a deeper explanation.

"Perhaps. But I believe this is an iceberg that goes far, far below the surface," Monzon said, watching Knight's eyebrows raise. "I have the feeling there is something much more serious this time, and that Fidel might be aware of it. With communism crumbling, he knows he is in a precarious position."

Knight leaned forward and put his elbows on his knees, resting his chin on one hand. He was drawn in, but now he didn't care; he wanted to know more.

"What makes you think that?"

Monzon dropped the *Time* on the floor between his legs and

looked sternly at Knight. His soft blue eyes took on a grayish tinge.

"I have heard you are well versed in Cuban politics, Mr. Knight. It is not a subject that is easily understood. It cannot be taught in a classroom at a university. But you have studied it in the best of all places—on the streets of Miami, and among the hundreds of Cuban exiles you must have spoken to over so many years.

"You have been involved in your business long enough to follow the patterns of people and events, to watch them develop and evolve. We both know that is the only way to understand how the past casts its shadow on the present and the future. The writers of books on Miami that come here for six months or a year to write on the drugs, the cultural changes, and the politics in this city have no conception of how Fidel's Cuba directly relates to everything that happens here." He paused to set his coffee cup down. "It is an evolutionary process, but I believe you understand this as well as, or perhaps better than, any gringo in Miami. And possibly more than most Cubans here."

Knight hesitated to respond, reluctant to expose the thoughts that pushed to the front of his mind. Though he agreed with Monzon's analysis, he detected an underlying thread that mystified him. There was more than a suggestion that Monzon knew more of Knight than his reputation as a fair and honorable man. But the message wasn't clear, and Knight cautioned himself about engaging his conspiratorial gears. He shrugged his shoulders without speaking, signaling Monzon to continue.

"Your perception of the events you mentioned is obviously correct, Mr. Knight, but you, and most history books, are too selective. Consider how many Soviet leaders have held that role since 1959—five! And during that time, Cuba has had only Fidel! Is this not a significant fact?

"You see, if you look at the rhetoric, the economic and military assistance, the Cuban adventures in Africa, the surrogate military role imposed on the people of Cuba, you cannot escape the conclusion that Fidel Castro has been frustrated under the yoke of the Russian bear. Whether you consider him an egomaniac or not, that yoke has made him suffer bitterly. I know it is not necessary to give you a history lesson, but you must know this: Fidel has never liked the Russians. Never. It is a myth to believe that he ever enjoyed a symbiotic relationship with the Soviet Union. Stories of a romantic dalliance between the two countries, at any time, are fairy tales, propaganda fed to mindless souls and nations."

Knight wondered whether he was listening to a litany of propaganda. Still, he had heard fragments of this speculative theory before, but it always fell apart because no firm evidence was ever marshaled to support it. Yet he followed Monzon's recitation as if it was a lawyer's opening statement, with promises of facts to prove his case. He was anxious to see whether Monzon could present any hard evidence.

"That's an interesting theory, but it doesn't seem to fit the historical facts. Castro may not always have been on the best terms with the Soviets, the whole world knows that, but he's still economically dependent on them. And they need him. There may be earthquakes of change rumbling through the Soviet Union and the Warsaw Pact countries, but whether it's the destruction of the Berlin Wall or some form of democracy in Poland or Hungary, the Soviets have a strategic base in this hemisphere as long as they keep some control on Cuba. Do you really think they'd give that up? They'd be crazy to even think of it.

"Look, no nation is situated better than Cuba to interfere with vital sea lines of communications going to and from the United States, as well as resources like Mexican oil in the Gulf of Mexico. And I can't imagine the Soviets would give up those deepwater ports and electronic listening posts Cuba has on the back door of the United States. Even the Pentagon knows we could be strangled in a matter of days," Knight said, hoping his comment would provoke Monzon to come on stronger. He leaned back in the chair to listen.

"Yes, Mr. Knight, you make a strong argument indeed for the Soviet Union to maintain their presence in Cuba." He lowered his voice. "But let me ask you this—what do you know of the DLN?"

"DLN? I've never heard of it." Knight's narrowed eyes showed his puzzlement.

"Aha. The DLN, the Cuban Directorate of National Liberation; you never heard of it. I'm not surprised, but I will explain it to you." Monzon drained his cup.

"Of course, you know how the KGB took over the DGI, the Cuban intelligence service, in 1968, when the Soviets put the ultimate pressure on Fidel to walk the line they drew. From then on, every DGI activity was directed by Moscow, as it is today, under the complete authority of the KGB.

"But before 1968, Fidel had a degree of autonomy over the DGI. He had a cadre of loyal officers, most of whom had great animosity toward the Russians in Cuba, especially those of the KGB. It is a well-kept secret, but some DGI men took violent actions against the Russians, with Fidel's tacit approval. These Cubans hated the Russians as much as the Germans did in World War Two, but they were at great risk when the KGB took over. Fidel knew he had to protect them, so he created the DLN in 1969 and gave them all new identities. He told the KGB that these men had all fled Cuba, but that if any were caught on the island, they would be executed."

"And the KGB bought it? What did they do about the DLN? Was it supposed to be another intelligence arm?" Knight asked.

"The KGB was too involved putting into place their methods of control over the DGI. They brought DGI officers to Moscow for training and put those selected men in charge of the DGI and in Cuban embassies all over the world. In many cases, those officers transferred their loyalty from Fidel to the Soviets, making the takeover complete.

"But the men in the DLN remained in position, primarily training revolutionaries from other countries in terrorism and guerilla warfare. By 1973, that function was given to the Cuban army, and the DLN was disbanded. Fidel then discreetly placed the men in different posts in the government, but they still retained their intense animosity toward the Soviets. And I believe they will do anything for Fidel, anything he asks, especially if it is against the Russians." Monzon looked at Knight and a thin smile stretched across his mouth.

"So. Do you believe me, Mr. Knight? Or do you think I am just another crazy Cuban? It is an interesting story, no? But please, do not mention it to anyone else. They might think you are crazy, too." Monzon erupted in a roaring laugh that sounded too loud to come from his small frame.

Knight's head jerked back. What? A story? What the hell is this? Maybe Monzon *is* crazy. Who the hell is he? Christ, I've got more important things to do than listen to this kind of bullshit.

Knight stood up. "Thanks for the coffee, and the entertaining story. It was a very interesting evening, but I really have to leave now." He made no effort to hide his sarcasm, nor did he reach out to shake hands.

Monzon looked up from the chair, his face now grim. "I apologize for my childish humor, Mr. Knight. But what I have told you is not a fabrication, nor an exaggeration. Fidel Castro does have an anti-Soviet network concealed in his own government, I am positive. Who or exactly where, I have no idea. And I cannot tell you why, because it is a feeling, a hunch you might say, but I believe very strongly that Castro's problems with the Soviets are more severe than ever before." His expression pleaded with Knight to accept his word, but his voice was still firm.

Knight walked to the fireplace and rested one arm on the mantel. Monzon's tale had the ring of truth, but it confused him. With his experience dealing with informants and double agents and the information passed to him about the Cuban regime for so many years, he could not understand why he had never heard of the DLN, or a supposed elite group of anti-Soviet Cuban officers. How could Monzon know of it? And even if it was true, why did Monzon tell him?

Knight left that question for one more practical: What difference does it make if I have Monzon's information? I couldn't do a damn thing with it even if I wanted to.

He was more concerned with his own problems, not Fidel Castro's. There was no point in pursuing Soviet and Cuban political intrigue when he had to deal with murders and surveillance cars in Miami.

He looked toward the front door, but glimpsed a glass-framed certificate on the mantel and made out the large letters of several words: METRO-DADE POLICE DEPARTMENT, OFFICER OF THE MONTH, JENNIFER FERRER. Knight took it to read the small print. "For her courage and bravery in subduing and arresting three armed robbers without assistance while on midnight patrol, Officer Jennifer Ferrer is awarded this Certificate of Honor. . . ."

Knight held the frame up to Monzon. "This was given to Jennifer?"

"And three or four, maybe five more. She hides them, but I convinced her to give me one. She is a very strong, brave woman, Mr. Knight. I raised her since her parents died years ago. She is a remarkable young lady," Monzon said with patent pride.

Knight read the certificate again, silently, and put it back on the mantel. There's more to this girl than I thought, he mused. Then he turned to Monzon.

"What you told me is very intriguing. But whether it's true or not, it really doesn't mean anything to me. Let the CIA, the politicians, and the bureaucrats play with it if they want to. I'm sure they'll screw it up, just like everything else they do," Knight said, smiling cynically.

"Perhaps." Monzon didn't return the smile. His voice was still grave. "But it is something to be aware of, Mr. Knight. I still believe something is going to happen in Cuba, something that may affect all of us. It must be watched very closely."

Knight reached for his coat and smoothed the damp wrinkles. "Thank you again for your hospitality. Tell Jennifer . . ."

Monzon stood up quickly. "Jennifer! Mr. Knight is leaving! Come out and say good-bye!"

Jennifer came out of a room. She wore a blue sweatshirt with the sleeves pushed up, blue sweatpants, and floppy white socks. Her hair was swept back and tied in a ponytail, with wispy bangs. She looked as if she were eighteen. Knight took a deep breath as she shuffled toward them.

"I didn't know you were still here," she said, as if he was an intruder.

"Your uncle is an interesting man. We had a pleasant conversation," Knight said, looking at Monzon. "I'm sorry I stayed so long. And I'm sorry about tonight, Jennifer."

"Don't worry about it." Her words froze in the air.

"Jennifer, did you know Mr. Knight used to be with the FBI? He was in law enforcement, like you. You two have something in common, no?"

"The FBI? How nice. But that doesn't mean we have anything in common." Her expression had not changed since she had walked into the room. She stood with her hands clasped behind her back.

Monzon said. "You know, I knew an FBI agent from many years ago. He was in Miami before your time, I think. His name was Randall, Henry Randall, a gringo like you. But he did not understand the Cubans like you do, Mr. Knight. He was not very well liked in Miami."

Knight recalled the name. Randall had been on the same counterintelligence squad before Knight came to Miami. He had heard that Randall was a nine-to-fiver whose only motivation was to get close to superiors who could advance his career in the Bureau. The last he knew, Randall had been at FBI headquarters in the Intelligence Division, on the Soviet Desk.

"I've heard the name, but I don't know him. He might be at headquarters now," Knight said, moving toward the door.

"No, no. He's at the American embassy in Madrid. He calls me sometimes, to ask questions."

Knight stopped and his coat slipped out of his hand. He didn't pick it up. "He calls you? Why? What does he want?"

"You know, so many Cuban drug dealers and fugitives go to Spain. I think he tries to locate them there. He knows I hear things on the street that might be helpful, so he calls."

"He must be a Legat, in the Legal Attaché's office. They do a lot of that work overseas," Knight said.

Monzon stared at the ceiling for an instant. "It was about three weeks ago he last called. He wanted to know about a man named Torres, Miguel Torres."

"Miguel Torres?" Knight gasped. "You know about Miguel Torres?"

"Miguelito? Of course, I know him well, but I haven't seen him in three or four years. He lives in Spain, just outside of Madrid."

Knight felt his knees buckle. Vertigo spun Monzon's face, and Knight grabbed the doorknob to keep his balance. Monzon moved toward him, but Knight turned without a word and trudged to the driveway, oblivious to any memory of his meeting later with Harrison Witham. He stayed in his car five minutes after Monzon closed the door. His shirt collar clung to his neck, soaked from profuse sweat. The rain had stopped. He rolled down the window and inhaled the damp, cool air.

My God, if Miguel is alive, I've been deceived by my own government for years. Worse, Miguel must have been a part of the deception. How could he do that to me? But maybe Monzon's wrong; maybe he's talking about another Miguel Torres. There must be at least twenty in the Miami phone book alone . . . but Monzon mentioned Spain. That's a link to my Miguel. And if it is Miguel, why was Henry Randall calling about him. Wasn't Randall in the Miami Division Office, then the Intelligence Division at headquarters? But I can't remember when! Think, dammit!

108

Monzon stood behind a curtain and watched Knight back slowly out of the driveway. Jennifer's door was closed and he heard the television from her room. He walked quickly to the kitchen telephone and dialed a number.

"He just left. I told him about Torres. He didn't say anything, although his reaction was what I expected. Now we must wait." Monzon hung up the phone without waiting for a response.

ELEVEN

Harrison Witham stepped out of the shower in the steamy, cramped bathroom and opened the door to let the moist air escape. The thin towel barely made it around his shoulders as he rubbed it hard on his back. Condensation rivulets streaked down the medicine-cabinet mirror. He grabbed another towel, stepped into the coolness of the bedroom to finish drying himself, and dialed the telephone.

Damn, an answering machine. He waited for the beep. "Mr. Knight, this is Harrison Witham. I wanted to confirm our meeting tonight. Let's meet at The Fish Market on South Dixie Highway at eleven-thirty. Sorry it has to be so late, but it's essential we talk before I go. I'll be in the lounge." He spoke precisely but with a detectable drawl.

Standing naked in front of the Skyways Hotel window, Witham gazed across Lejeune Road at the palm-lined entry road and sparkling lights of Miami International Airport's terminal and high-rise parking lots. He was sorry he had to take the time to see Knight, but he had to get the information to him. It was an obligation now, an unexpected but necessary detail that could not be avoided. He had resolved his initial conflicts, and felt confident about the course he had chosen.

Though this was his last night in Miami, he had decided to stay in the room and relax until eleven. *The Green Berets*, with John Wayne, was on television in an hour. He had seen the movie over a dozen times, but he never tired of it.

God, I love that man, he thought, anticipating the dead movie star's presence on the twenty-inch screen. He looked at the bathroom mirror fifteen feet away, admiring the similarity of his build to that of his celluloid hero. *The Sands of Iwo Jima* had once been his favorite movie; three months after he saw it in 1953, he had enlisted in the marines. But when Wayne made the film about those elite warriors in the Vietnam War, Witham's preference changed.

He smiled at his reflection in the mirror. Only one difference, Duke: I was there in real combat. The real goddamn thing!

He held his hands up, sighting his image down the imaginary barrel of an M16. "Pow! Pow, pow, pow!" Then he ducked, taking himself out of the line of imaginary return fire.

Four loud raps on the door startled him, and he crashed the toes of his right foot into the leg of a walnut-veneered coffee table, wincing in pain. "Jesus!" he bellowed, hobbling toward the towel he had tossed on the couch. It wouldn't stretch to tie around his waist, so he held the corners together and limped to the door. His belly hung over the wet cloth.

"Who is it?" he growled, peering through the fish-eye security viewer in the door.

"Tom Lewis, Mr. Witham. We talked earlier about coming to see you tonight," a voice answered.

Goddamn it! It's the guys from the Office of Security, Witham remembered. They want to talk about the Costas thing. Just what

I fucking wanted to do tonight. What the hell, I'll tell them what I know and get their asses out of here.

He took the chain off the latch and opened the door. Two men in gray suits walked into the room with embarrassed smiles on their faces. Witham looked down and saw that the front flap of the towel had fallen away.

"Sorry, men, I just got out of the shower. Stand at ease," he said, hoping they hadn't heard his imitation gunfire. He dropped the towel and strode to the bathroom to put on his robe, tying it tightly. Behind the door, he switched on a wireless receiver connected to a voice-activated microcassette recorder hidden under a pile of dirty clothes. Then he returned.

Both men held their credential cases at arm's length. Witham inspected each one closely, then they slipped them back into their inside pockets.

"I'm Tom Lewis, Mr. Witham," the man with glasses said. This is Al Rubin. We're both from OS."

Witham shook each man's hand, dwarfing them in his massive grip. He noticed that Rubin had manicured nails. Each was at least five inches shorter than Witham. He gauged both to be in their early thirties. Christ, he thought, where did the Agency pick these guys up? They look like goddamn soft-bellied accountants. I bet neither one has been in fatigues since Camp Peary, probably barely passed hand-to-hand combat, for Chrissake.

He forced his mouth into a smile. "Gentlemen, please, sit down," he said, motioning to the couch. "Can I get you something from room service, a drink, coffee?"

"No thanks. This shouldn't take long. We've just got some basic questions; you know the routine," Rubin said. He sat close to a lamp and took a legal pad from a narrow leather folder with the initials ASR on the flap.

Witham stood until both sat down, then pulled up a straight-backed chair. He crossed his leg and massaged his red toes. A drop of blood oozed from one toenail, but he was more concerned with the tiny transmitter under the coffee table. He hoped it hadn't been jarred so loose it wouldn't pick up the conversation.

"Should we explain the procedure, Mr. Witham?" Rubin asked.

"Don't bother. Where's the consent form?"

Rubin handed him a paper and pen.

Witham glanced at the title and signed the document that authorized the recording of the interview. He knew he had no choice, but that wasn't even a factor to consider. Though he had been through countless, sometimes brutal, Office of Security witch-hunts before, he knew this wouldn't be one of them.

Rubin recited the names of those present, the date, and the location into his recorder, and set it on the table. He made some notes on his legal pad as Lewis began the questioning.

"State your full name, date, and place of birth."

"Harrison Arthur Witham, 10 July 1935, Odessa, Texas."

"What is your present occupation?"

"I'm a security consultant for Global Risks International, 4518 Clair Street, Fairfax, Virginia. I've been there for the last six years."

"Have you ever been employed by the Central Intelligence Agency?"

"Yes, from January 1960 until November 1976." And don't ask me what I did. If you want to know, check my fucking two-oh-two file. And good luck in trying to find it.

"Mr. Witham, we're investigating the apparent accidental death of Anthony Peter Costas, an employee of the Central Intelligence Agency, on December 17. Normally, I'd continue in a detailed question-answer format, but why don't you just give us a narrative of what you know. I'll jump in with questions as we go along if I think there should be some clarification. Sound okay?"

"Fine with me. Mind if I have a drink? Sure you don't want one?" Witham watched them shake their heads in unison, then went to the dresser. He grabbed a handful of ice from an ice bucket, dropped it in a glass, and filled the tumbler from a half-empty bottle of Johnnie Walker Black. He took a long gulp, then sat down.

"All right. I came to Miami for a Brigade reunion, that's the

Cuban group that went to the Bay of Pigs. I was a case officer for them, for the invasion in sixty-one, training them here and in Nicaragua. I was even on the first boat that landed at Red Beach at Playa Girón. You probably know that I got hell for that from Bobby Kennedy. But I also got the Intelligence Star personally from Allen Dulles, just before JFK ran him out of the Agency." Witham looked each man in the eyes to underline the importance of the CIA's medal for "acts of courage performed under hazardous conditions."

"But I got real close to the Cubans, like a brother, and I have been ever since. There's a reunion dinner every four or five years here in Miami, and I always come in for it. We always have a great time reminiscing. When we're together, it's like time never passed. It's a hard feeling to put into words. You can't really understand it, if you've never been in combat." He watched Rubin shift his weight on the couch and write something on the legal pad.

"Anyway, this time they decided to have it in my honor. To tell you the God's honest truth, those guys love me, for what I did for them. They've never forgotten that, and they won't let me forget it. Most of them would die for me, whether I asked or not." Witham paused, staring into the glass. He stirred the ice with his forefinger.

"When did you come to Miami?" Lewis asked.

"The afternoon of the fifteenth. I always come a day early to meet with some of the men I'm particularly close to; there're about six of them. We all had dinner at Fabio Camacho's house, you know, all their families, aunts, uncles, kids. They had a roast pig, buckets of paella, tons of arroz con pollo, a real spread. You can see the result," Witham said, putting both hands on his stomach. "I didn't get back to the room until about three in the morning, and I spent the next hour on the john." He smiled as he took a sip from his glass.

"Did you know Anthony Costas?"

"Know him? Not like a friend or anything, I mean I met him

maybe once or twice, just before I left the Agency. I may have run into him by accident a few other times that I came to Miami, I guess. I'm not real sure about that."

"Do you know what he did in Miami?"

"Worked for us—I mean the Agency. I just assumed he was Domestic Contacts Division, but I don't really know. It wasn't important to me, what he did. Remember, I was out of it by seventy-six."

"Why was he at the reunion dinner?" Lewis shot the question in a harsher tone, but it had no effect on Witham.

"I can't tell you, specifically." He tilted back on two legs of the chair. "Look, the guy worked here. He's got his contacts, sources, friends, whatever. A lot of them are probably *Brigadistas*; that's nothing new in Miami. It's always been like that for the outfit down here. Maybe he just wanted to get out of the house, schmooze, have a good time. I remember seeing a couple of Customs agents there, too. One got so plastered, they carried him out."

"I know, we've interviewed all of them. But Costas, did you talk to him at the dinner?"

Witham took another sip—picturing the faces of the Customs agents, where they were sitting, who they were with, trying to remember whether he had seen Costas talking to any of them— before he answered the question.

"You know, it was really crowded, shoulder to shoulder, until we sat down for dinner. I was at the head table; it was kind of like a dais. Costas came up to me and we shook hands. It was just, 'How're you doin', how've you been,' real short. He congratulated me on the award they were giving me. That's about all I remember."

Rubin leaned over to show Lewis a note on the legal pad. Lewis nodded.

"You're sure? You don't recall him asking any questions, mentioning any names?"

Witham caught the skeptical look, but he felt certain Lewis was fishing. Don't pull that trick on me, Mr. Office of Security; we all went through the same interrogation class in training.

"*Nada*. Nothing. There wasn't anything like that we had in common to talk about. Like I said, I hardly knew the guy."

"What about other people. Did you see Costas spending more time with anyone, talking to one person more than another?"

"Jesus, Lewis, there were almost three hundred people there. I can't even remember everyone I talked to; how am I going to remember whom Costas or anyone else was talking to?" He laughed. "You know, with all those cigar-smoking Cubans, I could barely see halfway across the room."

"Yeah, I think I know what you mean," Lewis said, grinning. He glanced at Rubin, then back at Witham. His eyes hardened and his face was devoid of humor.

"One last question, Mr. Witham. When you spoke with Costas, did he mention Miguel Torres?"

Witham felt his stomach muscles instantly contract. His mouth went dry and he gulped the rest of his drink, hoping the Office of Security men didn't notice the slight tremor that jiggled the ice cubes. He held the glass in both hands and rested it in his lap.

"Torres? Miguel Torres?" Witham looked over their heads, pulling his thoughts together. "You know, I don't think I've ever heard that name . . . wait, maybe . . . no, hell, I never did. And I'm damn sure Tony Costas didn't say anything to me about a guy with that name. No, that's something I would have remembered." He managed a wan smile and rubbed his forehead.

Lewis and Rubin stared at him. Witham recognized the ploy and leaned forward, pouring another drink. The gurgling bottle was the only sound in the silent room. Then he stood up quickly, regaining confidence from his towering height advantage. The panic passed and he wanted the two men out of his sight—now! But he maintained his composure with a level voice.

"Well, fellas, I guess that's it. Not much more that I can tell you. I wish I could, honest, but that's all I know. If something else comes up, why don't you get back to me? You know where to find me."

He reached to shake hands with Rubin and pulled him up from the couch. Lewis shuffled his papers into his briefcase, eyeing Witham with a slight smile.

"Right," Lewis said. "We know where to find you."

Witham walked them to the door and double-locked it when they left. Panic returned and sweat began to seep from his pores. Jesus, he thought, what the hell do they know about Torres? Why the fuck did they ask me about him? Have I been made? Do they know that I'm El Aura?

He took three deep breaths and the throbbing in his head eased. He had the answer. There's still a little time, he thought. I'll get a message to Jorge tomorrow. He felt better now, relaxed, and smiled to himself. Christ, I might even get a fucking medal out of this one!

Witham checked his watch—8:55, it's almost on. He padded to the table and pulled off the transmitter, then went into the bathroom, rewound the tape, and shut off the recorder. He put the devices into a hollowed-out book in his suitcase. Then he turned on the television and stretched out on the bed with another Johnnie Walker Black in his hand. As the opening credits came on, Witham hummed along with the familiar theme music of *The Green Berets*, certain that Jorge would be proud of his solution to the problem.

When he met David Knight later, he would tell him that Miguel Torres was alive; then Knight would do anything to find him. No matter what the CIA knew, they would never think Witham was using Knight. Torres was the key, and Knight was the path to Torres . . . and Witham was certain Torres would tell Knight. Then Witham would have both of them on the mat, and one or the other would give him what he wanted. With that information, the plan to assassinate Fidel Castro could not be stopped.

TWELVE

Knight slumped in the chair in his apartment. He purposely left the lights off, to match the bleak darkness of his mood. Monzon's startling revelation about Miguel still had his mind reeling, but it also set him thinking about past conflicts he had tried to overcome when he was with the FBI.

From the beginning, Knight had received high accolades for his triumphs as a counterintelligence agent, from his group supervisor in Miami to the Assistant Director of Intelligence at FBI headquarters. But he found himself addicted to the act of deceiving others, and it soon became not only the means to an objective; it was an end in itself. Yet perversely, he also instilled instant loyalty in those men he controlled and blind trust in other people he deliberately deceived. With the faith, respect, and admiration he commanded from each, Knight easily led them to commit despicable acts and deadly betrayals. His mastery of manipulation was consummate, and more remarkable because his talent needed no honing to create or maintain its sharp edge—it was a God-given gift, as natural as his ability to throw a football.

Painfully probing this conduct, Knight slowly extracted the truth from his reluctant conscience. When it stood in full view, he was incredulous. For the first time, he saw the shrouds of deceit in which he had wrapped himself. With incisive fury, he realized he had become a skilled practitioner of those traits of mankind he detested: He had used people and had played games with their lives by lying, deceiving, betraying, and manipulating them. In some cases, he knew his actions had caused even the deaths of known and unknown persons he had used as pawns.

That insight illuminated a chilling conclusion, however: Until now, Knight firmly believed that, in some unknown way, he had been responsible for the death of Miguel Torres. Unable to find the true reason behind that mystery, his uncertainty only fueled the condemnation he heaped upon himself. And not a day passed that anguishing guilt about Torres failed to jab at his conscience.

Still, he saw himself as a guardian, battling evil with evil's methods. At times, the moral conflicts were agonizing, yet the justification for his acts and conduct boiled down to the one belief that sustained him through risks and doubts: *Someone has to do it. If I don't, who will?* It was on that standard of personal commitment that he built and sustained his faith and confidence in himself.

His forced resignation from the FBI nearly destroyed his idealistic fervor, and his search for the scattered pieces often seemed hopeless. Relentless despair dissipated his self-confidence, transforming it into numbing apathy. Yet one remnant—his need to learn what had happened to Miguel Torres—had remained an unyielding, torturous link to the past.

Now, Knight once again wrestled with his conscience. And again, Torres was central to the conflict. His mind was still numb from the intensity of his memories and the shocking statement Felix Monzon had tossed at him so casually. Yet the sheer possibility that Torres was alive in Spain and might have had contact with Henry Randall stimulated his desire to seek the facts that would dispel a theory of mere coincidence. Moreover, he was certain Torres, if alive, would shed more light on Roger Estevez and the CIA polygraph fiasco. And possibly Tony's murder.

Spurred by that hope, questions raced through his mind. How did Monzon know Miguel? What did he know about Miguel? Why was Miguel reported dead? Why wasn't I told he was alive? Why didn't Miguel ever contact me? And the bitter question that Knight had asked himself every day for the last three years: Why was Miguel taken away from me?

He knew there were no immediate answers, but he was certain of one thing: He had to try to find them. He could do no less, given the monstrous deceit played on him. And if, by any chance, he found Torres, those questions and more just might unravel like loose threads on an old sweater.

He walked to the refrigerator for a beer and noticed the answer-phone's red light flashing. I can't listen to it now. It's probably Paul, checking up on me. Jesus, I can't talk to him or anyone else tonight, not in this mood. Anyway, it's 11:10, too late to call him back. Whatever he wants, it'll have to wait until tomorrow.

Knight stared at the answer-phone. All right, Paul, talk to me. Maybe your voice will help bring me back to reality. He pressed the message button, but it was not Paul. He listened for a moment before he recognized the stranger's voice.

My God, that's Witham! Meet at 11:30? Knight froze, trying to pull his thoughts together.

How the hell can I talk to him like this? Should I ask him about Torres or Monzon? Can I trust him? What about Milian? Dammit, I have to see him; I need to talk to him about Tony. I can't put it off—it's too important.

A rush of panic spun him around and his hand knocked the open beer can to the floor. A sharp pain ran up his neck and circled around his head, squeezing tightly. He changed shirts, shoved on his shoes, and flew out the door, trying to calculate the quickest route to The Fish Market.

Knight swung open the door of the seafood restaurant, banging it against the outside cement wall. A strong grip locked on to his forearm as he rushed toward the lounge. He turned around to see a mountain of a man and recognized Witham from television interviews. The ex-CIA man was much bigger than Knight had envisioned.

"Hey, slow down there, Mr. Knight. I was just on the phone calling your damn answer machine again. I would have waited at least half an hour, but you're only ten minutes late. Take it easy," Witham said. His voice was low, and it had a calming tone. He gave Knight a long look. "Damn, looks like you had a helluva night. I hope she was worth it." Witham laughed, slapping Knight on the back and gently pushing him toward the lounge.

The room was smothered in shades of red: red leather bar stools at a small L-shaped bar, red vinyl captain's chairs around red shiny-topped tables, and opaque red lamp shades that hid low-watt bulbs.

Knight suspected the five bar patrons were regulars. They were crowded together, buying rounds for each other, calling the bartender by her first name. A boisterous laugh erupted as he and Witham passed them, walking to a tiny table in the rear, where the voices from the bar were muted. Brilliant-colored tropical fish swam through coral crevices in a fluorescent-lit fifty-gallon saltwater tank behind their table.

Before they sat down, Witham extended his hand. "It's a real pleasure to meet you, Mr. Knight. I've heard a lot of good things about you."

"Thanks, but that always depends on the source, doesn't it?" Knight shook his hand and smiled. Thoughts of Miguel Torres still echoed confusion in his mind. He fought for clarity, hoping it came before he said something he might regret.

"Guess that's true." Witham's tinkling chuckle seemed incongruous to his size. "Look, if you don't mind, let's use first names. We may have more in common than you'd think, and I'd feel more comfortable if I could call you David."

"Sure, no problem."

A waiter interrupted them. Witham ordered a refill of his Johnnie Walker Black and Knight asked for a vodka and tonic with two slices of lime.

"I'm glad you could make it, David. I don't know when I'll be back in Miami, but it's important we have this talk now." Witham leaned his elbows and forearms on the table. His shirt cuffs rode up a few inches, exposing a battered Rolex GMT, the unofficial badge of some CIA employees who fought the clandestine wars against Fidel Castro in the sixties. Those that received it were a select group, chosen because of their courage, bravery, and ability. Witham and others wore it with the same pride as a Purple Heart, the Distinguished Flying Cross, or the Medal of Honor. For many it was a symbol of brotherhood that kept their hearts linked and their memories alive in a union of spirit that transcended time.

Knight knew that some men who wore it simply thought the GMT was a souvenir and a watch that kept good time. But from what he knew of Witham, he didn't think the man would fall into that category.

It wasn't that he knew Witham well; in fact, what he had heard was only by reputation. Passing comments by Cuban exiles made Witham a living legend, ranking him with José Martí, the leader who fought for Cuban independence against the Spanish in the late nineteenth century. Even now, Knight had heard, a crowded room of Cuban exiles would stand at attention in silence if Witham put his foot in the door. Grayston Lynch and William "Rip" Robertson, two other CIA officers who trained the exiles for the invasion and landed with them at the Bay of Pigs, were idolized but were dwarfed in stature when the name of Harrison Witham was mentioned in Little Havana.

However, if Witham expected the same reverence from Knight, he would not receive it. Knight could not remember the last time he was awestruck by any person of any rank, title, or reputation, other than when he was ten years old and shook hands with Ernie Banks, the Chicago Cubs All Star shortstop. He also recalled the comment by Tony Costas that Witham was "a pain in the ass." While that didn't make Witham a bad guy, it did take him off of a pedestal. Knight decided to make up his mind after this meeting. Anyway, he was more interested in what Witham had to say than what he was.

"Well, Harrison, you're a pretty well-known person yourself in this town. I'm pleased you made the time to talk to me. You must be on a tight schedule." Knight gave him that much.

"More than well known, friend. I guess you know about my background, so there's not much reason to go into that. I don't think I have to impress you with my bona fides, do I? If they were good enough for the Kennedys and Lyndon Johnson, they should be sufficient for the FBI, right?" A smirk hid behind his glass as he raised it to his lips.

Knight looked into his eyes. "I'm not with the Bureau anymore. I thought you'd have known that. I left six months ago. I'm just a lawyer now."

"Yeah, that's right. I heard you went through a rough time with the Agency and Burack. He's a bastard, always has been." Witham let the words hang as he drained his glass.

Burack? How did Witham get the name of the polygraph examiner? I'm not surprised he knew what happened, but how much more does he know about me?

"Well, it's all over now. I'm out of that bureaucratic bullshit, trying to make some money." Knight toyed with the swizzle stick, bending and unbending it in equal parts. He decided to get the question out now.

"Harrison, I'm not sure why you wanted to talk to me about Tony Costas. I knew him, and even helped him out a few times. That accident, my God, it shocked the hell out of me. But we hadn't talked in over a year, I guess. That's why I'm wondering why you wanted to meet, if you want to talk about Tony." Knight opened the subject like a boxer walking around the ring in the first round, sizing up his opponent.

"You know, David, in my time we never worked with the FBI. Never felt we could trust them. Back in the sixties, some of your guys went a little overboard chasing Cuban exiles they thought were violating the Neutrality Laws. You remember how a few exiles would set off in a launch from the Keys with a few hand grenades, maybe a beat-up .30-caliber machine gun.

"But some of those Bureau agents stepped on our operations, blowing our sources and screwing up our plans. Got into some real pissin' matches, let me tell you." Witham's voice rose, but he toned it down quickly.

"What I'm trying to say is, even though you're not FBI anymore, I still don't trust anyone from the Bureau. Now you say, at least what it sounds like, you didn't know Tony so well. That makes me a little suspicious, David, especially because of what I wanted to tell you. I was hoping we could trust each other." He rapped his knuckles lightly on the table in a slow cadence, then folded his hands around the glass. His eyes, black in the shadows, met Knight's.

"Maybe I should put it this way. We have to trust each other. Neither of us have a choice. And we don't have time for games, David. We can't operate like that."

The conversation wasn't going the way Knight had expected. Witham had control and Knight felt as if he was getting backed into a corner. Wait a minute, he thought. Maybe you're too defensive, maybe your guard's too high. Ride with him for a while, see where he's going. You don't have to give up everything, just enough to draw him out.

"So what's it going to be?" Witham asked. His arm was in the air, waving at the waiter.

"I guess I'm just being overcautious. It gets to be a habit, not always a good one. But I'm not trying to play games. I'm just not sure where I stand, or why this should be important to me, but let me clear something up. Tony and I were good friends. In fact, I saw him earlier that day. He said he was going to the reunion dinner, that he wanted to talk to some people, but I honestly don't know why.

"But I'll tell you one thing: I don't believe it was an accident. Call it a hunch, a gut feeling, but I think he was murdered, and I think it's being covered up, for some reason. That bothers me, and it bothers me that there's not a damn thing I can do about it. But that's it, Harrison. I'm not hiding any secrets, I don't have any to hide. If you've got any questions, take your shots. I'm an easy target." Knight had focused on the bridge of Witham's nose while he was talking, but now he looked away and saw the waiter taking an order at another table.

Witham gave a smile of satisfaction. "All right, I'm glad you cut the bullshit. I understand why you're careful; I like that. Now we can get down to business. But we've got to keep this tight. There are some heavy problems, and one is the Agency. Two guys from the Office of Security hit on me earlier tonight. I didn't tell them anything that I'm going to tell you. That's one of the reasons I have to be able to trust you, David, because if it goes anywhere else, I'm in deep shit. The Agency can't do anything to me officially, but they can make things damn miserable. I guess I don't need to explain that to *you*."

"No, not at all." Knight sighed deeply. "But I still don't understand how I fit into this. So I knew Tony? So what?"

Witham sat up straight and pursed his lips, shaking his head to tell Knight to stop talking. The waiter stood behind Knight's chair. They ordered another round, and Witham leaned closer as the waiter walked away.

"Your hunch is right, David: Tony was hit. And I think I may know why." He paused for a reaction and got one.

Knight leaned forward with his hand at his mouth, hushing his voice. "My God! Even though I thought it might be, I didn't want to believe it. How long has it been since someone from the Agency was murdered? Welch in Greece in seventy-six is the last I remember. But why Tony? Who'd have the balls to take an outfit guy down, especially in the United States? I can't believe the KGB or even the DGI would hit one of our guys; they play by the rules of the game. Did you get anything from the OS people? How did you find out?"

"Those are the same questions I asked myself," Witham said, in the same loud whisper. "I wasn't sure at first, but I wanted to check it out. I may not get to Miami that often, but I've got sources no agency's ever heard of, and they don't bullshit me.

"Let me back up a little. When Tony came to Centro Vasco that night, it was early and not too crowded yet. He pulled me off to the side and we started talking about what's going on in Miami. Mostly who's doing what now, where's old so-and-so, stuff like that.

"Then he asks me if I've heard anything about a plot to hit Fidel. I tell him I used to hear that half a dozen times a year, but it's always that same old crap. Remember what Julio Cruz said at a bond hearing in court, when a cop testified Julio threatened him? 'Judge, you know Cubans, we just talk a lot of shit.' Most of the time, that's how it is here, you know that.

"Anyway, Tony says this is different. Supposedly there's some new blood, young guys, maybe even one or two women, who don't even use a war name for their group. But Tony hears they're hell-bent to do it, and he needs more information before he passes it on to Langley."

Knight interrupted. "Harrison, wait a minute. You know that's FBI jurisdiction. It goes to the antiterrorist squad for investigation. They've got the wheels for those cases. It's their responsibility; the Agency's got to back off."

"Sure. But we both know how it works in Miami. If some CIA guy's got something like that, how often does he really turn it over, especially without clearance from Langley? Remember what I said about trusting the Bureau? You've been around long enough to know that's how it is."

Knight thought of the relationship of trust he had had with Tony, which contradicted Witham's statement. Then he realized that he was out of the FBI when Tony developed the information, and he knew there was no one else at the Bureau with whom Tony was that close. Witham had a good point.

"Okay, go on," Knight said.

"So Tony asks me, can I help him? I tell him I'll check around and get back to him. I see him talking to different people at the dinner, but I don't know if it was about this or not. Next thing I know, BOOM! Sirens, red and blue flashing lights, and Tony's dead." He leaned back, staring at the group at the bar. They were quieter now.

"But why tell me? Where am I in all of this? I still don't understand, Harrison." Knight thought he knew the answer, but he wasn't sure he wanted to hear it. Still, it might reveal what Witham knew about him. Better to get that out now.

"I'm getting to that. While I'm talking to Tony, he says you're the only one from the Bureau he ever trusted. I don't know why, but he must have known he was in dangerous territory with this plot against Fidel business. Anyway, he says if anything happens to him, I should tell you. But here's the real kicker: He says, 'Promise me you won't say anything to Langley, not a damn thing.' That blew my mind, but I figure he's got his reasons. I respected Tony, and I'm keeping the promise. He trusted me, and that's why you and I have to trust each other. Because there's more."

The two drinks had Knight's head throbbing, and his eyelids scraped like sandpaper. He wanted to fold his arms on the table and go to sleep. He knew he was losing his edge, but he had to go on.

"Look, from what you've told me, I've got no problem trusting you. Let's keep on going." He wetted his fingertips with ice and rubbed his eyes, then dabbed them with the cocktail napkin.

"Good. Like I told you, I've got my own suspicions about the accident. I start to wonder if it's tied into what Tony told me, so I go to my sources. What I get back makes it sound like he was on to something big, so big it even scares me. I can't get the whole picture yet, but here's what it looks like so far.

"There're maybe ten young Cubans from Miami, all around thirty, that've been training to hit Fidel sometime soon. I don't know if that means a week or a month. Almost all have been in Special Forces, the SEALs, or something like that. It's supposed to happen when Fidel goes to another country. I think he's got a trip coming up to visit four or five, so we can't even pin that down yet. These guys are fanatics, worse than the shooter teams the Agency used in the sixties and early seventies.

"It's bad, David. We can't find out where, when, or how they're going to carry it out. And it gets worse."

"Worse? Harrison, there's only one thing to do. Give it to the Bureau right now, let them get on it. You can't take a chance to lose time, not even a day. We can call the duty officer right now." Knight was emphatic. This was out of his league and Witham's. He could deal with Torres on his own. Even if there was a link to Tony, Witham's information had to take precedence.

"No can do. I said worse. This team was put together by some high-powered exiles here, real movers and shakers in Miami— politicians, bankers, I don't know who else, but they're tapped into everything—the White House, the Agency, the Bureau, you name it. If it goes to anyplace like that, they'll know it." Witham ran both hands through his gray, wavy hair and massaged his forehead. "I've thought about it, but I don't know what the hell to do. I've still got a few friends at headquarters in Langley. When I get back to Virginia tomorrow, I might try something with them. But I'm still leery about whom to trust up there."

"My problem's just as bad here, but different," Knight said. "No one trusts me. And if what you say is true about these Cubans, whatever I say will get jammed down my throat, one way or another." The same sense of immobilizing frustration he had suffered before gripped Knight now. The disclosures from

Witham were reason enough to trust the man, and now it looked as if his only option was to join Witham's team.

"So where do we go from here? Is there any daylight?" Knight didn't see any from his view. "What can I do?"

"I'm not sure. The way Tony talked about you, it seemed there might be something you knew that fit into this thing. Maybe you can figure it out, think about what you two talked about. If you come up with anything, you can let me know the next time we talk.

"But let me see what happens tomorrow. I need time to think this through before I approach anyone." He scribbled on a napkin. "These are three numbers where you can reach me. Wait for me to call, but if you don't hear from me by noon, try these numbers."

Knight saw no other choice, but he felt himself drawn into a vortex that was already spinning out of control. He needed more than a night to make sense of everything whipsawing his mind. It was 1:00 A.M., and he knew the morning would come too soon.

"I'll wait for your call, and I'll see if I can come up with something down here. What about your sources? Should I contact anyone?"

"No . . . wait. I'll give you a name just in case you can't reach me. Gus Suarez . . . do you know him?"

"Suarez . . . from the Keys, a *Brigadista*? I think he was a CI source years ago."

"Maybe, but I worked with him in the Agency. So did Tony. He's good people, you can trust him." He wrote another number on the napkin.

Witham paid the bill and they walked outside the restaurant. Two curving arc lights cast a white light that accentuated their shadows as they stood a few feet from the front door.

"We'll talk in the morning," Witham said. "Oh, there is one thing that could be mighty important. One of my guys gave me the last name of a Cuban who might know the connection between the hit team and some of the big fish. Trouble is, no one knows where to find him. They think the guy might be in Spain."

Knight shuddered. His voice came out in a whisper, tremoring. "What's his name?"

Witham gazed at the cloudless sky, pausing to remember. Then he looked down at Knight's ashen face.

"Torres."

THIRTEEN

December 18
Marco Island, Florida

His body glistened as he ran on the packed sand, damp from wavelets inching up the beach at low tide. Tiny shells and crushed coral crunched under his bare feet, but the only sound he heard came from his rhythmic deep breaths. As he began the last four hundred yards of his two-mile run, he lengthened his stride, pumping his arms and legs like pistons. His muscled thighs burned when he changed to a sprint, but he took an athlete's pleasure from the pain.

He stopped when he passed the scrub bush higher up on the soft yellow sand that marked the distance for his early-morning jog. Walking another half mile, he swung his arms in circles as he cooled down. When he reached the wooden steps that led to the condominium pool and buildings, he grabbed his towel off the railing and draped it around his neck.

The pool was still shaded from the sun by three 12-story condos that surrounded the circular cement deck. It was too early for any of the inhabitants to compete for the thirty-odd chaise lounges with their oil-slathered bodies. Their absence was more reason why he enjoyed the solitude of rising at seven and completing his outdoor exercise before eight.

He dropped his towel on the pool coping and dove into the deep end. The water was cooler and more refreshing now, before the sun heated it to bathwater temperature. He swam the twenty-yard width twice underwater without coming up for a breath. When he surfaced, he clung to the edge for a moment to clear the chlorine from his eyes. Then he sliced through the water with a smooth crawl, stretching to pull deeply while his feet barely broke the water with a powerful flutter kick. He stopped after he had crossed the pool eleven times and boosted himself out of the water. Drying his body roughly, he checked his Rolex. In five minutes, at eight o'clock, the call would come.

He shivered briefly as he walked into the cold air conditioning of the south building and took the elevator to the seventh floor. As soon as he closed the door of the apartment, he stripped off his bathing suit and threw it into the shower stall. He put on a red sweatshirt and a pair of white cotton shorts, and sat on the couch next to the telephone.

Sunlight streamed through the vertical fabric blinds that covered a twenty-five-foot wall of windows, brightening the combined dining and living room. But he faced away from them, staring through sliding glass doors that gave an expansive view of the beach and the Gulf of Mexico.

The phone jangled, but he waited until after the fourth ring to pick it up. He said nothing and listened to the female voice speaking perfect English.

"Mr. Baron, this is your answering service. We received a call from a Mr. John Arnold. He asked us to reach you and tell you that he sent the letter by express mail yesterday. He said he'd like you to pick it up as soon as possible."

"Thank you for calling. If you hear from Mr. Arnold again, tell him I received his message."

He stood up, walked through the glass doors to the balcony, and leaned on the railing. The Gulf looked like a vast shiny azure tabletop, reaching far to the western horizon. From the seventh floor, he could not detect a ripple except for the gentle waves breaking less than ten feet from the shoreline. He watched three dolphins cruising playfully in the water fifty yards from the beach. A mile south, a soundless motorboat towed a parasailer in front of a luxury hotel. On the beach below, sun worshippers were seeking choice spots to spread their blankets and set up sand umbrellas.

Noting the activity below, he realized he had to move quickly. But he hated to leave the safe house on Marco Beach, a sliver of peaceful paradise a hundred miles east of the tumult in Miami. Two days of rest and relaxation here seemed like a week, but it still wasn't long enough. He had hoped the call would have said he could stay longer.

Changing into a navy T-shirt, he took a dry towel from the linen closet and headed down to the beach. Outside again, he sidled between the people filling the pool deck, went down the wooden steps, and walked to the edge of the water. He stood facing the Gulf, then turned slowly to see whether anyone was nearby. People strolled on the beach, singles and couples, young and old, but no one seemed to be paying any attention to him.

He walked north slowly, sloshing through two inches of water. When he neared the scrub-brush jogging marker, he angled across the damp, packed sand and crushed coral to hot, soft sand. He casually looked both ways as he came closer to the bush. Just behind it, a ten-inch twig stuck straight up from the sand. He walked a few feet past it, toward denser patches of similar bushes. When he turned, he saw that the closest person was at least seventy yards away.

Kneeling quickly at the twig, he shoved both hands into the sand and felt a waterproof vinyl envelope. He pulled it out, slid it in his waistband, and covered it with his shirt. Then he retraced his route back to the condominium, again watching for eyes that might be focused on him.

Safely inside the apartment, he dusted the sand off the outer envelope and separated the Velcro fastener. A sealed paper envelope was inside. He slit it open with a paring knife and spread the documents on the kitchen counter.

The United States passport displayed his picture, but it showed him with a mustache and brownish-gray hair, instead of his natural black hair. The date of birth made him ten years older. His name would be Dennis Enright. A Virginia driver's license contained the same information.

The other document was also in the name of Dennis Enright. It was a one-way ticket to Madrid, aboard an Iberia Airlines flight that was scheduled to leave Miami tonight at six o'clock.

So El Aura believes the American is going to Spain to find Torres! That may be a very fortunate development. But to be sure, I shall check the reservations for all Miami flights to Madrid.

Glancing at a calendar on the kitchen wall, he noticed that Christmas was approaching fast. Colonel Jorge Posada hoped this operation would be quick and successful. It had to be.

FOURTEEN December 18
Miami

The morning shower cleansed him, but it had been far from refreshing. Knight's body ached from the long hours he had spent at his desk last night, mulling over the events of the last few days. In those dark hours, he suddenly remembered the story of Henry Randall's confrontation with the CIA in 1980. Guided by a whispering hope that Randall's attitude had not changed, he meticulously prepared his plan of action. When he finished at three o'clock, he called Iberia Airlines for a reservation on a direct flight to Madrid. But when he had finally fallen into bed, questions and theories had kept his eyes fixed on the ceiling, until they closed at 4:00 A.M.

Now, while he dressed three hours later, he was still certain this was an unalterable course he had to pursue; every fact and reason he considered supported his resolve. He knew it was the right decision—the only decision. He also decided to tell only Paul Singer that he was going to Spain. Yet he would not tell even Paul his hidden motive: to find Miguel Torres.

He heard the word-processing printer clattering as he entered the reception room. Jennifer was not at her desk, but her voice drifted from Paul's office. He stepped quietly until he was three feet from the doorway. When he heard his name, he strained to overhear her side of the telephone conversation.

"I've got to go now; we'll have to talk about it later. Knight isn't here yet, and I don't know when he's coming in. I'll try to find out, don't worry. I'll let you know when I hear something. *'Ta luego.*"

Knight hurried back to the reception room, opened the door and slammed it shut, then picked up the phone messages. He saw nothing from Witham. When Jennifer came around the corner, she seemed surprised to see him.

"Hi. I didn't expect you so soon. . . . I mean I didn't know when you were coming in. I didn't see anything scheduled in your book for today. I was just putting some files away for Paul." She looked at the messages in his hand. "Those are all his. You haven't had any calls this morning." She stood behind her desk with her hands on the back of the chair, pushing it aside to make room to sit down.

"Wait, I'd like to talk to you for a few minutes, Jennifer. Why don't we go into my office?" He motioned with his hand for her to go first.

As he followed her, he was surprised to feel a slight sense of disappointment. When he realized it was because she was wearing beige pleated slacks, a blouse buttoned at her neck, and a short brown tie, he became angry with himself. Dammit, Knight, what are you thinking about? She might be attractive, but you still don't know whether she's trouble or not. Get your mind back on track.

Last night, he had made a three-page list of questions, trying to gain some semblance of order from his earlier confusion. He had put the names of Torres, Monzon, Witham, Costas, and Ferrer as headings, with questions under each name. Now, he wanted the ones about Jennifer answered. He was confident he could couch them in sufficiently ambiguous statements so she would not suspect his true motivation.

Knight had developed and refined the technique after years of experience, and few of his subjects had ever realized that he always came away with more information using this surreptitious method than by direct interrogation. The touchstone of the process was quite basic, not at all unique: He relied more on listening than on specific conversational objectives, leading the speaker into expansive statements. Knight's oblique comments were brief, often designed to draw questions from his subjects, because what they asked might reveal more of what they knew. Yet during these seemingly rambling discussions, he might inject subtle intimidation to provoke unwitting disclosures.

He also used a sensitive third ear to hear what was not said: Omissions were often just as important as direct discourse. Though he might disregard mere oversights, Knight believed that information deliberately withheld was done for a reason; and that reason was usually deception. Once he found deception, he knew the truth hovered nearby.

From his conversation with Monzon, Knight believed the man knew more about Knight's past with the FBI than he had let on. Monzon's comments evidenced an awareness that Knight had worked on the foreign counterintelligence squad; but the weightier question of whether he knew specific details about Knight's clandestine labors required an indirect inquiry. He reasoned that the relationship between Monzon and Jennifer was close enough for the uncle to confide much of his knowledge in his niece. Talking to Jennifer, then, might give him information about both; and the one-sided conversation he had just overheard intensified that belief.

Jennifer sat across from his desk, her back straight and slightly arched away from the chair. Knight tried to read her expression to see whether her body language was a sign of tension or simply good posture. When he noticed that her eyes were enticingly soft and wide, he glanced away, wondering whether she might be spinning her own web.

"I wanted to apologize again for last night, Jennifer. I'm really sorry about the incident in the car. You can believe this or not, but I honestly don't know what it was all about. And I'll tell you this, it had nothing to do with what you said to me. I know it was upsetting, but it was just as confusing to me. Like I said, I just wanted you to know that I'm sorry it happened," he said.

"I guess I did come on pretty strong, but I was more angry than scared. I've seen enough to know crazy things happen in Miami, and I know how criminal-defense attorneys can make problems for themselves. But I heard what my uncle said about you. Maybe I overreacted; if I did, I'm the one who owes you an apology." For the first time since they had met, she smiled.

Knight was also surprised that her voice was so gentle and sounded so sincere. Though he hadn't expected this change in her attitude, he kept to his plan and changed the subject.

"I wanted to mention something your uncle brought up last night, even though it's not that important. Like he said, I was with the FBI. I resigned just a few months ago, after almost twenty years. But I covered a lot of ground over that time, and I didn't make too many friends. I'm not totally disregarding the possibility that the car incident had something to do with my past. I can't think of any specific reason, but you never know. I thought, maybe from your own experience as a cop, you might understand that."

Jennifer leaned back and crossed her legs. Her smile was gone. "I don't like to talk about that time in my life. Actually, I'd like to forget most of it." She paused, then tilted her head forward. "But I think I know what you mean. I never got into investigations, but I know detectives who had problems with the bad guys, usually the drug traffickers. Did you work narcotics? You look too clean-cut to be involved in that. What kind of work did you do?"

"It wasn't dope, I can tell you that. Mostly what we call general-jurisdiction crimes: bank robberies, interstate theft, some racketeering cases, things like that." Now he was ready to plant the land mine and watch her drive over it.

"But back in the seventies, I worked anti-Castro terrorist investigations. Some of those got a little dangerous. In 1976, they went crazy, even blew a Cuban plane out of the sky that killed ninety-three people and murdered an ex-ambassador with a remote-control bomb in Washington. They killed more people that year than all the Arab terrorists combined. I had some threats, but no real problems. Things have quieted down around here since then."

Stillness hung in the air. Knight fumbled for a paper clip in a drawer, trying to prolong the silence until she spoke. From the corner of his eye, he watched her shift in the chair. She sighed and smiled again, but this time he recognized an obvious release of tension.

"You must have had your hands full then. I don't remember too much about that time, but my uncle told me about some of the bombings here and outside the United States. He used to say a lot of the so-called terrorists were extortionists and drug dealers, but that most were really dedicated patriots who hated Castro. . . ."

Knight saw the opening and jumped in. "Well, I know some were decent guys, even likable. Sometimes I'd go out to interview one and he'd invite me in for coffee, introduce me to his family, and then we'd get into political and philosophical discussions. At the end, I'd say, 'Don't do what you're planning to do,' and he'd say, 'You have your job, and I have mine. If you catch me, that's the risk I take.' They weren't really like criminals. It was a strange relationship. I guess you could say we were 'friendly enemies' . . . something like that." His eyes wandered around the room, recalling some of those men he genuinely admired.

"In a way, I kind of respected them because they were doing what they believed in, even though they were violating the law. So I know what your uncle meant. Did he know any of them?"

Knight watched her eyes closely. She blinked rapidly for an instant.

"I think . . . I don't really remember. Maybe he mentioned some names, but I can't recall." She stopped abruptly, but Knight was ready.

"But you know, most of the time they were just plain stupid. I still don't know how they thought setting a bomb off in Miami, Mexico, Costa Rica, or anywhere else would make a difference to Fidel. He knew they were only hurting themselves, because we'd have to jump on them here. He was too smart for them; they were less bother to him, pardon me, than flies on a horse's ass. Fidel never even gave a damn about their farfetched plots to kill him. He penetrated their groups with his own agents, so he usually knew everything that was going down. They were goddamn crazy to think they could ever get to him.

"Honest, Jennifer, it got to be like a joke. They usually screwed up whenever they tried to get something going. And no one, I mean no one, ever took the assassination plots seriously. They may have been dedicated, but most of the time they acted like a bunch of clowns. I bet your uncle never told you that, did he?" Knight laughed, hoping it didn't sound as phony to Jennifer as it did to him.

She pressed her lips tightly. Knight saw anger rising on her face and waited for the eruption.

"Comedies? Clowns? Fidel is so smart? That's what you think? My uncle said you understood Cubans, that you knew how we felt and what we believed. Are you trying to make a fool of him, too? What you've done is to show me just how ignorant you are, Mr. Knight. You don't know a goddamn thing." She sat on the edge of the chair, firing her words at him.

"You must think it's all a game, that we've all resigned ourselves to a communist Cuba forever, that everyone thinks Castro's going to live forever. Did you forget that your own country tried to overthrow him? How many times did your CIA come up with some stupid plan to assassinate him? Remember, your government taught my people how to do it. Forget the Bay of Pigs, but do you have any idea how many Cubans died doing whatever the United States asked of them? Do you? And what did we get for that, for those sacrifices? Can you answer that?" She unleashed each question with unbridled fury.

Knight was taken back by her strident assault, but he thought she'd say more if he riled her with a few provocative statements. He jumped up and raised his voice in mock anger.

"You're goddamn right I can answer that. You got this!" He pointed his finger at the window overlooking Calle Ocho. "You got Miami! The Cubans have taken political and economic control of this city. Jesus, Jennifer, open your eyes. You're the only immigrant group to ever take over a city in the United States. And you did it in twenty-five years. That's a goddamn fact, isn't it? What does Uncle Felix have to say about that? Did he ever tell you how they did it? Did he?" Knight paused to lower his voice, but not long enough for Jennifer to speak.

"Dammit, the Cubans have got it so good here, how many do you really think would ever go back, whether Castro was there or not? Do you think getting rid of him would really make any difference to ninety percent of the exiles here? Be realistic, Jennifer. Read *The Miami Herald* sometime and see who's got the clout in Miami now." Enough, Knight told himself, it's time to cool it down.

Jennifer was standing, pressing her fists tightly to her sides, arms quivering. Her face was colored with rage, but Knight noticed her watery eyes. She turned her back suddenly and stared at the ceiling, silently. When she finally looked at him, tears trickled down her cheeks.

"You don't understand," she whispered. "Whether what you said is true or not, you don't understand. I don't care about that; it doesn't mean anything to me. I have my own reasons."

Jennifer sat down and wrapped her arms around her shoulders, sniffling to hold back more tears. Her head hung down, face to the floor. She looked weak and vulnerable. Knight wondered what sensitive nerve he had struck. He suddenly felt a protective urge to hold and comfort her.

She glanced at the monkeys on his desk, avoiding his eyes. "My mother was executed by a firing squad in Cuba in 1961. She was working for the CIA and Castro found out. I never knew exactly what she was doing and no one would ever tell me, not even my uncle. Sometimes I want to know, sometimes I don't . . . but I can never stop thinking about it." Her voice was steadier, still soft.

"Don't you see, I don't care about what's happening now in Miami. I can't leave the past; it haunts me every day and night. My uncle told me she never told them anything, that she was very brave and courageous. I guess he thought it would help me to know that, but it only makes me think of how she must have been tortured before she was killed." She held her shoulders when they began to tremble.

Jennifer's emotions suddenly connected to his own, an identification of latent pain that pierced him like a long needle. Though their circumstances were different, that distinction was irrelevant in the depths of the unconscious mind. There, all that mattered was the vestigial memory of an enormous loss.

Knight sensed their shared sorrow for an instant, then tried to push his emotions aside. He still had to be a professional, despite an intense impulse to give in to the feelings. But he didn't know how to get back.

"I'm sorry, Jennifer. I had no idea. . . . That's a terrible burden to live with. I wish I could tell you how much I . . . I mean . . ." His emotions kept tangling with his logic, but he knew it wasn't pity. It was pain.

She was up, pacing in the small room. "The only things I want out of life are sunsets and paydays and a man to love. That isn't asking for too much, is it? But I hardly even think of those things because of my hatred for Fidel Castro. I despise the man, Knight. If I had the chance, I'd cut off his testicles and jam them down his throat. I'd give my own life if I could watch him die a slow, agonizing death. A bomb or a sniper's bullet would be too good for that bastard and anyone else responsible for my mother's death." Her voice ricocheted off the walls like a bullet fired into a metal box, but she wasn't yelling.

"My uncle told me of some of the attempts to assassinate Castro, Knight. Probably more than you ever knew about, because some of his friends died trying. So don't talk to me about comedies and clowns when I know things that you don't have any idea about."

Knight didn't have to prompt her now. She continued the full-force diatribe on her own.

"You don't even know who my uncle is, do you? No, you didn't recognize his name. Well, did you ever hear of *El León*, The Lion? Maybe you've heard that before!" She stopped and glared at Knight.

Monzon is *El León*? He couldn't hide the surprise on his face. The name of *El León* was legendary in Miami. He had been known as one of the CIA's top Cuban exile assets, a fearless fighter who had infiltrated Cuba throughout the sixties, leading four-man teams that destroyed oil refineries and sugar mills. Some said he even had been involved in mysterious missions for the CIA in other parts of the world.

Wounded and captured in Cuba in 1966, he had escaped from Castro's maximum-security prison, La Cabaña, a year later. According to stories Knight had heard, *El León* kept operating for the CIA, but his specific activities had been cloaked with the highest levels of secrecy.

In 1974, *El León* supposedly dropped out of sight. Rumors abounded that the CIA had asked him to carry out an action to which he was bitterly opposed. After he refused to participate in that operation, he vanished, and no federal agency had heard of him since. But Knight remembered Tony Costas had mentioned *El León* once, and said the Cuban had been one of the most trusted operatives ever to work for the Agency. Tony, in a revering voice, once described him to Knight: "He was an honorable man, David, a very honorable and trustworthy man. If he was still

143

around, I would place the lives of my children in his care over anyone else." Knight had been struck by the awe with which Tony regarded *El León*, but Tony had never mentioned his true name.

Jennifer's disclosure stunned Knight, raising a sudden pang of anxiety. The CIA again? Could Monzon have gone back into the fold? Is the Agency using Monzon to take a run at me now?

But from what Tony had told Knight, Monzon had backed away from the Agency years ago, so bitter that he had vowed never to have anything to do with the CIA again. Then how and why did he get involved in the maze I'm trying to find my way out of? I can't assume it's just a coincidence. Could he be working for someone else now?

Jennifer watched him, eyes wide and waiting for him to speak. He turned to the window when more questions crowded into his panicked thoughts.

Why did she tell me Monzon was *El León*? Is it just because of her volatile temper, or is there a hidden reason? Is Monzon using her to spin a web around me?

Knight tried to think of anything else Tony had said. He needed time to sort out the pieces of this puzzle, but he had to respond. Back off and take it slowly, he told himself. Tell her anything.

"*El León*? No, I don't think I've heard that one before. I didn't come to Miami until 1975, so maybe he was around before then. What was he? What did he do? Was he someone I should have heard about?" Knight asked, and glanced at his watch. It was eleven. He wondered why Witham had not called.

Jennifer sighed. "No, I guess not. It isn't important; forget that I brought it up. It probably wouldn't make any difference to you. Let's just drop it. I don't want to talk about this anymore. Besides, I've got work to do." She slammed the door when she left the room.

Knight wanted to call someone immediately to get more background on Monzon, *El León*. He looked at the numbers Witham had given him. It was too early, but this couldn't wait. Witham would have to know something about Monzon, Knight was certain.

Something held him from making the call, however. He looked at the last question he had written under Witham's name. *"Why should I trust him?"* He still could not come up with an answer to satisfy himself, and until he did, he could not risk giving Witham information he developed on his own.

It was also something he would not feel comfortable talking about on the telephone. If all the hard-wire illegal phone taps in the buildings on Brickell Avenue were pulled out, most of the structures would tumble down. They weren't just law-enforcement or intelligence-agency bugs: Lawyers, bankers, businessmen, and stock brokers listened in on each other's conversations daily. Tidbits of gossip and insider knowledge often gave them information to obtain a competitive edge, or questionable conduct conducive to a threat of blackmail.

Knight blamed himself for not having given Witham the number of a phone more secure than his office or apartment. But he was curious why the problem had not occurred to Witham. He wondered how safe the numbers were on the cocktail napkin he held in his hand, another reason not to make the call.

He buzzed Jennifer to ask when Paul would be in. Soon, she said curtly. He hoped she was right.

The conversation with Jennifer did not answer all of his questions; it raised more. But as uncomfortable as their dialogue was, Knight considered he had come out ahead. Her comments increased his data base with additional information to test theories by hypothesis as well as speculation. By twisting, turning, and juxtaposing these new facts, he hoped to find reasonable inferences that would lead him to irrefutable conclusions.

He learned more from Jennifer than he had expected. Now he knew that Monzon had been active in the CIA in the early seventies. He also knew that Henry Randall was on the Miami Field Office's counterintelligence squad at the same time. Monzon said he had known Miguel Torres, and that Randall called him from Madrid to ask about Torres. Knight reasoned that Randall would not have made that contact unless they had had a previous relationship; and the fact that Randall asked about Torres was clear evidence that he had to know more of Miguel. And according to Monzon, Randall was a Legat at the American embassy in Madrid.

Knight also had Witham's comment that a Cuban exile named Torres, supposedly in Spain, might have information about the anti-Castro assassination plot. Jennifer said that Monzon had known of past assassination plots by exile activists. From the way she said it, Knight thought it was possible Monzon had participated in some of those attempts. If Knight believed Witham, another plan to kill Fidel Castro was far past the planning stage. And if the conspirators were as young as thirty, Knight speculated they would need mentors—someone like Felix Monzon.

Knight felt as if he were playing chess with pieces all the same color, not black and white or even shades of gray. He had no way to tell who was on which side. Worse, he could not distinguish a pawn from a bishop or a queen.

"Hey, David, what's happening?" Paul Singer boomed the greeting into Knight's office.

Flustered from deep thought, Knight looked up in surprise. "Paul, am I glad to see you. I have to talk to you right away." He stood up and hurried to the door.

"Slow down, buddy. C'mon in," he said, striding to his office. He sat down with a big grin on his face.

"Take it easy, David. Hey, I just won the motion to suppress on the Pratt case. It was great. I had the prosecutor so pissed, the judge really came down on him. I got the cop so confused, he—"

"Paul, listen, this is important," Knight said, lowering his voice as he closed the door.

"All right, just sit down and relax. Tell me what it is. You look like it's something serious." Singer took his smile away.

"It is. I need to do something. I have to be away for a few days."

"You want some time off, a little vacation, take it. I think that's a great idea. Clear your head; you'll feel a lot better when you get back. I can hold the fort. Where you goin'? Key West, Sanibel, the Bahamas?"

"No, it isn't like that. This isn't a vacation."

"Uh-oh. Don't tell me you're goin' on one of your missions again. David, what's wrong with you? You gotta get yourself together. Please, take my advice, take a vacation. Whatever you're up to now, it's just not gonna help you get what you want, whatever the hell that is. How many times do I have to tell you? . . . Jesus, I should know better; every fuckin' time I do, it doesn't do any good. Okay, you wanna tell me about it? Or is this more 'top secret' bullshit?"

Knight took a deep breath. "I'm going to Madrid."

"Madrid?" Singer bellowed. "You are crazy, absolutely fucking crazy. What the hell are you going to Madrid for? David, for Chrissake, you're taking this stuff too far, honest to God. I gotta figure some way to bring you back to reality. You're going off the deep end now."

"Paul, I'm going to Madrid. I'll probably be back in three days. You don't understand, and I can't explain it to you. But someone has to know, and you're the only one I can trust. You have to believe me that I wouldn't do it unless I really had to. No one else can know, not even Jennifer."

"Bullshit. Whatever you're up to, you can't do this. The crap you get into here is bad enough, but you can't do it in a foreign country. You got no protection, no backup. If you get into a jam, you can't run to the embassy and say 'I'm J. Edgar Hoover, help me.' You got nothin', zero." Singer's voice reeked with exasperation.

"I know all that, believe me. But I don't have a choice. I've got to find someone and talk to him—that's all I can tell you. I need you for this, Paul, maybe as much as I've ever needed you." Knight knew Singer could not resist that entreaty.

"No choice? That's one of the most ridiculous things I've ever heard you say, David." He turned toward the windows, then looked back at Knight. "Jesus, all right, so you're goin' to Madrid. And I'll keep my mouth shut and cover for you. What else?"

"Nothing. If I need something, I'll call you. I don't know what you'll be able to do, but I have to have a contact I can reach. That's it, nothing else." Knight held his hands out, palms up.

"Wonderful. Sure, 'nothing else.' You know, if I didn't love you so much, I'd run your ass outta here and tell you not to come back until you've grown up. But I'll be here if you need me, you know that. And do me a favor."

Knight was standing. "Sure, what is it?"

Singer stepped directly in front of him and hugged Knight's shoulders, unembarrassed.

"Watch your ass. Be careful."

Knight nodded. They smiled as they shook hands, and Singer patted his back as he walked away.

"Good luck, you crazy fucker. Hey, how soon are you leaving?"

"Tonight, at six. I've got a flight on Iberia," Knight said as he left Paul's office.

By 1:30 P.M., Witham still had not called. Knight was relieved.

He left the office an hour later for a quick search at the Coral Gables library. Indexing Henry Randall's name surfaced three *Miami Herald* articles; he scanned them on the microfilm viewer and found two that held information he thought would be useful. After he copied them, he drove back to his apartment.

From past experience and the plans for Madrid set in his mind, he wanted to prepare for the strain of international travel. Once he landed in Madrid, he would not have time for a leisurely recovery. Flying seven hours through different time zones was tiring enough, but this trip would require physical endurance and maximum mental acuity for a sustained period of time. He could not allow fatigue to tire his body or cloud his judgment.

Changing into a bathing suit, he spent half an hour stretching and going through light calisthenics, then he went to the pool and swam fifty lengths. The exercise relaxed his mind and body, easing the tension and taking enough energy and stimulation from him to induce a restful sleep after the first hour in the air.

Back inside, he listened to slow jazz and read three past issues of *Sports Illustrated* cover to cover, purposely drawing his mind away from the trip. He also drank three quarts of purified water. At 4:00 P.M., Knight began to get dressed.

FIFTEEN December 19
Madrid

The flight attendant touched Knight gently on his shoulder. His blanket slid to the floor as he jerked upright, rubbing his eyes. She held a hot, damp cloth in tongs. He took it and toweled his face, then pressed it hard with both hands. She told him the flight was an hour from Madrid.

Staring out the window, he saw a saffron glow edge over the eastern horizon, chasing the darkness behind him. Land in muted, brown winter tones soon appeared below. As the plane streaked over Portugal and into Spain, he hoped his plan would finally chase the shadows that followed his footsteps day and night.

Clearing customs at Madrid's Barajas Airport was painfully slow. In four teams, uniformed inspectors opened every passenger's bag and suitcase, waving detector wands and rummaging through neatly packed articles. Yet Knight understood the zealous searches and waited with stoic patience. He remembered reading that the Party of God, a pro-Iranian Lebanese terrorist group, had attacked a van of the Civil Guard near Torrejon Air Base a week ago, killing thirteen soldiers. He also knew that the POG had been held responsible for setting the bomb that allegedly killed Miguel Torres in 1986.

Knight had last been in Madrid in 1983. As the taxi wound its way through the city's outskirts, he marveled at the burgeoning growth of modern condominiums and office buildings, though he had a greater appreciation for the classical European architecture in the central business and government areas of old Madrid. The United States Embassy was located on Calle Serrano, a fashionable boutique-lined avenue two miles from the Spanish National Palace. Knight directed the driver to the Los Galgos Hotel, a five-minute walk from the embassy, where he checked into a suite.

It was nine in the morning, almost time to initiate the first step of his plan. First, however, he stripped to his undershorts and went through a brief set of calisthenics, then stretched out on the bed. He needed to acclimate himself to the time change and to allow his mind a respite before he brought it to full concentration for the task ahead.

When the travel alarm buzzed him awake an hour later, he felt sluggish and disoriented. He padded into the bathroom and splashed cold water on his face, then let it run hard on his wrists. Drying himself with a thin towel, he sat on the edge of the bed and placed a call to the United States Embassy.

"I'd like to speak to Henry Randall, please. He's in the Legal Attaché's office." He waited for the call to go through the switchboard.

"Randall." The voice was polite but official.

"Henry Randall?"

"That's right. Who is this?" Randall asked with a hint of irritation.

"My name's David Knight. We've never met, but I used to be with the Bureau in Miami."

Silence. Then, "David Knight? From Miami? Do I know you?" The voice was harsher.

"We've never met, but a mutual friend told me to call you if I got to Madrid. I'm practicing law now, and I finally made enough money to take a European tour. I've been to London, Paris, and Rome, and this is my last stop. I'm leaving tomorrow and wondered if we could get together for a drink or two." Knight prayed Randall wouldn't ask the name of the fictitious "mutual friend."

"Who's the friend, Mr. Knight?" Randall's tone dared Knight to answer.

Knight felt his stomach muscles tense. He remembered Randall's reputation as a ruthless interrogator, but he hadn't expected to be faced with a grilling before he left the dugout. If he wanted to score, he at least had to get into the batter's box. He swallowed and cleared his throat.

"I was hoping I could tell you when we met. See, this friend wanted me to find a book for him," Knight said, planting a phrase from counterintelligence squad's code. Whenever an agent mentioned "find a book," it meant "I have to talk to you about something sensitive." He was confident Randall knew the term, but less certain that Randall would respond favorably.

Another brief silence. "Oh. What was your name? David Knight? . . . Well, maybe I can help you. There's a bookstore where you should be able to find what you're looking for. But the best time to go there is five-thirty, before it gets too crowded." Knight sighed in relief. Randall had answered in the same code as Knight's message: 5:30 meant he would meet Knight at 4:30. Randall then gave him a street number eighty digits less than the true address.

"Thanks . . . Henry."

"Sure. My pleasure. Look, I'd like to meet with you, but my day's really jammed. If you're still here tomorrow, give me a call. If not, tell our friend I said hello." He hung up without saying good-bye.

Knight wiped his forehead with the towel. He wished the meeting could have been earlier, but at least Randall agreed to make the contact. Then he remembered that in Madrid, where the siesta hours were observed as religiously as Sunday mass, every business establishment would be closed from one until four. Still, he had accomplished his first goal: getting Randall alone and away from the embassy.

He pulled on a burgundy crewneck sweater to wear beneath a navy windbreaker. Though the sun burned brightly in a cloudless sky, the temperature hovered at sixty degrees. Knight checked a street map and saw that the address was about a mile from his hotel; he wanted to check out the location of their meeting place this morning. Besides, he thought a long walk in this weather and the higher Madrid altitude might tire him enough to take his own siesta.

His inner alarm had him awake a few minutes before three, the time he had set on the travel clock. He was surprised that he woke smiling and in a calm, pleasant mood. He remembered dreaming about Jennifer, but the details slipped back into his unconscious before he could fix them in his mind. He forced his thoughts away from trying to recall the dream; the next few hours were too important to be hindered by distractions.

Knight left the hotel dressed as he was for his earlier reconnaissance stroll, but the temperature had dropped nearly twenty degrees by late afternoon. Christmas decorations hung from streetlights and on storefronts, but lent little cheer to holiday shoppers scurrying in a chill drizzle. Dour *Madrileños* hunched their shoulders under a tarnished-pewter sky, hiding their faces in turned-up collars and pulled-down hats.

Knight ducked his head into the wind and stuffed his hands in his pockets. He turned a corner and trudged another block on Calle Bavamo until he reached the canopy of the small restaurant and bar, where he took off the windbreaker and shook it. Stepping inside, he thought he recognized Randall leaning against the near end of a standing-room-only long bar. The man wore an Ivy League suit and had a Burberry trench coat draped over his left arm. His head turned slowly and he moved away from the bar as Knight cleared the revolving door.

"You must be David Knight," he said, extending his arm. "Not exactly Miami, is it? I'm Hank Randall."

Knight shook his hand and looked into pale blue eyes partially hidden by lazy eyelids. His thin black hair was streaked with gray, cut short, with a few strands falling on his forehead. A blue three-button suit covered Randall's narrow frame, although barely noticeable bulges gave Knight the impression that the Legat worked out with weights on a regular schedule.

"You know how blood thins out in Miami. My God, it's cold here. But really, thanks for coming to meet me. I hope I'm not taking you away from anything."

"Do you want to tell me about the book?" Randall asked icily.

Knight looked away and rubbed the back of his neck, startled by the abrupt question. He glanced down the bar, then around the crowded, smoky room and noticed a few empty tables in the rear.

"Can we, ah, sit down for a few minutes?" he said hesitantly, pointing to the back of the room. "I don't feel comfortable talking right here."

"Sure, Mr. Knight. Lead the way."

Knight sidled through the tables, listening to boisterous Castilian Spanish voices laughing and raising toasts, aware of the dialect so different from the Cuban bodegas in Miami. The din diminished when he found a corner table. Both men sat with their backs slightly angled to the wall. A waiter in a white apron appeared instantly and Randall asked for Courvoisier straight up. While Knight ordered, he scanned the room carefully. He turned back when the waiter left.

"So, Mr. Knight-errant, are you ready to cut the bullshit? I did a little background on you today. From what I heard, I should have called you back and told you to go to hell."

He had a menacing look on his face that made Knight want to get up and walk out immediately, but he shook off Randall's blatant intimidation and asked the question that instantly jumped into his head.

"Then why didn't you? Why are you here with me now?" Knight said forcefully.

Randall tilted back on two chair legs. "Not bad, not bad. . . ." His lips drew into a thin smile, but he kept talking. Now, though, his voice was more subdued.

"Well, let's just say I'm a little curious. Maybe I'm wondering why you called me. Maybe you're a plant." He leaned forward with his elbows on the table, his face a foot from Knight's, his voice suddenly hushed. "Maybe I'm wondering why an agent who flunked a CIA polygraph test and then resigned from the Bureau would want to come all the way to Madrid to talk to me."

Knight glared back, anger building, but he caught himself when he remembered what he wanted from Randall. He had the opening now. He pulled the copied newspaper clippings from his pocket and spread them on the table.

"You son of a bitch," Randall said, glancing at the articles. He read the headline of one out loud: "'FBI AGENT DISCIPLINED FOR VOUCHER PADDING.' Those fucking bastards! What do you know about this?" He drained his glass and looked at Knight with venom in his eyes.

Knight took a deep breath. "Enough to know that's bullshit. Enough to know that was how the Bureau covered your problem with the CIA. And enough to think you might help someone who was set up and hung out to dry by the Agency."

Randall's expression changed. His eyes narrowed and he tilted his head to the side. Suddenly, he erupted in a laugh that drew quizzical looks from patrons at three nearby tables, then he lowered his voice.

"So that's why you're here," he said, smiling. "You want to talk to the FBI agent who has a hard-on for the CIA bigger than a California redwood, because you were screwed by them, too. I'll be damned, David Knight. You are one smart agent."

Knight grinned nervously, relieved that the stories he had heard about Randall and the CIA were true. He was also pleasantly surprised that Randall had made the connection so easily. But now that he was on track, Knight didn't want to tell Randall he had done it all on a guess, a hope, and a prayer.

"I don't know who told you what was behind that 'voucher' crap; it doesn't matter now. But then you probably know how the Agency tried to ream my ass when they found out I was running one of my sources in Rome on an unauthorized counterintelligence operation. That's how it started."

Knight nodded, anxious for Randall to tell the tale.

"The CIA wanted the Bureau to nail me, but they didn't want to let anything out that might compromise national security. Our headquarters really thought we were in deep shit because of what I'd done, even though we got three KGB agents kicked out of Italy. So they laid it off on the old 'padded voucher' story. You know how they use that when they want to cover up something more serious. Then this article came out," he said, tapping the table. "But that was before I turned it around."

"How'd you do that?" Knight asked, sensing that Randall wanted to tell the whole story.

"When we were in Italy, my source developed fantastic contacts. I sent him back to Rome on his own when the Bureau had me under wraps. You'll like this one," Randall said, grinning. "He came back here with solid information that the Agency's station chief had been whoring around with a member of the Red Brigade, a twenty-year-old gorgeous Italian girl." He laughed. "Literally, a bombshell. She was the terrorists' specialist in timing devices for their bombs.

"Anyway, the CIA went bananas over their man, and then agreed to whitewash everything I did. But I never forgot about how they wanted to crucify me. Damn near ruined my reputation." He paused and fingered the news article, then smiled. "The best part was that the Bureau was so happy we caught the Agency with their collective pants down, they gave me anything I wanted. That's why I'm here. I love Spain." He turned and caught the eye of the waiter and waved him to the table.

"That's a helluva story, a great ending. But I need your help. That's why I'm here," Knight said, his eyes pleading.

"David, let me tell you something else that's just between you and me. I work with some CIA guys here, but most are afraid of me because they know I can't stand them. Anytime I can fuck them over, I do it, as long as it doesn't involve national security. What do you need?"

Knight felt a sudden release of tension. Now he had to swing for the fence; it was time for a home run.

"I'm trying to locate someone. If I do, I think I can ram that polygraph down the Agency's throat. Some people have told me he's here, in or near Madrid, but I don't know where to start looking." Caution told him not to say anything about the lead coming from Felix Monzon.

Randall leaned forward again. "What's his name?"

"Miguel Torres. He's a Cuban from Miami." Knight's chest pounded in anticipation.

"Torres . . . Torres." Randall dropped his eyes to the table, thinking, and rubbed his chin. He looked up quickly with a smile. "I think you're in luck, David Knight."

"Why? You've heard of him?"

"I'm pretty sure it's the guy. A month ago, I got a request from Bureau headquarters to put a trace on a Miami drug dealer with that name. Someone gave them information he was a fugitive living over here. We have to run this stuff past the Agency to see if they have any interest; they've always got dopers doing something for them. I made a few calls first, just checking around.

"But when I finally ran it by the deputy station chief, Eric Steiner, he almost went through the ceiling because our cable had the guy's new identity and his address here. He said he was one of theirs and to stay away. God, was Steiner upset! So I just said fine, it's less work for me, and I didn't pay any more attention to it. Figured headquarters would handle the problem. But I'm sure his name was Miguel Torres, and I remember the address. If you want his phone number, I can probably get it tomorrow from one of my friends in the Spanish Directorate of General Security."

Randall looked at Knight's stunned face, waiting for him to answer. "David? What's wrong? Did you hear me?"

Miguel's alive? Is it really true? Is it really Miguel Torres . . . my Miguel?

Dazed, Knight muttered, "Phone number? Right, I could use it. That would help me get a better make on this guy." The words sounded distant to him, as if someone else were speaking, while the questions throbbed in his mind.

Knight gave Randall a brief sketch of his polygraph session while they had one more drink, but he said nothing more about Miguel Torres. They left the bodega ten minutes later. During the ride back to the Los Galgos Hotel, Randall told Knight he was leaving tomorrow afternoon for three days leave on the Costa del Sol; but he gave Knight directions to the address and promised to call him before ten o'clock in the morning with Torres's telephone number.

Inside the hotel, Knight sat in a lobby chair next to a window. Watching the hazy headlights of cars driving by in a fine mist, he thought about the next morning, planning what he'd do with the phone number from Randall. Suddenly, an image of Miguel flashed into his mind and the plan changed.

He walked to a pay-telephone bank, thumbed through the directory, and called a car-rental agency. Then he took the elevator to his room and packed quickly. He walked down a stairwell that opened to the lobby and was out of view of the front desk and left by a side door. I'll be damned if I'll wait until tomorrow; I'm going to find out who this Miguel Torres is tonight, he thought, waving down a taxi.

It didn't take long for him to adapt to the Seat's confusing controls, but the layout of the Madrid streets at night presented greater difficulty. He finally found the *Autovía de Rozas* highway and headed east. The city lights were soon far behind and he sped by vast stretches of black farmland. Within minutes, the *Maja Dahonda* exit sign loomed brightly ahead. He cut off the highway onto a dark cloverleaf, then followed the road that led directly to the *Monte Clara* subdivision.

He turned in the entrance and wound past new homes that looked strangely like 1960s-style row houses in the United States, but one was easily distinguished from the others: Glaring security lights lit the corners and it was surrounded by an eight-foot wrought-iron fence with an electronic gate. The address matched the one given by Randall. When Knight parked the car and got out, two large rottweilers snarled menacingly on the other side of the fence.

He hesitated, then pressed the gate buzzer.

"Who is it?" the familiar voice asked through an intercom.

Knight began to pant nervously. It is Miguel!

"Who is it?" the voice asked again, angrily.

Knight took a deep breath. "Tomcat. How are you, my friend?" he said, using the code name that had been buried for years.

"*El Lanza*? David! Is that you? *Coño*, tell me it is!"

"Yes, Miguel. I've come a long way to see you."

Knight pushed through the gate when he heard an electric click. Looking up the walkway, he saw the image of a portly man standing in the shadow of the doorway. When Miguel Torres stepped forward into the light, Knight stopped. He blinked his eyes to focus, but Torres was running to him.

"David, David, David!" Torres wrapped his arms around Knight, lifting him to his toes. When he let go and stood back, Knight saw tears trickling down his cheeks. Torres pulled the speechless American into the house, wiping his face with a white handkerchief.

"I can't believe it's really you, David, I can't believe it. I'm so glad to see you, I don't know what to say. There's so much I must tell you. Come in, come in." His face was flushed with happiness.

Knight looked at Torres solemnly and studied his sparkling eyes. He followed him into the living room, where Torres switched on two lamps and embraced Knight again.

"Sit here," Torres said, patting a plush white couch. "Let me get you a drink. Wait here; I'll be right back." He waddled from the room with short, fast steps.

He returned with a tray of glasses and bottles of vodka and Spanish brandy and set it on a mirrored-top table in front of Knight. Taking his snifter off the tray, he sat in a cushioned chair directly to Knight's left.

"To us," he said, holding the glass at arm's length.

Knight reached to clink glasses, but he did not join the toast. He let the vodka touch his lips, then put the glass down. The emotional drain of seeing Miguel weakened his defenses. His thoughts of Torres were bound tightly by conflicting threads of joy and anger, lacing his throat with knots that captured his voice. Torres was an apparition from the past: For a moment, Knight thought he was an illusion that would vanish like a fast-fading dream.

"I'm surprised but happy they finally told you where I was. When did they tell you?"

Knight stared at Torres, breathing heavily, wondering who "they" were. No words came.

"David, what's wrong? We're together again. Aren't you glad to see me?" A pained expression replaced his smile.

"Jesus, Miguel. See you? I never expected to see you again. I thought you were dead."

"Dead?" Torres jumped up. "Dead? Why did you think I was dead? It was all part of the plan, David; you knew that. You had to know; they told me they explained everything to you." He sat down with anguish still on his face.

"You didn't know, did you? No one told you anything. All these years, all this time, you thought I was dead. Why did they do that? It doesn't make sense, David. I don't understand. Why? Why?"

Knight's shoulders fell. He tried to arouse a sense of smouldering anger, but fatigue swirled his emotions. For an instant, he wanted to give up, walk out, and forget why he had come to Spain. Staring at a seven-foot elephant tusk on a pedestal across the room, his ears barely registered Torres's voice. But he couldn't shut out the words that revived tormenting questions.

Dammit, Knight, you wanted answers before you came to Spain. Now you're with the man you once trusted with your life, and he can tell you what you want to know. You know you can believe him. Don't fall down on yourself.

Knight took his jacket off and tossed it on the couch. Leaning with his forearms on his thighs, he looked at the tray of bottles, then at Torres.

"Miguel, wait. Can you get me some coffee? We have a lot to talk about, so let's forget the booze. It's going to be a long night."

Torres smiled enthusiastically. "Instant, if that's all right. It only takes a minute," he said, already on his way to the kitchen.

Knight had his sweater off when he returned. He took the cup, dropped in an ice cube, and forced the warm coffee down his throat. He catalogued the questions in his mind, sorting them into a chronology. Torres sat with his back straight; Knight knew he was anxious to start the debriefing. Just like old times, he thought.

"Okay, Miguel. Let's start from the beginning." Knight smiled for the first time since he had greeted his old friend.

SIXTEEN

Knight took a second cup of coffee as Torres settled in his chair. Stimulation from the caffeine and the presence of his old friend charged him with subdued excitement, but not enough to curtail his methodical precision. There was only one place to start: at the beginning.

"Miguel, we were so close to taking down the network in Cuba. I don't understand what happened. What was this 'plan' you mentioned? How did you get involved in it?"

"Ah, yes, 'the plan.' The 'plan' that never was. Let me tell you. Remember the last day I was in Key West, when I told you I just wanted to spend the night to relax? That's when they made contact with me.

"You know Carlos Alvarez, the *Brigadista* who lives in Key West. He called me and said one of his friends in the CIA wanted to talk to me. I thought it wouldn't hurt, so I met the man in his room at the Casa Marina. When I walked in, a man from the FBI was with him. He showed me his credentials and said he was from the Bureau's Intelligence Division in Washington. Right there, I started to get nervous. Honest to God, David, I wanted to walk out and call you right away."

If only you had, Knight thought. He downed the coffee. "Go on," he said.

"Anyway, they started telling me . . ." He paused to take a deep breath. "*Coño*, you won't believe this. They told me they knew all about what we'd been doing: dates when we met, dates when I went to Cuba, even that weekend when I went to visit my mother in California."

Knight leaned back and stared at the wood-beam ceiling. "Bastards," he muttered. All that time I thought I was running it on my own, that no one else knew. They watched me, played with me. But who? Why?

"How?" Knight asked, turning sharply to Torres. "How could they know?" He hoped Miguel had the answer.

"I don't know." Torres shook his head and looked at Knight for sympathy. "David, I didn't know what to think or what to do, I was so confused. But they kept saying, 'Don't worry, it's all right.' They said they were grateful for what I'd done, but that some things were happening that I didn't know about. Of course, they didn't say what.

"Then they said the whole operation had become too complicated, that the CIA had to take it over. I was so surprised, I couldn't think of anything to say. But they said it had been cleared at the highest levels of both agencies." Torres shrugged his shoulders.

"David, you know how I feel about the United States government. I love it. If they say there's a reason for doing something, I never ask why. I believe whatever you or any agent tells me, if it's what the government thinks is best."

Knight knew exactly what he meant. He had controlled few informants who were as loyal to the government as Miguel

163

Torres, and none had ever been asked to go as far as he had directed Miguel. But, Knight thought, where was his loyalty to me?

"Why didn't you tell me? Couldn't you at least have gotten word to me somehow? Didn't you owe me that much?"

Torres bent forward, holding his head. "Yes, now I know I should have. But David, they told me they would explain everything to you, that you would know all about it. I believed them! Why shouldn't I? They were from the government; I thought we were all on the same side. I didn't question what they told me. I never questioned you, did I?" he said weakly.

"No, Miguel, never. I guess that's part of the problem. You always trusted me and I never gave you any reason to doubt my word. You believed them the same way. You did what you thought was right. I can't blame you for that."

Silence invaded the room. Both seemed to realize that the relationship of trust they had held so dearly between one another had caused crushing mutual pain since Miguel had disappeared. Yet it was the fault of neither; nor was it irreparable. Their separation by time and place had vanished. They were together again and the healing process had begun. For Knight, answers were just questions away.

"What was the rest of the plan? Is that why you're in this house?" Knight asked.

"Yes, yes. The CIA man said they needed me for an operation in Spain. The bombing was part of my disappearance, and my new identity, and—"

"Slow down, Miguel. What was the operation? Who was running it?"

Torres stood up and paced the room, clasping his hands as he walked, fading in and out of the shadows. Sweat beaded on his upper lip and he wiped it away with a handkerchief.

"That's the strangest thing of all, David. I don't know. I never found out. They never asked me to do anything after I got here. The SRF people, they handled everything. They're the ones

164

who planned the bombing that supposedly killed me. That was to be the beginning of their plan—at least that's what they told me."

Of course, Knight thought, SRF would have been involved. He remembered the bland acronym for Special Reporting Facility, the term for deep-cover CIA employees operating overseas without benefit of State Department credentials. In foreign nations, they performed the clandestine tasks that required "plausible deniability" to protect the Agency's people working in a United States embassy or consulate. Still, Knight was surprised SRF would go to this extreme.

"They planned the bombing? In Madrid? How the hell did they get away with it?" he asked incredulously.

Torres stared ahead. "They coordinated it with the Spanish DGS, the Directorate of General Security. . . . I think it was the Security Section. No one was killed, but they set it up to blame the POG. The DGS took an unidentified vagrant's body from the morgue and the SRF men put my papers on it. No Spanish general was killed; that was just for the press. The bomb went off when they were positive no one would be around to get hurt, but the body was blown into small pieces. My identification was found in the debris, and from then on I was dead. That was the purpose, the only reason for the bombing." He paused and studied his palms, then looked at Knight.

"But you were supposed to know all this. A man from SRF, Otto something, told me that. He said they would explain everything to you, but that I should never contact you. I had to follow his instructions, David; I didn't have a choice. He said if anyone found out I was still alive, or that I had any contact with you, you would be killed. I never asked why, but I didn't want anything to happen to you. I couldn't take that chance. I thought I was protecting you. What else could I do?" His wide eyes asked the same question, imploring Knight to exonerate him from guilt.

Knight reached to touch Miguel's arm. "They had you locked

tight. You couldn't do a damn thing. None of this was your fault, my friend. But you were put here for a reason; I see that now. I just can't figure out why." Knight thought for a moment. "What about the CIA's operation? Are you saying nothing ever happened?"

"Nothing. After the bombing, they put me in this house with my new name and gave me money every month. I kept asking Otto when something was going to happen. He'd just say, 'Wait and be patient. We're getting ready.' After a while, I stopped calling, but they'd still come to check on me to find out how I was doing. Then a few months ago, they started asking me if I'd heard from you. I said, 'No, are you crazy?' They seemed to be satisfied, but whenever one of them left, he'd say, 'Remember, no contact with Knight.' It sounded almost like a warning. David, there wasn't anyone I could talk to and I started to become afraid. Of what, I don't even know." Torres wiped his forehead and sat back in the chair.

"But now you're here. What has happened to us? I don't understand any of it. What was the CIA trying to do?" Miguel asked.

Knight stood up and stretched his arms toward the ceiling, working a cramp out of his back. He stepped to the back of Torres's chair and put his hands on his friend's shoulders, massaging gently.

"That's why I'm here, Miguel. That's what we're going to find out. We may not get all the answers, but we're sure as hell going to look for them. How about some more coffee?"

He watched Torres shuffle to the kitchen. Confusion still kept a check on Knight's optimism, but renewed energy coursed in his veins. He drew strength from talking with Miguel, someone he could trust and believe, and he felt his sense of isolation ebbing. He smiled when Torres returned with the coffee.

"Now, tell me about Victor Milian," Knight asked softly.

Torres's hand shook, jiggling the cup on his saucer. Surprise flushed his face and he looked away from Knight's inquiring eyes.

"Who? . . . Milian? Why do you bring up that name?"

"You gave it to me, dammit. You told me about him after you bumped into Roger Estevez in Havana, remember? Don't get evasive with me now, Miguel; we don't have time."

Torres sipped his coffee, hand still trembling. He set the cup and saucer down. His lips pressed together in a tight frown, as if he was deliberately holding his words.

Knight knew Miguel was thinking of a cogent response, but he wanted the answer immediately. "Now, Miguel. Tell me." His voice was still calm.

"David, please, let me explain." While he took a deep breath, his eyes wandered around the room and settled back on Knight. "He was my cousin; well, actually, my second cousin. I have not talked to him in ten or twelve years, not even after he went to the United States. He never tried to contact me, I swear. You must believe me; I'm telling you the truth. I never had anything to do with him," Torres said anxiously.

"Calm down, relax. He's just a doctor, isn't he? Why are you so upset I asked about him? . . . Is it because the CIA told you he was killed in an accident a few days ago?" Knight's last question was tinged with sarcasm.

"Yes, they advised me of his death. And I told them it could not have been an accident. He was murdered, of that there is no doubt in my mind. *That* is what is upsetting to me." Torres tensed and recoiled simultaneously. He reminded Knight of a turtle following a primitive instinct, pulling in its head to protect itself from nearby danger.

"I understand," Knight said. "But why do you think he was murdered? Who was he?"

Miguel spoke, rasping the words. "Victor was thirteen years older than I. He had been in the revolution with Fidel, from the very beginning. He was always—at least from what my family told me—he was always very close to Fidel Castro. They said Fidel used him for highly sensitive missions that Fidel trusted only Victor to carry out." Torres opened his palms to Knight. "But no one in our family knew what those missions were or what he really did, just that he worked in some ministry in Havana. My mother once told me that sometimes even Raul Castro did not know what Victor was doing for Fidel.

"When he came to the United States, I found out. I knew it had to be on Fidel's orders. But I never saw him or talked to him; I didn't even tell my family. Maybe they knew, but no one ever spoke about it. I stayed as far away from Victor as I could, believe me." His voice dropped to a whisper. "I was afraid, David. That's why I didn't tell you more about him when we talked about Roger Estevez." Shame cloaked his face. His eyes dropped into his lap.

Knight tried to hold in his rumbling anger, but it seeped through when he spoke. "Jesus, Miguel! How could you keep that from me? Fidel's personal agent in Miami? Do you know what we could have accomplished if I had turned him? Dammit, what the hell were you so afraid of that you couldn't tell me?" His rage smouldered as he thought of the lost chance to make Milian a double agent.

The words stung Torres; his eyes reddened. "I was afraid that if you knew about Victor, you wouldn't let me work with you anymore; that you'd blacklist me. I thought if someone in the government found out one of my relatives was a Cuban agent, I would not be trusted. I couldn't allow that to happen, David; working with you meant too much to me. If I had to, I would die for you, but I would have taken this secret to my death." He stared into Knight's eyes. "Can you understand that?"

"Yes, my friend, I can." Knight sighed, then let a thin, sympathetic smile cross his lips to ease the anxiety clinging to Miguel's confession. He felt no anger at Torres for failing to disclose such vital knowledge about Milian; and he realized it was useless to speculate about what he might have done if Torres had told him years ago. Ironically, the information was just as timely and important in the present. Knight would use it to fill in some of the mysterious gaps he had been trying to plug.

Now he had reliable evidence that Victor Milian *was* a Cuban intelligence agent; more significantly, he had been a confidant of Fidel Castro. Did that mean he was DGI? ICAP? Or was he from another arm of the Cuban intelligence service? From what Torres said, Knight concluded that Milian operated at a much higher level than the common Cuban agents skittering around Miami trying to pick up stale gossip about prominent exiles. And Torres had corroborated his theory that Milian was in Miami for a clandestine purpose. If he could decipher that secret, he would be closer to the motive for Milian's murder. He decided to probe Torres for more details.

"Miguel, this is very important. Think, try to remember anything you heard about Victor, from anyone, whether you believed it or not. There must be something else."

"That's all I can recall. You see, no one wanted to talk about him because they knew what he did, and that he was very close to Fidel. You know what the Cuban newspapers and radio stations do in Miami if they find out you have a relative working for Fidel. They would have made my family's life miserable; the threats never would have stopped. Perhaps one would have been carried out. We had to stay away from Victor, especially when he went to Miami." Torres suddenly stared ahead and furrowed his brow, as if he was trying to grasp a distant thought, then turned to Knight.

"There is something. . . . I don't remember it that clearly, but perhaps it will help. Do you remember when my grandfather died? Yes, you went to the funeral with me. Well, I was with him alone in the hospital about a week before he died. He was rambling, almost delirious from a pain shot. He was talking about his life in Cuba and ranted on about some of our relatives. One time he pulled me close to the bed—he still had strong arms—and whispered something about Victor." He nodded to himself. As he remembered the eerie quiet in his grandfather's room that faraway night, his jaw muscles tightened his lips and puffed the skin on his cheeks.

"I can't recall his exact words, but he said that Victor belonged to a secret organization in Cuba under Fidel's direct control. I always thought he had meant the DGI . . . but now I'm not so sure he was talking about the DGI or any other official Cuban intelligence organization. Everyone in the family just assumed he was DGI and left it at that. So if Victor was DGI, why would my grandfather think it should be a secret to be told on his deathbed? I'm sure he knew more, David. Do you know anything about Milian that might explain what he was trying to tell me?" He slumped in the chair but kept his eyes on Knight.

The last question puzzled Knight; it sounded as if Miguel was fishing, casting a line to see whether Knight grabbed the hook. But he passed over that thought, focusing on a phrase he had just heard: ". . . a secret organization in Cuba under Fidel's direct control." The words sent him back to the meeting with Felix Monzon and his description of the DLN. Knight had thought Monzon's tale was more fiction than fact, the product of an imagination that fashioned hopeful reality from distorted wishful thinking. Now, Miguel's information lent credence to the statements of Monzon, but Knight wasn't sure whether he should mention the DLN. His cautious intuition told him to hold back until he covered more ground with Miguel, and he decided to raise another subject.

"Miguel, I know you've been out of Miami for a long time, but something came up a few days ago. I heard a rumor about a new plot to assassinate Fidel. Have you got wind of anything like that?"

"Another one?" Torres's belly bounced when he laughed. "David, you're not falling for one of those three-man, Little Havana street-corner conspiracies again?"

Knight didn't smile. "I wouldn't have mentioned it if I didn't think it was serious. What would you say if I told you Harrison Witham might be involved in it?"

"Witham? I'm sorry I laughed. I do not know him, but I have heard enough to believe he is a very dangerous man. Everyone knows he hates Fidel. I'm sure he helped the exile terrorists in the seventies when they were setting off bombs in Miami and killing Cuban diplomats in other countries. A friend once told me, 'When Witham comes around, someone's going to get hit.' I don't know if that's true, but I do know he has frightened many people." Torres picked up his cup and swirled the coffee, watching a tiny whirlpool form in the center.

"Tell me what your gut says, Miguel. Is it possible Witham's involved in a plan to kill Fidel?" Knight used one of their techniques from the past, when he'd rely on Torres's intuition almost as much as his own, trying to reach beyond an analysis of facts and logic alone.

Torres responded tersely. "Everyone thinks Witham resigned from the CIA in 1976, but some say he is still operating for the Agency. Others say he gets protection from his friends in the CIA. It has even been rumored that he blackmails them. I do not know if any of those are true. He is very controversial, David, very . . . eni—, eni—"

"Enigmatic?"

"Enigmatic, yes, I always liked that word when you used it. But he has many disciples who treat and adore him like a god; they will do anything for him." Torres patted his stomach. "If he is involved with the terrorists again, my gut tells me it is quite likely he is working with them on a plot to kill Fidel. It would be an opportune time, when you consider the far-reaching effects of the weakening of the Eastern Bloc and Fidel's adamant resistance to the Soviet Union's glasnost. I believe his demise would not be looked upon as tragic, nor undesirable, to the Soviets." Torres leaned forward, elbows on his knees.

"Witham has a large network of trusted people, David. It is not inconceivable that he would undertake such an operation. And I know there are wealthy and powerful figures in Miami who would provide him with considerable support, if he asked. Whether they are behind him now, I cannot say, but I do not believe he would do it on his own. He would require strong backing from someone with great influence." Torres stopped abruptly. "Why are you so interested in Witham? What makes you think he is involved?"

The questions unnerved Knight. Now Miguel *is* fishing, he thought. Why? For what? He's trying to get something out of me. I better go slowly until I see where he's coming from.

"I'm not sure, Miguel; I'm just digging around. You know how I get caught up in Cuban conspiracies. I guess I can't break the habit, probably never will," he said, forcing a smile.

Torres nodded, but his countenance was still serious.

Knight said, "So let's take this just a little further. Is there any way you can get me more information about this? Not only on Witham but anything about the terrorists acting up again, whether it's a plot against Fidel or something else?"

"I was waiting for that," Torres said, rubbing his chin. "Remember Samuel Pineiro, the drug dealer who jumped bond a few years ago on a two-thousand-kilo cocaine case? He lives four miles from here; we golf together every weekend. In the late seventies, he gave some anti-Castro terrorists money to protect his marijuana shipments. He's always having people from Miami coming to see him. I'll talk to him in the morning and find out what he knows."

Knight grinned. "I should have known you'd still have some sources in your bag of tricks, amigo." A grateful sense of relief rushed through his body. Miguel was at his side again; he wasn't alone anymore. They were accomplishing more than he expected, and he realized the years apart had not diminished Miguel's uncanny ability to anticipate his questions and be waiting with the right answer.

Still, he sensed Miguel was holding something back. That subtle suspicion aroused a vague uneasiness, causing Knight to tread lightly into the next question. He also decided to keep his own knowledge about the subject hidden, for now.

"Let's keep going, Miguel, we're on a roll. I've got another name I thought you might be able to help me with: Felix Monzon."

Torres straightened his back and folded his hands in his lap. "Monzon. *El León*. You are moving in strange directions, David. What do you know about him?" His voice was suddenly cold.

"Hey, that's my question," Knight said, taken aback by Miguel's tone. But he knew he struck a sensitive nerve. "You sound defensive; is there something—"

"No, no, it's just that I'm surprised you mentioned that name. I thought Monzon disappeared before you came to Miami. It seems strange that you'd be interested in him now," Torres said.

Disappeared? What the hell is he talking about? Monzon told me he talks to Miguel almost regularly. Dammit, Miguel's flat out lying to me! How can he do that? What the hell is he trying to do?

Knight sipped his coffee, hiding his shock, while he gauged the hanging curveball Miguel had just thrown. Another thought struck him: What if Monzon was lying? He decided not to swing at the pitch until he saw what else Miguel had to offer.

"Hell, that's why I'm asking you," Knight said. "I'd never heard of him until an old source mentioned it, but he didn't know much. Miguel, look, if you don't want to talk about him . . ."

Torres smiled. "I'm sorry. I know you have your reasons, David. I'll tell you what I can, but it may not be too helpful.

"If Witham is enigmatic, Monzon is a jigsaw puzzle without colors on the pieces. Few people knew what side he worked on; some say he played for everyone at one time or another. When he was operating, he was called 'the consummate spy,' whatever that means. I don't know if anyone ever knew exactly who or what he was, just that he was very effective at what he did. Supposedly, though, he had a reputation as a quiet, efficient killer." The words hung between Torres and Knight in a brief silence until Miguel spoke.

"But that may just be a fable, like so many that fill the mouths of the Cubans in Little Havana." Torres paused, staring into a dark corner of the room. When he continued, his eyes had a glazed look. "I once heard a comment about Monzon that seemed strange, but I was told it came from someone who knew him well. The person said Monzon was 'an honorable man, a dedicated man who could be trusted.' Did you ever hear that?" Torres asked, turning to Knight.

Knight felt his throat tighten. Damn, that's how Tony described Monzon! Why would Miguel say that and tell me he thought Monzon had disappeared? Wait, wait, don't get excited. He could have heard it from anyone in a Miami street-corner conversation. I don't want to bring Tony's death into this yet. Play it safe.

"No, that's what I'm telling you, I'm trying to find out more about him." Knight shifted on the couch, still trying to figure out whether Miguel was sparring with him. And why.

"I don't know, maybe it's not even worth pursuing. After all, you said he disappeared a long time ago. He might be dead now, for all we know. Whatever he is—I mean was—it's probably not important now, anyway. At least you've told me enough to think Monzon was too much of a mystery to try to figure out," he said, wondering whether Miguel would accept his lie.

Torres hesitated, tilting his head, eyeing Knight closely. Then he nodded.

"Yes, I believe you're right, David. We have so much more to talk about. I want to know what's happened to you over these past years."

Knight glanced at his watch. I need time to go over what Miguel said tonight and figure out why he's not opening up to me, he thought.

"Look, it's late," he said, yawning. "I'm having trouble keeping everything straight. I'm exhausted, Miguel, it's been a long day. Why don't we begin again in the morning?"

Torres sighed. "I suppose you are right. I hate to see you leave, but I can see you need rest. Tomorrow we can take as much time as we need."

Knight rose, then sat down quickly. He didn't want to leave before he asked the most important question he had traveled to Madrid to ask.

SEVENTEEN

"Sind sie verrückt?" "Are they crazy?" Jorge said to the man at the next window. A flashlight beam had glanced off the side of Torres's house, a flagrant breach of security. It came from the two-man team on the south side of the fence. Jorge wondered whether the team on the opposite side had seen it.

The lapse was unusual for experienced agents of the STASI, the Ministry of State Security of the East German intelligence service. He had worked with them in two previous operations, and found their proficiency nearly the equal of the KGB's. But these men were hard-line renegades who had bolted from the STASI when the Soviet Union's glasnost spread through the Warsaw Pact countries. Not only had staunch Marxist leaders been deposed; the Eastern Bloc intelligence agencies had been decimated, scattering their agents like the gestapo after World War II.

175

Still, with his KGB contacts, Jorge had found the men with the required skills for this operation; and he was confident his command ability would keep the team on the course he so carefully had plotted.

Jorge told Dieter, the young German, to contact the team to verify its status. Though not even a shadow was visible in this vacant house, he thought he saw the man sneer at him. He had felt the air of resentment from all five men this morning during the briefing session, an undercurrent of haughty condescension at the thought of a Cuban taking them through a European operation. At least he had surprised them with his fluent German, and he was certain none had the number of medals he had received from the KGB. Didn't they realize he would not have been put in charge if his record and qualifications were not superior?

Still, he did not want a subtle conflict between nationalities to interfere with the effectiveness of this assignment. The six-man team, including Jorge, was dressed in black: shoes, pants, sweater, and stocking mask, with no indicia of rank. Two of them had Steyr machine pistols with silencers and four flash grenades each; Jorge carried a Beretta 93 in a black shoulder holster. All the weapons were loaded with 9mm ammunition made in the United States.

So far, every detail had been carried out with a watchmaker's precision. Jorge admired the techniques of the Germans but cared little for their attitude. Yet as a consummate professional, he had no desire to cause friction tonight. He had only one objective: to accomplish this mission.

He asked Dieter for the night-vision binoculars, though the security lights of the Torres house made them all but unnecessary. With the wide lens, he viewed the front door to the southeast corner of the building, then panned two houses in each direction. There was no activity. When he had watched the greeting between Torres and the American fifteen minutes ago, he knew the surveillance would not be short.

Jorge went into the windowless bathroom. Unfolding a plot

plan of the Torres house, he scanned the red markings of the E-field perimeter alarm system with a penlight. It is so rudimentary and poorly installed, he thought. The wire supports ten meters apart make it almost defective before we disable it. He doubted Torres or anyone else had tested it by crawling or rolling under the lower sensing wire, or jumping over the top sensing wire of the system. If they had, surely they would have been aware of its ineffectiveness. He measured the layout and distances of the alarm system again. Puzzled, his forehead tightened when he looked closer. I do not understand how someone could be so inept; it almost appears as if someone designed it to fail.

He went back to the other room when he heard a low crackle from the two-way radio. Dieter did not hear him approach in his rubber-soled shoes, and looked up in surprise at Jorge standing above him.

"The men are secure, comrade. The garage has been checked and the wife's auto is gone. No lights have been on in the child's room since dark. We must assume Torres and the American are the only people in the house."

"No, Dieter, we must not make that assumption. What we must do is be patient. It is an error to make assumptions on limited or incomplete data. We cannot afford to make such errors, especially this early. I think we are in for a long evening. We must wait. Be thankful you are inside this house, with me." Jorge spoke as if he was gently lecturing a son.

He sat on the floor, resting his back against the wall, and closed his eyes. Not to sleep, but to review the plan again. The American had made the operation easier by parking in front of the house. Jorge was surprised at his carelessness, especially his failure to make a simple visual check for surveillance before he got out of the seat. For Jorge's team, however, they were fortuitous omissions that now simplified the operation.

Jorge had been involved in twenty kidnappings, eight as team leader. The way the American was setting himself up, this one offered the fewest difficulties of any other. But Jorge did not communicate his opinion to the Germans: He did not want them to lose their edge, nor did he want them to report that he was taking the mission lightly.

The daytime surveillance team had verified that the front gate was the only exit available from the small compound. Depending on the direction the American drove, either the north or south team would fall in behind him. Jorge had calculated it would take less than thirty seconds for Dieter and him to catch up. Three-quarters of a mile from the Monte Clara exit, at a construction access road hidden by four or five tin shanties, Jorge and Dieter would run the American off the highway while the tail car pinned him from the rear. The entire action would take only ten minutes, and less than an hour later, Jorge and his American prize would be on a plane to East Berlin.

He was less enthusiastic about the contingency plan. If the American did not come out of the house by two hours before sunrise, they would have to go in for him. Jorge was certain Torres had weapons. If any alarm sounded before the Germans made entry, the risk factor would be magnified geometrically. But if they bypassed the alarm system, the surprise factor would greatly increase their odds for success. The American would still be taken, perhaps somewhat damaged, but certainly not dead.

As for Torres . . . well, he was not included in Jorge's assignment. The Germans would have to solve that problem on their own. He looked at the luminous hands on his Rolex, then peered at the house across the street. Jorge was sorry they hadn't had time to put a listening device in at least one of the rooms. *Coño*, he thought, I wish I knew what they were saying to each other.

David Knight tilted his head back and stared at the ceiling.

"There's one more thing I wanted to ask you about, Miguel." He closed his eyes and inhaled deeply, trying to calm himself. When he exhaled and looked at Miguel, he saw that Torres had inched forward on the chair. Their eyes met and locked.

"What do you know about the CIA polygraph?"

Torres slumped back into the cushions as if he had been punched in the chest by Knight's question. His face flushed and he grimaced from instant pain.

"I . . . I . . . I don't know what to say. I was so shocked when I heard, I wanted to call you immediately. You can't imagine how badly I felt, how much I wanted to know what and how it had happened. I pleaded with them to let me—"

"Hold it! Back up! Who told you? Who wouldn't let you talk to me? The CIA again?"

Torres sighed. "Of course. He came here—I think it was a month or so after—to tell me you had resigned. When I asked him why, that's when he told me about the polygraph. I was so upset, I yelled and screamed, believe me, to get him to tell me—"

"Dammit, Miguel, who? Who told you?" Knight glared at Torres. He knew Miguel was growing more uncomfortable when he saw his friend's left eye twitching.

Torres looked at the floor. "His name was Steiner. Eric Steiner, he was from the embassy," he said softly.

Steiner? That was the deputy station chief, according to Henry Randall. My God, why didn't I recognize it when Randall mentioned his name?

Steiner's face flashed into his mind. It had been four, maybe five years ago when they had met in Mexico City. Knight had gone to the embassy there to meet one of his sources for a day-long debriefing. The Legat working with Knight introduced Steiner when they passed in a hallway, and said that Steiner was using the cover of an assistant economic attaché. Steiner said he was leaving for another assignment and told the Legat to bring Knight to his going-away dinner that night. When Steiner walked away, the Legat told Knight that Steiner was one of the most effective CIA case officers that ever operated in Mexico.

Long after dinner, when most of the well-wishers had left, Knight and Steiner talked for an hour by themselves, discussing their common interest in the activities of Cuban exiles in Mexico

City. Knight came away from that brief conversation with the distinct impression that Steiner was in favor of any action the exiles took against Fidel Castro. He also thought that the CIA man was a little too sympathetic to their violent actions; in fact, Knight had strongly suspected that Steiner had probably provided the exiles with assistance when they operated in Mexico.

Now, as he looked at Torres, the memory of Eric Steiner roamed in his mind, but Miguel's distant voice drew him back.

". . . But I couldn't get him to tell me what happened to you, even though I told him it was impossible for you to fail a polygraph." Torres paused. "He had a funny reaction, though. It seemed very strange to me at the time."

Knight looked at him quizzically.

"David, he seemed sympathetic . . . almost sad when he told me about it. He even said you were 'a fine agent,' and that your resignation was a loss to the country. When I asked him what he meant, he wouldn't talk about it anymore. And I finally just stopped trying. That night, I cried because I knew what you must have been going through. It hurt me; I can't tell you . . ." Torres whispered as his voice faded.

Knight shook his head, chagrined at the thought of a compliment from the CIA deputy station chief. But Miguel's answer to the polygraph question pushed Knight into a dark room with more locked doors. Frustration and exhaustion suddenly swept over him; his back and neck ached from tension. He needed time and rest to clear his head before he continued with Miguel. He knew an attempt to go on tonight would be futile. Points he wanted to clarify and go over in detail would have to wait until tomorrow.

Standing up, Knight reached for Miguel and pulled him to his feet. They embraced and patted each other's backs lightly. Words were unnecessary to express their deep feeling about this unusual reunion. Then Torres led Knight to a small room past the kitchen, where he sat at a desk. Knight turned to his right and saw an open closet, lined with shelves that held four handguns, two shotguns, an Uzi machine pistol, and a .308-caliber hunting rifle with a powerful scope. One shelf was jammed with boxes of ammunition. On the floor, he recognized a night-vision head-set and a pair of fourteen-inch hunting boots.

"I see you took up hunting, Miguel; I always thought you didn't like guns," Knight said, nodding toward the closet.

Torres looked up from the map he was drawing for Knight. "Gifts from the CIA. They said I should be prepared for any type of prey that might come into the vicinity," he said, smiling. Then he turned serious.

"David, you must be very careful. I have never seen anyone following me, but I suspect I am often under surveillance. Perhaps it is just the SRF people checking up on me; but I always take precautions, and you must also. Take this," he said, reaching into the closet.

He handed Knight a four-inch Smith & Wesson .357 revolver and a box of cartridges. While Knight placed six rounds in the cylinder, Torres continued drawing on the paper. Finished, he turned to Knight.

"Here, follow this map. The route takes you back to Madrid a shorter and faster way. And leave your car here; I have another for you."

He pushed back and led Knight to the garage, then through a heavy wooden door with two dead-bolt locks. They descended a stairway twelve feet below the floor. Knight couldn't understand why Miguel was taking him into a basement until Miguel opened a steel door and switched on the light. Before them, a damp but well-lit tunnel stretched at least a hundred yards.

Torres chuckled when he saw the surprise on Knight's face. "This used to be a safe house for CIA defectors," he explained. "I don't know if the tunnel was ever used by them, but I find it an occasional convenience. When you reach the end, you will find a ladder that leads to a trapdoor. It opens to a concrete room that looks like a tin shack from the outside. There is a Mercedes in it with a remote control under the dash that opens a sliding panel.

181

But be sure to use the periscope before you go out; it is on the right wall when you come up.

"In the morning, do not go back to the shack, just park in front of the house. I'll take care of the Seat." He handed the car keys to Knight, who mouthed "Thanks." They shook hands.

"Be careful, *El Lanza*. I want to see you in the morning. We have much, much more to talk about."

Knight put his hand on Miguel's shoulder. "Don't worry, my friend, I'll be here at nine." He turned and walked down the tunnel. He took several steps, then looked over his shoulder and waved. Miguel was smiling.

Yes, Miguel, we have much more to discuss tomorrow, Knight thought. And the first thing we'll start with will be Roger Estevez.

Torres hurried back into his study. Opening a small wood panel in the wall, he turned on the closed-circuit television monitor and switched to the camera mounted outside the shack garaging the Mercedes. He watched the sleek German car lumber over weeds and hard-packed ruts, then head slowly down the dirt road. His trained eyes watched the fuzzy black and white screen at least sixty seconds after the Mercedes left his view. Satisfied that David Knight was not followed, he turned the monitor off and replaced the panel.

He went to another, larger, concealed panel and removed it, revealing a combination wall safe two feet wide and four feet high. The tumblers clicked as he gently twisted the dial. Pulling the heavy door open, he reached inside and took out a small aluminum suitcase. Torres placed it on his desk and opened the top, then set the knobs and switches for the scrambler telephone resting in a cradle on the bottom. He punched in a number on the keypad, staring at the shuttered window nervously while he waited for a response.

"*Hola!* David Knight was just here!" Torres said. He listened to the voice speak.

"No, no, he didn't ask about Estevez, but he was persistent; he asked many questions. You said you would talk to me before he arrived! Why didn't you tell me he was coming so soon? I was not prepared for him," Torres said, breathing heavily while the voice responded.

"Yes, of course, so I told him a story about Victor and my grandfather. It was the only way I could think of getting around his question; I had to say something. *Coño*, and he asked me about Felix! I lied, but I am certain I can clear that up tomorrow when he comes back. Everything else I told him was the truth. But I don't know what he thinks about the DLN."

Listening, Miguel's face grew red with exasperation.

"Then you must be here and gone before Knight arrives! I will not lie to him again, do you understand? It is time for Knight to know all of the truth. There will be no more deception; you must promise me that much," Torres said adamantly, but the voice soothed him and he became calmer.

"Knight will believe me tomorrow. That will not be a problem, I assure you. Oh, I almost forgot—he mentioned Harrison Witham. From what he said, your theory about Witham is correct." He sighed impatiently, anxious to terminate the conversation.

"Yes, I agree. When Knight knows, then the operation may continue. But you must keep Steiner away, for now."

Torres listened while Colonel Eladio Ruiz gave him the final instructions.

"Yes, of course, I understand. Everything will be in place tomorrow. *'Ta luego.*"

He glanced at the closet and took out the Uzi. Then he closed the small suitcase, put it back in the safe, and replaced the panel. He took the Uzi and walked to the living room. As he poured himself a full glass of brandy, he noticed his hand shaking. He gulped the drink quickly.

Miguel was glad his wife and son had gone to Marbella for a few days. If she was here at the same time as David Knight, he would have to explain too many things to her, things that she had no need to know. Miguel also wanted solitude to plan for the meeting tomorrow. He knew he would sleep restlessly, if at all, but much of his worry would be relieved when he met with the colonel in the morning before Knight arrived. *After I tell my friend David the truth, everything will finally be the same again.* The thought gave Miguel immense pleasure. He smiled, anticipating a happy morning.

EIGHTEEN *December 20*

━━━━━━━━━━━━━━━━ Knight's eyes twitched when slivers of sunlight splayed on his face through dusty venetian blinds. He stirred and rolled over, then propped himself up on one arm. Groggy and disoriented, he looked at his watch: 10:15! Dammit! I forgot to set the alarm! He bolted out of bed and dressed quickly. He was glad he had stayed at the small hotel by the city university: It was only five minutes from the *Autovía de Rozas*. If he hurried, he could make it to Miguel's in forty minutes.

Knight spun through the *Maja Dahonda* exit at 10:45 and accelerated toward the *Monte Clara* subdivision. When he turned onto the winding street that led to Miguel's house, he braked abruptly. Residents milled on the sidewalks and lawns and in the street, talking and looking toward the tall wrought-iron fence two blocks away. Knight observed a police barricade of metal sections that looked like bicycle racks angling across the street a block ahead. Three yellow Civil Guard emergency trucks, doors hanging open, crowded on the sidewalk, abutting the black fence. The Seat was parked in the same place he had left it, just beyond the trucks. Uniformed men stood at equal intervals outside the fence, while others wearing business suits bustled in and out of the front door Knight had entered last night with Miguel. Two men emerged with a sagging black body bag.

Knight tried to swallow past the knot in his throat, but his mouth was as dry as parched earth. His pulse thumped so hard, it shook his body, sending a shiver from his thighs to his shoulders. Consciousness began to fade into the sound of rapid deep breaths.

"Move your car!" A Civil Guard soldier rapped hard on the windshield. "Get off the street! *Andale!*"

Startled, Knight turned the ignition, but the car was still running and the starter cried out a grinding whine. The soldier jumped back, angrily motioning Knight to turn the car around. He backed the Mercedes to an empty driveway and pulled forward to park on the roadway grass. Before he got out, he loosened his tie, took off his jacket, and reached into his bag for a pencil and a small notebook.

He felt his stomach shrinking as he approached the house, still breathing heavily. Another Civil Guard ran up to him, but Knight flashed his Florida Bar card in the man's face.

"Press, UPI Madrid. My boss sent me out here to cover this story. I need to talk to the officer in charge." He put the card away quickly.

The soldier nodded his head toward the house and directed Knight through the barricade.

But Knight did not want to talk to the lead detective, nor to any of the plainclothesmen. Showing his face to a police officer who might easily see through his ruse would be a mistake he could not afford. He stopped when he got to the yellow tape marking off the crime-scene perimeter, five feet from the fence, where two Civil Guards were talking.

Knight approached and gave them the same line about UPI. "What happened here? What's going on?"

The soldiers ignored him.

"Look, I've got a deadline. I don't need much, just a little bit." He pointed to a television news station's van parked near the Mercedes. "It's going to come out soon, anyway. Look. You tell me now, I'll put your name in the paper."

The man on his right beamed, throwing back his shoulders and smiling at his partner. "I'm Corporal Diego Medina. My wife is Celia; I have three children, one boy, two girls, and my wife is pregnant." Medina's smile broadened.

Knight wrote everything down. "I don't know about the children, Corporal, but I'm sure I can mention your wife in the article. Now, tell me why *you* are guarding this house."

"The house was occupied by José Castillo, a notorious Cuban drug dealer from Miami who had been living here for three or four years. He had been running his operation from Madrid and Barcelona, a thousand kilograms of cocaine a month to the United States. Apparently, he stole a great deal of money from the Colombians he was doing business with, and they retaliated with him this way, about four this morning," Medina said, spreading his left arm toward the house. "Castillo's body was found in the empty swimming pool. He was tortured before he was shot. But that's the way the Colombian gangsters do things. They are very ruthless."

Knight turned his back when the tears welled in his eyes. Numbness stifled every emotion, but he kept his composure and maintained a reporter's inquiring demeanor.

"Corporal, I appreciate your information. It sounds as if you are part of the investigating team. Have you been in the house?"

"No, no. I do not investigate. Before we arrived here, we were all told what happened, and this is what we were to tell anyone who asked questions. I have no personal knowledge of anything."

"Then your information comes from the detective in charge. Is he here now?"

"No, not the detective. We were told by Captain Riverte before we came here. He never goes to a crime scene."

Puzzled, Knight pursued this apparent anomaly. "Who is Captain Riverte? Where can I find him?"

"Riverte is in Madrid, at headquarters. He is the Chief of Intelligence of the Department of General Security."

Knight sucked in a breath. "That's the DGS?" His voice was barely audible.

"Yes, of course. I was curious myself that he addressed us about a homicide. In fact, it was the first time I had ever seen Riverte," Medina said. "Usually, he only deals in matters of state security."

Knight felt a needle of panic. The DGS had helped lay the legend that Miguel was dead in 1986. Now Miguel *is* dead, and the DGS Chief of Intelligence was selling another deception. His mind jumped to the Seat. If the house had been under surveillance when Knight arrived last night, the killers would have thought he was in the house when they attacked. And if Knight had been a target last night, the killers would certainly come searching for him today.

He thanked Medina for his help and strolled back to his car, watching for any face that paid particular interest to him. When he sat behind the steering wheel, he was sweating profusely. He unlocked the glove compartment and pulled a map of Spain from under the revolver. Madrid was not a safe destination. Scanning the routes and distances, he decided on Valencia, where the map showed an airport. Though it was a long drive, he would be traveling on an *autopista,* a modern expressway. He hoped he could get there before dark.

An hour later, Knight pulled away from a service station in Tarancón. He gunned the engine until it hummed at eighty kilometers per hour, heading southeast toward Valencia. Without sunglasses, the glare from the bright concrete highway and the hood of the Mercedes strained his eyes. He glimpsed in the rearview mirror and saw a black car a mile behind. When he looked again a moment later, it had drawn so close, he noticed the BMW hood ornament. His eyes left the road as he reached for the revolver and put it on the seat next to his leg.

A sudden jolt threw him against the steering wheel. The BMW had rammed the rear bumper of the Mercedes. Knight checked the mirror and watched the BMW drop back, then come closer for another hit. He pressed the accelerator to the floor and pulled away, but the BMW swung into the left lane, gaining on him. The passenger hung his head and arms out the window, holding a small rifle. Afraid he might lose control if he picked up the revolver, Knight swerved in front of the other car. He heard two loud pops as bullets struck his trunk, and he knew the shots were not from an automatic weapon.

The blond shooter leaned farther out the window. Knight serpentined the heavy Mercedes down the highway, but four more shots hit just above the right and left wheel wells. They're not trying to kill me, they're trying to stop me! Why? Who are they?

Knight got into the right lane and slowed enough for the BMW to draw abreast. He glanced at the two men and briefly held up both hands as a sign of surrender. Slowing down, he brought the car to a stop on the level part of a grassy shoulder that pitched six feet into a culvert, and kept both hands high on the steering wheel.

The BMW came to a halt a car length ahead of him. The blond passenger exited with the rifle and the driver got out holding a semiautomatic pistol at his side. They walked to the Mercedes, looking up and down the desolate highway.

Knight eased the door ajar and slid the revolver under his thigh. When the driver was three feet away, Knight swung his legs and kicked the door into the man, knocking him on his back. Tumbling out with the Magnum in his hand, he scrambled on his knees to the rear of the car. The blond man ran toward Knight with the rifle pointing to the sky. Just as he leveled it, Knight brought his head and arms over the trunk and pulled the trigger. The Magnum roared, flashing white fire. The bullet blew a gaping hole in the blond man's neck, lifting him off his feet. Knight didn't have time to watch his body roll into the culvert.

He stayed low and rushed to the right side of the car. Peeking through the windows, he saw the driver craning his neck both ways to see around the Mercedes. The Magnum still smoked from the hot loads he had put in it. Knight scraped up gravel from under the car and tossed it at the right-front fender. The driver took a wide step to his left, pointing his pistol at the sound, but his move brought him into Knight's line of sight. Knight fired and the Magnum roared again, blasting the driver in the left shoulder, spinning him halfway into the expressway, but the man didn't fall. Dazed, he raised the pistol in his shaking right hand. Knight didn't hesitate; his next shot hit the driver's right temple, splattering blood, hair, and brain tissue onto the white concrete.

Knight dropped the revolver into the Mercedes, then dragged the driver off the expressway and pushed him into the trunk of the BMW. He got in the car and eased it down the slope, where he dumped the other body into the trunk and searched each pocket for identification. Nothing, not even a matchbook. Then he drove the car a hundred yards farther until he found tall grass to conceal it from the highway.

Dusting himself off, he slid into the Mercedes, eased it off the shoulder, and sped away. He ripped off his shirt and mopped the sweat from his body. When he tried to unzip his bag for another, he could not grasp the zipper because his hands shook so violently. An hour passed before he put on a clean shirt.

The powerful German car ate up the afternoon miles, but the endless arid countryside offered no visual distractions to occupy his thoughts. With only the low hum of rubber rolling over pavement to break the monotony, Knight tried to remember the events that had occurred since he had arrived in Spain. But he couldn't concentrate. As an FBI agent, he had learned the skills that had kept him alive, but as a human being, no training could have prepared him for the devastation the act of killing wreaked on his conscience. Instinct had saved his life, but reflection now made him ill. And trying to force away the images of the two dead men did little to ease his torment.

Thoughts of Miguel Torres plunged Knight back into chilling isolation; the Mercedes became an ice floe, caught in gusting winds that drove him into abject despair. The polygraph and the death of

Victor Milian had drawn him to a lost friend; and now that compulsion had caused the death of Miguel Torres. Yet to survive, Knight had employed the ultimate sanction by killing two unknown enemies. And still, he was no closer to the motives for any of these acts. His own pursuit of truth had swept him into a black hole of insidious treachery, and it seemed to be closing in on top of him.

Dusk darkened the outskirts of Valencia. Building lights flashed on, casting a soft orange glow to the sky. He found his way to *Plaza Redondo* and parked the Mercedes on *Calle San Vicente*. With a cloth from under the seat, he wrapped the revolver and dumped it into a garbage can. He walked two blocks and turned east, where he shoved his torn shirt into another garbage can.

Strolling to the spotlighted plaza, he hailed a taxi from the circling traffic and asked the driver to take him to the airport. He combed his hair and smoothed his clothes during the fifteen-minute drive, trying to look like an average businessman taking an evening flight. After what had happened today, he had no desire to act or dress in any way that might call attention to himself.

Still, the Civil Guards routinely patrolling the airport made him apprehensive. He strode from the taxi to the Iberia ticket counter, with his eyes focused on the clerk behind the counter. She told him the next Iberia flight to London left in an hour. With a two-hour layover at Heathrow Airport, he could make a connecting Pan Am 747 flight to Fort Lauderdale.

The clerk directed him to a stall of pay phone booths. He placed a call to Paul Singer at home. No answer. He called the office, but the answering service could not raise Paul on his car phone. Knight waited fifteen minutes and called his home again. Still no answer. He checked his watch.

The flight was boarding soon. Time compressed his thoughts. Panic clutched his stomach. He had to contact someone in Miami before he left. Whom? Reluctantly, but with no other choice, he dialed the number of Sarah Costas. She answered.

"Sarah! Thank God you answered. It's David. I need your help," he said, relieved.

"David? . . . David, please, I can't talk to you now. I'm leaving Miami; the cab just arrived and I've got to get—"

"Sarah, this is important. I can't reach Paul; I need someone to . . . wait, you said you're leaving?"

"I'm sorry, David, I can't help you. I have to go," she said curtly.

"Why won't you listen to me? Look, I don't have much time; there's no one else I can reach. Sarah, please!"

Knight listened to silence, but he knew she had not hung up on him. Sarah's voice came back after a few seconds.

"David, call Felix Monzon. You can trust him, believe me. Don't ask me anything else. Call Felix. He'll help you."

This time, he heard the phone disconnect. Sarah was gone.

Knight's thoughts raced. Trust Monzon? Tony said it, Miguel said it, now Sarah said it. Should I? Do I have another choice?

He heard his flight number in a garbled message over the terminal loudspeaker—last call for boarding. He pushed the keypad quickly.

"*Hola!*"

"Monzon, this is Knight. I'm in Spain. I don't know why I'm calling you, but I had to reach someone." He guarded his words. "I've run into severe difficulties here. I can't get a hold of my partner, and I was hoping you might help. My plane arrives in Lauderdale at midnight, but I'd like to talk to you when I get in."

"I understand, Mr. Knight. Someone will meet you." Monzon's voice was somber, devoid of any cheer. "Give me your flight information and I shall make the necessary arrangements."

Knight responded hurriedly, hung up, and ran to the boarding gate. Stumbling through the plane's door, he paid no attention to the startled flight attendant. He collapsed into his seat just as the Iberia DC-9 began to taxi, anxious for the aircraft to get off the ground. He couldn't leave Spain fast enough.

NINETEEN

As the Pan Am 747 headed west into the jet stream at 37,000 feet, Knight poured his third rum on the rocks into a small plastic glass. A fourth miniature bottle stood at attention, uncapped, on the seat-back tray. He had not had rum in five years, yet the burning, bittersweet drink barely affected his exhausted mind and body.

He drank for self-medication: to sleep, to forget, to numb himself into a drugged stupor, to find an ethereal state where his mind would soar higher than the stars above, where mortal problems disappeared into a meaningless black void—a place to escape the inner torment of guilt.

Knight watched the ice cubes dissolve into slivers, cursing the stark realization that his personal quest over the CIA polygraph might have caused the murders of two close friends. His journey to Spain had been for a specific purpose: to find Miguel Torres, with the hope that Torres would help him find a solution to the polygraph debacle. Before the trip, he had also asked Tony Costas for help for the same reason, and Tony had been killed. Now, Knight ached to blot the memories from his mind, but the liquor did little to relieve his soul-searching agony.

Yet an unyielding need to find the relationship between the deaths, if one existed, pummeled his brain. He could not accept his own pursuit, the polygraph riddle, as a sufficient motive for murder; it had to be deeper, more insidious. He forced himself to remember the details of his conversations with each man, looking for a common thread that linked their deaths and the well-hidden reason for killing them.

It had to be something they knew, something that would be dangerous to others if Tony and Miguel acted on their knowledge, Knight surmised. What did they tell me that could be so sensitive? What secret was so frightening that two men were killed to keep it quiet?

He stared at the fourth bottle of rum, wondering whether he should ask the flight attendant for a Coke to sweeten the drink. Then I'd have a Cuba libre, he thought, snickering at the name given during the Spanish-American War. Suddenly, his muscles tensed and he grabbed the small bottle. The answer crashed into his mind as he stared at the amber liquid.

Cuba libre! Free Cuba! Oh my God, I talked to both Tony and Miguel about a plot to assassinate Fidel Castro! Each one thought it was plausible; Miguel even said it was "an opportune time" to do it. That's it; that must be the reason Tony and Miguel were murdered! They must have known something that would have uncovered a conspiracy to kill Castro . . . and possibly the identities of the conspirators.

Hazy details of the past three days struggled for recollection, but he analyzed each with precision, seeking to separate a consistent pattern from a web of deception. One quickly spun out and pointed at the CIA.

The Agency had taken over Knight's operation with Miguel

Torres; it had fabricated his death in 1986; it had given him the house he was killed in; and two of its legendary warriors in the battle against Fidel, Harrison Witham and Eric Steiner, cast shadows over a treacherous landscape like ominous, circling prehistoric birds.

Still, Knight saw a flaw in his reasoning, a speck of doubt that cautioned against a rash conclusion. Not only had the CIA's plots against Castro been exposed by the Church committee in 1976; credible sources had gone public in 1978 and said the CIA was entertaining plans to assassinate him in Mexico, using Cuban exiles. And in 1984, Castro's own double agents allegedly foiled the CIA's attempts to collect data on his schedule and movements for the purpose of another assassination conspiracy. Knight remembered similar failed plans that never reached the public's eye; and he also knew that Fidel Castro gave intense consideration to those ill-fated schemes.

If any of these public allegations were true, would the CIA be so arrogant as to continue those efforts when they always seemed to surface in a harsh light? Or were renegade elements of the CIA operating again with their favorite Hessians, the Cuban exiles? Those allies had surfaced in the Contra arms and drugs scandal in 1987, but they were never punished for those grievous transgressions. Were they at it again, with Fidel as the target? Or could it be a band of Cuban exiles, using disinformation tactics and old Agency ties to blame their triumphant act on the CIA? From his own experience, Knight had seen their prowess as master manipulators.

And what about a powerful drug lord or drug cartel? Rumors of Castro's involvement in narcotics had emerged periodically since the early days of the Cuban revolution, but were now considered as hard facts. The idea that a crazed, vengeful trafficker might attempt to kill a head of state was not beyond comprehension in the vast subterranean network of international drug dealing. That possibility led Knight to a startling thought: the United States government had discussed openly the feasibility of assassination teams not only for the heads of narcotics empires but also was reconsidering their use against foreign political leaders.

He remembered the Cuban reaction to the United States invasion of Panama to oust General Manuel Noriega. Thousands of Cubans had rallied outside the U.S. Interest Section in Havana to vent their fervent nationalism and strong anti-imperialist sentiments, protesting the attack on the sovereignty and territory of a Third World country. But few other socialist nations reacted so stridently; did the Bush administration believe Castro was now an isolated icon who could be easily disposed of by assassination?

Knight felt his palms sweating and dried them with a cocktail napkin. Jesus, maybe the government *is* involved, he thought. That fits my scenario that the plan to kill Fidel was hatched in the United States.

That wasn't the only reason for his theory, however. The other ingredient was Victor Milian: From what Torres had told him, he thought it likely that Milian had been sent to gather intelligence in Miami by a direct order from Castro. Though hundreds of Cuban agents salted the exile community in Miami, Milian's role as a personal emissary attested to the gravity Fidel attached to this possible new attempt on his life.

As he tied the threads together, Knight sighed. Now he saw a reason for the murder of Tony Costas. It was a rare fear of agents, but not unheard of in the clandestine chess games intelligence services played: retaliation by the Cuban DGI. You take one of mine, I'll take one of yours. Tony for Milian, bishop for bishop. Then call it even.

As for Torres's death, the rationale was frightening, but not difficult to fathom. He simply knew too much. Like Julio Cruz, he had become a liability, a living time bomb filled with explosive knowledge, capable of wreaking devastation on a convoluted conspiracy to kill Castro.

Following these hypotheses, Knight saw the compass needle again pointing at the CIA. If his theory held true, then it had to be the CIA chasing him. His own problem had begun with the hidden motive behind the polygraph incident at Langley, when he had been set up. The Agency wanted him out of the game then, and now that he was back in it, he was a threatening player. But a threat to what? The discovery of another plot to assassinate Castro? What did the CIA think he might do if he did uncover it? He remembered Tony telling him that he knew too much, that he was considered dangerous, that no one would trust him. This all made more sense to him now.

Knight got up and paced in the dark aisles, noticing the peaceful sleeping faces and silent laughter from passengers listening through earphones to the in-flight movie. He longed for the same contentment, but knew he would never have it if he kept tilting at the deadly windmills that spun his thoughts with fear and apprehension. He sat down, thinking of the choices: Stop the windmills, or stop trying. His decision came quickly.

He had always been driven by a compulsion to seek the truth. At times, not even intense introspection gave him a clear-cut reason for this obsession. Yet it was often a source of extreme frustration, for he found that most people didn't care what was true, while the others didn't want to know the truth. But for David Knight, its pursuit was vital and life-sustaining. That relentless goal had pushed him into his search for answers to the polygraph, and now it propelled him again: If he discovered the truth about a conspiracy to assassinate Fidel Castro, he knew it would also lead to the murderers of Tony Costas and Miguel Torres. And only then would he expiate his own guilt.

Yet another reason of larger scope also shaped his will. Because of his familiarity with the political instability of the Caribbean and Latin America, he knew that the murder of Castro would throw those regions into violent turmoil and upheaval. Though Fidel seemed to be an anachronism in an era of communist glasnost, his stature and popularity in lesser-developed Third World countries was only slightly diminished. Millions still idolized him. If the blame for his death fell on the United States, the worldwide repercussions would be unfathomable.

Despite the overwhelming odds against one man pitting himself against such vast unknown forces, Knight's ingenuous determination was unswayed. No inner voice questioned his motivation, nor did it argue with his decision to join the battle.

Sparkling lights of the southeast Florida coastline grew brighter as the 747 passed over Palm Beach County, then began its approach into Fort Lauderdale International Airport. Knight glanced out the window and spotted familiar landmarks: Port Everglades, Pier 66, Bahia Mar Marina, and the I-95 expressway. With the recognition of those sights, he felt a sense of relief common to air travelers returning home. But that euphoria was short-lived, yielding to his last memory of Miguel and grave apprehension about the action he knew he had to take.

Exhaustion lined his face as he straggled down the gleaming white concourse at the end of a horde of deplaning passengers. He walked sluggishly, slowed by the thought that he was now placing his trust in Felix Monzon, and he wondered what arrangements Monzon had made for his homecoming. Knight scanned the noisy crowd greeting the flight arrivals as they strolled into the terminal, looking for some sign or signal of recognition. When he saw none, his shoulders sagged.

"Knight! David Knight!"

He heard his name above the clamor and looked to his left. Jennifer elbowed through clumps of hugging friends and relatives, waving her hand. Her face was drawn, but his mood brightened when he saw her and his steps quickened.

"Welcome back. How was Spain?"

Her grim expression and the question whirled his thoughts back to Miguel's black body bag and the terrifying incident on the road to Valencia. He fought to keep his voice calm.

"Not good. I found Torres, but he's dead. Murdered." He didn't want to mention the two men he had killed.

"Oh, no!" She put her hand to her cheek. "How? What happened?"

He looked around. "I don't want to talk here. Let's go to your car," he said, taking her arm and leading her toward the exit.

A blast of hot, humid air sapped his energy when they passed through the sliding glass doors to the passenger pickup area outside. Knight loosened his tie and hung his jacket on a finger over his shoulder. Still holding her arm, he hustled her across the street.

"I'm over here, in short-term parking." She pulled her arm away and led him to a blue Honda Prelude.

When she started the car, Knight switched the air conditioning on high. He stayed silent until after she paid the parking attendant, drove away from the airport, and turned onto Federal Highway.

"It's a long story, too long to go into all the details. Torres was living under a new identity that he got from a government agency. We talked for a few hours one night, and I was supposed to see him the next day. When I got there in the morning, Spanish police were all over. I didn't tell them who I was, but one of them told me Miguel was a drug dealer who was killed by Colombians." He paused, remembering the police milling around Miguel's house, then went on.

"It was a goddamn setup, but I have no idea why or who did it. I got out of there as fast as I could and drove to Valencia. That's when I called your uncle."

Jennifer started to speak, but Knight continued as if he were talking to himself.

"It's crazy; the whole thing doesn't make any sense. I've tried to find out what's going on, and so far I've seen three people, two of them my friends, murdered in a week. I'm sick about it, Jennifer; I can't help but think that somehow it's my fault, that I . . ." He stopped and stared ahead, surprised he had opened his inner feelings to her so easily. "I'd rather not talk about it now. Where are we going? To your uncle's house?"

"Yes. Why, are you too tired from the trip to see him tonight?" Her voice was consoling, but she kept her eyes on the road.

"No, I need to talk to him as soon as possible. Listen, I tried to call Paul from Spain, but I couldn't reach him anywhere.

Couldn't even get him through the answering service. Is he out of town on the Tampa case?" he asked, turning toward her.

Jennifer's eyes darted at him, but she quickly looked back at the cars ahead of them on I-95. "David . . ." Her voice was soft and hesitant. She couldn't complete the sentence, but she tried again, stretching her neck to swallow.

"I have to tell you something. I didn't want to; I was hoping my uncle would do it, but it isn't fair to you to wait." Her jaw quivered and she gripped the steering wheel tightly with both hands, bracing herself.

"Jennifer, it can't be that bad. Take it easy. What is it? What's wrong?"

When she looked at him, he saw a tear on each cheek. Her eyes were as soft as a doe's, but her voice trembled.

"Paul was murdered today."

Knight's jaw went slack. A rush of air blew through his parted lips, as if a steel fist had driven into his stomach. Every muscle in his body collapsed and his head fell back against the window. He grabbed his shoulders and doubled over, trying to cope with the piercing pain that ran to the tip of every nerve ending. When Jennifer touched his arm, he jerked away and held his face in his hands.

"No, no, no! Not Paul, my God, not Paul!" He pounded his fist on the dashboard, moaning his friend's name. Then he punched the roof of the car with both hands. His eyes glazed over with fury, and he looked around for something to tear apart to satisfy his rage.

Jennifer pulled off the expressway and switched on the blinking hazard lights. Knight opened the door and pushed himself out. He walked into the glare of the Honda's headlights, kicking stones and ripping weeds from the roadside. When he bent over, hands on his knees, she eased the car forward.

Panting, he got in and slumped in the seat. "How was he killed? What the hell happened?" he rasped through deep breaths.

"I called in the morning around nine and told Paul I'd be late, that I wouldn't be there 'til one. When I got there, the door was locked, but as soon as I walked in, I knew something bad had happened. The reception room looked like a tornado had hit it: papers, files, drawers scattered all over. Then I saw that all the Lanier disks were missing."

"Dammit, what about Paul? What happened?"

"I didn't even think he would have been there when it happened. I called the police to report a forty-two, a burglary, then I walked through the rooms. When I got to his office, I found him." She shuddered as if a cold wind wrapped around her neck.

"The dark-out drapes were drawn. But he must have fought like hell. His desk lamp was across the room, and the chairs and tables were knocked over. The lights didn't work; I almost didn't see him. When I went in to open the drapes, I saw him. His body was sprawled out on the couch, and his head was hanging over one end. I didn't touch anything—I know better—but I took a close look. He had cuts and bruises all over his face and head. His nose was broken, and the blood had run down and soaked his shirt. The killer must have used that football trophy in the fight, because it was covered with blood. It was terrible, David; I don't think I've ever seen anything so brutal. But I stayed and talked to the police and the medical examiner."

Knight turned to the window, staring at access-road warehouses as the car neared the Dade-Broward county line. A daylight burglary in an office building on Brickell? That doesn't make sense, he thought. Something's missing.

"Jennifer, are you saying he was beaten to death? Is that how he died? What did the ME say?"

"No, listen to me; I'm not finished. I knew before the police came." She inhaled deeply and turned to Knight. "He was shot. A bullet in each eye. From the size, I'd say it was a twenty-two, probably with a silencer, because there were no exit holes. It wasn't a simple burglary; it had to be a hit," she said, in a tone of sympathy he had never heard before.

Jennifer continued. "I talked to one of the detectives later. He thinks it was probably one of Paul's clients who put out a contract for ripping him off on a fee, or someone who wanted something out of his files. They're going through everything in the office to see if something like that turns up, and they want to talk to you." She paused. "But there's one thing I don't understand: If the hit man wanted something of Paul's, why did he ransack your office, too? You don't even have clients. What could you have that he would want?"

Knight couldn't speak. He closed his eyes to a black void, shutting out any thought that tried to enter. But he couldn't prevent a repeating image of the tarnished football trophy tumbling off Paul's shelf, breaking as it hit the floor.

TWENTY December 20
Miami

Rosa Suarez shook her head, chasing away the drowsiness that pulled on her eyelids and dropped her chin to her chest. She drove the desire to sleep from her mind, determined to stay awake until the meeting was over. Though she had been up since 5:30 this morning, toiling ten hours sewing seams at a piece-goods plant in Hialeah, her dedication to Gustavo took precedence over any personal concern. And if the gringo Witham had come to their house to talk to Gus and Eduardo Canaves, she knew the discussion in the kitchen was not just idle conversation; it meant that her husband of twenty-six years would be leaving soon on another mission.

Gus was a *Brigadista* who had been a squad leader at the invasion in 1961. His men had demolished three tanks before he was captured, and his outspoken, venomous denunciation of Castro at the kangaroo tribunal for the invaders had almost put him in front of a firing squad. But the same attitude sent him into solitary confinement in a tiny damp cell at *El Principe* prison for eight months before the Brigade 2506 prisoners were released in December 1962.

From 1964 until 1975, the short, wiry firebrand had been a member of a CIA contingency team with four other exiles. On a few hours notice, they would be called to action on black missions, destinations unknown until a briefing on the plane long after takeoff. During those years, Gus's team had been sent to Central America, South America, Mexico, Cuba, Africa, and Vietnam, yet they were rarely gone for more than a week at a time.

From 1967 until 1969, Harrison Witham had been the CIA case officer in charge of the team. In 1968, he gave the five exiles their euphemistic designation: the "Z Team." Though they were trained in the most sophisticated black arts of clandestine warfare, their assignments were limited to one function: assassinations. But when the Pike committee began to hold congressional hearings in 1975 on CIA activities, and with the gathering thunderheads of the Rockefeller Commission and the Church committee on the foreboding horizon for 1976, the CIA hastily disbanded the "Z Team" and destroyed any record of or reference to it.

Yet the devotion Gus gave to the Agency was not forgotten. By pulling only a few strings, it had placed him in a high-ranking position with DISIP, the security service of the Venezuelan government. This chess move was also a boon to the CIA, because Gus had access to intelligence information from countries that did not share their knowledge readily with the United States. Still, he was homesick for Rosa and Miami, so he left Venezuela in early 1978.

Rosa's knowledge of Gus's activities for the CIA was thorough, but it did not result from the two-inch height and thirty-pound weight advantage over her husband. They passionately loved and adored each other, and the closeness of their relationship left no room for secrets. That shared bond also encompassed respect and admiration and Rosa's willing desire to do whatever she could to help Gus, whether he asked her or not. Serving as a lookout for him tonight was as natural and gratuitous as a good-night kiss.

She placed his Colt .45 on the coffee table when she stood to look up and down Northwest Nineteenth Street from the front window. It had been four, maybe five, years since she had been Gus's lookout, but she hadn't lost the ability to notice the slightest suspicious sign of surveillance. The street was dark and silent, and she had seen no movement near any of the small stucco houses since midnight, an hour ago. Rosa stretched, sat down, and put the Colt back in her lap.

Witham poured another cup of coffee from the pot on the stove and turned to the table where Gus and Eduardo scrutinized the map of Havana. A small seal and the words *Central Intelligence Agency* in the lower left corner authenticated the map and showed that it had been printed in 1986. Gus traced the yellow-highlighted route as they murmured in Spanish to each other, recalling familiar locations they had not seen in the almost thirty years since they had left Cuba.

Standing back, Witham let them pore over the entire map to observe sites and landmark name changes since the revolution. In central Havana, they saw the former home of the Cuban presidents, now the *Museo de la Revolución*, that documented the course of Castro's rise to power; *Parque de Lenin*, a botanical garden and cultural center that was once a rock-strewn swamp; and the *Plaza de la Revolución*, a huge square where Fidel kept up to a million people enraptured with tirades and inspirational speeches on national holidays and at times of political crisis.

Witham listened to their shock and surprise, followed by bitter comments about the communist influence on buildings, parks, plazas, and streets in the city in which they were born and grew to manhood—and from which they fled to escape the tyranny of Fidel Castro. Anger and resentment resonated in rapid exchanges, coupled with forceful finger jabs on the map. A renewed, heart-wrenching pain of nearly thirty years in exile stung Eduardo as distant memories of happier days in his homeland rose to conscious recognition. When a tear dripped on the oilcloth map, Eduardo turned away and wiped his eyes with calloused knuckles.

When their voices quieted, Witham swung his leg over a chair back and sat across from them at the table. His silence was deliberate. He stared into the brown eyes of each man, sensing their nervous anticipation, confident they would eagerly accept his proposal.

"My friends, we are going into action again."

Gus and Eduardo smiled broadly in unison and almost fell off the vinyl chairs as they slapped each other's shoulders. Excited questions tumbled from their mouths, one voice echoing the other.

"When? How? What are we doing? How soon do we start? Is there anyone else involved? How long will it take?"

"Whoa, men, slow down. I thought you might react this way, but give me a chance to lay it out for you. It's complicated and more dangerous than anything you've done before. If you want to back out after I tell you what the target is, I'll understand. And I don't have to tell you about the consequences if there are any leaks."

Both men nodded and leaned on the table with their forearms on the map, sweaty palms rubbing together.

"You might have guessed from the map that we're not going after refineries, sugar mills, or patrol boats. And we're not going to try to pull off a prison break, either. We're after the biggest fish of all: *El Caballo*."

"Fidel?" Eduardo gasped. "Are you serious?" He looked to see whether Gus had the same sense of astonishment. But Gus kept his eyes on Witham, with a smirk drawn across his lips.

Eduardo had never worked for the CIA, but his dedication to *La Causa*, the exile terrorists' war against Fidel Castro in the seventies, had given him respect and a reputation for ruthlessness. His skill at making bombs was on a par with terrorists from the IRA, the ETA, and the violent factions in the Middle East. But more importantly, he had Gus's absolute trust. He was at the meeting tonight for both reasons; still, Witham's announcement shocked him and caught him off guard.

Gus tugged Eduardo's elbow. "Be calm, Eduardo. Witham is serious, I assure you. We must listen to him, but I have many questions. Perhaps they will be answered when he tells us more." He turned to Witham and said, "We are willing to listen to your plan, Harrison. Coming from you, I know this is not some outlandish scheme. But why now, after all these years? That is what is very puzzling to me."

"I'm surprised, Gus, I thought you would have seen it coming, or at least something like this, when George Bush was elected. Remember when he was the director of the Agency? January 1976 till January 1977." He looked at Canaves. "Eduardo, you know what happened then. Gus wasn't part of CORU, but you were. Think about it."

Eduardo gazed over Witham's head, remembering. "La Coordinación de Organizaciónes Revolucionarias Unidas. The Coordination of United Revolutionary Organizations, the umbrella group that brought us all together. Finally, five of our patriotic groups joined to fight Castro. I was from the Frente, the FLNC. Bosch brought in Acción Cubana, then there was the Cubana Movimiento Nationalisto, the Brigada 2506, and Fuerza-14. We divided the Western Hemisphere into five zones to attack Fidel's people at will, wherever they were.

"Until we all got together in July of 1976, in the Dominican Republic, we were splintered and often fought over actions and territories. But as CORU, we were a force Fidel greatly feared, powerful enough to carry out bombings all over the world if we wanted. And we did, but then the government of the United

States put so much pressure on us. Grand jury investigations here and in Washington, after the Orlando Letelier assassination in Washington and the Cubana Airline bombing in October, brought too much exposure. Bosch was jailed in Venezuela until 1988; the CMN was decimated after the Letelier trial." He looked wistfully at Gus. "There was so much we could have done, but it ended so quickly."

"Your memory is quite good, Eduardo," Witham said. "But who in the government put the pressure on? Who was on your tails in the United States and everyplace else?"

"Well . . . it was the FBI. They were on us like bears going after honey, relentlessly." His face twisted into an unasked question.

"Did you ever get any problems from the CIA?" Witham asked.

Only the faint tick of the kitchen clock's second hand broke the silence. Eduardo watched it, then shook his head.

"I don't think so. Some of us thought they might have assisted the FBI, but we were never certain. But why do you ask such questions now? That was many years ago. Things have changed now; it is not the same as it was then."

Witham let Gus give the response. "Eduardo, you do not understand what he is saying. When CORU was most active, George Bush was the director of the CIA. CORU did whatever it wanted outside the United States, until those *estúpidos* got on in Caracas and set the time pencil detonator on the Cubana plane so that it blew up in the air when it took off from Barbados. That was not supposed to happen; it was meant to go off while the plane was still on the ground, before the passengers got on. If they hadn't made that mistake, CORU never would have had the problems that destroyed it. That and the *stupidos* of the Cuban Nationalist Movement who, with the crazy Chileans, bombed Letelier in this country's capital, ended everything we worked for. *Coño*, Eduardo, without those incidents we might have achieved our greatest glory—the downfall of Fidel."

His tone of exasperation changed as he continued. "But now, George Bush is President. He is not only sympathetic to the Cuban exiles; he owes many favors to those who helped to elect him. Look at those he has made part of his administration, and the political power of the Institute of Cuban Policies, the group started in Miami only five years ago. Yes, Eduardo, times have changed. They may be better for us now than they've ever been." Gus paused and turned to Witham. "Is that not what you are telling us, Harrison?"

"Couldn't have said it better myself, Gus. We've got the support and backup we always wanted, all the way to the White House. We won't be out on a limb this time, I'll guarantee you that. But we still have to go by the same rules of secrecy and compartmentalization. You two and I are the only ones who can know how far our protection goes. I mean it. No one else Gus, not even Rosa."

"So there are others involved," Gus said. "Who are they?"

"Can't tell you yet. I still have to recruit a few more. But they're younger, no one else from your days. I've done my research on them. You two will be the senior members of the team, but you won't have any difficulties with the others. And remember, they won't know as much as you do, even though you can trust them. Now let me show you how we're going to do it."

Witham got up and walked between Gus and Eduardo. He took out a pen and pointed it at the highlighted streets on the map.

"You know that we still have well-placed sources in Havana, in the government. In the late afternoon on December 25, Christmas, Raul Castro is flying to Moscow for a meeting with Boris Ponomarev, the head of the International Department of the Soviet Communist Party. We think we know why, but that's not important. This is," he said, tapping on the map.

"We're not sure of the exact time, but that morning Fidel will go to Raul's house in *Nuevo Vedado*. The last seven times he went there, he took this route, with no deviations." Witham traced his pen along the yellow line. "He goes down Fifth Avenue, turns on Forty-second Street, then to Forty-seventh Avenue to cross the Almendares Bridge.

"On these two corners, at Forty-second and Nineteenth Avenue, there's the Miramar Market and a bakery." He drew two small boxes on the map. "They'll be jammed on the twenty-fourth, Christmas Eve. People are all over the sidewalks and the streets. As much of an atheist and communist as Fidel is, he doesn't interfere with the people who still celebrate Christmas. Anyway, that's where your team will be on the twenty-fourth."

Gus looked over his shoulder at Witham. "But you said Fidel was going by there the next day. Why are we going to be there a day earlier?"

"Because, my friend, that's when you're going to place the bomb."

"A bomb?" Eduardo said. "Witham, that's crazy. You expect us to put a bomb somewhere on that corner with all those people around? In broad daylight?"

"Relax and let me finish with the plan, Eduardo." Witham put his massive hands on each man's shoulder. "Three of you will infiltrate on the coast near Corralillo, the other three will go in just east of La Isabela, but I'll tell you more about that and your rendezvous later. You'll be taken to a safe house near Columbus Cemetery for the night. We've got six of the yellow jumpsuits worn by men of the Work Safety Directorate, and one of their trucks hidden in a garage." Witham stepped back to his chair and sat down so he could watch their faces as he explained the final details.

"Around noon, when the market and the bakery are filled, you'll drive to that intersection and put up yellow barricades around a manhole near the market. It's on the side of the street Fidel will be driving the next day. You've got to plan to be in and out of there in an hour, not a minute longer," he said, slamming the side of his palm on the table.

Eduardo finally smiled. "An hour? I can do it in half that time. But what about the explosives?"

"That's what I want you to think about. You have to let me know by the day after tomorrow, and it'll be in the safe house— RDX, PETN, dynamite, C-Four, detcord, whatever you want. But it's got to be powerful enough to blow a crater in the street."

Gus looked at Witham with steel eyes. "So it's going to be remote control if you're talking about detonation the next day. Are we supposed to stay around for that? Harrison, I don't like that idea; it's too dangerous. G-2 will be all over those streets if Fidel is taking that route."

"Gus, you'll be out of there that afternoon. The remote will be handled by a guy on a balcony half a block away. No one from your team will be around.

"See, we know that Fidel's limousine will have two Alfa Romeos in front and behind, with four bodyguards in each car. We need someone at a high vantage point who can see the cars coming and set it off just as the limo starts to cross the manhole. But don't worry about it, we've taken care of that part of the operation."

He looked at Eduardo. "But you have to give me your specs on the remote. I guess the easiest would be a Fanon-Courier, but that's your specialty, Eduardo. We'll need a five-hundred-yard range, just to be safe. Any problem with that?"

"No, I don't think so. I have never done that distance before, but I can do it, don't worry."

"Look, this is your baby. If you're as good as Gus says, I'm not worried. You're the key player; you screw up, we lose everything—and everybody. I know I'm not giving you much time, but it's the best I can do. It's in your hands, Eduardo." Witham dropped the awesome responsibility in the man's lap, waiting for his reaction.

"Harrison, I told you, *no problema*. You are giving me the opportunity I have dreamed of for thirty years. Believe me, I shall not fail." He said it as an inevitability, not an entreaty, in a voice brimming with confidence and authority.

Witham smiled and nodded, then looked at Gus. An uncomfortable silence hung between them. He knew Gus was bothered, but he couldn't read his impassive face.

"What is it, Gus, what's wrong? I know you're thinking about something. Get it out. We can't afford to play around with doubts or secrets in an operation like this."

Gus shifted his weight and leaned back on two chair legs, folding his arms. He stared at the map, then at Witham.

"You still haven't answered my question. Why are we doing this now? If you say the U.S. government is behind us, what is their reason? I want to see Fidel dead as much as you, Eduardo, or anyone else, and I am glad I am going to be in this action. But are we not entitled to know more?" He held his arms out to Witham, palms up.

"Harrison, this is not 1961 or 1963, there are no plans for an invasion. Am I correct? Then what is the assassination of Fidel to accomplish? Why is the United States government taking this extreme measure now? Why can't we know that?"

Witham suppressed the urge to shout his answer. "Gus, you know the game, especially when it trickles down to us. Everything begins at the top of a funnel, and when it goes down the sides, it gets narrower. We're at the rock bottom of the need-to-know end; we don't get anything but the assignment." He burned his eyes into each man. "Look, I don't even know; if I did, I couldn't tell you. But it's always been that way; you know how it is.

"When we finish, maybe we'll find out; maybe we won't. Jesus, Gus, what difference does it make? Fidel will be gone; you guys will be goddamn heroes. You'll be able to have anything you want in Miami. What's so bad about that?"

Witham's statement brought a huge smile to Eduardo's face, but Gus showed no reaction. He had another question.

"You're sure we're not going to have problems with the FBI? No surveillance, no taps, no visits? They'll stay away from us?"

"Positive. I told you, we've got protection all around. Don't worry about the Bureau, Gus. If anything does come up, let me know. I'll take care of it." Witham rubbed his tired face with both hands, then stood up. "That's enough for tonight. I'll meet with you tomorrow and bring you up to date. Eduardo, if you've got any info by tomorrow, give it to me."

Gus and Eduardo rose together, falling in behind Witham as he headed for the kitchen door. When he stopped abruptly and turned around, they stumbled, almost bumping into him.

"I forgot to tell you something that may cause a problem. There's an ex-FBI agent sticking his nose into things he shouldn't, and I think he might be getting close to us. I don't know what the hell he's trying to do, but he could be dangerous. Ever hear of David Knight?"

"Coño, of course!" Eduardo said, exchanging a nervous look with Gus. "He was like a tiger smelling meat when he was after us years ago, but when we stopped our actions in 1982, he never bothered us again."

Gus jumped in quickly. "He was one of the best they had. I know—I worked with him when I was in Venezuela. But if he's not with the FBI now, why should we worry about him? Why would he be dangerous? What could he do?"

"I'm not sure." Witham glanced at the clock and ran his fingers through the hair on the side of his head. "He's up to something, but I don't know whom he's working for."

"But you said we had protection, that no one in the government would bother us. How can that be, if Knight is investigating? I don't understand you, Harrison," Gus said.

Witham lowered his voice. "That's the problem. If he's not working for the government, whom is he working for? Do you see what I mean? Maybe he's working for—"

"Fidel!" Eduardo said. "Is that possible? How can we find out? What should we do?"

The corners of Witham's mouth curled up when he looked at Gus.

"What usually happens to Fidel's agents in Miami? You know, don't you, Gus?" He paused, now frowning. "But let me see what I can dig up. I'll handle it for now."

Witham walked through the dark rooms to the front door. "Rosa, *muchas gracias* for your help and hospitality." She stood up and he gave her a gentle embrace.

Then he shook hands with Gus and Eduardo. "*'Ta luego*, gentlemen. It was a pleasure. We'll talk tomorrow."

He smiled as he walked to his car in the still night. They bought it, he mused; they believed every fucking thing I told them, like bears lapping up honey. Wait 'til I tell Jorge how I handled those suckers; *goddamn*, were they gullible!

Although Witham had first objected, he now saw Jorge's reason for feeding David Knight the story that an anti-Castro exile plot to kill Fidel was beyond the planning stage. With Gus, Eduardo, and the others woven into the skein, Knight would have to follow the false trail leading to the CIA and the exiles. Not only would he be out of Jorge's way; in the end, he'd be the best witness to testify that the United States government assassinated Castro.

I've got to give the fucker credit; Jorge's a genius, a fucking master of the game.

TWENTY-ONE

The headlights of Jennifer's Prelude shined on Monzon as she pulled in the driveway. He hurried down the porch steps, opened the door for her, and waited for Knight to walk around the car.

Knight's face was frozen in a mask of despair. His red, tired eyes were glassy and swollen. Furrowed lines of tension stretched across his forehead and jawline. Dry, caked saliva cracked on his partially open lips.

He leaned forward, shoulders hunched, and shuffled toward Monzon. When the older man extended his hand, Knight grabbed his arm for balance. Monzon took Knight's left wrist and put his other arm around his back while Jennifer held Knight's right arm, guiding him into the house. They sat him on the couch, where he crumpled like a puppet without its strings. When Monzon went into the kitchen, Jennifer eased Knight's arms out of his suit coat and pulled it off, smoothing the wrinkles against her body.

Returning with two cups and a pot of coffee on a tray, Monzon poured one for Knight, who took it with both hands. He stared at the brown liquid, then sipped it cautiously. No word had been uttered since his outburst in the car, and no one made an attempt at conversation now.

Color crept back into Knight's face and he leaned back against the couch, feeling the tension drain from his body. Yet the same sensation made him weak and dizzy. He finished the coffee in two gulps and set the cup on the seat cushion next to him.

"I'd like to use the bathroom," he whispered.

Monzon led him to a small door in the hallway and switched on a fluorescent fixture. Knight entered, shielding his eyes from the harsh light. Monzon turned on the cold water and closed the door behind him.

Knight splashed water on his face and neck, rubbing hard, and let the cold water run on his wrists until his mind began to shed the numbness of the last hour. He shut off the faucet and sat on the edge of the bathtub, elbows on his knees, head in his hands. Paul's face flashed before him and he recalled Jennifer's description of the brutal murder scene.

Because of me, all because of me! Tony, Miguel, Paul, my closest friends, all dead in one week because of something I started. He suddenly felt alone, helplessly groping with the abject pain of abandonment that brought tears to his eyes.

One poignant insight slipped through his emotions, deepening his sorrow. He realized those three friends were the only people who had truly cared for him, who had tried to help him, who were there when he needed someone. Now they were gone. And now he had no one.

He stood and leaned on the sink, looking into the mirror at eyes filled with self-pity. A ravaged image stared back, craving an answer to his confused emotions.

At first, it came slowly, then grew with intensity as tumultuous thoughts shoved his pain back to the black depths of his mind. Within minutes, they galvanized into anger, consuming him with bloodthirsty rage.

His answer was bold and primal: He could not allow those deaths to go unavenged. Whoever killed his friends would have to suffer the same fate at his hands. Though he knew his objective would involve risk and danger, he resolved to take every action to further that goal with clarity and considered determination. His first step, he decided, required him to discover the motivation behind the murders. He would have to manipulate people and use any other means, legal or illegal, to find that answer. No price—even his own death—would be too high to make peace with his furies.

He found a small bottle of Murine for his eyes and brushed his hair, then splashed Monzon's Old Spice on his face to sting his cheeks. With a last glance in the mirror, he straightened his shirt in his pants and left the bathroom. The first two people he would use for his immediate objective sat twenty feet away.

Monzon and Jennifer were talking softly when he came into the room. She had changed from her dress to tight black jeans, cowboy boots, and a red blouse with a stand-up collar. He stood in front of them and they stopped speaking to look up. Their expressions of sympathy seemed genuine.

"I feel better now," he said, bending to pour his own coffee. He took the same seat on the couch and looked at Monzon. Tony, Miguel, and Sarah had said he could be trusted; if Knight believed them, he had to make the leap of faith now.

"Paul's murder changes everything; the stakes are higher now. I've been running around in the dark too long and I need more light. Somehow, these other murders tie in—I'm sure of it. But whatever's going on, I have to believe it's leading up to some kind of action or operation. One way or another, I'm going to find out how it all fits together." He stopped to sip his coffee, then made the jump. "But I'll need your help, Felix."

"Mr. Knight—"

"Call me David."

"Well, David . . . are you sure you want to do this? Look at what you've been through. These murders, the danger—"

Knight interrupted again. "Don't try to reason with me, Felix. Yes or no, that's all I want, unconditional. I know I'm putting you on the spot, but I also know you know more than what you've told me. You can help me; the question is, do you want to?"

"Yes."

Knight leaned back when he heard Jennifer's voice answer. She had been out of his view while he was talking to Monzon. He glanced sideways without looking directly at her.

"Jennifer, I was talking to your uncle. You've already been helpful, but I'd like the answer from—"

"She speaks for both of us, David. We are willing to assist you in any way. We talked about it earlier, before you got back. It is a joint decision."

"That's very nice, Felix, but I need your help, not Jennifer's. You know how dangerous this is—you said it yourself." He turned back to Jennifer. "I appreciate your offer, but I'd rather not take it. It's better if you don't get involved, thanks anyway," he said curtly.

Jennifer stood up quickly, hands on her hips, stretching the blouse across her firm breasts. But her angry eyes, thin lips, and tightly set jaw short-circuited the impulse of sudden desire Knight felt. Her harsh voice drove his hopeful daydream away.

"You heard my uncle. This is a joint decision, Knight; we're both in on it. If you want help, that's the way it has to be. I'm involved or you're completely on your own." She took three steps to Monzon. "Uncle Felix, give me the Browning."

Monzon reached under a folded newspaper and grasped the pistol by the barrel, then handed it to Jennifer.

She pressed the magazine release and the twelve-round magazine slid into her left hand. Then she ejected the round in the chamber into her right hand. Placing them on the table in front of Knight, she leaned over and began to disassemble the weapon. Her hands blurred as she popped out the ejector rod, slid the receiver off, drew the barrel out, and took off the spring. With the pistol in pieces, she picked up the magazine and ejected each round into her left hand.

Jennifer stood over Knight, rattling the rounds in her palm. She looked at him, then filled the magazine and reassembled the Browning with the same speed. When she finished, she cocked it and let the hammer down gently against the firing pin. After she handed the weapon back to Monzon, she sat down. Less than ninety seconds had passed since she had taken it from him.

"You see, David, Jennifer may be more of an asset than you'd have expected. The skill you witnessed is only exceeded by her ability on the firing range," Monzon said, smiling. "But she is right; if you want any help at all, she must be included—in everything. And I believe it will be to your advantage if you accept our proposal as we presented it to you."

Knight stared at the miniature boxes on the far wall. Monzon had a strong point: Knight had no backup if he found himself in a threatening situation. He knew he had been lucky on the road to Valencia; with a partner, his odds would have been doubled. With Paul's murder in Miami, he was certain someone was still looking for him here. Whoever it was, there was no question they were ruthless killers. And Jennifer had a street cop's savvy, something he needed but sorely lacked. He took a deep breath and glanced at Jennifer's award on the mantel.

"All right, she goes. But understand this: I call the shots; I make the decisions. This is my game. If you want to back out, at any time, let me know. I'm playing this one to the end, no matter what happens. Understood?"

Monzon looked at Jennifer. With her elbows resting on the arms of the chair, she made a tent with her fingertips. Then she nodded an assent.

"Agreed," Monzon said.

"All right." Knight tried to muster a sign of enthusiasm, but his guard was still up. It was too soon to take Monzon and Jennifer totally into his confidence. First, they had to be tested. Knight had cards to play, but he had to keep most of them facedown for now. He had too little time and too much ground to cover for a dissertation on every detail.

"Let me begin with a conclusion, then we'll go back and look at some facts. From everything I've heard and everything that's happened so far, I'm as positive of this as of any investigation I've ever done: Someone is plotting to assassinate Fidel. But we're on a short tether. I'm certain whoever is behind it has gone far beyond the talking stage. I think we're looking at a very short deadline, maybe just a few days."

He watched for a reaction. Their faces remained impassive, showing no sign of shock, surprise, or faint interest. He paused, deliberately, to wait for the silence to break.

"David, if you are correct, is this not an appropriate matter for the FBI or some other agency? If you were able to make this deduction, don't you think much of the same information is in the hands of the government?" Monzon asked.

Knight expected the questions. "Felix, don't patronize me with the obvious. You know damn well I wouldn't even be here if I thought the Bureau was investigating and had everything. If they do, that's as much of a problem as anything else. It's bad enough that I'm persona non grata with them, but I'm sure as hell not about to tell the FBI what I know."

"What are you trying to say? We're not mindreaders. If you're making a point, get it out," Jennifer said.

"A point? This is the goddamn point! I'm telling you there are damn good reasons for me to think that the United States government is going to hit Fidel Castro. And if I'm right, what the hell do you think the Bureau's going to do if I give them my information? Jesus, that's why I'm reluctant to tell you two everything . . . I'm trying to protect you."

"Such an accusation cannot be made lightly, David, even when we consider the attempts made in the sixties by the CIA and the Mafia. But those ridiculous exploits were brought to light many years ago. Surely you don't think the government is taking that course again?" Monzon said, setting his cup on the table to his side.

"Look, remember whom you're talking to. Play devil's advocate if you want, but I'm not some crazy paranoid who sees a diabolical government conspiracy behind every covert action. But I have seen enough of them to know the government creates more devious plans than the people of this country would ever believe." A short fuse set Knight off and he voiced his true thoughts.

"You just mentioned the mob and the CIA going after Fidel. Add these to the list: the Kennedy assassination, Watergate, Allende in Chile, the Contra scandal. Throw in dope and money laundering and organized crime. Where do you think the money came from to build the banks and condominiums on Brickell Avenue?" Knight got up and paced in front of the fireplace.

"If you want to name one common location where the seeds of all these conspiracies were sown and flourished, what do you come up with? Miami. If you try to find one common group in all of them, who do you see? Anti-Castro Cubans. And it sure as hell is no secret that the only way Miami became an international center of finance was because of narcotics, after the exile dope dealers made the Colombian connection." He punctuated each phrase with a stab of his right hand.

"Name any other city in the United States that was taken over by an immigrant group; give me any other nationality in exile that wields the kind of power in the White House the Cuban exiles have. You can't, Monzon. Do you think your people could have done it without help, and protection, from the United States government? My God, that's been going on since 1960. You know that as well as anyone, Felix." Breathless, Knight stopped.

"I remember a similar conversation a few days ago," Jennifer said. "It may be true, but what does all that have to do with a plan to assassinate Fidel now? I still don't understand what you're trying to prove."

Knight took a deep breath to calm his voice. "I'm simply trying to convince you that the possibility of a conspiracy by the government and the anti-Castro Cubans to kill Castro is very real."

"And if it is, why are you so concerned? Perhaps there are valid reasons why the government has made such a plan. Who are we to say?" Monzon asked.

"Because there's a lot more to it that doesn't make sense, Felix, things I can't explain." Knight rubbed the back of his neck with his left hand. "Dammit, within days after I first heard of it, three of my best friends were killed. When Tony Costas and Miguel Torres talked to me about it, the next thing I knew, they were dead. Why?"

He focused his eyes on Jennifer. "And I don't buy the theory that Paul was killed by a 'disgruntled' client, I don't care what the police say. But I think I know why the killer ransacked my office. Whoever murdered Paul was after something; something someone thinks I have."

When the air conditioner clicked off, the room filled with stale silence. Monzon and Jennifer followed his movements, waiting for him to continue.

Knight took Jennifer's Officer of the Month award off the mantel and stared at it. His voice tremored when his eyes rose to look at her.

"If my government is killing people, my friends, to shut them up because of a plot to kill Fidel, I want to know why. I have to know why. And I won't stop until I do."

"But that isn't the only reason." He paused to put back the award. "If I don't find out fast, I think I'm going to be next."

TWENTY-TWO

Monzon inched forward on his chair. "Sit down, David; we have work to do. I just wanted to hear your reasoning, and I agree with everything you said. But time is short, and we must move quickly. We must consider every fact and every possibility, but you must guide us."

"I think we should take a closer look at the murders, Uncle Felix," Jennifer said. "The links are there, all we have to do is find them. Then we'll have a track to run on."

She addressed Knight. "You must have done most of that by now. Why don't you tell us what you've come up with so far? Bring us up to your level."

Knight grabbed a dining room chair and straddled his legs around the seat, sitting so his arms hung over the back. He nudged the chair forward to form an equilateral triangle with Monzon and Jennifer.

"When I met with Costas, he told me he had heard of a group of young Cubans planning an assassination of Fidel. I thought it was a joke—who the hell talks like that anymore?—but he was dead serious. He said he hadn't told the Agency about it yet, that he wanted to try to get more information. Then he goes to the Brigade reunion that night and winds up the victim of a hit-and-run.

"The next day I talked to his wife. She got a visit from the Office of Security. For some reason, they don't seem to pick up on her suspicions that it wasn't an accident and slough it off, more or less. But I don't know if she found out anything more."

Monzon cleared his throat. "So you have a CIA man who tells you about a plot to kill Fidel, then gets killed under suspicious circumstances. His own Agency does not appear to be too interested in classifying it as anything but an accident. Go on. What about Torres?"

Knight hesitated, unsure of how much he wanted to disclose of his relationship with Miguel. But at this point, he wondered, how much do I have to lose? He decided to go with most—but not all—of the story as a method to take a shot at Monzon because of the ambiguous statements from Miguel.

"Torres was an asset of mine." He used CIA terminology for Miguel's role, rather than calling him an FBI informant. "We got very close after a few operations, almost like brothers. He was the best I ever worked with.

"We had something going that would have blown a DGI network running between Cuba and Nicaragua, but for some reason the CIA pulled him away from me in eighty-four. The bastards never told me why, and the next thing I hear, he's supposed to have been killed by a bomb in Madrid in 1986." Knight turned the chair around and sat down.

"When I got to Spain, I found out he was alive, and I met with him. He told me the Agency was responsible for taking him away from me for one of their operations in Spain. They put him up in one of their safe houses, but they never do anything with him—

except to warn him never to contact me, because it might be bad for my health."

He uncrossed his leg and leaned toward Monzon, choosing his next words carefully. His eyes narrowed when he spoke.

"Felix, you're the one who told me he was in Spain, remember? But Miguel told me he didn't know you; only that he thought you'd disappeared. That doesn't make sense, does it? Maybe you better explain before I go any further," Knight said with blatant skepticism.

Jennifer began to speak, but Monzon held up his hand. He sat back and looked at his hands folded in his lap. His eyes were apologetic when he turned to Knight.

"Yes, David, I think I owe you that much. Many years ago, when I was somewhat active for the CIA, Miguel Torres was a young man who made enemies easily, primarily because of his violent temper.

"Our families were good friends in Havana, and when we came to the United States, I took a protective attitude toward Miguelito. His father was quite old, and did not understand his son's propensity for self-made problems. To make a long story short, Miguel had a problem with the police here in 1971. I spoke to some friends and pulled him out of it. Since then, he always felt as if I was an older brother, someone he could come to for advice. Actually, it may have been my influence that led him to become, as you say, 'an asset' for you." Monzon let a smile slip across his lips.

Knight felt a rock in his throat. "So you knew he was working for me. Did he tell you . . . I mean, did he talk to you about what we were doing?"

"Sometimes. But please, believe me, he never talked in specifics. I never knew precisely what you and he were doing. You see, he was extremely loyal to you, David. It is true that he loved you like a brother, and I know that he never would have betrayed you. Not even to me." Monzon hesitated, then continued. "But perhaps his fear that you would reach such a conclusion prevented him from disclosing his association with me . . . perhaps if you and he had talked in the morning . . ." His eyes glazed over and he regained his voice.

"But he never told me why he went to Spain, although he called me at times. Of course, on the telephone, he was even more secretive. I understand the ways and means, so I never inquired of him. But when I received the call from Henry Randall, I became very concerned. It was innocuous enough, but his characterization of Miguel as a drug trafficker was very strange and it made me highly suspicious."

"Your concern wasn't unwarranted, even though I think Randall was just doing his job," Knight said. He didn't want to go into the details of his discussion with Randall.

"But what about Paul?" Jennifer asked, drawing his attention away from Torres. "He was killed when you were coming back from Spain. Does his murder fit into all this?"

"I'm sure it does. Paul was the only person I told that I was going to Spain, but I didn't tell him why. But from what happened there, someone else had to have known. I don't think the killer expected me *or* Paul to be in the office." Knight stopped for a moment, thinking. "Didn't Paul have an arraignment that day? Wasn't he supposed to be in court?" he asked Jennifer.

"Yes, but it was canceled," she said. She shifted in the cushioned chair and sat on one leg. "I keep thinking about how he was shot. Bullets in the eyes, you know what that usually means?"

"No, not exactly, but I have an idea. 'Close your eyes because you know too much,' something like that?"

"Right. Organized crime uses it a lot, and some of the exiles have picked up on it. It tends to fit the police theory, but it might have been done just as a cover to blame any number of Paul's clients," she said, wrapping her hands around one knee.

"But if we think of it as part of the pattern you've suggested, then it might have been a message to you, that *you* know too much."

"Dammit, Jennifer, that's the problem. I talked to Tony and Miguel about a plan to assassinate Fidel just before they were murdered. Why not just kill me, too? Whoever killed them must have known I met with them. Maybe I had a little luck getting out of Spain, but I still traveled under my own name. And I'm still alive. That's why I think they want something I'm supposed to have . . . or know. That's why my office was ransacked; that has to be the reason. But what is it? I've tried to think of everything I've been involved in 'til now, but nothing comes to my mind."

"You must think harder, David," Monzon said. "Let us help you analyze everything. If they believe you have something, it must be of critical importance. Search your mind out loud."

I have to tell them, he thought. I can't hold it back any longer.

"All right, let's see where this goes. About six months ago, I was picked to run an operation for the CIA. Someone at Langley must have really resented it, because an Agency polygraph examiner clobbered me, accusing me of everything from homosexuality to breaching national security. It was all a fabrication, but for some reason the Bureau went along with the Agency and pushed me into a corner. That's why I resigned."

"What was the operation? That might be very significant now." Monzon said, leaning forward.

Do I have a choice? Knight took a deep breath.

"I don't have all the details. I was supposed to get more information after I went on board with the Agency, so I can only give you part of the big picture.

"The CIA hasn't had any asset worth a damn in Cuba for over fifteen years. Castro doubled most of the ones they sent in, and has blown just about every network the Agency set up. I sent one of my guys, Roger Estevez, into Cuba in early seventy-seven, when George Bush was director of the CIA. But in 1982, someone in the Agency complained that I was using my man operationally and that I was usurping their foreign-intelligence function.

"So the Agency took over his control. He was the only asset we've had that penetrated the Politburo, and he gave us incredible information. Then in the fall of eighty-four, he told his Agency control he wanted to get out of Cuba, to come back here. The

Agency told him to stay put and kept him working. A few years later, they got worried that he might have been doubled.

"That's when I got the call. The guy told the Agency that they had screwed him over, and that I was the only person he'd trust. The Agency called the Bureau and asked for help, so the director tapped me for the job. They worked it out so that I'd be detached to the CIA and set up an operation to find out if he had gone over to Fidel. If he hadn't, I was supposed to bring him home. Instead, I got my teeth kicked in. And I still don't know why."

A calm sense of relief came over Knight when he realized he had finally unlocked the dreaded secret that had caused his downfall. He felt his forehead sweating and wiped it with the back of his hand.

Monzon rubbed his chin. "In 1984, he wanted to leave Cuba. Remind me, when was Miguelito taken away from you?"

Knight's shoulders sagged. "My God, the same year. But I wasn't sent to help the Agency and its man in Cuba until eighty-six, so I never put the two together. And then I got nailed by the polygraph charade. Dammit! Somehow it all ties together, doesn't it?" he asked, hoping for a confirmation.

"It appears so, yes," Monzon said. "I suspect you were a threat to someone long before last week, David. You were isolated years ago, either because of what you knew or because of what you might have discovered. And because of that, you have been the victim of a grand deception."

Knight closed his eyes and nodded silently.

Monzon continued: "I understand how you must feel. But you know as well as I that layers and layers of lies cover this deception. So we must first find the lies and peel them away as quickly as possible. It should not be too difficult to do that. With our knowledge of your deception, we have an advantage. The truth always hovers near the deception." Monzon reached out to touch Knight's shoulder. His voice was soft but stern. "David, I believe we are coming closer to the truth. We must go on, please."

"Is there anything you've left out, something you might have missed?" Jennifer prodded.

Knight blinked when the thought flashed into his mind. "Yes! Victor Milian. His murder, that's what got me started. That's why I went to Tony in the first place, to ask him about Milian. But he didn't want to talk to me about it. He told Sarah that if I looked into it, it could be dangerous for me."

"Did he say why?" she asked.

"No, she said he didn't tell her. When I asked him about Milian, he told me to stay away, that it would just cause me problems. And I never got to talk to him again." He folded his hands in his lap and looked at them.

"But I did talk to Miguel about Milian." He pictured the comfortable house in Maja Dahonda and remembered their conversation. "Miguel said Milian was very close to Castro, and often did sensitive missions for him. He talked about some secret organization Milian might have been in, but . . ." Knight suddenly jumped from his chair and grabbed Monzon by the shoulders.

"Felix! The DLN, you told me about it! Castro's secret group, the anti-Soviet people he has stashed all over his government." He released his hands and his eyes widened as all of his thoughts meshed in synchronization.

"That's it, isn't it? Milian was in the DLN. He must have been here on Fidel's orders, with something about the assassination plot. That's why he was killed. But what did he have or know that was so important? Why was he killed?"

Jennifer sent a questioning look to Monzon, but he ignored it and spoke to Knight.

"If he was part of the DLN, David, that may be the most important clue to this enigma. I cannot answer your questions about Milian . . . not yet. But I believe it will assist us if you know more about the DLN." He drew a deep breath and straightened his narrow shoulders before he continued.

"To fully explain the DLN, I must give you its history. It is lengthy, but important, so please be patient. But once you understand what I am about to tell you, I believe you will be much closer to the truth than you could imagine."

TWENTY-THREE

Knight moved to the couch to be more comfortable. Monzon, to his right, sidled over to make room. Jennifer stayed in the chair on his left, her slender legs stretched out and crossed at the ankles. He glanced at the silver metal tips of her boots, then turned when he heard Monzon's voice.

"Before I go into the DLN, David, it will be instructive to consider an aspect of President John F. Kennedy's policy toward Latin America. This has nothing to do with the aborted fiasco at the Bay of Pigs, that ludicrous folly created by the Eisenhower administration and dropped into the lap of the naïve young President. While Kennedy accepted responsibility for the invasion's failure, the blame should have been placed at the feet of Richard Nixon. But that is another story."

One that I'd like to hear, Knight thought.

"The Cuban revolution, as you know, was not a revolt by the masses because of severe governmental oppression. Nor was it due to economic hardships suffered by the people; at that time, Cuba had the highest per capita income of any country in Central America. Fidel's revolution was purely political, in the sense that his small cadre attracted those who desired to rid the country of a corrupt despot." Monzon spoke like a history professor, but he held Knight's rapt attention.

"Conditions in the other Latin American countries were, however, deplorable. Their economies were shambles. Living conditions, education, and health care were among the lowest in the hemisphere, with little hope of improvement under regimes like that of the Somozas.

"One would have thought that if a rebellion was to take place, it would have been in one of those countries. In fact, Fidel did send men into Peru, Colombia, Venezuela, Panama, and the Dominican Republic in 1962, hoping to foment insurrections that would overthrow those established governments. Of course, he was unsuccessful."

"Felix, where does John Kennedy come into this? How does he relate to the DLN?" Knight asked impatiently.

"I am getting to that. You see, Fidel and President Kennedy shared similar beliefs about the problems in the countries south of the United States. It is, perhaps, the greatest irony in the political arena of this hemisphere that these two great men appeared to the world to hate each other, yet held such compatible beliefs about solving the issues that afflicted millions of downtrodden people."

"Compatible beliefs? You're losing me. What the hell did those two have in common? How could they share anything?"

"Ah, David, bear with me and listen. Surely you remember President Kennedy's Alliance for Progress, his elaborate plan to help these countries? Land reform, technical assistance, student exchange programs, long-term development funds, all designed to provide the type of assistance that would improve the economic and societal status of the people in Central and South America.

"Was that not also the goal of Fidel in his early years? To rectify the substandard living conditions of those people? Actually, Kennedy's program was meant to compete with Fidel's theory of revolution, to solve the problems peacefully rather than with violence.

"Obviously, they differed in their methods, but their objectives were identical. Don't you see the irony? Had Fidel and the President ever discussed their ideas and come to an agreement, can you imagine the strides that could have been made? Years later, Fidel said he admired the idea of the Alliance for Progress, and thought that Kennedy was a wise man to have recognized the economic and social situations that could lead to violent revolution."

Monzon stood and stretched his arms. When he sat down, Knight thought he noticed a wetness in his eyes.

"But then Kennedy was assassinated. The Alliance for Progress died when he died, and it was never resurrected. That, David, is the cruelest irony of all."

Stillness pervaded the room. A bitter sadness struck Knight, and his chest swelled with a heavy sigh. Painful black and white memories of the televised funeral in 1963 flooded his thoughts. The irony was worse than cruel; in retrospect, he realized it was devastating.

He looked at Jennifer while Monzon wiped his eyes. She tilted her head slightly, and he thought he saw a wan smile. He followed her gaze back to Monzon.

"Felix, I understand your sentiment. I feel the same way. But I'm still waiting to hear about the DLN."

Monzon gave Knight a sharp look.

"Now I am going to tell you something that very few people know. It has been one of the most-guarded secrets you will ever hear, so listen to me carefully. I shall not repeat one word," he said, almost whispering. His expression did not change.

"In early 1962, Fidel was almost overthrown by members of the Communist party in Cuba. These men, led by Anibal Escalante, were communists long before the revolution, strict adherents to the Soviet voice. They did not fight with Fidel; they did not participate in the overthrow of Batista in any way.

232

"They sought to push Fidel aside, to allow him to be a figurehead but nothing else. It was their intention to install a chemically pure Soviet-style government in Cuba. As you might imagine, Fidel was too smart for them. He turned the tables and sent Escalante and his comrades into exile."

Knight looked surprised. "But Fidel was a Marxist. He admitted that openly in 1961. Why would communists in Cuba try to get rid of him?"

"David, please. Yes, he is a Marxist. But he is first, and always has been, a Cuban. Regardless of his ideology, his revolution was indigenous. He did not ask for, nor did he need the support of the Soviet Union. In his egomaniacal mind, he overthrew Batista for the Cuban people. Events that followed were not necessarily of his choosing."

Knight leaned closer to Monzon. "Then someone must have been backing Escalante. The Soviets?"

"The truth remains hidden. I believe Fidel knows it was the Russians, but he has always been too inscrutable to let them know what he knows. He was fiercely independent and wanted absolute control of his revolution, without any interference. After he banished Escalante, he became very distrustful of them. Yet at the same time, they were offering aid to him. And though he was still riding the crest of his revolution, he reluctantly accepted it.

"Here is another historical irony: Had the United States not enforced its embargo so stringently, it is quite possible that Fidel would not have fallen into the Soviet grasp so easily."

Knight said, "If he didn't trust the Soviets, why did he deal with them? That sounds like a contradiction, Felix, especially if he thought they were trying to get him out of power."

Monzon reached forward and poured two cups of coffee. He offered one to Knight.

"To understand Fidel, you must realize that he has survived for the last thirty years by being a contradiction, no matter whom he deals with. He thrives on deception and keeping his opponents— and friends—off balance. That is the most important trait that has kept him in existence all this time," Monzon said. He paused for a breath.

"But allow me to continue. As you remember, in October 1962, the missile crisis occurred. There is still much confusion and controversy about why the missiles were placed in Cuba. The truth, however, is that Khrushchev convinced Fidel that Kennedy was planning another invasion of Cuba. Fidel was duped and went along with that fable, allowed the missiles, and the crisis erupted. Kennedy then humiliated Khrushchev by getting him to withdraw the missiles, supposedly in return for a promise not to invade Cuba."

"Supposedly?" Knight said, raising his eyebrows. "What does that mean? After all these years, is there some doubt that Kennedy made that commitment?"

"David, for all purposes, that was an empty promise. It was never put in writing—anywhere. You see, the President never had any intention of making another mistake like the Bay of Pigs. He realized, long before the missile crisis, that Fidel could not be overthrown. If he sent American troops to Cuba, how could he prevent the Soviets from moving into West Berlin or some other country in Western Europe? Kennedy had many faults, but he was not geopolitically naïve," Monzon said, flicking the back of his hand to emphasize the point.

"But more important is this, and you will never find it recorded in even the most classified document. During the crisis, when Kennedy was communicating with Khrushchev, he sent a secret emissary to meet with Fidel. The emissary convinced Fidel that the Russians had tricked him with the invasion theory. Fidel was irate, but he could not allow the Russians to discover what he had been told. So the assurance that Cuba would not be invaded by the United States was given to him before it was ever discussed by Kennedy and Khrushchev."

Knight's palms were sweating. He knew Monzon was far from finished, and he wondered what other revelations were coming. He was anxious to hear them.

"That set the stage for a unique relationship of trust between

Fidel and President Kennedy. A month after the crisis was over, the emissary again met with Fidel. But this time, Ché Guevara joined them. They talked for two long days about the tactics the Soviets had been using on Fidel, particularly the Escalante incident and the missile charade. And Ché expressed his concern at the way the KGB was setting up the DGI, making many Cuban intelligence officers more loyal to the Soviet Union than to Cuba. Finally, they came to an understanding."

"What was it?" The words spilled from Knight's mouth.

"Fidel and Ché concluded that the Soviets could never be trusted, and that they had to be constantly vigilant for any attempt to oust Fidel from power. They realized that if the Soviets found it expedient, they would not hesitate to cause a coup d'état of a so-called friend.

"So Ché and the emissary came up with the idea that Fidel needed his own anti-Soviet loyalists to protect him. As much as Ché denounced the United States and fought its influence, he and the emissary liked each other immensely. And you must also realize that Ché was the most outspoken critic of the Soviet Union. He had no love for the Russians," Monzon said emphatically.

"So the DLN began in sixty-two?"

"No. Fidel soon became so involved with running the government and trying to solve its economic problems, he did not fully implement the plan. Ché kept after him, but Fidel directed his efforts to leading and inspiring the people, trying to show them that the revolution was educating, feeding, housing, protecting, and caring for them better than at any time in the history of Cuba. Besides, after the great hurricane in 1963, Fidel had no choice but to accept some of the aid offered to him by the Soviets."

When Monzon paused, Knight spoke. "And that's how the umbilical was fastened. From then on, the Soviets had an economic leash on Cuba. Fidel sold out; the rest is history."

Knight could not hold in a yawn and tried to conceal it with his hand. He hoped Monzon did not take it as a lack of interest.

"Not all history is recorded, David. Fidel always fought to remain independent, even from the Soviets. As late as 1967, he still believed he could become economically self-sufficient, and was not concerned with the loss of Soviet support. As we know, that quickly changed.

"But now I am going to tell you how the DLN was created. It may sound incredible to you, but I assure you it is the truth." Monzon's professorial tone was gone, and he sounded like a commanding officer about to give a briefing.

"Despite the assistance he was receiving from the Soviet Union, Fidel made secret inquiries about restoring relations with the United States. The Kennedy administration responded affirmatively by speaking to one of Fidel's closest aides. Perhaps you are unaware of another tragic irony: On the day of the President's assassination, a French journalist brought Fidel a secret message from Kennedy about opening a dialogue to overcome the tensions between the two countries."

Monzon fell silent. Knight thought of responding, but held his voice and waited until Monzon looked up.

"Then in 1964, Fidel gave hints, mostly through newspaper interviews, that he was interested in improving relations with the United States. He was chafing under the Soviet yoke. Unfortunately, he was rebuffed by the Johnson administration, which was becoming preoccupied with the problems in Vietnam."

"But he was sending people to other countries to promote revolutions during those years. Why would he approach our government when he was doing that?" Knight asked.

"To use your term, he wanted to sever the *umbilical* with the Soviet Union. Ché Guevara went to Moscow in November of 1964, after Khrushchev was deposed and replaced by Leonid Brezhnev. When he returned, he was convinced the Soviets no longer stood for true revolution in Cuba or any Third World country. His hatred of them turned to rage.

"You see, Ché knew they were not pleased with the course the Cuban revolution had taken, and believed they were planning to topple Fidel. Not necessarily immediately, but at some time in the future. He saw how the KGB had taken over the DGI, and was afraid of the power the Soviets had inside Cuba. That was when he finally persuaded Fidel to implement the plan he and the emissary had conceived."

"Felix, that doesn't make sense. If the KGB had such power and influence in Cuba, how could Fidel get away with it? The Soviets had to be watching him so closely, how could he set up anything without them knowing it?"

"Of course, that was a severe problem. But you may remember that Ché disappeared from Cuba in early 1965, for reasons that have never been explained. His departure from Cuba has always been veiled in secrecy, and even today Fidel refuses to discuss that subject. But now, I shall tell you the truth about that mystery."

Knight inched closer, straining to hear Monzon's low voice. He didn't want to miss a word.

"It is true that Ché left Cuba. He was accompanied by nearly one hundred of the most loyal anti-Soviet men and women in Cuba. But they did not go to other countries to foment rebellion. They went to a secret location in Costa Rica for one year, where they trained to become the DLN."

Knight glanced sidelong at Jennifer, pressing his lips together, then looked back sharply at Monzon. He was speechless. Felix was right: The story was incredible. He had never heard anything so preposterous, so totally unbelievable. But his counterintelligence intuition held on, reminding him that any scenario is possible until proven otherwise. But how could he test the credibility of Monzon's tale?

"Honestly, Felix, that's probably the most bizarre story I've listened to since I became an agent. The premise is fascinating, but you don't really expect me to take you seriously? This is too far-out," Knight said, shaking his head.

"You are surprised, David, no? You do not believe me? I thought so; it is what I expected. But bear with me and allow me to convince you," he said calmly, and a thin smile slid across his lips. Then he rose quickly and left the room.

"He'll be right back. I think he's getting something to show you," Jennifer said. She sat in the lotus position, easily crossing her forelegs in spite of the heavy boots.

"I guess I should start calling you David since we'll be working together. That is, if you don't mind." Her voice carried a hint of shyness that surprised Knight.

The light from the table lamp bathed her face with a soft radiance that made him think of a Key West sunset shining on it. For a moment, he imagined standing next to her on a balcony at the Pier House, holding her tightly while they gazed at the sparkling Gulf of Mexico at dusk.

"Do you mind?" she asked, breaking his trance.

"No, no, of course not," he said coldly. Jesus, he thought, that came out all wrong. Why can't I talk to her the way I feel? What's wrong with me?

Jennifer gave him a hurt look, then glanced at Monzon walking back into the room.

He stood in front of Knight and handed him four faded 8 x 10 black and white photographs. He pointed to the first one, which depicted two men, from the waist up, standing next to each other.

"Do you recognize those men?"

Knight examined the picture closely. "Isn't that Fidel? My God, no beard, dressed in a suit and tie? This must have been taken at least thirty-five years ago." He looked at Monzon. "Who's he with? I don't recognize the other man at all."

Monzon and Jennifer laughed. "He's standing in front of you, David. That's me! The photo was taken in Mexico in 1956, before we left for the attack on the Moncada Barracks. I think I look somewhat dashing, don't you?" he said, laughing again.

Knight was too engrossed in the other photographs to hear Monzon's question. Now the faces were familiar. Fidel in fatigues and beard, flanked by Ché Guevara and Monzon, smiling gleefully and holding rifles at their sides. The next showed Castro shaking hands with José "Pepe" Figueres, the President of Costa Rica at the time of the Cuban revolution. To Fidel's left, in the background, Monzon talked with Ché Guevara. The last photo looked like a publicity still of Ché, his arm upraised in a clenched-fist salute. Knight made out the scribbled Spanish inscription at the bottom: "To Felix, my dear friend. Long live the revolution. Ché."

Knight flipped through the pictures again as Monzon sat on the couch. He had a sensation of not just holding reminders of the past but of seeing and feeling the beginning of a historical period that had woven living threads into his own life for the past twenty years. The thought overwhelmed him. His pulse quickened; he became light-headed and felt his mind spinning, until he heard Monzon's voice.

"I hope those photos will help my credibility, David. The success of what we must do depends on your total faith in me. I realize your work has made you suspicious of everything you encounter, but there are often times when you must base your judgment only on faith. I have more to tell you, but it is of utmost importance that you listen to me without skepticism obstructing your mind. Can you do that?" Monzon sounded like he was appealing to a jury. If he had been, his sincerity would have led them to any conclusion he wanted.

Knight rested the photographs in his lap and folded his hands on top of them. The commitment Monzon asked for was more than a quantum leap of faith; it meant that Knight would have to let down his guard and collapse the few defenses he had kept so inviolate. But he stopped himself from thinking of it as a surrender. If he wanted to know more, it was a necessity.

"All right, Felix, I'm with you. Keep going. These are impressive, but you don't have to explain them. I can see how you probably got your information, if you were that close to them," Knight said, handing the photos to Monzon.

"Thank you. To continue, Ché left the United States in late 1966, after he met with the emissary. He had made his decision to go to Bolivia. Then—"

"Wait a minute. You keep talking about this emissary, but who was it? You make him sound like a major operator, but you never say his name. What was he, CIA? Someone I shouldn't know about?"

Monzon sucked in a deep breath and exhaled slowly. His face suddenly had a sad and distant look.

"No, it is not a secret. It is just that I have painful memories when I say his name. The emissary was"—his voice dropped to a whisper—"Robert Kennedy."

"Jesus! Bobby Kennedy and Ché Guevara! I don't believe it!" Knight fell back against the couch. His eyes rolled to the ceiling and he put both hands to the sides of his head.

Thoughts of June 5, 1968, thundered into his mind: a brilliant image of a law-school professor rushing into the library, tears streaming down his face, wailing, "Bobby Kennedy's been shot!" Knight felt his body reeling now, as it had at that frozen moment so many years ago. He touched his cheeks and found the same tears that had sent him sobbing into the book stacks. And the pain, the terrible pain that had thrown his stomach into spasms then, doubled him over again.

Two gentle hands massaged his shoulders. "Easy, David, easy. It's all right. Let it out," Jennifer said.

She stood back when he raised up. He slumped against the back of the couch, tasted salt in his mouth, and rubbed his eyes. He looked at Jennifer through a watery film.

"You know, I remember someone once asked Bobby what he'd be if he wasn't a politician. He said, 'I'd probably be a revolutionary.' Now I know why." The pain subsided and he sat up, trying to bring his mind back into focus.

"Yes, I remember that statement, too," Monzon said softly. "I know it is late, but I must finish, David. I'm coming to the most important part."

"Go on. I'm okay now," Knight said. He turned to Jennifer and mouthed "Thanks."

Monzon's voice rose and he spoke faster, with a tone of urgency.

"Because of his desire to lead the Bolivian peasants to revolution, Ché failed in a most important regard. He did not take steps to structure the DLN force in Fidel's government. When the group secretly returned to Cuba without Ché, they were totally disorganized."

"Then what happened? What did they do?" Knight asked.

"Nothing. Fidel could not take control of the group, so it remained dormant."

"But you said it's in existence now, Felix. Someone must have put it together."

"Of course. But because of Ché's disappearance, the Russians suspected he had been doing something against their interests. It is commonly accepted that Ché was captured and killed by Bolivian Rangers and CIA operatives in 1967. What is not commonly known is that the Bolivian Communist party, under Soviet instructions, set him up to be captured. Two KGB officers participated in his torture, hoping he would disclose his activities in 1965."

"Jesus! The CIA and the KGB, working together. I know it's happened in the past, but I never thought the Soviets fingered Ché." Knight looked around the room, then brought his eyes back to Monzon.

Monzon said, "Fidel learned the truth that December and was enraged. In fact, he dedicated 1968 as 'The Year of the Heroic Guerilla,' in Ché's honor. But the Soviets brought more pressure on Fidel. Anibal Escalante had returned and instigated the 'microfaction' that again sought to remove him. Raul Castro developed evidence that Escalante had been meeting with KGB men in Cuba, and Fidel quickly put him and his followers on trial. With the support of the people behind him, Fidel outwitted the Soviets and prevented a coup d'état. It was then that Fidel gave life to the DLN."

Monzon was hoarse when he stopped. His face was tired and haggard, but his eyes still gleamed. He asked Jennifer for a glass of water and continued talking when she returned.

"Fidel was uncertain about how to proceed with the DLN, so he arranged a secret meeting with Bobby Kennedy in Cuba. Kennedy was making his decision to run for the presidency, but he understood the urgency of this matter.

"As a result of their meeting, Kennedy sent a defector from the Czechoslovakian intelligence service to Cuba to organize the DLN. It was as dangerous as it was necessary, because the KGB nearly had absolute control over the DGI. Anyone who professed an anti-Soviet attitude quickly disappeared, and Fidel was virtually powerless to prevent it."

Monzon suddenly sat erect, jaw jutting forward, in a military bearing. His voice was clear and strong.

"But by June, the DLN was in place. To my knowledge, it has never been called to action, but I believe it is ready if circumstances now require its deployment." He held his position and stared at Knight, then at Jennifer, as if he was mesmerized by his closing statement.

"Incredible," Knight finally said, breaking the silence. "Yet it's still hard for me to believe that you could have all this knowledge. If you were working for the CIA in the sixties, how did you find out about all this? How can you be sure it's accurate if there was nothing ever written about it? Did the Agency tell you?"

Monzon gently took hold of Knight's forearm and turned so their faces were a foot apart. His gaze was intense and burned into Knight's eyes.

"From 1963 until 1968, I was Bobby Kennedy's personal bodyguard. Wherever he went, I went. I attended every meeting he had with Fidel and Ché. I was with him constantly, except for one 2-week period, when I went to the Yucatán to meet with the Czech after he had finished his work with the DLN.

"You see, David, on June 5, 1968, when Robert Kennedy was in Los Angeles, I was in Havana." Monzon swallowed and his stone face shattered. When he got up to leave the room, Knight saw tears in his eyes.

TWENTY-FOUR

Knight turned, to see Jennifer standing at the front window, fingering a faded drapery. She snapped off a loose thread and spoke with her back to him.

"That's the first time I heard that. I know he's been involved in things he'd never talk about, but I never imagined he was so close to Bobby Kennedy. Or this business about the DLN, whatever it is." She faced Knight. "There's so much I don't know, that I don't understand." She faced Knight. "Why is he bringing it up now? What's it supposed to mean, David? Do you have any idea?"

Knight had been asking himself the same questions since Monzon left the room. Yet his blurred thoughts were becoming more distinct; as analytical rays of clarity sliced through confusion, illuminating images appeared in his mind. But he knew he could draw the focus more sharply by thinking out loud, using Jennifer as his sounding board.

"Maybe. Let's just hypothesize and brainstorm it for a while. First, assume Milian was DLN, here in Miami on a mission for Fidel. Why? What was it? It would have to be something Fidel didn't want the Soviets to know about, something so sensitive he couldn't take the chance that it might leak out or be intercepted."

Knight concentrated, looking away from Jennifer while he spoke. He didn't want to be distracted by the intensity in her eyes.

"More and more, intelligence services are getting away from sending information electronically for covert operations. It's gotten too risky and dangerous: no matter how sophisticated the equipment is now, someone always seems to have a device that's just a little better. Any code can be deciphered. Some take longer than others, but it's only a matter of time before they're broken.

"Ever since we intercepted the messages from Qaddafi to the East Germans and vice versa in eighty-six, when the bomb went off in a tavern in West Berlin, most intelligence services and terrorist groups have gone back to the most secure method of passing information: word-of-mouth or hand-delivered messages."

He looked directly at Jennifer. "So I think Milian was trying to get a message from Fidel to someone here. But who in Miami knows about the DLN? Whom could Fidel trust with such a personal message?" Knight paused, then answered his own questions. "I can think of only one person who might know what to do with it, Jennifer. It has to be Felix," he said, with the anticipation of a pitcher waiting for the batter to swing wildly at his hanging curveball.

Jennifer didn't bite, though. Instead, her face turned into a question mark and she responded in hesitant yet measured words.

"Uncle Felix? No, I can't believe that; it doesn't make sense. I'm with him so much, I'm sure I'd have seen or heard something that fits your theory, if it was true. Anyway, what could he do if he got a message from Fidel? Why would Fidel go to him?"

"Jesus, Jennifer, you heard Felix. During the revolution, he was close to Fidel. He helped set up the DLN; he knows all about it. Miguel Torres was related to Milian. He never got to tell me everything he knew, but I know he wanted to talk to me about Felix. And now I find out that Felix was practically Miguel's big brother. What more do I need to reach that conclusion? Unless I'm missing something, all the pieces fit. Who else is there?" Knight argued.

He suddenly lowered his voice, backtracking in his mind. "But you may be right about what he could or couldn't do. I don't have an answer for that. At least not now."

"I do," Monzon said. He entered the room and sat on the straight-back chair. "Jennifer is right, David. There isn't anything I could do. *Nada*. But I overheard you, and I agree that Milian was here to pass a message to someone. For whom it was intended and what the message was are clearly the most pressing questions.

"Please bear with me. Perhaps we are overlooking the obvious. If someone from the DLN had a mission, it is quite possible the KGB was aware of it and was close behind. More precisely, I believe the KGB was after Milian to find the same answers we are searching for. But I also believe they have not been successful." Monzon cocked his head and gave a slight shrug of his shoulders, gesturing to Knight for a response.

Knight held back, pausing to consider Monzon's statement about the KGB. In his own slippery quest, he had not brought the KGB into the puzzling equation that already contained so many X factors. But now, he realized the theory might not be implausible.

"All right, I'll concede that possibility, Felix, if the DLN is really involved. And if the Soviets had any suspicion of activity against their interests, from Fidel or anyone else, they'd try to smother the operation with a bear rug. I see what you mean, but it's still just speculation. There's nothing solid to support it," Knight said.

Jennifer moved to the couch next to Knight. He caught her citrus fragrance and it heightened her presence.

"David, you've been chasing around the idea that the CIA and the anti-Castro exiles are planning to assassinate Fidel," she said. "Turn it around. What if the Russians are behind it, using that as a deception? Isn't that possible?"

His eyes narrowed as he leaned back and exhaled audibly, camouflaging a jolting thought. During this intense discussion, he had never mentioned Harrison Witham, nor had he brought up any detail Witham had told him about the exile plot. Knight quickly decided not to disclose his contact with the ex-CIA case officer. It was the only card he could keep facedown for now, but it might prove useful later. And as long as it stayed hidden, he could make the choice to play it at the most advantageous time. Satisfied, he responded to Jennifer.

"The Soviets hitting Fidel? For what reason? Because he gave them a hard time about glasnost? Because he's an obstinate son of a bitch and won't go along with it? He's always played that game. Jennifer, I think you're stretching the DLN theory a little too far. I just can't imagine Fidel trembling in his combat boots, afraid of being knocked off by his meal ticket."

Monzon interjected. "She may have a point. Look at how Fidel is using Ché's memory now. Huge posters of his face, slogans reminding the Cuban people of Ché's sacrifices decorate Havana and other cities. There is a reason, David. And remember what happened to Ché in Bolivia and how he was set up by the Russians," Monzon said.

"That was over twenty years ago, Felix. Major powers don't do that anymore—"

"No? Then what of your theory that our government is behind it? Your premise would make that equally invalid, would it not?"

"Got me," Knight said, flashing a reluctant smile. "But still, I don't think the Soviets would go that far. What would it accomplish? And who would replace Fidel? Do you think the Cuban people would sit still for a Soviet surrogate? I sure as hell don't." He looked at Jennifer for agreement, but her face was impassive.

Monzon said, "Those are questions that would take hours to

answer, David, valuable time that we cannot afford. But you must accept Ché's resurrection as a signal that Fidel is preparing for something. So our immediate concern is to find out what Victor Milian was attempting to do in Miami. As you said, our time is very limited. We must move quickly."

"Felix, it's late. I'm exhausted, wiped out. Let's sleep on it and figure out what to do tomorrow. My mind is in a fog, and I'm running on empty. I can't think this through tonight," Knight said plaintively.

"No! We do not have that luxury. Remember, I told you about the Czech who organized the DLN. He now lives in Mexico City, but he still has many contacts. When I left the room, I called him. He is expecting you tomorrow. You must meet with him; that is the only way to reach into the DLN, the only way to learn more about Victor Milian."

Monzon nodded at Jennifer. "David, that is why Jennifer must go with you. She can identify the Czech, and he will feel safer talking to you in her presence. In fact, that was a condition he demanded."

The urgency in Monzon's voice did not detract from his commanding tone. Knight felt trapped, but he had no strength, nor any desire to argue against Monzon's order. Moreover, he had no alternative to offer.

He wrapped his arms around his shoulders and pulled hard, stretching his tight back muscles. Then he shrugged one shoulder after the other, loosening his upper body.

"When do I leave?"

"I made reservations for you and Jennifer on Mexicana. The flight departs at nine. Pick up your ticket at the counter. She will meet you on the plane."

Knight looked at Jennifer apprehensively. She avoided his eyes, but he realized one advantage in having her on the trip to Mexico: A man and woman traveling together would certainly draw less suspicion, and it would be easier to deflect if any arose. He also considered another factor: With Jennifer at his side, he might discover whether Monzon had an ulterior motive for insisting that she accompany him.

He glanced quickly at his watch; if he was lucky, he might get four hours of sleep. Jennifer and Monzon rose. His body aching, Knight followed them slowly to the door.

As he drove south on Tigertail to his apartment, Knight's thoughts refused to quiet. He tossed Monzon's plan over and over, and from every view it appeared logical. The DLN now loomed as a much larger piece of the puzzle than he first had imagined. Hopefully, the trip to Mexico would put it in place.

However, he was uncomfortable with the thought that the decision had not been his; an unsettling hesitancy that he could not dispel made him question his judgment in accepting the plan so readily. In Mexico, nothing would be in his control, and that concern brought on anxiety that gripped him with icy fingers.

The winding street in Coconut Grove, so scenic during the day, was eerily desolate under the harsh arc lights casting shadows through the tall ficus and poinciana trees. An approaching Porsche, bright headlights glaring, wove across the center line twice as it quickly closed the distance to Knight's car.

Flashing his high and low beams, Knight slowed to a crawl and pulled to the side, hoping the drunk driver would pass without careening across the street. The driver must have seen Knight's warning, because his car turned and sped along the gravel shoulder on the opposite side a hundred yards ahead. When the Porsche's lights suddenly shone on a parked Ford directly in its path, it swerved, wheels throwing up clouds of dirt and pebbles, then it caught the pavement and skidded past Knight.

His heart thumped, both from the near-collision and the images he had seen illuminated in the parked car. The heads and shoulders of two men sitting in the Ford had been turned to watch the Porsche, but now they looked toward Knight.

Knight heard their ignition start. When he saw the car move, he accelerated and switched off his lights, watching in the mirror as it turned around into his lane. He made a quick right on Aviation Avenue, then a left, and another right back to Aviation. His tires squealed as he raced up the exit ramp of the 2735 building into the under-building parking area, stopping behind the elevator entrance, hiding in its shadows. Keeping his head down, he eased out the door and crept to the three-foot retaining wall. The tail car stopped at the intersection below. Knight thought his breathing sounded as loud as the car's rumbling engine.

The men in the car scanned the area for an agonizing minute, then pulled forward and headed north on Twenty-seventh Avenue. Knight sat on the cold concrete, chilled by the sweat on his back soaking against the wall, and rested his chin on his knees. He checked his watch. Five minutes later, he drove out of the building.

With his lights off, he cruised the streets near his apartment, carefully looking into parked cars and watching for any movement on the sidewalk. Feeling safe but not totally secure, he pulled into the rear-entrance parking lot of the condominium next to his complex. He closed the door quietly, pushed through the bushes to his building's parking lot, and took the dimly lit stairwell to the third floor. Inside, he packed a small suitcase in the darkness of his bedroom, scanned the streets and the parking lot from the windows, then retraced his steps to his car.

Twenty minutes later, Knight checked in and entered the room at the Airport Ramada. He stripped off his clothes, set the alarm, and turned down the bed. His mind was numb, devoid of thoughts of Monzon, Mexico, or car chases. He lay on top of the sheets, staring at the black ceiling, sweat from his neck and legs soaking into the cool cotton. When his eyes finally closed, the first image in his dream was of Jennifer standing over him, sneering and laughing loudly. In his sleep, he was not aware of his body shivering and thrashing.

TWENTY-FIVE *December 21*

Knight woke early to shower and wash his hair. He had brought with him the rarely-used hair-coloring kit he kept for his infrequent undercover roles, and now he massaged the foamy mousse through every strand on his head. When he rinsed and dried his hair twenty minutes later, it was stringy and black. He covered it with Vaseline and slicked it straight back with a wide-toothed comb. Then he slipped on three T-shirts. With an oversized shirt on top, he looked twenty-five pounds heavier. He decided to wait until he got to the airport to put the cotton in his cheeks.

Knight took a taxi to the airport at eight and got off at the far-north end of the terminal. Strolling slowly, with his head down, he walked the length of the inner terminal toward the Delta ticket counter, glancing casually at the faces of other travelers. At each concourse, he entered a shop or boutique and circled out, trying to glimpse someone he might have passed earlier, but he recognized no one.

He sat in the coffee shop adjacent to Concourse H for ten minutes. At 8:30, he went to the Mexicana counter and picked up his ticket. Then he walked back to the entrance of the international concourse and leaned against a pillar that partially hid him yet gave a direct view of everyone approaching the security checkpoint. When his tension gave way to relief, his empty stomach growled, making him anxious for the in-flight breakfast.

Thirty yards away, he saw Jennifer, wearing a short denim dress and navy high heels, striding into the concourse. As he backed farther around the pillar to stay out of her view, he saw a stocky, swarthy man approach her. Knight fought to squelch his panic when they both stopped and engaged in conversation.

My God, I know him; that's Gus Suarez. What the hell's going on? Why is she talking to him? What are they saying?

A minute later, they parted and Knight watched Jennifer pass through the magnetometer. Dammit, is this a setup? Though he doubted that either Jennifer or Suarez had seen or recognized him, his mind whirled. Should I get on the plane? Is this a trap? But they don't know I saw them; maybe I can use that to my advantage.

With that edge, he gambled he could turn this possible near-disaster around. Seeing Gus Suarez confirmed his belief that Monzon had a concealed reason for the sudden trip to Mexico. He needed to know why, but he also knew there was only one way to find out. At least he now had an element of surprise that might turn out to his benefit.

Knight calmed himself, made sure Suarez was out of sight, and followed Jennifer three minutes later. As he walked down the tunnel and passed through the gaping fuselage door, he wondered whether he was stepping into the jaws of a lion.

Carlos Holman stood at the broad expanse of windows in his office on the forty-seventh floor of the Bank of the Americas on Brickell Avenue. Smoke-tinted glass covered the east, south, and west exposures, presenting an observer with panoramic vistas of the Atlantic Ocean far past the deep blue shipping lanes, south Florida down to the inlets and channels on Key Largo, and west into the Everglades, beyond the distant Dade-Collier county border.

Holman often paced along the windows, like a medieval monarch surveying his kingdom from a high parapet of his castle; his attitude was not dissimilar. As president of a bank that had grown from a small building in Hialeah into the largest financial institution in Florida in the short span of eight years, he considered everything he viewed below to be his domain, a fiefdom he had conquered and now controlled with his ruthless economic genius.

As his financial base had grown, so had his status in the south Florida community. He was a ranking member of the Greater Miami Chamber of Commerce, one of the few Hispanics on the prestigious Orange Bowl committee, and a director on the boards of two universities and seven public-service organizations. Local and national politicians groveled for his support and backing for their campaigns, and returned the favors by obsequiously responding to his exacting requests.

In that short time, he also had established Edge Act banks in eight Central and South American countries. The tentacles of his economic holdings reached into real estate, shipping, agricultural, and manufacturing conglomerates scattered throughout Latin America. From this economic base, the pulse of Latin American finance throbbed at his fingertips.

Appearing to accomplish these feats by using textbook methods and dictates for capitalistic enterprise, Carlos Holman had become one of the most powerful men in the state of Florida. But for one well-concealed fact, his success could have been a classic example of a Cuban exile following the footsteps of Horatio Alger. For behind that facade of an American dream come true, Holman was the Miami *residentura* of the Directorate of General Intelligence, the Cuban counterpart of a station chief of the Central Intelligence Agency.

He glanced at the desk-set clock and realized his 9:30 appointment would be arriving in four minutes. He straightened his tie and suit jacket, then sat behind his marble desk and twirled a sharp letter opener in his hands.

"Mr. Holman, Peter Baron is here to see you," a female voice announced over the intercom.

Holman pressed a black button. "Show him in, please."

He rose from his chair when the secretary opened the door. A well-dressed man with neatly trimmed hair followed the instruction she gave with her arm and strode across the room to Holman's desk.

"Mr. Baron, it is a pleasure to see you," Holman said, smiling as he stepped around the desk with his hand extended. He watched his secretary close the door and listened to the latch click shut.

Jorge did not return the affable greeting. His jaw was set tightly and his dark eyes flicked around the room. When he shook Holman's pudgy hand, it felt cool and clammy, like a wrung-out wet rag.

"I told you I did not want to meet you here. Now I am certain it was a mistake," Jorge said icily.

Holman kept his nervous smile. "Please, comrade, do not feel so insecure. You are quite safe here, believe me. There is no danger of discovery. I assure you we are not under any surveillance. *Claro*, we are better off in my office than a bodega or a park bench."

Jorge circled the room while Holman spoke. He stayed four feet away from the windows as he examined the furnishings, lifting up couch cushions, feeling under the two tables, looking into lamps, and sliding pictures and plaques to see behind them, checking for small bumps and hidden wires.

"This office is swept twice a day, at night at eight and in the morning at six, including weekends. Do not be concerned about soft- or hard-wire devices. The windows are coated on both sides with an acrylic compound impervious to laser microphones, and they are also checked daily. These and other countermeasures were installed and are maintained by East Germans. I should not have to remind you of their technological expertise. And you should not be so paranoid, my friend," Holman said, taking a thick cigar from a desktop humidor and snipping the end with a gold cutter. He moistened the wrapper with his tongue, then drew both ends through his lips and lit it with a long wooden match.

Jorge stood rigidly, unimpressed by Holman's curt, condescending explanation. He also detested the stifling aroma of even the best Havana cigar, and he quickly noted that Holman's choice was not even close to prime Monte Cristo caliber. His disgust of cheap cigars was similar to the degree of respect with which he regarded Holman.

Yet, while both held the military rank of colonel in the DGI, Holman held an edge of superiority because of his position as *residentura* in Miami. Jorge, as a field operative of the Illegals Center, was technically subservient to the chief of any DGI unit in a foreign country. But it was a role to which Jorge had never acquiesced. And with a mission of this magnitude four days away, he had no intention of bowing to such regimentation now. Moreover, he knew that Holman was not aware of the entire details of the plan, and that fact placed Jorge in a position to exert subtle control.

"Your assurances may satisfy Moscow and Havana, but I am still uncomfortable in this setting. As you know, I am here only to receive information from you, not to discuss the operation with you. I would like to make this visit short, so please provide it to me as quickly as possible." Jorge remained standing, ignoring Holman's gesture to sit down.

Holman cleared his throat. "May I remind you, comrade, that all of our operations in the Western Hemisphere come through this unit first. Miami, not Mexico City, is now the major operational base outside of Havana, and I have direct authority over—"

"Colonel, do not attempt to exercise that authority over me. We both know what our responsibilities are, and we also know that Miami has a limited function in this operation. Let us not quarrel about bureaucratic authority." Jorge smiled sardonically at Holman, then paced to the expansive windows and leaned his hands on the marble sill. He wheeled around sharply, eyes on fire, and jabbed his finger at Holman.

"Coño, I do not have time for your games and your supercilious attitude. Soon you will understand why, but for now, get on with it. My patience is thin, comrade, and my task is far from finished." His voice crashed into Holman, thundering in the sumptuous office.

The banker's hands began to sweat and tremble. The ash on his cigar, an inch long, broke off and spilled on the floor. He stumbled when his toe caught the fringe of the Oriental rug in front of his desk, mashing the ash into the fabric.

Holman did not know whether Jorge was tracking a target, but he did know of his reputation as the most cold-blooded killer in the DGI. The thought brought a noticeable tremor to his voice that he tried to conceal with levity.

"Please, do not kill the messenger," he said, chuckling nervously. "I am only the conduit, but my news is not favorable. Our friends in Moscow are not pleased with your performance in Spain. Specifically, they are quite upset that David Knight not only slipped your grasp but also killed the two East Germans."

Jorge felt the salt pour into his open wound, but his face stayed impassive. He remained silent, waiting for Holman to continue.

"They believe Knight is an ominous threat to the plan—whatever it is. Unfortunately, they do not know why. But they want you to use whatever means necessary to find and stop him. That is to be your priority, and it must be accomplished before any other step is taken. That is a direct order—"

"Thank you for telling me everything I already know," Jorge interrupted. His neck muscles bulged against his collar button and tie, drawing a tinge of red to his face. His anger was also directed at the men who had lost Knight just six hours earlier, but he hoped that that failure had not yet reached his Soviet masters.

He took three intimidating steps toward Holman. "Now tell me something I don't know, Colonel."

Sweat beaded on Holman's upper lip. "Purely by chance, our airport surveillance saw Jennifer Monzon board a Mexicana flight to Mexico City. But they did not see Knight, nor was he listed on the passenger manifest. They made no attempt at contact, although they did observe her meet briefly with a *gusano* exile. We identified him as Gustavo Suarez," he said proudly.

"Suarez?" Jorge pictured the stocky man. "He is one of our worst enemies, one of the most dangerous exile terrorists in the sixties and seventies. Fidel hates that man!" His voice exploded, but an urgent question ran through his mind. Why didn't *Witham* tell me this? I must contact him immediately.

"Where did he go? Was he followed?" Jorge asked anxiously.

"Only to see him get into a taxi. It moved too quickly in the airport traffic for our people to initiate mobile surveillance," Holman said sheepishly, apprehensive that Jorge would launch a tirade about incompetent Miami DGI agents.

However, Jorge walked slowly to the west windows and looked into the sky. He watched an airliner climb eastward over downtown Miami, then bank as it passed over Miami Beach, heading north up the Atlantic coast. When it became a speck, his thoughts focused on the Mexicana DC-10 heading west.

"So Jennifer Monzon is going to Mexico City. And first she met with Gustavo Suarez," he said, barely whispering. His face was grim when he turned. He walked toward Holman, but stopped ten feet from the *residentura*.

"Well, Colonel, do you have anything else to tell me?"

Holman sighed in relief. The meeting was over.

"No, comrade. But, for the sake of the revolution, I wish you good luck."

Jorge nodded and strode from Holman's office without saying a word. When he reached the building lobby, he found a pay telephone and made an urgent call to Mexico City.

TWENTY-SIX *Mexico City*

━━━━━━━━━━━━━━━━━━━━━━━━━ Knight spotted Jennifer in a window seat next to the wing of the DC-10. The plane was only two-thirds full, so he headed for the A seat across the aisle and two rows behind her. As he passed Jennifer, he noticed she was flipping through the pages of the in-flight magazine. She didn't look up, or give any sign of recognition.

When the overhead seat-belt indicator flashed off, he tilted back and glanced at Jennifer. Her face leaned against the window, watching the ground fall away. He saw no need to speak to her. Within minutes, the drone of the plane's engines lulled his senses and his eyes closed involuntarily.

But his mind would not rest. Jennifer's meeting with Gus Suarez at the airport foreclosed any possibility of sleep. He remembered Suarez from the late seventies, when he was known in Cuban exile terrorist circles as "The Naval Commander." An expert seaman and marksman, he had conducted hit-and-run attacks in the Florida Straits on Fidel's fishing trawlers, which some believed to be sophisticated electronic listening posts. Once, Suarez and three others even strafed a Soviet freighter with a fifty-caliber machine gun mounted on a twenty-three-foot open fisherman.

Those actions quickly brought Suarez to the attention of the FBI's counterterrorist squad. He became a prime target, but every time the Bureau came close to gathering enough evidence to present to a grand jury, the Special Agent in Charge in Miami received a not-so-subtle message from the CIA: "Hands off; he's one of ours." Knight also recalled a 1984 marijuana mother-ship operation off the Georgia coast in which Suarez had been identified; then, the Drug Enforcement Administration got the same admonition from Langley.

Knight shifted uncomfortably in the narrow seat and looked at Jennifer. Her head rested on a small white pillow propped against the bulkhead and she seemed to be sleeping. He leaned forward to see her profile, surprised that he suddenly felt attracted by her beauty, then chided himself for the thought.

Keep your mind on business, Knight. You can't afford to let her looks throw you off course. You have to keep a sharp edge ready for everything, especially after you saw her with Suarez, he warned himself.

He focused back on Suarez. Monzon had never mentioned him or any exile activist, but Jennifer's comments about Castro assassination plots led Knight to believe Monzon might have had past associations with some; and Suarez fit the profile she had described. If the plot to kill Fidel was coming from the exiles, Gus had the tools and the background to be a player. Older now, but he'd still have the expertise to carry out the mission—or to train others to do it. Equally disturbing to Knight was the past protective shield the CIA had provided Suarez, a strong testimonial to the trust and confidence the Agency had placed in him.

Knight turned toward the window, conscious of his deep, rhythmic breathing. If . . . Christ, why are there so many goddamn ifs? If it's an exile plot, Jennifer must be in on it; if it isn't, Suarez must be helping Monzon. But how? Why did he meet Jennifer? What did he tell her?

As much as he wanted the answers, he knew he would tip his hand if he confronted her with those direct questions. Then it would go right back to Monzon, and that was an eventuality Knight had to avoid. As long as she wasn't aware that he saw her with Suarez, he decided it would be safer to let the facts play out. But he hoped the answers would come soon.

Knight looked at Jennifer again, wondering what other secrets she concealed behind the image that attracted him. He hoped they were few and less sinister than he feared, but he couldn't dislodge his unsettling belief that she was also hiding whatever Monzon didn't want him to know.

Fatigue began rolling over him. His thoughts grew fleeting and obscure, wandering and drifting into denser confusion. He fought to stay awake, but sleep finally overcame his futile effort.

Two hours later, Knight woke to Jennifer's gentle tugging on his arm. "Look, you can see the city," she said, pulling him toward the window. She had ducked into his row at the rear of the plane after the pilot had announced the beginning of their descent.

The sight was not pleasant, even from the descending flight path. Though the sun shone brilliantly on surrounding mountains and lower plateaus, thick smog and pollution hung over Mexico City like an ominous gray cloud of disease and pestilence. Knight thought of the teeming 10 million people, most of them at poverty-level existence, and wondered how long it took to turn their lungs as black as the air they breathed. His mind shifted quickly, hoping he and Jennifer would still be alive and breathing when they left Mexico City.

Within minutes, they were on the ground. Jennifer, moving with the passengers in the front of the line, had cleared and walked into the terminal. Now, a tall, thin immigration officer with a Pancho Villa mustache compared Knight's passport photo with the man before him. Knight had a mock look of impatient disdain on his face, mentioning something about an old picture, but he sighed audibly when the officer stamped the entry permit and told him to move on.

Hurrying through the grimy, cavernous terminal, he found Jennifer outside. They found the taxi stand and a hustling driver who shooed them into his vehicle, to the hoots of drivers farther ahead of him in the taxi line.

"The Maria Isabella," Knight said.

He looked out the side window, focusing on faces, styles of dress, and cars that appeared clean and less than five years old. When the taxi pulled into a traffic jam outside of the airport, he turned and carefully inspected the vehicles behind.

Jennifer had pushed herself into the corner of the backseat. When Knight finished looking out the rear window, she glared at him.

"What is wrong with you? Did you see something? Do you know something you're not telling me about?"

Knight stared ahead. "I'm just checking, Jennifer, just being careful. Does that bother you?" He made no attempt to hide his sarcasm, but he quickly regretted it.

"Uh-oh. There is something going on." She inched to the edge of the seat cushion so he could not avoid her eyes. Her voice was angry, but not loud, when she continued.

"Listen, I'm in this, too. I don't know what's going to happen, but I do know there are a lot of other things I'd rather be doing. So don't keep things from me, and get rid of your damn 'silent treatment' attitude. Don't play games with me, David. You can't afford to, believe me."

Was that a threat? Knight wondered. He turned slowly, thinking about his response.

"There are no games, Jennifer," he said sternly. "We both know this is dead serious. Sorry for the pun. I've just been thinking about everything, trying to put the pieces together, so we can get what we're after without getting hurt. But I can't guarantee that we won't."

The taxi shuddered as it swerved around a stopped school bus, sliding Knight into the door. The driver looked in the rearview mirror and threw his hands up in a sign of apology. Knight swore under his breath and glanced outside at the thinning traffic before he went on.

"I don't like that thought any better than you do, so I'm trying to plan ahead. I'm sorry if I didn't ask your opinion, but remember, you volunteered. I call the shots."

Jennifer did not back down. "Wait a minute. I'm here to help you, don't forget that. Felix told you why. If you want to make the decisions, fine, but you better include me before you make one. There's too much at stake to let everything ride on your macho ego. And remember this: You need me, no matter what shot you think you should call."

He knew it was useless to continue arguing, but he did not want to let Jennifer know he agreed with some of her points. Knight used a tactic that had served him well in the past; he bent with the wind—but only so he could move behind it and use it to his advantage at a later time.

He sighed heavily. "All right. But let's get settled at the hotel first, then I'll go over it with you."

"Good. And then you can wash that slop that looks like black beans out of your hair," she said, relaxing with a smile that suddenly made him wish they were on a vacation together.

Perhaps the best-known hotel in Mexico City, the Maria Isabella stood tall on the broad tree-lined *Paseo de la Reforma* at the *Plaza del Oro*. Its modern edifice rose thirty-four stories, and the rooms facing the *Reforma* overlooked the *Zona Rosa*, a square-mile section of exclusive shops, gourmet restaurants, and outdoor cafés frequented as much by local artists and professionals as by the foreign tourists crowding its avenues. Adjacent to the hotel, a high steel fence surrounded the massive United States Embassy, where a line of visa applicants stood at the entrance and stretched down the sidewalk with hopeful expectations.

Knight took the sights in with a hurried glance as the taxi pulled into the semicircular drive in front of the Maria Isabella. He carried his and Jennifer's carry-on bags through the revolving door. The lobby bustled with businessmen running to meetings, while others waited anxiously at the checkout counter. At 10:30 A.M., it was still too early to see arriving and departing tourists beginning their beehive activities.

"Why don't you make the call now, before we check in?" Knight said to Jennifer, nodding toward a bank of pay telephones.

He followed her, looking back at the entrance and around the lobby for eyes that might be glancing at them with more than casual interest. When Jennifer placed the call, he leaned against the wall next to the phones, with a clear view of everyone in the long room. A sudden charge of adrenaline surged in his body, heightening his senses. He felt more alert than he had in the last three days, and he welcomed the sensation. An internal switch had clicked on, preparing his mind and body for action.

"What are you grinning about?" Jennifer asked, hanging up the phone.

Knight's smile widened. "I don't know. Just some thought I can't remember."

She cocked her head and narrowed her eyes, trying to read the silly expression on his face.

"I'm fine, really, don't worry about it." He nudged her toward the reservation counter with one of the bags.

"Did you reach him?"

"Yes. He wants to meet at the National Museum of Anthropology, at one."

Knight remembered the museum, world famous for its extensive collection of pre-Hispanic exhibits and artifacts that traced the tumultuous history of the Mexican people and their culture.

But he also recalled that it was a huge building, with two floors divided into towering halls and minute exhibit rooms.

He stopped walking. Jennifer took two more steps before she turned back to him.

"What's wrong?"

"Where in the museum are we going to meet him?" he said.

"Where? I don't know, he just said he'd find us."

"Do you know how gigantic that building is? Do you have any idea how many people will be roaming around there?" Knight hid his real concern: He knew how easy it would be to get set up in some obscure corner of the museum.

"David, don't worry. I know he'll find us," she said, and strode to the reservation desk.

Jennifer checked in and declined a bellhop's offer of escort. In the room, while Knight showered, she changed into a yellow blouse, faded jeans, heavy white socks, and sneakers.

With his hair back to its natural color, brown with flecks of gray, he dressed in navy slacks, a white button-down-collar shirt, and a navy V neck sweater. When he came out of the bedroom, Jennifer was sitting at the window. She turned and noticed his hair.

"Well, the real David Knight is back—thank God. Now what? When are we going to talk about your plan, or whatever you've been thinking about?"

Knight checked his watch. "We've got a little over an hour. I don't want to wait in the hotel. I've been to the embassy five times in the last four years, and I stayed here each time. I'm afraid someone might recognize me if we hang around the lobby or the coffee shop. Let's take a walk, then we'll take a taxi to the museum."

He tossed his windbreaker to Jennifer. "You might need that. The temperature won't go much above seventy at this time of year. And take it easy. We just went from zero altitude to nine thousand feet; you can get tired from walking a few blocks if you don't take time to adjust your body."

He watched the blouse stretch across her breasts as she slipped into his jacket. He blushed when their eyes met, but this time Jennifer just smiled.

Minutes later, they dashed across the six wide lanes of traffic and the grassy median of the *Paseo de la Reforma*. Knight stopped and bent with his hands on his knees, gulping for breath, while Jennifer stood by. Her face was slightly flushed, but her breathing showed no sign of labor.

Knight stood up and managed a grin. "See what I mean about the altitude?" He panted. He noticed how the wind had tousled her hair, loosely framing her radiant cheeks. She looked like a cover girl posing for a high-fashion magazine.

"I don't know about the altitude, David. Maybe age?" She laughed, but her eyes eased the chagrin he felt when she called attention to their fourteen-year age difference. He shrugged his shoulders, trying to understand why he felt hurt by her comment.

Impulsively, he grabbed Jennifer's hand and pulled her along as he stepped over a short wire fence and walked on the grass toward the Zona Rosa. She didn't resist, and he didn't let go until they reached a sidewalk café two blocks away.

They sat at an outdoor table, Knight with his back to the Paseo and the Maria Isabella. Strangely entranced by Jennifer's nearness, he fought to keep his mind on the purpose for coming to Mexico City. A fleeting thought of spending the rest of the day and night with her in the hotel room intruded, but he forced it away and tried to talk about the upcoming meeting with their contact.

Still, his tension ebbed. Jennifer's presence brought on a mood of relaxed pleasure. But when he watched her animated lips, Knight felt an arousing desire. It was not that he had been celibate since Kathy's death eight years ago, nor was it simply physical attraction. He was lured by the same arcane sensation he had had when he first met Jennifer in Paul Singer's office. The intuitive closeness he had experienced then had returned. And despite one inner voice warning him that she was still too much of a mystery, that the Suarez meeting was a danger sign, another told him that he could confide his trust in her. That unconscious bond urged him to surrender his scarred defenses and to ease open the gates of his stirring desire—but logic and self-control held him back.

He restrained his emotional conflict with bantering conversation. They rambled on about people they knew in Miami and spoke of the sights and attractions in Mexico City each wished they had time to visit. He listened selectively, waiting for a telltale slip or lapse, hoping he didn't hear one. Engrossed by her words, he failed to notice another presence until an unseen powerful hand gripped his shoulder and jarred his concentration.

"David Knight, it is you! I thought I recognized you."

Knight looked up, but the sun sent a black spot into his eyes, briefly obliterating the man's features. He squinted and raised his hand to block the sun. The man took a step to the side and his face became visible under the shade of an awning.

Knight's startled expression was not due to his failure to identify the man; instead, when he matched the face to the man's name, it translated to an ill-concealed sign of panic because of the shocking recognition. But what unnerved him more chillingly was the question that suddenly throbbed in his head: *What the hell is Eric Steiner, the CIA deputy station chief in Madrid, doing in Mexico City?*

TWENTY-SEVEN

The iron chair grated noisily on the cement when Knight pushed it back to stand up. He forced a thin smile and grabbed Steiner's hand. It was like squeezing a rock.

Steiner looked like an aging fireplug fullback: Muscular shoulders leaned forward, straining against the fabric of an ill-fitting gray suit coat. A once-aquiline nose, now bent and bulbous, was the result of four years as the only Jewish football player at Holy Cross and a career-long drinking problem. But he had established a reputation in the intelligence community as a bulldog, sinking his teeth into a project until it was accomplished, and his opponents always knew they had been in a bitter fight when Steiner finished with them. Though he never disguised his contempt for enemy intelligence services, neither did he take measures to conceal an air of menacing intimidation from friends and acquaintances. Knight was no exception.

"I'll be damned. Eric Steiner? I thought you were long gone from here, maybe even retired by now. How many years has it been since that party? Three, four?"

"Three years, seven months since we had that red-eye conversation, but I remember it like it was last week." Steiner gave a hesitant glance at Jennifer, dropping his eyes to her left hand. Then he looked back at Knight.

"I travel a lot now, David. Here, there, it's always some goddamn thing. The State Department likes to keep me hopping—you know how it is," he said, signaling Knight to go along with his CIA cover. His eyes flicked to Jennifer again.

"I'm sorry, Eric, this is my fiancée, Jennifer Ferrer." Knight waited while they greeted each other, trying to plan his explanation, but Steiner interrupted his thought.

"So what brings you two south of the border? Must be a good reason to leave sunny Miami in December and come to Mexico City. You here on business? Vacation?" Steiner pressed.

Knight had no immediate answer. He felt a lump bobbing in his throat, blocking his voice.

"It's because of David's law practice, Mr. Steiner," Jennifer said, rescuing Knight.

"Eric, beautiful lady. Law practice? Oh, that's right, I heard you left the Bureau. You must be doing damn well to get a case down here. But isn't that a little unusual? I mean, you can't really practice out of the United States, can you? Don't most American lawyers just get a Mexican lawyer because the judicial systems are so different?" Steiner asked, tilting his head at Knight with a look bordering on disbelief.

"No, I didn't mean legal business here," Jennifer said, drawing Steiner away from his target again. "It's just that David's been so busy, we're trying to fit our own plans into his hectic schedule. The only way we can have a honeymoon is to do it now, before the wedding. If you know David, you know he never does anything the way it's supposed to be done. And anyway, I kind of like the idea." Her eyes danced as she laughed infectiously and reached across the table to squeeze Knight's hand.

Steiner snickered and jarred Knight with a stinging slap on his arm. Steiner's eyes, hard and penetrating above an obviously false grin, met Knight's glare.

"You son of a bitch. I should have known once you left the government you'd be raking it in. I've heard there's gold in those mountains of cocaine in Miami; glad to see you're getting some of it. And a gorgeous young lady to go along. Sure sounds good to me." Steiner paused. "But it must keep you running, David. You doing any other traveling?"

Reel it in Steiner; you're not going to catch me on that rusty hook. But I'll nudge it, just to see if you jerk the rod, you eager bastard, Knight thought.

"As a matter of fact, I just got back from Spain last week. It was strictly business, but I did run into a few old friends from Miami. They filled me in and brought me up to date about things that have been happening since I left the Bureau.

"But I'm not really interested in that whorehouse gossip now. I've got more important things on my mind," he said, moving to stand behind Jennifer. He kneaded her shoulders with his fingers.

Steiner's voice mellowed when she glanced at him from under her long lashes. "You don't have to convince me. I'd say Jennifer's enough to get your mind off old war stories and keep you occupied for a long time. A real long time," he said, reaching to shake hands with Knight.

"Well, folks, I have to get running. No time to play when you're on Uncle's time, always moving. Right, David?"

But Knight wanted time to push Steiner into his own trap, to encircle him with a bait net of questions about why he was in Mexico City. Steiner, according to Henry Randall, had clearly known Miguel Torres was in Madrid. Steiner had even called Monzon about Torres. And Monzon sent Knight to Mexico City. Now Steiner shows up here, on this street, suddenly appearing at his side. Knight knew that deputy station chiefs, laden with in-country paperwork and other bureaucratic responsibilities, do not hop from continent to continent without a high-priority assign-ment. And rarely would a man like Steiner be given a field oper-ative's function of making a covert contact, especially out of the country.

When he turned these facts around in his mind, Knight's sur-prise at the contact by Steiner changed to chagrin: How could Steiner be so blatant? Did he think Knight would not be aware he was breaching strict Agency mandates and policies? Steiner's con-duct was so incongruous, it almost lent credence to a theory of coincidence.

Maybe that's the design, Knight thought, a deception to throw me off balance and into confusion, so I won't know when I'm walking into his snare—if he's setting one.

The answer would not come from Eric Steiner. He shook Knight's hand and left abruptly, striding around a near corner. Knight reached for Jennifer and pulled her up from the table.

"What was that all about?"

"We've been made. I don't know what the hell's going on, but he's not supposed to be in Mexico City. He's CIA, from Spain." Knight looked furtively both ways on the street.

"You have to call the Czech, call off the meeting. It's not safe now; we've got to change plans. Don't tell him why, just tell him . . . Jesus, what if he's being watched? Look, just tell him 'We lost the violin.' He should know what that means." Knight felt certain the Czech would recognize the KGB code for cancel-ing a meeting.

He paid no attention to the puzzled look on Jennifer's face when he motioned toward a pay phone at the nearest intersection. They walked quickly, but Knight tried to appear calm.

Jennifer held the receiver to her ear, but irritation grew on her face as the intermittent buzz went unanswered. Finally, on the ninth ring, a voice responded. She spoke hurriedly, eyes flicking to Knight. She hung up and looked at him with a trace of panic.

"It's too late. His wife said he already left. He told her he was going out to buy some groceries, that he'd be back by three. I'm sure he's going to the museum. What should we do?"

Knight chewed on his lower lip, breathing heavily. He remembered his personal commitment, to go for the win no matter what the consequence. There was no choice but to make the contact; he was too close to important answers to turn back. His decision contradicted a basic rule of tradecraft for any intelligence operative: Call off a proposed meeting when you have advance knowledge the other side is watching. But he had to take the risk. He grabbed Jennifer's arm and pulled her with him.

A dozing taxi driver jerked up when they rushed into his parked Chevrolet. Knight barked an instruction and the taxi squealed from its space.

The National Museum of Anthropology was two miles from the *Zona Rosa*, a direct drive west on the *Paseo de la Reforma*. Knight glanced at the Modern Art Museum on the left as they crossed the *Melchor Ocampo* and *Mariano Escobedo* intersection, then spotted their destination less than half a mile ahead. He directed the driver to take the next left, on *Calzada De La Milla*, into Chapultepec Park. Following Knight's directions, the taxi wound through the park's rolling wooded grounds. Giant cypress trees, centuries old, grew over a hundred feet into the sky. Smaller oaks and elms with barren branches crowded together on leaf-strewn brown grass, giving Knight a sense of déjà vu and memories of Chicago's Lincoln Park in the fall. The taxi glided past the drained Don Quixote Fountain, a poignant reminder of the windmills Knight had tried to tilt for so many years. He hoped this quest would not be as futile as the follies encountered by that misguided mythical hero.

When he saw the zoo through the right-front window, Knight told the driver to stop. They were at the *Paseo*, two hundred yards west of the museum. If surveillance was following, he reasoned it would be easier to detect if he and Jennifer were on foot. It would also give him more time and the opportunity to abort the meeting before they made contact with the Czech. Knight dropped two hundred pesos in the front seat and hustled Jennifer out of the taxi.

They strolled toward the museum entrance in silence, except for the crunching dry leaves on the sidewalk. Tourist buses jammed the museum's drive. Throngs of sightseers crowded around a bubbling fountain and the scattered cement benches on the broad expanse leading to eight glass entry doors. Taking Jennifer's hand, he jostled through the people and pushed her inside one of the doors.

"Easy, David. If they didn't see us before, they have now, the way you ran in here," Jennifer said, pulling her hand from his tight grasp.

Knight scanned the area outside the doors. "That's why I did it, to see if anyone changed their pace to follow us inside. But I don't see anything unusual out there. Did you?"

"Nothing. Look, the man from the CIA could have been a coincidence, couldn't he? I mean, don't you think you're a little too paranoid. Coincidences do happen."

His eyes burned into hers. "Listen to me. In my life, there are no coincidences. There are reasons for everything. I learned that the hard way, and it's a lesson I'll carry until the day I die. I can't live any other way. And as long as you're with me, I intend to keep a healthy paranoia around us. Believe me, it's a helluva lot safer to have it in this business. Whether you like it or not, that's the way it has to be. Got it?"

Jennifer's expression registered an apology to his rare show of temper. She nodded sheepishly and turned her face away. Knight surveyed the interior of the museum. He had seen it as a tourist four years ago, and even in that three-hour span he had made it through only half of the exhibits.

He damned himself for consenting to the museum as a contact location. Twelve halls radiated from the main-floor patio, displaying Mexico's early civilizations; on the second floor, numerous dioramas depicted the country's indigenous cultures; and on the top floor, ten exhibition halls described the development of Mexico's modern cultures. Outside gardens held replicas and scale-model reproductions of ancient sites throughout Mexico.

Too many rooms, too many corners, too many people with too many different faces, Knight thought. If someone is watching us, how the hell am I going to pick him, her, or them out in this maze? And if the Czech shows, how is he going to find us?

Jennifer had drifted away, but Knight caught up to her near the Aztec Room. Before he uttered an admonishment, he saw what had drawn her to that hall. A huge Aztec calendar stone on a wide black pedestal emitted a golden glow from three ceiling spotlights. More than any other exhibit, it personified a cultural period when the grandeur of Mexico was as resplendent as that of any country in the world.

When Knight had seen it years ago, it had held a magnetic fascination for him. Now, he felt the same pull. He glanced at Jennifer and ushered her toward it with a slight pressure on her back. They walked within two feet of the pedestal. Jennifer reached out tentatively and touched the cold intricately carved stone.

"It's magnificent," she said softly. "I remember reading about the Aztec calendar and I've seen pictures of it. But this is breathtaking . . . and it's where we're meeting Emil."

"What? Why didn't you tell me? What are you—" Before he finished, he saw her eyes widen and look over his shoulder. A smile broke her smug expression.

She brushed past Knight and hurried to the steps at the base of the Aztec calendar, where she embraced a tall, gaunt man with thick silver hair. Beneath a drooping brown sport coat, he wore a turtleneck sweater. His blue trousers bunched at the waist, hanging loosely on his legs.

"Ah, Jennifer, how beautiful you've become," the man said, holding her shoulders at arms' length. "It must be at least twelve years since I saw you last, when you were a rambunctious teenager. You are now, what, twenty-five?"

"Thirty, I'm sorry to say, for both of us," she said shyly, nodding at Knight.

"And you are David Knight, of course. I am Emil Pavlicek. That is a Russian name, but that is my father's fault, from his heritage. I was born in Prague." Pavlicek's voice was low, but rapid and authoritative. He made no attempt to shake hands. The sparkle in his eyes when he spoke to Jennifer was gone.

"Felix has told me much about you, Mr. Knight. I must admit, however, I was reluctant to meet with you at first. But Felix has a very persuasive manner. I'm sure you know what I mean. He explained the necessity for this meeting, but unfortunately, I believe it is more than necessary. It is urgent that I pass vital information to you, but we have very little time."

Pavlicek led them away from the calendar stone and out of the Aztec Room. To a casual observer, he looked like a professor of anthropology conducting a private tour for an American couple. His pace was unhurried and he pointed to relics, sculptures, ceramics, and other exhibits as they walked to a courtyard garden with a replica of a pre-Hispanic house in Oaxaca. The only anomaly in the scene was a modern stainless-steel drinking fountain on a patch of brown grass.

Pavlicek said, "We are more secure here. There is only one entry and exit, so we can see who comes this way. If anyone does, just talk about the exhibit."

Knight was impressed with Pavlicek's professionalism, but he was impatient to get his information. "If what you have is that important, you better start now. I hope it's something I can use before it's too late."

Pavlicek dismissed Knight's comment with a pained smile to Jennifer. He tested his weight against a wooden fence rail around the exhibit. When it held, he leaned back and folded his hands at his waist.

"Felix told you the background of the DLN, so I shall not discuss it or my role in its creation. Obviously, however, I still have contacts within that organization who are intensely loyal to me. But my interest had waned until recently, perhaps four or five months ago. I began reading of certain Soviet overtures in Mexico, so I made some discreet inquiries. Then, coincidentally, I received the call from Felix."

Jennifer shot a raised-eyebrow look at Knight, but his face was impassive, waiting for Pavlicek to continue.

"And now you are here, Mr. Knight. Other than Felix telling me that you can be trusted, I know little of your purpose or involvement in this matter. But from what I have learned here, I believe my information will be quite useful to you." The intensity in Pavlicek's steel gray eyes emphasized his last phrase.

"I'm listening," Knight said, moving closer to Pavlicek.

"What do you remember of Thomas Mann?" Pavlicek asked.

"Thomas Mann? The German novelist?" Knight shrugged his shoulders, puzzled by the question.

Pavlicek covered his mouth when he laughed. "No, Mr. Knight, not *that* Thomas Mann. I'm speaking of the Under Secretary of State for Latin America during the Johnson administration. Does that help you? Do you have any knowledge of Operation Thomas Mann?" He said sternly.

Knight looked at Jennifer, then shook his head at Pavlicek. The question marks in his eyes grew bigger.

TWENTY-EIGHT

Pavlicek raised his palm. "Excuse me. The altitude and low humidity at this time of the year parches my throat when I'm outside." He leaned over to sip from the water fountain and then turned back to Knight, wiping his mouth with his cuff.

"Before I defected, I was a captain in the Czechoslovakian intelligence service. From 1964 until 1967, I conducted many operations for Department Eight. It may be more familiar to you as Department D."

Knight nodded. "Yes, *dezinformatsia*." Department D was the designation used to denote a Soviet-bloc intelligence division that handled disinformation operations, or active measures, against the West. Although each service gave it a different numerical designation, Western intelligence agencies always called them by the letter *D*.

Knight was more than familiar with Department D special operations. Detecting disinformation ploys created by the KGB and the DGI had been one of his responsibilities as a counterintelligence agent. But it had never been an easy task: The aim of a disinformation scheme was to deceive the United States by feeding false information, hoping that policy-making officials would use it as a basis for reaching conclusions the Cubans or Soviets wanted them to reach. That conscious distortion was designed to taint the natural flow of information to, from, and within the United States. To penetrate such a web of deception before it was acted on by government officials, Knight would first build a border around it by ferreting out feedback links, security locks, and channels of communications, hoping to find common denominators in overt activities. If he succeeded, he would then have the tools to decipher the disinformation message.

Now, as he looked at Jennifer sitting on a small cement bench in the shade, he wondered whether Pavlicek would give him the chisel he needed to wedge open this consuming deception. Knight walked to her, put one foot on the bench, and rested his forearms on his thigh. He readied his mind for another history lesson, eager to find its relevance to the present.

Pavlicek coughed hoarsely into a handkerchief. "The Kennedy era, particularly the missile crisis in sixty-two and the Khrushchev humiliation, caused the Russians to reevaluate their intelligence activities. Until then, they had maintained a generally passive, information-gathering role. But there was a shift in priorities after Kennedy was assassinated. The Soviets conceived the theory of ideological subversion, to counterbalance the Western powers' attempts to promote democracies in lesser-developed countries. Kennedy's Alliance for Progress is an example that comes to mind.

"One result of that thinking was the establishment of Department D's. Obviously, the Soviets could not and did not want to show an overt presence in noncommunist nations, so they resorted to using surrogate intelligence services to achieve their goals. We, the Czechs, and the East Germans were sent to countries in Africa and Latin America with specific directives to use disinformation to influence political affairs, economic conditions, and the effects of American policies."

Pavlicek coughed again, hacking loudly, and his eyes teared. He took a pill from his pocket and swallowed it at the fountain. Knight and Jennifer exchanged worried glances.

"Are you all right?" she asked.

"Yes . . . no, but that is not your concern. I am not well, so I must finish quickly. Let me go on to Operation Thomas Mann."

"Now I remember," Knight said, jabbing his finger at Pavlicek. "Mann was the Assistant Secretary of State under Johnson and was responsible for setting the President's policies for Latin America."

"Precisely. And that is why the Czechoslovakian service, at the direction of the KGB, created a massive disinformation campaign to discredit the United States in that region.

"The operation began in early 1964, with the disinformation objective to show that U.S. foreign policy toward Latin America had radically changed after Kennedy's assassination. Our directives were to prove that Thomas Mann, with President Johnson's approval, had designed a policy that called for more economic exploitation and more blatant interference in the internal affairs of Latin American countries."

Pavlicek waved the back of his hand above his shoulder. "Of course, there were specific details and tactics, but to mention them would serve no purpose for your present interests." He paused and folded his handkerchief.

"What may be of great interest to you, however, is this: One of our major tracks was to label the CIA as the cause of in-country meddling machinations to implement the new U.S. policy. Primarily by the use of forgeries—one, Mr. Knight, even purported to bear the signature of J. Edgar Hoover—we attempted to convince the Latin American people that the CIA planned to topple the governments of Uruguay, Brazil, Chile, Cuba, and Mexico.

Our task was made much easier after the coup in Brazil that April, when we publicized the names of so-called American agents responsible for that incident. Yet it was all a fabrication, a total deception to blame the United States." His voice was low and raspy, and he blotted his neck with the handkerchief. His breathing was heavy and labored.

Knight took his foot off the bench and stood with his hands clasped behind his back. The thought slashed into his mind like a lightning bolt.

"I think I know where you're going. For some reason, you believe a similar deception is being played out now, another plan to discredit the United States."

Pavlicek's face had turned pale gray, but he looked at Knight sharply. "And the Central Intelligence Agency, Mr. Knight. Of that, there is no doubt in my mind."

Knight considered Pavlicek's emphatic statement but gave no response. Eric Steiner's image flashed into his mind. He decided not to ask Pavlicek whether he knew Steiner.

Jennifer broke the silence. "But why, Emil? Look at what has happened in Eastern Europe. The Communists are out of power; their influence is minimal. And with Gorbachev shaking hands with everyone in the world, people sincerely believe that glasnost is reshaping the entire Soviet bloc with political pluralism. Why would they be planning a deception to discredit the United States in Latin America now? How could that be possible?"

"My dear Jennifer, you must realize that in the world of global politics and superpowers, what is said publicly is always done for a hidden reason. To paraphrase a late chief of counterintelligence for the CIA, 'deception is a state of mind—but it is also the mind of the state.'" He held up his hand to keep her from speaking.

"Please understand, I am not saying that Mr. Gorbachev is not sincere, nor that his desire for glasnost is not honest. But when he says his economic reforms have failed, he is telling the West exactly what it wants to hear. You must also realize that he is a very proud man and a fervent Russian nationalist. He does not renounce communism; he simply seeks to rejuvenate it with the free world's economy. What happens after that is the subject of worldwide speculation. My personal belief is that it is but another charade, though perhaps much more complicated than in the past.

"You see, there are additional factors. Not all of his comrades in the Kremlin and Eastern Europe are in favor of his policies. But that is not a secret, is it, Mr. Knight?"

Knight shook his head. "No, of course not. He does have enemies, or at least opposition to contend with in his regime. There must still be at least twenty million hard-line conservatives in the Soviet Union. And I can't accept it as a fait accompli that the KGB and its cousins in the Warsaw Pact have gone out of business. They're not going to just kiss and make up with the CIA. That's not even probable." He stopped and took a deep breath. "Then what you're saying is that those elements may be, or are, behind this deception, whatever it is. Or possibly Gorbachev himself?"

Pavlicek smiled. "It is only an old man's theory. But yes, I strongly believe it. And I also believe their plan involves Mexico."

Knight's expression changed to surprise, puzzled by the mention of Mexico. He had hoped the meeting with Pavlicek would lead to answers about a Castro assassination plot, but now he felt like a quarterback who forgot whether he called a pass or a run after the huddle broke. All he could do was call the count, take the ball, and hope to make the play by watching what the other players were doing.

"I don't follow you. Why Mexico?"

"As I said, I have my contacts and sources. And I pay close attention to geopolitical items that appear in the press, especially when they mention this country. With your background, Mr. Knight, I would expect you to understand the importance of that regimen." He did not wait for Knight's response.

"I read prolifically, every newspaper and magazine I can find. At my age, I have little else to do. But several months ago, an article in *Excelsior* mentioned that the Soviets opened consulates in Hermosillo, Ciudad Juárez, and Monterrey. The stated reason was because of the Soviet interest in commercial trade with Mexico. That may be a valid premise, but I doubt it is the true purpose."

Jennifer asked Knight's question. "Then what is the real purpose?"

Pavlicek paced away from the fence rail, turning his back to Jennifer and Knight. "I cannot give you that answer. I can only tell you that anytime the Soviet Union opens a consulate, it is staffed with a full complement of KGB officers. And I should not have to tell you that *their* presence is not to promote goodwill or trade relations with a host country."

Knight directed his comment to Jennifer. "The KGB has only two purposes in a foreign country—intelligence gathering and subversion. But if Emil's theory runs true, it also includes disinformation. Probably, it's a combination of all three."

He looked at Pavlicek. "You must have some ideas, at least speculation. What do you think they're doing in those three cities?"

"Ah, Mr. Knight, I have racked my brain for months to decipher the reason. But even a hypothesis escapes me. The medication I take for diabetes and emphysema wages a losing battle that affects my memory and concentration."

Knight shoved his hands in his pockets and kicked at a small branch on the stone pathway. He stared at the redbrick wall surrounding the courtyard. The trip to Mexico City had yielded no answers, only more questions, and little prospect for solutions. The thought of raising the issue of a Castro assassination plot seemed ridiculous. He had a sudden urge to go to the airport and use his MasterCard for a six-month vacation in Hawaii.

With a deep sigh, he looked at Jennifer and shrugged his shoulders, signaling frustration and resignation. She stood and walked to him, reaching for his hand, but both turned when they heard Pavlicek's voice.

"I have made arrangements for you to speak to one of my contacts, who may provide you with the information you seek. This person is a member of the DLN, but works as the Cuban Fisheries attaché in Mérida, in the Yucatán. But you must leave immediately."

Knight could not conceal the startled look on his face. Pavlicek cut him off before he asked how the contact should be made.

"We will leave separately, you two first. I will watch carefully for surveillance." He moved to Jennifer and took her hand, then kissed her cheek. "It was so good to see you again, my dear. Please give my love to Felix." Pavlicek shook Knight's hand, then disappeared into the museum.

Knight took Jennifer's hand and walked quickly inside, through the interior exhibit room to the main hall, where he shouldered past a guided group waiting at the entrance to the Mayan Room. They slowed to a steady pace, rounding the marble circular dais in the lobby. He pulled Jennifer into the crowded museum bookstore and stood behind a postcard rack, craning his neck to observe the glass front doors. Turning, he looked back into the throngs moving from exhibit to exhibit, but he did not see Pavlicek.

Jorge folded the *Excelsior* to the financial page and crossed his legs, shifting his weight on the tufted-fabric couch. His polished wing tips glistened in the sun's rays falling from a narrow skylight. He peered over the newspaper to check his view of the Maria Isabella's revolving doors, then glanced at his watch.

The corners of his mouth drew into a faint smile when he pictured the looks that would be on their faces when they burst through those doors. He was not concerned with their meeting; whatever the old Czech had told Knight would be extracted when the interrogation took place. Pavlicek had been a tiresome meddler of little consequence to the KGB for years, who, according to the most recent report, had only six months to live. More important now was David Knight's imminent return to the hotel—and the bonus of Felix Monzon's niece. With both in his grasp, the mission would finally be assured of success.

After I have what I want from the American, I will personally put the bullet through his brain, Jorge thought. But the girl . . . she is quite beautiful. I will let her live a little longer.

Jorge turned the *Excelsior* so the front page faced the revolving doors, signaling the other four men in the lobby to ready themselves for the abduction. The pounding in his veins told him it was but minutes away.

Knight told the taxi driver to stay in the right lane of the *Paseo de la Reforma* and to drive slowly. As other vehicles honked and sped by, he tossed a five-hundred-peso bill into the front seat to soothe the disgruntled driver. Jennifer sat sideways, watching out the rear window.

Looking through the windshield, Knight saw the Independence Monument looming two blocks away. He stared at the Maria Isabella just beyond it, around the traffic circle, and thought of Eric Steiner. He made his decision before the taxi began its turn to enter the approach lane for the hotel.

"Go straight! Stay on the Reforma!" he snapped.

The driver cut back across two lanes of traffic to the sounds of screeching brakes and Spanish obscenities. He directed two of his own at Knight, but accelerated past the Maria Isabella and the United States Embassy.

Knight turned, straining to look behind at the front of the hotel. "Take us to the airport."

"What are you doing?" Jennifer said tensely.

"I don't like it; something's not right. We can't go back to the hotel now. It's not safe," he said, scanning the entrance and the cars parked in front.

Fear flashed into Jennifer's eyes for an instant, but she nodded as she looked at the hotel. "I think you're right. We'd be taking too much of a risk if we went back there now."

Knight studied the driver for a reaction, but the man kept his eyes ahead, intensely negotiating the traffic at a speed he obviously enjoyed. Knight prayed silently that the driver had not understood or paid attention to their brief comments about the hotel.

He instructed the driver to let them off at the international section of the terminal. Once inside, they walked on opposite sides back to the Aeromexico counter, scanning the area forward, behind, and between them. Knight stood twenty yards away while Jennifer bought two one-way tickets to Mérida for a flight leaving in thirty minutes. They separated again before they reached the boarding lounge.

From a worn vinyl chair, Knight watched Jennifer wade into a conversation with eight men and women carrying Bibles. They were dressed casually, similar to Jennifer's attire. Their fair skin, blue eyes, and earnest expressions made him think they were Midwesterners, possibly from Iowa or Minnesota, probably on a religious retreat.

Nice move, Jennifer; now you're getting into the game, he thought.

She boarded Aeromexico DC-9 with her adopted group, but Knight waited until the lounge had emptied and the gate attendant made the last passenger call. He took one last look and then walked down the tunnel.

TWENTY-NINE December 21
Mérida, Mexico

Sixty-seven minutes later, the fuselage door opened in Mérida to an aluminum airplane ladder. The late-afternoon sun still burned hot and yellow in a cloudless sky, casting long shadows of the passengers as they loped across the blistering tarmac to the terminal.

Jennifer had stayed with the religious group on the plane, helping an encumbered mother by carrying one of her children. She glanced over her shoulder and saw Knight standing at the top of the ladder.

He left the plane last, shedding his sweater and squinting at the terminal as he walked down the ladder. The subtropical climate of the Yucatán, so different from dry, brisk Mexico City, suffocated his first few breaths. He smelled, then noticed, gasoline fumes shimmering from a red fuel truck pulling up to the DC-9. Humidity squeezed his skin, raising splotches of sweat on his chest and back, while heat from the white concrete seeped into his shoes as he hurried into the building.

Jennifer was giving a good-bye kiss to the mother she had helped when Knight purposely stepped into her line of vision. When he angled his head, she left the group and followed him to a bank of telephones.

"Look up the address of the consulate. We've got to get there before they stop doing business for the day," Knight said.

She touched her finger on her tongue and leafed through the pages quickly. "Here it is. Let's find the cab stand." Jennifer grabbed Knight's hand and pulled him toward the doors.

The air in the taxi was stifling, thick with the scent of stale cigar smoke. The driver chewed on an unlit Havana Royale still wrapped with its red and blue band. When he took it out of his mouth to look at the two American passengers, brown spittle dribbled from his lower lip.

"*Cuatro-uno-ocho Montejo, el consulado americano, por favor,*" Jennifer directed.

The driver nodded, clenched the cigar between his teeth, and jerked the taxi through three gears as they sped toward the airport exit. A hot breeze from the open windows swirled Jennifer's hair around her face, but she made no motion to brush it away, staring impassively at the dusty road ahead.

Knight looked to his left and saw that she was sitting slightly forward with her hands tightly folded in her lap. He wondered what she was thinking, but his own thoughts of their mission in Mérida held his attention. Glancing nervously at the driver, he decided to tell Jennifer his plan. She was looking at him when he turned to her.

"What have you got in mind?" she asked, speaking first.

"I've been thinking about something that just might work. We've got to make contact with the man Emil told us about if we want to make any headway. I may be stretching our luck, but I'm betting we got here undetected." His voice was barely audible in the rushing wind.

"God, I hope so. But—"

"We just can't go to the Cuban consulate, knock on their door, and ask for the Fisheries attaché. Besides diplomatic protocol, they'd probably turn us inside out to find what we're really after. We can't afford that; we can't afford even to show our faces there. Especially mine."

"But we're going to show our faces to the American consulate. Isn't that a risk, especially after the Steiner incident?"

"Maybe. But if we do it quickly enough, we might pull it off. Remember, Emil said he already told his contact we were coming. I'm gambling his man is waiting for us."

Knight looked out the window, musing on his choice of words. He never had had any interest in games of chance like poker, horse racing, or even football-wagering cards. He never even entered office betting pools for the Super Bowl or the World Series. Yet his career in counterintelligence had been based on risks, percentages, and playing the margins. Though he was aware of the irony, he had never tried to analyze or understand it.

Jennifer shook her head. "You're right—it does sound like a big chance. Maybe it's too big, David. Maybe we should get out of it now. Felix and I thought I could help you, but whatever you're involved in is getting out of control. I don't know how much more I can take." The emotional toll of the day cracked her voice and etched her face with fatigue.

Knight sensed a vulnerability in her words. He felt a tender poignancy from deep within translate into a yearning to take care of her. He wanted to touch, stroke, and caress her, to tell her not to worry. He wanted to hold her closely in his arms and to feel her softness against his body. More than anything else, he wanted to protect her.

He could not bring himself to reach for her hand, however, not even to say the words that would tell her how he felt. He suddenly pictured her meeting with Gus Suarez at the airport in

Miami and wondered how he could think of Jennifer so tenderly when he still wasn't certain how far he could trust her. The thoughts confused him, but he had no time to dwell on distractions. Perhaps someday, but not now, not with the unknown mental, emotional, and physical demands he knew he would need to ensure their survival.

"*Esto es el consulado americano,*" the cigar-chomping driver announced proudly. He pointed to a white colonial-style mansion with six porch pillars rising to the second floor. It looked as pristine as if it had been uprooted from antebellum Atlanta. Lush bushes, laced with pastel flowers, bordered the property as a waist-high hedge. But two marines in combat gear and with M16s on their shoulders, stepping off paces on the porch, shattered the image of tropical tranquillity.

Knight gave Jennifer his hand to assist her from the taxi. He paid the driver, looked at the consulate, and buried a sigh with his thought: If this doesn't work, it's all over. He moved closer to Jennifer, speaking softly.

"I don't think we'll have a problem. Just follow my lead and put on your sexiest smile. As long as the consul keeps looking at you, he won't even pay attention to what I'm saying. And take off your ring."

"How's this?" She lowered her eyes and licked her lips, letting her tongue linger until she drew it in quickly.

He grinned nervously when he felt his loins stiffen. "You do that and he'll never let you leave," he said, pulling her toward the porch.

A third marine in dress blues emerged from the consulate and greeted them. When they reached the front door, Knight noticed it was made of heavy metal, and saw the slits in the jamb for another metal door to slide in front of it.

"May I help you, sir? I'm Lance Corporal Henson," the marine's baritone voice boomed.

"We'd like to see the consul. I'm a writer, and I was hoping he could point me in the right direction for some research I'm doing on an article," Knight said.

"You folks are from the States?" The marine looked at Jennifer from head to toe, in obvious appreciation.

Knight said, "Yes, right. But it's getting late and I wanted to talk to the consul before tomorrow."

Henson finally turned back to Knight.

"Sorry, sir, the consul's in Washington. But the chargé d'affaires is here. Maybe she could help you."

Jennifer did her best to hide her grin.

"Well . . . yes, I'd like to talk to her," Knight said. He whispered to Jennifer, "At least your smile got us past the front door."

The chargé d'affaires met them in an upstairs office. An open window behind her desk overlooked a manicured tropical garden, with gnarled eucalyptus and gumbo-limbo trees climbing above the roof. A gentle breeze wafted the scent of flowering royal poincianas into the room.

The furniture, unlike other State Department offices Knight had seen overseas, was an eclectic mix of teak and mahogany, lending a subtle informality to the office. But the chargé's voice brought the United States government into the room.

"Miss Ferrer and Mr. Knight, welcome to Mérida. My name is Sharon Karafotas. Please sit down. How may I be of assistance?" She stood and motioned them to the cushioned-back wood chairs in front of her desk.

Knight gauged her to be in her late twenties or early thirties, close to Jennifer's age. Ash blond hair, almost touching her shoulders, fell in damp curls. In a drier climate, she could have just stepped out of a shower. She wore a white blouse and a white skirt, hemmed at mid-calf. Black-rimmed glasses framed her eyes. He noticed she did not wear a ring on her left hand.

Knight explained their purpose for coming to Mérida. Smiling freely, he told Sharon Karafotas he was a free-lance science writer doing an article on a species of sea turtle indigenous to Mexican waters that had recently been discovered in the Florida Keys. This unusual migration, he said, was producing an unfortunate decrease in the lobster and stone-crab catch of the Keys commercial fisherman. He went on to say that his sources believed the fishing industry of the Republic of Cuba had a great interest in this sea turtle, and he was hoping to get that information without the hassle of traveling to Cuba.

"Jennifer and I took a quick diving vacation to Cancún, and I thought that since we were so close to Mérida, with a Cuban consulate here, maybe there'd be someone I could interview about the turtles. Maybe a fisheries expert, someone like that," Knight said, summoning a smile that gleamed through his tired eyes.

He noticed a slight blush on the chargé's face when she removed her glasses to polish the lenses with a tissue. He kept smiling, even when he felt a kick on his calf from Jennifer's shoe.

Karafotas set her glasses on the desk and raised her eyes to Knight. She picked up a pencil and tapped the eraser on a green desk pad, pausing before she spoke.

"I think I can help you, Mr. Knight. Maybe a phone call will suffice, but it's getting quite late. I'll see what I can arrange before the close of business. I can't promise you anything, but at times the Cubans can be quite accommodating. There is a marine scientist at their consulate who may be able to provide you with some information.

"If you'd like, I can call you at your hotel tonight . . . if it won't interrupt you," she said, watching for a visual reaction from either Jennifer or Knight. Seeing none, she smiled at Knight again.

"Where are you staying?"

"Ah, we'll be at . . ."

"The Holiday Inn," Jennifer answered for Knight. "We've already checked in with our bags."

Sharon Karafotas glared at her, then relaxed her gaze and adjusted the glasses on her nose. The prim voice of the government returned.

"Fine, you're nearby. Well, I'll call you as soon as I know anything. But I can't guarantee it will be before the morning."

"Miss Karafotas, Sharon, I'm really grateful. I'm glad we got to see you, and I'll look forward to your call." Knight stood and reached across the desk to clasp her hand with a tight but gentle pressure and a full smile.

Knight walked down the stairway from the chargé's office alert and confident. Jennifer remained a step behind with a sullen look on her face, ignoring Lance Corporal Henson's attempt to find out where she was staying in Mérida.

On the street, waiting for the taxi Henson called, Knight whistled an unrecognizable melody. Jennifer grabbed his arm and pulled hard.

"Will you stop it? What's gotten into you? Do you think the State Department's Greek goddess is going to come beating on your door? We don't even have a room yet. I saved your ass when I said the Holiday Inn, just because I saw it on a billboard."

Knight yanked his arm away when he felt her fingernails dig into his flesh, but he kept smiling. "This is part of the show, dammit! We have to go with the flow," he whispered harshly through his teeth, then turned from her when the taxi pulled up. He opened the door with a flourish, bowing when Jennifer entered the backseat.

"*Come mierda,*" she muttered, and slid across the seat, folding her arms tightly on her chest. She stared out the window, apparently oblivious to Knight's directions to the driver.

Knight had the taxi stop two blocks south of the tree-shaded Plaza de la Independencia, at the *zócalo*, Mérida's largest market, hoping a change of pace might relax both of them. He quickly located a pay telephone and used Jennifer's MasterCard to make a reservation for the last available room at the Holiday Inn: a suite with a king-size bed and a balcony overlooking an atrium dining area.

Strolling through stands and tables of jewelry, hammocks, straw purses, and exquisite linens, Knight persuaded Jennifer to buy an embroidered blouse and skirt, and a pair of leather sandals. When he tried on an undersized bright pink *guayabera*, she began to giggle, then burst into an uproarious laugh. But when Knight offered to pay for it, she pushed him away from the approving Mexican vendor.

Walking to the nearest corner, Knight checked the street markers and calculated the Holiday Inn was about four blocks away. Jennifer seemed more at ease, so he led her along a narrow sidewalk away from the *zócalo*. He was surprised when she clung to his left arm with both hands as if she were a bride on her honeymoon.

As the market's garish lights dimmed behind and the dark spaces between sparse street lamps lengthened, Knight felt her grip tighten, however. He listened to the night sounds and his eyes searched the deepening street shadows. A creeping, uncomfortable sensation that danger might be waiting for them around any corner tightened his chest. He felt the same tension in Jennifer. Hand in hand, they walked faster, until they were almost trotting. Knight slowed and noticed her taut face. Looking ahead, he finally found relief in the shape of a Holiday Inn marquee flashing high above. It was less than a block away.

Knight thanked the desk clerk for holding the reservation and found Jennifer sipping a wine cooler in the bar off the Holiday Inn's lobby.

"We got a message from the chargé," he said, handing her a small piece of paper.

She read it once to herself, then aloud. "'Mr. Knight: I can make the introduction you requested in the morning. Would like to meet you for breakfast first. Bring your companion, if necessary.'"

Sparks lit her eyes. "'Companion? If necessary?'" She

crumpled the paper and pushed his hand down when he motioned her to lower her voice.

Knight grabbed the note off the bar, unfolded it, and tore it into pieces. He looked away from her face when he felt the smile coming to his lips.

"What's so funny, Mr. Security, Mr. Secret Agent? If you're going to an early breakfast, you better get to sleep right now!"

She slid off the bar stool and took a step toward the lobby. Knight lunged and grabbed her wrist, twisting it, and she stumbled. He pulled her close so the flame in her eyes met the ice in his.

"Stop it! What the hell's gotten into you? I don't have the time or the patience for your sorority-girl games. Did you forget why we're here?"

She didn't flinch. Yanking her arm from his grasp, she stomped on his toe and stormed into the lobby.

Knight noticed the bartender, fifteen feet away, smiling at him. He returned the look, shrugged his shoulders, and made a circling sign with his forefinger at his temple. Then he rushed after Jennifer.

They stood on opposite sides of the elevator, separated by a giggling American couple in their sixties. Jennifer stared at the elevator buttons. When the door opened at the fifth floor, Knight stepped out and looked at Jennifer.

"Follow me. I hope I get what I paid for."

The elderly couple went silent, dropping their clasped hands, and the wife cupped her mouth in shock. Jennifer's face flushed with rage, but she jumped into the hallway just before the door hissed shut.

Knight was in the suite's bedroom when she came from behind. With both hands, she grabbed his right shoulder and spun him around, then slammed her right fist into his chest. The blow from her left hand glanced off his raised arm. She suddenly lowered both arms and looked up at his face, tears trickling from her eyes. Her body sagged like a deflating balloon.

Without a conscious thought, Knight wrapped his arms around Jennifer's quivering shoulders and pressed her head to his chest, stroking her hair. He held her tightly, gently rocking her as her body heaved with sobs. When she stopped, he tilted her head to his face. Her eyes were closed. He eased her face past the stubble on his jaw.

"I'm sorry, so sorry about all of this. I didn't want to get you involved, I never thought it would go this far," Knight whispered.

He touched his lips to her cheeks, tasting her salt with his tongue, feeling the coolness of her skin next to his. He shut his eyes and brushed his lashes on the side of her face, savoring the scent of her hair, sweat, and tears.

Jennifer curled her right hand around his neck and guided her mouth to his. She licked his lips, barely touching them with her tongue. Stroking his cheek with her left hand, she pulled him closer and pressed her lips harder, letting her tongue roam deeper into his mouth.

Muted light from the courtyard below filtered through a thin curtain into the dark room. Her hands groped to his back, fingers digging into the flesh under his shoulder blades. Holding him, she pushed him back toward the bed, slipping one hand inside the front of his waistband, tugging at his belt buckle with the other. As she bit his lower lip, he felt her frenzied gasps forcing hot air down his throat.

Knight braced his calves against the bed and held her waist. "Easy, Jennifer, easy," he whispered, pulling his head away to reach for the spread. He threw it back with one hand and circled her waist with his other arm, guiding her gently to the cool cotton sheets. She pulled on his arms, trying to draw him down, but he kneeled on the bed above her and slowly unbuttoned her blouse. Then he stroked the sides of her head, running his fingers through her silky strands, his eyes speaking deeply into hers, silently saying "I love you."

His hands massaged her neck and shoulders, then moved to her breasts. She pressed her hands on his, moaning as he caressed her nipples. He lowered himself next to her and slid her clothes off, then his own.

Their naked bodies entwined, twisting, stroking, holding each other, while their lips touched areas of arousal that brought shuddering crescendos of pleasure. Whenever Knight felt Jennifer peaking, he eased back, sensing her desire each time she reached higher for the edge, and waited before he took her over. Finally, when she arched her back to meet the cresting wave, he pushed her into its churning curl of ecstasy. Her body shook with spasms, then relaxed. Within minutes, he brought her into it once more. But when she arched for the third time, he released, flooding his mind with her name and a brilliant shower of cascading white lights, falling on him with a warmth he thought he had forgotten so many long years ago.

Jennifer curled into a fetal position under his arm, nestling her head on his shoulder. He felt her rhythmic soft breaths on his chest and pulled her closer. He had not realized how badly he had wanted her, nor had he imagined how tightly his emotions had been bound to the past, until they joined. All he could think of was their oneness, a physical and spiritual unity that shielded them from the harsh intrusions of a distant outside world.

Knight looked at her face, brushed a few wisps of damp hair from her cheek, and grazed it with his fingertips, then touched them to her lips. In her sleep, she kissed them and rolled into his chest, sliding her leg between his. He felt himself hardening again.

He fingered her erect nipples. When she stirred, he rubbed his hand along the insides of her thighs. She whimpered through a thin smile and stroked his neck with her left hand.

A loud knocking sat them up, tangled in legs and arms. Surprise registered on Jennifer's face and Knight put his hand to her mouth. He motioned her to the bathroom, scooping up her clothes and dropping them into her arms. He switched on the nightstand lamp and climbed into his pants, then padded to the door.

"Who is it?" His voice had a slight tremor.

A woman's voice answered. "I am from the Cuban embassy, Mr. Knight. My name is Adelfa Rivera."

"What do you want?" he called, glancing at the disheveled bedroom. He ran and grabbed his shirt.

"I am the Cuban Fisheries attaché. I received a message from your consulate that you wanted to see me."

Tonight? His neck broke into a sweat, but he smoothed his hair, tucked his shirt in his pants, and opened the door.

"I'm sorry to disturb you . . ."

"No, no, you're not disturbing anything. Come in, please."

She stepped in and he shut the door. Adelfa Rivera was as tall as Knight, but slender, almost willowy, and wore a tan blouse and tan slacks. He noticed she had on brown rubber-soled boat shoes and carried a package wrapped in brown paper.

Knight turned on a floor lamp. The dim bulb cast a low light, so he walked to a table lamp near the window.

"No, this light is sufficient," she said softly, but with a command in her voice. She studied the room until her eyes fell on the light inching out from beneath the bathroom door.

"You are alone?"

"Ah, no, my companion is freshening up. Let me see if I can hurry her—" Just as he took a step toward the bathroom, the door opened.

Jennifer walked out. Her hair was tied in a ponytail and her face was scrubbed and radiant in the soft light. Her eyes locked into Knight's and she smiled, then glanced away to look at Adelfa Rivera.

"And you are Miss Ferrer . . . Jennifer, I believe," she said, extending a long arm to shake hands.

Knight said, "I thought we were going to meet in the morning, Miss Rivera. We didn't expect you this evening."

Adelfa looked quickly at the window, then back at Knight. "Mr. Knight, I did not expect you to be in Mérida. But Emil called and told me it was urgent that we meet. He mentioned your need to know more about . . . the DLN, so I made the decision to contact you immediately after I received the message from Miss Karafotas." She hesitated, glancing at Jennifer, then spoke sternly. "I do not believe it is safe for you to stay here. I have made other arrangements."

Knight and Jennifer exchanged puzzled looks, but Adelfa Rivera continued.

"We must leave now. Do not take your belongings. But you may need these," she said, handing Knight the paper package. "It was Emil's suggestion."

Knight tore off the brown paper, opened the box, and tossed crumpled newspaper on the floor. He lifted out two clear plastic bags, each containing a handgun. Knight recognized a Colt Python .357 Magnum revolver in one and a Browning Hi-Power 9mm pistol in the other, identical to the one Jennifer had field stripped in Monzon's house. The latter also held two additional filled magazines.

Jennifer took it from him with less assurance than when she had handled the one in Miami, but she removed it from the bag and examined it carefully. Knight sat on a chair and pulled on his socks and shoes, then slid the Python in his belt at the same spot Jennifer's hand had been an hour ago.

"Be careful with that," Jennifer said with a nervous smile.

Knight shifted the revolver to the small of his back, under his jacket, and looked at Adelfa.

"We're ready. Now what?"

"Wait two minutes after I leave. Then use the stairway to go to the ground floor. Do not stop at the door with the number One on it; that leads to the mezzanine. On the floor below, you will exit to a hall that leads to the rear of the hotel. There, a door opens to an alley. I will be waiting for you." Her voice was like ice. Then she left.

"Don't ask me," he said when he saw the pained quizzical look on Jennifer's face. He turned off the lights in the suite except for one by the door and stood in the shadows away from the window view.

"I'm going to anyway, David. I don't like this." She walked to him and put his arm around her shoulder, glancing at his watch. Her eyes were lime green when she looked at his face. Then she asked the question for which Knight had no answer.

"Why should we trust her?"

THIRTY *The Yucatán*

━━━━━━━━━━━━ The blades from the Soviet MIL Mi-4 helicopter battered tall grass and whirled up clouds of dirt as it jostled
down on its balloon tires. Shielding his eyes, Jorge jumped from
the door and ran, hunched over, with long strides. Shadows enveloped three men standing fifty yards away from the bouncing
glare of the chopper's landing lights. The uniformed man in the
middle held his hands behind his back, slipping his fingers from
one palm to the other.

Jorge halted abruptly in front of them, surprised to see a Soviet
colonel in the Yucatán. He jerked his hand to salute, but he did
not recognize the face below the gray, black-visored cap. Returning Jorge's gesture, the colonel turned to the Cuban captain on his
right and spoke in Russian. Jorge waited for the translation and felt
sweat from his forehead drip down his nose and temples. His
stomach tensed when the interpreter nodded and looked at him.

"Comrade, the colonel wishes me to inform you that the KGB is becoming quite concerned with your failures to apprehend the American. He says—"

"Captain, tell the colonel he is—"

"Comrade, I am sorry to interrupt you. I am aware of your rank, but I must insist that you allow me to continue." He motioned to the third man. "He is a Soviet translator, present to monitor everything that is said in Spanish. I suggest you think carefully before you speak."

Jorge took a step backward and glanced at the short, grim-faced Russian, then at the colonel. He bowed his head deferentially to hide the anger spreading on his face.

"*Gracias.* Now, the colonel says the American and the girl are in Mérida. Our units believe they know where they are staying and hope to have them in custody within the hour. However, he says the American embassy in Mexico City has dispatched SRF personnel to locate them, and that you must appreciate the paramount necessity of finding them before the Americans do."

When the colonel turned his head to the captain's ear and spoke, Jorge said, "Yes, of course I understand. But I would like you to tell the Colonel this is my—"

The captain's voice rose to cut him off. "Comrade! The colonel wishes me to advise you that you are not to participate any further in this operation. That is a direct order from the KGB. He realizes that you are an efficient and highly regarded operative, but he also knows that you have a much more important role to play in the next few days.

"You are to return to Havana immediately. Arrangements have been made for you to depart within the hour. Your vehicle is waiting, comrade."

Jorge knew he had been dismissed. His jaw tightened and he ground his teeth when he looked at the three men, but he did not respond. He held his thought and saluted, then executed an about-face and began to walk away. *Maricones*, he thought. Anyway, I have other details to attend to. First Havana, then Key West. And then . . . He grinned to himself, then stopped. Turning his head to glance back, he spat over his shoulder. He continued with a leisurely pace, paying no attention to the string of Russian expletives rising in the damp night air.

Adelfa Rivera's topless jeep bounced through the narrow side-streets of Mérida, jerking from stops and starts designed to detect surveillance vehicles. Knight, secured by a cross-chest seat belt in the front, looked over his shoulder at Jennifer. Her legs were spread wide, bracing on the seat supports, and her left arm was wrapped tightly around the rear roll bar. She managed a look that told Knight she was all right; he didn't see it change back to fright when he turned to the front.

The jeep spun onto Paseo Montejo and headed northward, past Moorish and rococo mansions built nearly a hundred years ago, when Mérida's production and exportation of hemp gave it luxuries and the title "The Paris of the Western World." The wide boulevard that streamed with traffic during the day was almost desolate, yet it took on an amusement-park brilliance under its pale pink streetlights.

With the wind buffeting his ears and tearing his eyes, Knight hunched to the center of the jeep, and glimpsed a long object between the console and Adelfa's seat. Looking closer, he recognized a Chinese AKS assault rifle and two 30-round magazines, taped together upside down for immediate reloading.

When Adelfa came to the Route 180 bypass, she reversed directions and backtracked on 180, then followed it east away from the city. The lights of Mérida dimmed quickly behind as the jeep sped into the black Yucatán countryside.

A sudden blast of cool air covered them like a sheet. Knight grabbed his shoulders and twisted to look at Jennifer. Her face was white, ghostly in the glow of the dash lights. Shivering, she ducked behind Adelfa's seat back for refuge, but her eyes sought an answer from Knight. It came from Adelfa.

"It's a *norte*," she yelled above the wind. "A bad storm that comes from the north with rain and cold winds. Not very enjoyable in a car like this. I think it just gave us a kiss hello." She smiled for the first time, baring her teeth to the chilling air.

Knight clamped his jaws shut to keep his own teeth from chattering. He leaned forward and studied the dash controls for the heater. When he pulled the levers, he felt no rush of hot air.

"Doesn't work," Adelfa yelled in his ear.

He grimaced as drops of rain stung his cheeks. Looking up, he watched fish-scale clouds skate across the sky, then swirl into towering thunderheads. Illuminated by distant bright flashes to his left, the highway looked like a black ribbon of asphalt leading them into a blacker netherworld. An earsplitting crack rocked the jeep, but Adelfa kept the vehicle steady as she switched on the windshield wipers.

Knight reached behind the seat to touch Jennifer. She huddled between the front and back seats, hands covering her ears. He pulled her collar around her neck, then rubbed her back, trying to keep her warm. He felt her pounding pulse through the thin wet fabric on her back.

"Have you got a towel or a rag?" Knight hollered to Adelfa.

She nodded and pointed to the metal console between their seats.

Knight lifted the lid but the dash lights were too dim to shine on the contents in the box. He put his hand inside and felt a coarse, heavy cloth wrapped around a cylindrical object. Fumbling with the cloth, he touched a metal can. At first he thought it was a soft-drink container, but it was heavier than he expected. He fingered the can and felt it taper to a narrow handle. When he pulled it into the glow of the dash lights, he examined it closely, surprised at his discovery.

It was a Soviet RPG-6 anti-tank grenade, similar to one he had studied during a seminar on terrorist weaponry at the Redstone Arsenal in Alabama. Though the course was eight years ago, he recognized the grenade's distinctive markings immediately.

"My God, Adelfa, this is a Russian grenade! What are you doing with it? Is it live?"

Adelfa smiled again but held her face forward. "It's just a souvenir—from Angola. I'm going to use it as a paperweight in my office." Her eyes flicked to Knight. "I don't know if it's been defused. Never thought to ask. Don't worry about it."

Knight took a deep breath and disregarded her fatalistic nonchalance. Holding the grenade gingerly between his thighs, he wiped Jennifer's back with the cloth, then rewrapped the small bomb and gently placed it back in the console.

They rode silently for another thirty minutes, then Adelfa slowed the jeep. The temperature rose noticeably when the rushing wind fell to a stiff breeze, but it still swept a stinging mist against their soaked clothes. At ten miles an hour, Adelfa turned off the pavement to a mushy dirt road. She wrestled with the steering wheel until the four-wheel-drive vehicle's knobby tires grabbed hold, propelling it forward, up a narrow trail. Branches from dense underbrush glanced off the windshield, springing back like metal whips, barely missing the jeep's ducking occupants.

Five minutes later, Adelfa drove into a large circus ring–sized clearing. On the opposite side, another trail led higher. Knight noticed smudge pots in a wide circle, suggesting a possible drop site for drugs. But when he saw streaks of flattened grass in the middle, a flash of euphoria buoyed his spirit.

Thank God, maybe we're leaving from here! Adelfa must have a chopper coming for us, he thought. He decided to let her tell Jennifer the good news.

Adelfa opened the console and took the cloth from the grenade. She dried her face and passed the cloth to Jennifer. The rain had stopped but the wind picked up again, chilling them with icy gusts.

"I apologize for this experience. I had no choice but to get you out of Mérida any way I could. We are safe here for a short time, then we shall begin again," Adelfa said.

"Begin again?"

The shock in Knight's voice startled Jennifer. He grabbed her hand when she reached for him.

"Yes, of course, we will not stay here for long. Someone is to meet us here to take you to Kantunil, perhaps another half hour's drive. A pilot will take you to Cancún in a small plane, and from there you can go to Miami," Adelfa said.

Knight sighed and smiled at Jennifer.

"I am curious about why you met with Emil," Adelfa said, pausing to take the towel from Jennifer. "He told me you knew about the DLN, and I assume that is why you came to Mérida. But there is something more . . . or am I wrong?"

"That's what I thought you'd tell us, Adelfa. I thought you had the answers. I thought Emil talked to you about that," Knight said, raising his eyebrows. "The only thing he told us was that he believed the Soviets were involved in some type of massive disinformation operation. . . ."

Adelfa paced away, squishing in the wet grass. She leaned against the front fender of the jeep, rubbing her forehead.

Jennifer hugged Knight around the waist. "Let's just get out of here, David. We've had enough. We'll go back to Miami, you put your lance away for good, and we'll—"

"*El Lanza!*" Adelfa cried. "Of course! Knight, The Lance, *el lanza*, the lance! You are *El Lanza*! That must be why Emil sent you here."

She ran to Knight and Jennifer, her eyes wide and gleaming, breathless from shouting her revelation.

"*El Lanza?* Adelfa, slow down, I don't know what you're talking about," Knight said.

"You have been called *El Lanza* before, yes?"

Knight tipped his eyes at Jennifer and shrugged.

"Well . . . sometimes, but only a few people ever called me that." One, Knight thought: Miguel Torres.

Adelfa lowered her voice. "You do not know, do you?"

Knight shook his head. "What should I know?" He felt Jennifer gripping his hand tighter.

"You are the person Victor Milian was trying to contact in Miami."

Knight stared at Adelfa. A cold breeze wrapped around his body and shook his shoulders. The wind wailed through drying leaves and branches, its mournful dirge the loudest sound in the clearing.

He walked from Adelfa and Jennifer, clenching and unclenching his hands, locking and unlocking his fingers. For a moment, his mind went blank and he forgot where he was, but the image of Miguel Torres startled him back to reality. He turned and approached the two women.

"So Milian is . . . was DLN. And he was on a mission for Fidel?" he said to Adelfa.

She nodded.

He took a deep breath. "But why me? What does Fidel want with me? Tell me, Adelfa!" He grabbed her wrist, but Jennifer stepped between them and separated his grasp.

"I am sorry. I do not know, sincerely."

Knight threw his head back, rolling his eyes to the sky. When he looked down, they were filled with anguish.

Adelfa spoke quickly. "But I will tell you what I know. Several weeks ago, the DLN learned that some KGB dissidents were plotting to kill Fidel. We believe they recruited one of our own DGI agents, but we have not been able to identify him. And worse, we think the assassination is planned for Christmas, four days from now."

Knight bit his lower lip. Monzon's fanciful theory raced into his mind on the legs of a thoroughbred. He glanced at Jennifer, trying to fathom her thoughts, wondering whether she knew this was fact before they came to Mexico—and why she met with Gustavo Suarez at the airport in Miami. But he voiced his most urgent concern.

"I'll ask it again: Why me? Where do I fit in?"

Adelfa slapped her hands together, linking her fingers. Her eyes jumped from Knight to Jennifer and back to Knight, pleading.

"I cannot tell you; I don't know, you must believe me. You must understand how compartmentalized we are, like any other intelligence organization. Only a few know everything."

"Right. I used to play by the same rules." His eyes roamed the clearing as he tried to sort his thoughts.

Yet even with this much, Knight had made his initial conclusions, and they centered on Miguel Torres: He was related to Milian; he knew Milian was in Miami, and probably knew Milian was DLN; he was the only person who called Knight "El Lanza"; he confided in Felix Monzon; and he was killed before he got to tell Knight everything he knew.

But one stumbling block kept Knight off balance, and it had come from Miguel's mouth: The CIA had deceived both of them. And it was the CIA that destroyed Knight's career in the FBI, yet another deception. *WHY?* his inner voice screamed.

Adelfa's voice snapped his concentration. "I believe I know what Emil meant when he mentioned a possible Soviet disinformation plan. We have learned that the KGB is also using a former member of the CIA to contact Cuban exiles in Miami, to use them for a false plot to assassinate Fidel, so that they can be blamed. But we have not identified that person, either. We do not even know if that person is American or Cuban; but we believe he, or she, is in Miami now, carrying out that part of the plan."

The image of Jennifer meeting Suarez again ran across his mind. He wanted to look at her to see her reaction to Adelfa's disclosure; the Soviet deception had been *her* theory. But why did she meet Gustavo Suarez at the airport? Whose side was she playing on? He could not bring himself to turn to her. His stomach cramped and a band tightened around his temples.

Suddenly, another thought struck him, crashing into his mind. If the DLN did not know if the ex-CIA officer was Cuban or American, then who. . . ? My God! Monzon had said the KGB wanted to know whom Milian was trying to reach and what was in his message. Those were Monzon's ". . . *most pressing ques-*

tions." What if Monzon is the KGB disinformation agent, playing out still another deception? Was the Mexican trip an elaborate setup to get those answers from the DLN?

"This is very important, Mr. Knight," Adelfa continued. "Whoever that person is, he has very high contacts in the CIA or the FBI, perhaps both. We discovered last week that this person has been able to find out everything about El Lanza—you—from those sources. That is why we made no attempt to contact you since Milian was murdered."

Knight stared at the ground. His shoes and pants were caked and spattered with mud. The *norte* whipped colder air around the clearing, but he felt his blood pulsing through his veins and arteries. Now he knew the reason he had been a target, and that it was the KGB and the DGI that wanted him in their cross hairs. Yet even with that, he still did not know why he was so important to the DLN; nor did he know why the DLN thought he was so important to a plot to assassinate Castro. But the time he needed to answer those questions was quickly running out in a cold rainstorm in the Yucatán. Until he had the answers, he knew he had to stay out of range.

"How do we get to Kantunil?" he asked. He gave Jennifer a sidelong look and held out his hand. She smiled and moved toward him.

Adelfa began walking toward the jeep, and he turned to follow her. Suddenly, Jennifer slammed into him from behind, knocking him on his stomach. Air burst from his lungs when he hit the ground and a black sheet started to draw across his vision. He heard two loud cracks, then a thudding sound smack into the mud and grass only inches from his head. Straining, he twisted his neck to see the object on the ground—and stared into the lifeless brown eyes of Adelfa Rivera.

THIRTY-ONE

Knight pushed himself to one elbow, shaking his head to focus his eyes. Jennifer kneeled with her back to him just out of his reach, next to the jeep's right-front wheel well. Her hair was matted in wet layers. She held the Browning in both hands, sweeping the pistol in a small arc toward the opposite edge of the clearing.

"What happened? What're you doing?" His voice came out in a hoarse whisper.

"Quiet! Keep down!" she whispered back.

He inched forward on his elbows, rolled to one side, and lifted the Python from his belt.

"The shots came from over there. I saw something move so I knocked you down, but I didn't see Adelfa get hit. Are you all right?"

"Yeah, I think so. Who are they?" Knight looked across the

circle but barely saw the black bushes. The only sound came from raindrops splatting on the jeep like a dozen tin drums. He pushed up and leaned against the tire, trying to concentrate and plan their next move.

"I don't know. But whoever it is, they want you alive, David," Jennifer said, her eyes still locked on the far shrubbery. "You have to get out of here."

He turned and clamped her shoulder. "Me? What are you talking about? We're getting out of here!"

She shook off his hand and jerked around. She glared at him as rain dripped from her eyebrows, four inches from his face. Her smoky breath blew in pants as she spoke.

"No! You can't let them catch you now. Whatever the reason is, it's too important, you heard Adelfa. If the Soviets succeed, the CIA gets blamed, and God knows what will happen in Cuba, Mexico, or this entire hemisphere.

"There's only one way you can make it, and that's if I stay here and cover you." She looked at the clearing and then turned back to him. "Even then, you might not make it. But it's the only chance we have."

"Bull shit!" He did not care who heard him. Any doubt he had about whom Jennifer was working for evaporated in a searing psychic and emotional pain. The thought of leaving her, of losing her, sent shivers of rage and panic through his body. I won't let this happen to me again, he vowed. Not this time.

He rose quickly, grabbed her arm, jumped into the jeep and pulled her in, stepping over the console and gearshift. As he started the engine, automatic weapons erupted, flashing white death, ripping ribbons of torn grass near the jeep's tires. The wheels spun, then caught the ground, and Knight speed-shifted toward the higher trail across the clearing.

Jennifer aimed at the spewing sparks and emptied the Browning. Her hands blurred as she shoved in the second magazine and fired thirteen more rounds. When she fumbled for the third magazine in her pocket, Knight pointed between the console and his seat.

"Here!" he shouted.

Jennifer grabbed the AKS and slapped in the double clip, narrowly missing the gearshift knob as she brought the barrel around. Bouncing in the seat, she drew back the bolt and turned to fire in one fluid motion.

Bullets pinged into the jeep's rear cargo door and shredded the exposed spare tire. Knight downshifted when they hit the incline, plowing through a low-hanging branch. Headlights from behind lit up the rearview mirror, followed by the chugging of a military four-wheel-drive truck.

Jennifer climbed into the backseat and kneeled on the floor, bracing her elbows against the back cushion. She unleashed a five-round burst from the automatic AKS, then stared at the rifle's sight when her shots fell short.

Suddenly, the gunfire from behind stopped. The following headlights drew closer, rising and falling as the truck dipped and climbed in the jeep's trailing path. Knight stayed in second gear, with his lights off, not wanting to send a signal with his taillights, but the slow speed he maintained to negotiate the twisting trail allowed the truck to close the distance between them.

Satisfied with her adjustment to the sight, Jennifer sat on a metal ledge over the wheel, bracing her back against the roll bar. As she raised the rifle, aiming at the truck's headlights, Knight spotted a level fifty-yard straightaway just ahead. The engine whined when he redlined second gear, and he tried to double-clutch into third for an extra burst of speed. The jeep bucked over a fallen log, tilting with its two right wheels off the ground, but it crunched down on all four wheels and sped forward.

The jarring impact knocked Knight's breath away and he slowed down, turning his head to check Jennifer's condition. The rear seat was empty. He threw the Jeep into neutral and stopped, searching with panicked eyes.

"David!"

Twenty yards behind, just beyond the glare of the truck's onrushing headlights, he saw Jennifer scrambling toward the jeep. The AKS was on the ground. Automatic-weapon fire kicked up clumps of mud just yards short of her heels.

"Run, Jennifer! Run!" Knight yelled. He looked around the jeep for another weapon. Nothing. Jennifer slogged through the mud and reached for the tailgate.

"No! Go around to the front! Stay down!" Knight screamed. As he waved his arm at her, he saw the console and remembered: the grenade! He ducked in the backseat and angled his arm to take it out. The pull ring, safety lever, and drop-out safety pin appeared to be intact and the stabilizing drogue was not even scratched.

He scrunched lower and turned his shoulders so he had room to throw. The weapons, surprisingly, had stopped firing, but he heard the heavy truck's engine grinding closer. He raised his head a few inches to gauge the distance—thirty yards. He would have to lead the truck like a wide receiver on a come-back pattern.

Knight gripped the handle in his palm, lightly wrapping his fingers around it. He cocked his elbow and felt the grenade's weight behind his shoulder. He arched his arm forward and the RPG-6 left his hand when he snapped his wrist. Please, he prayed, please!

The truck's lights caught the grenade's cloth streamers for an instant, but it sailed higher, out of view.

"Get under the jeep!" Knight yelled to Jennifer. He leaped over the side, rolled underneath the vehicle, and grabbed Jennifer, squeezing her to his body.

The flash from the fireball came first. A second later, the positive pressure wave hammered into the jeep, lifting it off the ground, exposing Knight and Jennifer. The same wave tumbled them over and over down the trail, their arms and legs flailing uncontrollably. Simultaneously, an enormous explosion sent peals of roaring thunder at the mottled gray clouds in the night sky.

Two minutes later, Knight staggered to his feet and found Jennifer crumpled at the base of a once-mighty tree, its massive trunk cracked at a right angle from the shock wave. Blood from a one-inch gash on her forehead trickled down her face. She opened her eyes, blinking rapidly, but they closed and her head fell against Knight's chest.

"Get up," Knight said, gently easing her to her feet. "We have to get out of here." He heard piercing screams and turned to see sharp flames flicking fifty feet skyward from where the truck burned. Men covered with fire ran into the forest, then suddenly halted and fell to the ground like fading fireflies on a hot summer night.

Knight held Jennifer as they stumbled to the jeep, now facing sideways on the trail. Miraculously, it was upright on four wheels. He wasn't sure whether Jennifer was fully conscious, so he lifted her into the passenger seat and strapped her in with the seat belt. The effort drained him and he rested against the front fender before he walked around to the driver's side.

The screams behind had subsided to loud moans, but then Knight heard voices. Angry, bitter voices, shouting above the sickening sounds of the injured. He didn't understand the words, but he cocked his head and listened, trying to recognize the strange language.

That's Russian! Those bastards are Soviets! What the hell are they doing with troops in Mexico?

As much as he wanted that answer, he had no time to think; he had to act. But this incident gave Knight all the corroboration he needed to believe the Soviets wanted him alive badly enough to use any means to catch him; and he knew they would keep on trying. Move! he told himself.

He climbed into the jeep and started it, stomping on the clutch as he pulled the gearshift into reverse. When he tried to go forward, his foot slipped off the accelerator and the jeep stalled. He started it again and began moving slowly. Behind, he heard Russian voices yelling what sounded like commands. Knight gunned the engine and headed up the steepening trail.

He drove without lights, whipping the jeep's gears and guiding its front wheels as it slid and slipped through blind turns and tortuous ruts, under grabbing branches and over gnarled roots, accelerator pedal pressed hard to the floor. Jennifer's eyes were still closed and her body flopped under the seat belt during the ride. Knight slowed once to hold her wrist. When he felt her pulse beating strongly, he resumed his breakneck speed. The uphill climb soon peaked and Knight began descending with the same deliberate abandon, downshifting in jerks as he splashed through deep troughs and watery bogs. His arms and back ached and his head throbbed, but he pushed away the pain and kept fighting the treacherous trail.

Twenty minutes later, the trail widened and leveled off. The underbrush thinned, replaced by tall Australian pines lining each side. The *norte*'s devilish rain had not reached this side of the terrain and the thick mud soon changed to dry, packed dirt.

Knight finally stopped the jeep and looked at Jennifer. She was still unconscious. He unhooked her seat belt and lifted her carefully into the backseat, folding his jacket for a pillow. He stood and stretched, craning his head around, trying to get a bearing, searching for any landmark, but he saw nothing but dark desolation. He threw the shifter into gear and sped onward.

The air was heavy with humidity, but cool as it blew against him. He turned on his lights and switched to high beaⅰs, now realizing that he had no idea where he was headed. But he noted the odometer reading and kept the speedometer at fifty. Resting his head against the high-backed seat, he spotted the Orion and Pleiades constellations shining in the clear sky and knew he was traveling northeast.

When he next looked at the dash, he calculated the elapsed mileage: thirty-seven miles. Ahead, his lights beamed on a concrete lip crossing the road two hundred yards distant and closing fast. He braked the jeep slowly, then stopped at the gray pavement of an east-west highway.

Knight hung on the steering wheel, shoulders sagging, wondering which way to turn. More than anything else, he wanted to sleep. He felt his head nodding down. His eyes closed but he jerked up and tried to shake himself awake by jiggling his shoulders. His motion rocked the jeep.

"David? What . . . where . . . where are we?" Jennifer murmured from the backseat. She rubbed her face and moaned when her hand touched the laceration on her forehead. The blood had dried, but a walnut-sized bump now protruded. She leaned forward, smoothing her hair, and put her hand on Knight's shoulder.

He shook his head. "I don't know. Somewhere out where Christ lost his shoes, I guess," he said, smiling wanly.

"David, don't joke. What are we going to—"

Knight suddenly held up his hand. "Quiet. Listen."

Within seconds, he heard the sound again, a faint roar, droning high above. He stared into the stars and spotted a large aircraft drifting across the sky, west to east on a line with the highway, and estimated it at six to eight thousand feet. Knight calculated quickly: From its size and at that altitude, it had to be heading for Cancún. He stood on the seat and looked east, straining his eyes, and made out a faint yellow glow near the horizon.

"That's got to be Cancún," he said, pointing his arm. "Maybe another hundred, hundred fifty miles." He looked down at the hopeful expression on Jennifer's face.

She reached and took his hand in both of hers, squeezing it tightly. "Do you want me to drive?" she asked.

"No, I'm fine. You rest. We still have work to do," he said with renewed energy. His mind was churning, planning what he had to do.

Knight threw the jeep in gear and lurched over the concrete lip, fishtailing on the pavement as dirt clumps spun from its packed treads. He eased it into fifth gear at forty-five miles an hour, then held it steady when he reached seventy. On the hard surface, it cruised like an ocean racer on glass-topped seas.

It's not over yet, Jennifer, he thought, glancing at her asleep in the backseat. I'm going to take this one into the end zone. That's a promise.

Finally, he had no doubt that Jennifer was on his side. And now he was certain she would answer his questions.

THIRTY-TWO
December 22
Cancún, Mexico

"Yes, I was part of it, okay? I already admitted that to you. But I didn't know what Felix wanted. How many times do I have to tell you that?" Jennifer said, exasperated at Knight's relentless questioning. She sat on the edge of the hotel bed dressed in a man's T-shirt that hung just above her knees. It was one of the items Knight had purchased that morning at the Plaza de Mexico mall in downtown Cancún.

They had arrived just after dawn. Knight found a McDonald's where they devoured a fast-food breakfast and waited until nine, when the tourist shops opened. While Jennifer bought two tickets to Miami at the Mexicana office, Knight went to the mall and then checked into a small hotel on Avenida Bonampak. At sixty-dollars-a-night rates, it was far removed in price and distance from the sprawling, sybaritic luxury hotels lining the beaches on Kukulcan Boulevard. But it was exactly what Knight desired.

The room had two twin beds, one of which Knight fell into ten minutes after they got to the room. He slept for five hours, rising before Jennifer to write notes on a small pad next to the telephone. He woke her an hour later, two hours before their 6:30 flight to Miami, and they snuggled in each other's arms for fifteen minutes. Then Knight had begun asking her the questions.

Now, glaring at him, Jennifer stood up and put her hands on her hips. As he watched the shirt ride up her thighs to mini mini-skirt length, he grinned.

"What's so funny?" she asked angrily.

"Look, I'm just trying to put things in place," he said, taking back his smile. He didn't want to tell her he was trying to catch her off guard.

"But dammit, you just told me that Felix set it up with Paul for you to work in our office—so you could keep your eyes on me and report back to Felix. And you expect me to believe that you didn't know why? That he didn't tell you? After everything that's happened to us since you walked into that office? After he sent you with me to Mexico?" The hard edge had returned to Knight's voice.

"Yes. Yes! I *am* telling you the truth!" Jennifer ran both hands through her hair and shook her head, sighing, then repeated what she had said before. "I didn't know. I didn't ask him. I trust him. It was important, that's all he said. He never told me why."

"What *did* he tell you?"

"Damn you, David—"

"Again. I want to hear you say it again." Knight got up from the chair and paced to the door, then turned to see Jennifer sitting back on the bed. "Tell it to me again," he said calmly, fighting to keep the lid on his rage. Though he believed her, what she had told him so far was enough for him to realize that he had been used, manipulated for some concealed reason. Now he wanted to find out why.

Jennifer looked at her palms. "He said he told Paul that he had a way to help you with your problem with the FBI, but that it involved national security. He told Paul I was working with him, but that you couldn't know what was happening until everything was in place. . . ." She paused, gulping air.

"Go on."

"He told Paul it would be better if Paul went away for a week, that the plan would work better if he wasn't around the office. . . ."

"And?"

". . . And Paul said no, he wouldn't leave, he wanted to make sure nothing happened to you."

"Jennifer, I want to ask you something I didn't bring up before: Why would Paul believe Felix? Why would Paul go along with this so-called plan?" He turned his back to her and the room fell into silence. He waited until she spoke.

"I can't answer that. All I know is that Felix has a lot of friends, some in high places. Maybe he had one of them talk to Paul . . . but I think we both know why Paul agreed."

"Why?" Knight looked at her sharply.

"He would have done anything to help you."

Knight felt his eyes tear. "He did, didn't he?"

"Yes," Jennifer said softly. She walked to him and held his arm in both hands, then stepped back. "David, did you ask yourself why he believed Felix? I mean, he did. Doesn't that make you think someone else probably talked to Paul?"

He knew she had a strong point, a consideration he had omitted in his haste to question her. Suddenly, a name came into his mind.

"What do you know about Harrison Witham?" he asked.

A startled look crossed Jennifer's face. She walked to the bed and grabbed a pillow, hugging it to her chest, and sat down.

"No, it couldn't have been him. Not Witham. Never, never, never!" she said, spitting out the words.

"Easy, Jennifer," Knight said, surprised by the intensity of her reaction to Witham's name. "Why does that upset you so much?"

She looked up, still clutching the pillow, rocking with it. "Because that's one of the reasons why I went to Mexico with you." Her voice was so faint, he barely heard it.

"What? What are you talking about?" Knight asked anxiously, but he waited until she was ready to speak.

"Remember what I told you about my mother, when we were in your office? I couldn't tell you everything then, but now . . . I don't know . . . it might fit in with what you're trying to find out." Her eyes went to the ceiling. "Felix thinks Witham had my mother killed."

"Why? How?" Knight could think of nothing else to say. He found the chair and sat in it.

She put the pillow down and continued with a stronger voice. "Felix always thought Witham was KGB or DGI, but he didn't tell me that until five years ago. Before that, I usually tuned him out whenever he talked about things like that. I didn't care and I didn't want to hear about the pro- and anti-Castro factions, about who was doing what to whom. I knew about what happened to my mother, but I wanted to forget it, to wipe it out of my mind. But I never could.

"Then one year, I don't remember why, Felix took me to one of the Brigade reunions. That's when I first met Witham. I could tell right away that Felix hated him, but it got worse when Witham tried to hit on me. If Felix had had a gun, he would've killed Witham—as it was, four men had to hold Felix back. He never went to another reunion after that." Jennifer paused, crossed one leg under her, and held her knee.

"Keep going. Finish it," Knight urged.

"Believe me, David, I don't know how Felix gets his information or whom he talks to, but he told me he'd been collecting bits and pieces about Witham for years. Everyone seems to know that he landed with the Brigade at Playa Girón for the invasion. According to Felix, most people think that Witham escaped by getting the Cuban underground to take him to Grand Cayman, to avoid capture—and, according to the CIA, that's where they found him two months later. He told them he stayed low because of some kind of bullet wound, and because of Kennedy's insistence that no Americans were involved at the Bay of Pigs.

"But Felix said he found out that Witham had been taken prisoner, and that Fidel was planning to execute him when the KGB stepped in and made Witham a double agent: They agreed to keep him alive if he worked for them. His first assignment was to identify every CIA agent he knew in Cuba . . . and one of the first he identified was my mother." Jennifer's voice began to tremble. She clasped her hands in her lap.

Knight walked to the bed and sat next to her, brushing a strand of hair away from her face. He touched her cheek, caressing it, then blotted three trickling tears with his thumb. He kissed her red-rimmed eyes.

"I understand your pain. But what does this have to do with the trip to Mexico?" he asked.

"Felix thought Witham might show up there, maybe with the KGB or the DGI. If he did, Felix said that would prove his theory about Witham, and . . ."

"And what?"

"And then I could take my revenge."

Knight sat straight and gripped Jennifer's shoulders. "Revenge? You mean . . ."

"Yes." Her voice was suddenly hard and cold. "I would kill him." She pulled away from his hands and walked to the window. The late-afternoon sun glowed through a dusty, white shade.

Turning, Jennifer said, "But he didn't show, David. What does that mean?"

"Maybe it just means we didn't *see* him show," he answered, but his mind was galloping ahead of his words.

If Witham is working with the other side, Pavlicek's theory about a grand deception against the United States and the CIA would make the story Witham told me about a CIA plot to kill Fidel a lie; and Witham could be masterminding the setup of the Agency.

If that's true, then Felix didn't send Jennifer to Mexico to kill Witham; more likely, he'd want Witham for himself. And I can't believe Felix would be so callous—no, careless—to let her go to Mexico without protection. But he gave me a different agenda and never mentioned Witham. Then why did Felix even think Witham might show up in Mexico? Something's missing, dammit. Wait . . . what about Suarez?

"Jennifer, I saw you meet with a man at the airport before you got on the plane. Who was it?" He prayed that she'd tell the truth.

"Gus Suarez—he's a friend of Felix. He just wanted me to know that someone would be around us in Mexico if we had a problem. But I guess they weren't, or whoever it was couldn't keep up with us."

"*We* would have protection, is that what Gus said? That someone would be watching *us* in case anything went wrong?"

"Yes, I remember that specifically. Why? What are you getting at?"

"Hell, what was the main reason for going to Mexico? To meet with Pavlicek, right? For me to get more information about the DLN, isn't that what Felix said? He never said you'd definitely see Witham, did he?"

"No, not in those words. Actually, at first Felix didn't want me to go. I heard him mention the possibility of Witham being in Mexico to someone on the phone. That's when I pushed him into letting me go with you. He tried again after you left that night, but I still wouldn't back down. Gus even tried to convince me not to go when we met at the airport, but then he gave me the message from Felix about the backup people."

The answer suddenly hit Knight. He stormed to the small closet and smashed his fist through its thin door. When he looked at Jennifer, he saw her face frozen with fear.

"My God, Jennifer, they weren't there to protect us. Whoever was working with Felix was there to get Witham. He never would have let you kill him."

"What do you mean? What are you saying?"

"You weren't supposed to be there, don't you see? Felix wanted me in Mexico alone, but when you insisted on going, he had Gus meet you with the story about the protection. Felix had someone there, but it wasn't just to keep you safe."

Knight took the shopping bag off the table and tossed it to Jennifer. "Get dressed. I want to leave with enough time to get through customs without any problems. I've got some unfinished business with Felix. I want to see him tonight," he said, tugging on the jeans he had bought for himself.

"I still don't understand, David. Why did he want you in Mexico by yourself?"

Trying to ignore her question, Knight walked toward the bathroom. He didn't want to tell her the frightening conclusion he had drawn.

"David! Answer me. Tell me why," she called to him.

"Not until after I talk to Felix."

"No! Now! I have a right to know."

He stepped back into the musty bedroom and stared at the mildew-stained carpet. When he looked up at Jennifer, his face was pale and haggard.

"Yes, I guess you do." He took a deep breath. "I think Felix was counting on Witham to surface in Mexico if he knew I was going to be there. Then Felix would spring his trap."

Jennifer still had a puzzled look. Knight drilled his eyes at her, but when he spoke his voice was weak, almost a whisper.

"Don't you see? Felix was using me as a goddamn chunk of bait to catch the shark—Witham."

THIRTY-THREE
December 22
Miami

Knight dozed fitfully on the flight back to Miami. Jennifer sat five rows directly ahead, but out of his sight. Even if they were sitting together, they would not be talking. Neither one had anything more to say.

From the time they had left the hotel until they had boarded the plane at the Cancún airport, Jennifer argued furiously against Knight's theory about Felix and the Mexican trip. At one point, as they waited in the passenger lounge, she deliberately slammed a pocketbook on the bruised hand he had punched through the hotel room's closet door. He winced as a knifing pain shot up his arm. Jennifer marched off, and they had not spoken since.

When the pilot announced the descent into Miami, Knight

again felt the same frustration he had during their argument. I need more facts, he thought, remembering Jennifer's most vocal complaint. He closed his eyes, trying to recall the events in Mexico. Something Adelfa Rivera had said stood on the edge of his memory, waiting for him to pull it into his conscious mind, but he couldn't bring it closer. You're thinking too hard, he admonished himself. You're too tired now. It's there, just let it drift in—but be ready to catch it when it does.

The terminal thronged with holiday travelers lolling in the lounges and rushing to catch the last evening flights. Knight scanned the area and found Jennifer waiting near an escalator opposite the international-flight concourse. He walked to her slowly, watching for eyes that might linger just a little too long on either of them. He saw none.

"I'm going to my apartment and then try to reach Felix. I'll call you—"

Jennifer held up her hand. "David, wait. Look, I'm sorry we argued about Felix. Maybe you're right, I don't know. But right now, I don't care. I know you have problems to solve and questions to answer, but I don't want to be involved in them anymore. I'll deal with Felix myself, but you do whatever you think you have to do. After that . . ." Her voice trailed off, but she took his bruised hand and touched her lips to it. Then she held it down and took her hands away. She looked softly into his eyes.

"After that, when you think you're done, then call me. I'll wait, don't worry. But I just can't handle it now." She turned quickly and stepped onto the escalator.

Knight leaned over the rubber railing and watched her go down. "Jennifer! Where are you going?" he called.

"Home. For a long rest."

Jorge nursed a cup of coffee in a doughnut shop on Kendall Drive near S.W. 137th Avenue. He knew he shouldn't be there now, not when it was so close to Christmas Day. His superiors would be irate if they found out he had deviated from the plan, but he was operating on his own now. He had the freedom and the authority to respond to exigent—and these were clearly exigent—circumstances.

For Jorge, they had arisen this morning when he had heard of the disastrous, monumental failure by the Soviets in the Yucatán. With all of their soldiers and equipment and their so-called expertise, not even *they* had been able to catch David Knight. And now they wanted him to simply disregard Knight and go forward with the assassination of Fidel. At times like this, he could not understand their slipshod mentality. Did they honestly believe that Knight would not still be a factor in the plan? That just because the final act was so imminent, Knight could no longer be an obstruction? That was ridiculous!

Jorge was too thorough to go along with their negligent assumptions, and that was why he had returned to Miami: to finally trap David Knight . . . and learn Knight's secret. He was confident he could do it within the next twenty-four hours, probably much less with El Aura's assistance. That would still give Jorge a day to prepare before he killed Fidel Castro.

Knight made his way to the lower level of the airport and passed through a glass pneumatic door to the outside passenger pickup curb. Oppressive humidity sapped him like a wet sauna, but he found a smiling Cuban driver who ushered him into a cab with an evergreen aroma. By the time they reached the airport exit ramp to Lejeune Road, Knight's head had slumped to the side. In his dream, he was running along a beach, laughing and calling to the girl in front of him. The sand slowed his strides, but he knew it was Jennifer and pumped his legs harder. Just before he reached her, she stopped. He wanted to wrap his arms around her, but she turned quickly and pointed the barrel of an AKS between his eyes. Her finger, squeezing the trigger in agonizing slow motion, filled his vision. . . .

"*Oye*, mister! We're here. This your place?" the driver barked.

Knight jerked up and felt his neck sopping in sweat. He grunted an answer, then fished in his pocket for the fare and stumbled out of the cab a block away from his apartment.

As exhausted as he felt, he brought his senses to a heightened awareness to surveil the area around his building. He walked on the opposite side of the street, moving quickly from shadow to shadow, scanning parked cars and tall shrubbery. From behind a thick oak, he examined the entrance of his building. Satisfied, he hurried across the street and ducked into the side stairwell, then stepped slowly and softly as he climbed the stairs.

The fingers on his right hand had stiffened, so he tried to fit the key in the door lock with his left. He missed twice, but the key slid in on the third try. He pushed the door open and stepped into the dark room. A narrow shaft of light from the hallway fell across the floor as he groped inside for the wall switch.

Before he touched the plastic plate, two hands grabbed his arm and slammed it to his side. A lightning bolt shot through his body when they twisted his arm behind his shoulder. He moaned, then heard the door shut behind him. The room went black. He lost his balance and careened into a small table next to the couch, but powerful hands kept him upright. When he offered no resistance, their grip eased and they guided him to the couch. His chin fell to his chest and he closed his eyes; he had no strength, nor any desire, to look at his assailant. The only sound in the room came from his gasps in the stagnant air.

He heard a click from the lamp on his desk. The lowest setting of a three-way bulb cast a dim glow across the gray carpet. He eased his eyelids open and saw the outline of a broad-shouldered man seated in his desk chair, but his face was hidden in a shadow. Knight sensed the presence of other men nearby but out of view.

"Allow me to introduce myself, Mr. Knight," said the man in the desk chair. His low voice rumbled from ten feet away. "I am Colonel Eladio Ruiz, of the Cuban Revolutionary Armed Forces."

What? A Cuban colonel in my apartment? Jesus, no, get the hell out of here. I don't believe this! Is this a joke? What the hell is going on? Knight's thoughts whirled from pain and fatigue, only heightened by the shock of Ruiz's announcement.

"Oh," he said weakly. "What's wrong, did Fidel run out of black beans and rice?"

Ruiz chuckled. "Very good, Mr. Knight. I did not expect sarcasm after what you've been through."

Knight thought of a question but did not have the energy to voice it. "I need a drink. Vodka."

"Yes, of course." Ruiz raised his voice and gave an order in Spanish.

A short man in a business suit stepped from behind Knight and went into the kitchen, returning with a glass filled with ice and vodka. Knight took it without looking at the man and sipped half of the liquid, then held a piece of ice on his knuckles.

"Well, Colonel, I guess I am surprised. But to tell you the truth, I don't really give a damn why you're here. You want to kill me, torture me, interrogate me, make me an honorary member of the Politburo, be my guest. Just do what you have to do and get the hell out of here."

Ruiz stood, moved the metal-framed chair two feet from Knight, and sat in it. He wore a tan poplin suit with a Kiwanis Club button in the lapel. His black hair was thick and wavy, without a visible strand of gray, but Knight judged him to be close to fifty. A distracting scar began between his brown eyes and ran three inches to his left cheek. He leaned forward with both elbows on his thighs and clasped his hands. Knight smelled the faint odor of cigars when Ruiz spoke.

"I have no intention of doing violence to you, Mr. Knight. I am here only to discuss a matter of utmost urgency to both of our countries. As you may have surmised, it has to do with the DLN." Ruiz paused, waiting for Knight to respond.

Knight exhaled loudly through his nose and finished the vodka. When he held the glass up, the colonel's aide took it into the kitchen for a refill. Knight looked at his lap and shook his head.

"The DLN. How nice, one of my most favorite subjects. How did you know that's just what I wanted to talk about tonight? When did the DGI start recruiting mind readers?" He looked up with a wan smile.

"I am not from the DGI, Mr. Knight; I am a member of the Cuban military. Our functions are usually quite dissimilar."

"Wonderful," Knight said, reaching for the second glass of vodka. "Listen to me, Colonel, I really don't give a rat's ass if—"

Ruiz grabbed Knight's wrist and vodka sloshed over the edge of the glass. "No, you listen! You must hear what I am going to tell you." His anger abated when he released Knight's arm. "Mr. Knight, you are the only person who can help us."

Knight slouched back on the couch and set the glass on the cushion next to him. He realized he was a captive audience, with no possibility of calling Felix to talk about Mexico. But Ruiz had mentioned the DLN. If he just listened, maybe Ruiz would give him the facts he needed to tie everything together.

"Talk to me," he said.

Ruiz allowed himself a thin smile and nodded appreciatively. "Thank you. But first, you have my sympathy for the ordeal you have undergone these past days. If only Victor Milian had not been killed, if he had reached you, none of that would have happened."

Thanks for nothing, Knight thought.

"But we have very little time. If you had any doubt, let me now assure you that the plot to assassinate Fidel Castro is quite real. It is to be carried out by one of our people who is working for the Soviets. Obviously, that is why the DLN is racing to prevent it.

"But, Mr. Knight, the larger Soviet scenario is much more ambitious and grandiose. It involves Mexico . . . actually all of Central America, perhaps the entire world, and a potential disaster to the United States of catastrophic dimensions," Ruiz said, touching the scar on his face.

Mexico? Knight pushed on the couch to sit straighter. His vision was clearer, and he noticed that Ruiz's face appeared drawn and tired. He tilted his head forward, anxious to hear what the colonel had to say.

"Living in Miami, I am certain you are more aware than the rest of your countrymen that Central America is a demographic centrifuge. The economic and political instability in those countries has sent hundreds of thousands of immigrants north to Mexico, most of them with the hope of entering the United States. It has been a monumental crisis for nearly a decade, but one that has been virtually ignored by your government. The primary reason, of course, is that illegal immigrants provide the cheapest source of labor for United States business interests. That, however, is not our immediate concern."

Knight took deep breaths, filling his lungs so oxygen would flow into his bloodstream and feed his tired brain. Ruiz's introduction tantalized him and he was thirsty for more information.

Ruiz leaned closer to Knight. "Is it not ironic that Mexico, third behind Canada and Japan as a trading partner of your country, has received so little attention from the administrations of your recent Presidents? Did you know that Mexico not only has the largest and closest oil reserves to the United States but that it has been the greatest supplier of foreign oil to the United States?

"Yet, Mr. Knight, Mexico is quickly becoming one of the most volatile countries in this hemisphere, a teeming population governed for years by epidemic corruption. And it shares an immense, porous border with the United States, whose immigration policy has yet to be formulated into a cohesive and consistent policy." Ruiz stood and paced away from Knight, then turned back abruptly.

"Consider this: More than six million Mexicans and Central Americans live at a poverty-level existence within ten miles of the United States border. Do you have any idea of the implications of that human time bomb? Do any thoughts come to your mind?"

Knight rubbed his temples, then his eyes. He blinked to focus clearly on Ruiz and a response moved to his lips.

"Mariel."

"Precisely! Fidel's ingenious scheme in 1980 to rid Cuba of its undesirables, over one hundred thousand delinquents and mentally ill dregs that he gladly dropped on Miami. And, as you so well know, hundreds of intelligence agents who have now dispersed throughout the United States."

Nightmarish memories skittered through Knight's mind: sprawling refugee tent cities in the Orange Bowl and under the expressways, an escalating violent crime wave, tinderbox racial tensions and raging riots, gun shops that looked like department stores two days before Christmas.

Miami had been a city gripped in an unrelenting vise of rampant fear. When a federal prosecutor told a local reporter that Miami was the 1980 version of Dodge City, the nickname stuck. National and international news media swarmed to south Florida, hoping to film live shoot-outs instead of the Orange Bowl parade and palm tree–lined beaches. With enormous drug profits, criminals found it easier to buy banks than to rob them, and massive money-laundering schemes brought riches and false respectability to scores of narcotics entrepreneurs. The only boon to Miami, though dubious to some, was a flashy television crime series that personified the pit in which the city fathers wallowed.

Knight massaged his neck. "But that was a decade ago. Things have changed since then; everything in Miami is much different now. Mariel is history. Those days are long gone and mostly forgotten."

Ruiz picked up a scruffy football from the floor and tried to read its faded inscription. He flicked his wrist and a perfect spiral sailed into Knight's hands.

"Yes, forgotten, along with the lessons that should have been learned." Ruiz held out his arms for Knight to toss the ball back. He caught it and spread his fingers on the laces, testing his grip. "You Americans treat history as if you are taking a college test: You spend two days cramming, trying to amass months of knowledge, and then two days after the test, nothing remains. Am I wrong, Mr. Knight?"

Knight smiled, remembering his law school all-nighters. He sighed and nodded in recognition.

The colonel continued, "But the Soviets view history as a vast continuum, a timeless dynamic crucible where every significant event must be pulverized until its meaning has been derived. It is time-consuming, but it is a necessary process that may take years of analysis to determine whether such an event has a useful instruction for the future.

"You see, Fidel used Mariel for an immediate purpose to solve an immediate problem—and he accomplished his objective. The Soviets, however, laboriously examined the Mariel episode with their historical microscope, searching for latent strategic opportunities."

Knight shook his head. "Colonel, I think you're forgetting something: glasnost. The Soviets changed the cold war game and they made up different rules. Look at Eastern Europe, if that's what it's still called. The United States is running in there like the miners during the California Gold Rush. We're all good friends now; everyone just wants to make big bucks. It's not like it used to be."

Ruiz spun the football toward the ceiling, but he was looking at Knight when it fell into his hands.

"I shall excuse your false naiveté, Mr. Knight. I know what happened to you in Mexico." Ruiz smiled briefly, then went on. "But to a great extent, you are quite accurate. The global political situation has changed drastically—and it is still changing. With your background, you must know that there are factions who resent the demise of communism and who strongly desire a return to the way 'it used to be.'"

Knight shrugged his shoulders. "I'm sure that's true, Colonel, but I don't see how they could accomplish it now. If they tried, they'd need an awful lot of luck."

"Perhaps," Ruiz said, nodding his head. "Unfortunately, they believe they found a suitable fortuity in Mexico. And they intend to implement it by the assassination of Fidel Castro."

THIRTY-FOUR

Ruiz's revelation about Mexico and the assassination plot triggered Knight's recollection of Adelfa Rivera's revelation that Victor Milian, of the DLN, was trying to contact him, apparently to give him information. He felt certain the message had something to do with what Ruiz had just told him. In Mexico, the Soviets had tried to catch him; it was certainly because they thought he had Milian's message. They had to know what it was. But it was a message Knight had never received.

Though his body ached, listening to Ruiz sharpened his senses. Fatigue faded rapidly as a second wind of alertness refreshed him. *If Ruiz is DLN, then he must have the information Milian wanted to give me,* Knight thought. *All I have to do is ask him—hold it! If Ruiz isn't DLN, if he's working for the KGB . . . dammit! I've got to play it out, let him come to me.*

Knight shifted his weight and eyed Ruiz sharply. "Take it a little slower, Colonel. I've seen enough to consider your assassination theory possibly valid, but Mexico? Where does that come from? What makes you think something's going to happen down there?"

Ruiz nodded approvingly. "Excellent questions, my friend. You must have those answers to fully understand why your role is so important to us."

Knight raised his eyebrows, but Ruiz quickly continued.

"Before I became chief of the Directorate of Foreign Relations of the FAR, I was the chief military attaché to the Soviet Union. I spent four freezing years in Moscow, using that time to my best advantage. But the details are boring and insignificant for our present purposes.

"Of immediate interest, however, is the intense fractionalization and the power struggles undercutting glasnost and perestroika. The Kremlin is not the monolith it once was, Mr. Knight. While it may not be crumbling, it is leaking. And I learned where and when to place the pail to collect vital drops of information."

Knight listened for a trace of smugness, but he heard none in the colonel's measured voice. The tension in his back had eased and he realized he was beginning to like Eladio Ruiz—but not enough to allay his apprehensions.

"So you've got Soviet sources—what makes you think they can be trusted?" Knight asked.

Ruiz's face hardened. "Please, Mr. Knight, do you think I would even be here if I suspected duplicity?" He paused when he heard Knight's snicker. "Well, perhaps if I was in your situation I might be somewhat more cautious. But I have verified the information my sources have provided, by collation and triangulation. I am confident the data is reliable, and I have faith in my own analysis. You must now have the same trust in me." Ruiz dropped the football on the couch.

The man's no slouch, Knight thought. But trust him? How can

I? He's supposed to be the goddamn enemy! Still, he did come here; but he's got to give me more.

Ruiz answered his thought. "Let me explain the Soviet plan to you, so you can appreciate its full significance. To use an American phrase, I shall place all my cards in front of you, faceup."

Ruiz opened a thin briefcase and unfolded a map of Mexico, setting it on the coffee table in front of Knight. He twisted the head of a small flashlight to widen its beam, then pointed to the map with a black pen in his other hand.

"After the Soviet-Mexican Mixed Commission for Scientific and Technical Cooperation in 1988, the Soviet Union opened consulates in Hermosillo, Ciudad Juárez, and Monterrey. The stated purpose was to advance mutual trade agreements entered into by both countries. In 1989, a month before the Berlin Wall crumbled, a Cuban exile in Mexico City acquired a portion of a KGB operational plan for those consulates. It came into my possession a few days later because of a family connection in Miami—you know how that happens here, Mr. Knight." A trace of a smile crossed his lips but he went on.

"That document calls for KGB operatives to infiltrate the massive Mexican and Central American immigrant population in the triangular area outlined by these three cities." Ruiz drew a heavy black line connecting Hermosillo, Ciudad Juárez, and Monterrey, then put in spokelike lines reaching north.

Knight leaned closer to the map and noticed that the area encompassed all of northern Mexico and the entire length of the United States border, from Brownsville to Tijuana. He checked the scale and quickly calculated a borderline of approximately 1,200 miles.

"According to the plan, Mexicans, Nicaraguans, Salvadorans, and Guatemalans have been trained by the KGB to foment insurrection in these locations. Their methods are to include sabotaging food supplies, polluting water, and assassinating popular politicians. Additionally, terrorists have been trained in the Middle East to assist, if necessary." Ruiz arched his back and wiped his brow with the back of his hand. "It will be a nightmare beyond belief, Mr. Knight. And it has already begun."

Knight looked up from the map. "You're losing me, Colonel. You said the KGB was going to assassinate Fidel, and that would kick everything off. Where does that part come in?"

"That is the first deception." Ruiz took off his suit coat and laid it carefully on the couch. "We do not know how or where, but we do know that unwitting Cuban exiles are to be used as decoys, set up by the KGB. Here, our information is sketchy, but I believe an exile team will be apprehended somewhere in Cuba after Fidel's assassination, with evidence of sponsorship by the CIA. By then, the KGB will have orchestrated a tumultuous outcry of rage and indignation against the United States, designed to tell the world that Fidel's death is the prelude to an overthrow of the Cuban regime by your country.

"I am certain you can imagine the reaction in Cuba. The people will galvanize their anger in a thunderous call for immediate retaliation. In that climate of hysteria, it will be useless to try to persuade them that the Soviets were responsible." Ruiz shrugged his shoulders and opened his palms in a show of helplessness.

Knight folded his hands, squeezing his fingers tightly. "Then what?" he whispered.

Ruiz sighed. "The now-dormant conservative KGB-military faction will rear its head to demand retaliation. That will provide it with a basis for ousting the glasnost leadership and for establishing a repressive, Leninist-elite dictatorship. They will then move to close the borders of Eastern Europe. You must remember, Mr. Knight, that there are nearly five hundred thousand Soviet troops still in that region, and I assure you that they will follow orders. Mass arrests of the leaders of those countries will occur, and they will be replaced with reliable puppets from the secret security police.

"At the same time, the new Kremlin leadership will play the second deception. They will threaten to use Cuban missiles to destroy all the Mexican oil reserves upon which the United States depends. More importantly, the use of that oil is the linchpin to the economic future of Mexico; without it, that country will become a wasteland of utter chaos, wracked with more human misery and devastation than a hundred Hiroshimas."

"Jesus," Knight exhaled, tilting his neck back. He stared at the ceiling, listening to the silence. Then he remembered. "But you said 'the second deception' . . . I don't think I understand."

Ruiz opened his palms to Knight. "That is my personal belief, that the Russians will not take such a drastic step. I wish I had sufficient facts upon which to base my opinion, but I have not obtained—"

Knight stood up and paced past Ruiz. "My God, you're just speculating? What if you're wrong, what if—"

"'What if' does not matter, Mr. Knight. Merely the threat of an attack on the oil reserves will be sufficient to produce the Soviets' desired result. That threat, combined with the KGB's subversive agitation in the northern regions of Mexico, will send at least a million illegal immigrants storming across the border into the United States. Your border patrol, your immigration service, your country will be powerless to stop that flood of humanity from seeking refuge.

"The threat will also throw the Mexican government into shambles, paralyzed and unable to cope with the resulting strife and disorder raging throughout the country. And because of the Soviet disinformation campaign about the CIA assassinating Castro, the Bush administration will suffer from a similar paralysis. All of Central America will turn against the United States, and then—"

"We're back in the cold war, but with more problems than we ever had before," Knight said, finishing the sentence. His shoulders sagged. The thought staggered him, draining his energy, and he sat on the couch.

Ruiz watched the football roll against Knight's thigh. "The scenario does not end in Mexico, though. What of the five, seven, or ten million illegal immigrants who then deluge the United

States? What effect will that have on the stability of your country? Can your government's social and economic resources deal with a problem of that magnitude? At what cost—if it could even be calculated—in dollars as well as the quality of life?"

Ruiz lowered his voice. "I know these are rhetorical questions, but they are not hypothetical. You mentioned the Mariel boat lift earlier. Mr. Knight, that incident will be a garden party compared to the havoc the Soviets have in store for the United States if Fidel Castro is assassinated."

"But why, Ruiz, why would they go to such an extreme measure? Why waste Fidel? How can they afford to lose him?" These were the same questions that had bothered Knight since Jennifer had first brought up the possibility of the Soviets behind the plot.

"Put simply, Fidel is of no further use to the Soviet Union. They know his revolution has failed. They tried to have him institute reforms in the spirit of glasnost, but he adamantly refused. His methods continue to drain their increasingly limited funds. Despite their past prodding and cajoling, he remains intransigent to their entreaties. Even Gorbachev decided long ago that Fidel was an albatross.

"Yet the assassination also serves the Soviet conservatives more insidiously. They know the Cuban people are tiring of Fidel and his cries for a return to revolutionary austerity. They fear that if the Cuban people somehow depose Fidel, Cuba may drift further from their sphere. But if the CIA is seen as the assassin, the Cubans will return to the Soviet fold like prodigal children." Ruiz slammed a fist into his palm and glared at Knight, but his voice remained calm. "You should not be surprised that the new leader of Cuba has been selected by the KGB. And his installation is to be in less than seventy-two hours."

Ruiz drew circles on the floor with the flashlight beam, then turned it off. His mouth was dry from talking, and his voice came out low and raspy.

"We need you, David Knight. You must help us and the people of the United States. You are the only person who can prevent the assassination of Fidel Castro."

Knight gazed across the room at a hanging wall unit that held his books, stereo, television, and four framed photographs. He narrowed his eyes when they would not focus. Each object he looked at had a fuzzy halo around it. Ruiz was a shadow sitting down in the desk chair. Knight heard him cough and clear his throat and knew he was finished talking. The room was dark and silent, waiting for Knight's response.

"David."

Startled, Knight quickly glanced over his shoulder. A man rose from a chair in a shadowy corner, but Knight recognized the voice. Felix Monzon stepped forward and put his hand on Knight's shoulder.

"Before you answer, I must speak. I must explain Mexico to you, David."

Knight wasn't as surprised as he thought he might be. He had figured most of it out while Ruiz was talking. But the dramatic disclosures by the colonel had softened him. As he stood and looked at the pained expression on Felix's face, any remaining trace of anger dissolved.

"An hour ago I'd have torn you apart, Felix. But I finally figured out why you did it . . . and for some crazy reason I don't understand, now I don't give a damn," Knight said.

Monzon nodded, then motioned Knight to sit down. When he did, Felix sat on the couch next to him.

"It is not easy for me to confront you, but I thought it would be easier if Eladio—Colonel Ruiz—talked to you first. By now, you obviously know that I have been working with the DLN on this matter of utmost urgency. As a professional, you know that I did what I felt was necessary; as a . . . a friend, I apologize to you. I put you, and my niece, at great risk, but it was not intended to be so—"

"Felix, I believe—"

"Please, let me continue. After your difficulty in Spain and

Miguel's murder, we thought we could institute sufficient controls in Mexico to avoid similar complications. That was the only reason I consented to Jennifer going with you. We were confident we could protect both of you and at the same time isolate the assassin if he came near. Clearly, we overestimated our abilities, which now necessitates this meeting and our request for your continuing assistance."

"Wait, Felix. You just confirmed my own thoughts about why you sent me to Mexico. I don't like it, but I said I understood your reasons. But at least now we know who the assassin is: Harrison Witham. Why don't you just have your people track him down and take him out?"

Monzon looked at Ruiz weakly, then back at Knight. "David, Witham is not the assassin. We still have not identified him. That is why Eladio is here tonight, urgently seeking your help."

"What?" Knight said, shooting his eyes at Ruiz.

"Felix is correct, Mr. Knight. That is why I told you the entire KGB plan in such detail. It is important that you know everything now." Ruiz leaned forward, resting his elbows on his thighs, and pressed his palms together.

"But there is something I omitted. Perhaps it will influence your decision. As a member of the Directorate of National Liberation, I have served Fidel Castro faithfully, often at great risk—now more so than ever, because of our hatred of the Soviet Union.

"Many of us, however, are extremely disenchanted with the failure of Fidel's revolution to meet the needs of our people and our country. Though some of his measures have provided us with higher standards of housing, education, and health care, we are no longer willing to accept his demands for sacrifice. More significantly, the generation behind us is dissatisfied with the regime. They are engaging in increasingly strident criticism, calling for an end to government corruption and more open forums to express their displeasure. And, Mr. Knight, many of us are listening to them.

"You see, if the KGB succeeds, we will once again be chafing under a dictator's yoke, regardless of glasnost and perestroika. We cannot allow that to happen, nor can we allow Fidel to retain his authoritarian rule. In short, we want to *and must be* the ones to depose him. With Fidel gone, we believe we can constructively restore relations with the United States, resume trade relations, and rid Cuba forever of the Soviet Union."

Knight rolled his head in a circle, loosening his neck muscles. "And if you don't stop the assassination, you'll never have that chance."

Ruiz dipped his shoulders and nodded. His eyes wandered away in a gaze of distant contemplation. Exhaustion hung on his face.

With a similar expression, Knight leaned forward and twirled the football between his hands. He cocked his head at Ruiz, then flicked his wrists, snapping the football to the colonel.

"I'm in," Knight said. "But I want some answers."

"Yes, of course—you are entitled to them. I must tell you why you are so vital to our success." Ruiz moved to the couch and put his hand on Knight's forearm. "First, however, it is essential that I explain something of grave importance about Miguel Torres before we delve into other matters."

Knight watched Ruiz take a slow, deep breath. He felt a firm pressure from Ruiz's hand. An uncomfortable fluttering sensation in his chest made him apprehensive about what Ruiz was preparing to say.

Ruiz swallowed. "Torres was one of us . . . one of the DLN."

THIRTY-FIVE

Knight jerked his arm away from Ruiz. His face froze in disbelief.

"It is true, David. There is no reason to mislead you now. There are no more games. We all have too much at stake," Monzon said.

Knight exploded from the couch. "Mislead me? Games? My God, who the hell do you think you are? This is the biggest goddamn game I've ever heard of! You can go to hell if you think I'm going to play this game!"

He stood over Ruiz, heart pounding through his chest, and grabbed Ruiz's throat with his left hand. As he drew back his right fist, Monzon grabbed his arm and twisted it, throwing him on the couch. Knight held his arm and glowered at the wall across the room.

Ruiz adjusted his collar and tie. "Your reaction is not surprising. I probably would have done the same. But we both know the saying in this business: 'Sometimes you make enemies of friends, sometimes you make friends of enemies.' We have no choice; we must be friends."

Knight refused to look at Ruiz. He thought only of Miguel, the man he had thought of as more than a friend. Brothers, they had called each other. But the bold letters of one word flashed like a neon sign in his mind: BETRAYAL.

"I know what you must be thinking, but please do not jump to rash conclusions. You must understand that the DLN is, above all, an anti-Soviet organization. Our actions are directed against them, not the United States. I can think of no instance when the DLN conducted an operation that damaged the United States in any way." Ruiz leaned toward Knight and touched his forearm again. "And I can assure you that Miguel Torres never betrayed you. Never."

Neither man flinched when their eyes locked. There was no bluster, no bravado, no intimidation. Instead, Knight felt a link connecting them far above any conscious level. It was a rare bond of instant trust, a sharing of confidence more binding than a legal contract, yet as indescribable as the sound of a butterfly's wings. But Knight knew it existed. A wetness in his eyes finally made him blink.

"I believe you, Colonel," he whispered.

Ruiz sighed and extended his right hand. When Knight took it, Ruiz placed his left hand on top. He smiled in relief at Herrera, then looked back at Knight with a broader grin.

Monzon stood up. "Gentlemen, please excuse me. I must make a call. I'll use the phone in the kitchen," he said.

Ruiz nodded, but spoke to Knight. "We have work to do, my friend. Let's begin with Torres and Operation Bull's-eye."

Knight registered no shock at the mention of the name of the operation he and Torres had been working on in 1984, when Miguel had been so close to exposing the KGB agent who had penetrated the CIA network. Nothing could surprise him now.

Ruiz got to his feet and stretched, long arms reaching toward the ceiling. He stepped quickly to the kitchen and splashed his face with cold water, then dried it with a paper towel. He walked back to Knight, rubbing his face with his hands and resting them on the back of the chair.

"You must realize that to us, the DLN, any Soviet activity in Cuba is a potential threat that we try to monitor closely. Their history of duplicitous dealings with Fidel is documented, but not nearly to the true extent. Anibal Escalante and the 'microfaction' incident is one widely known example, but there have been others of a more severe nature."

Knight remembered Monzon's explanation of the Escalante affair, but his thought jumped to Jennifer and their last good-bye at the airport. He shook her image away and listened to Ruiz.

"Operation Bull's-eye, as we both know, was your attempt to identify and expose the KGB agent penetrating the CIA network that had its origins in Nicaragua. Our intelligence service, the DGI, had known for some time that the objective of the CIA was to obtain detailed information on the flow of arms from Cuba to the insurgency groups in Central America. And because it dealt with arms and munitions, it fell within my purview.

"When I reviewed all of our intelligence reports, I came to the conclusion that the information being passed to the CIA was traveling through one source. Actually, it was a simple deduction." He paused and smiled, as if he was recalling the process before he recounted it.

"First, I collected the names of those who might have had access to the data. Next, from one of our sources in Miami, I obtained a general description of the agent. With my captain's help, we triangulated that knowledge with the dates and locations where the information was passed. When only one name surfaced in those three categories, I knew we had our man."

Knight nodded in appreciation. "Excellent, Colonel, classic counterintelligence work. But you're military . . . how did you come up with the triangulation method?"

"Well . . . at this point I have no reason not to tell you. I read. I have someone in Miami who sends me every book your American authors write on the CIA and other intelligence agencies, even the fiction. It has been quite an education, believe me."

Knight grimaced, then grinned. "I'll be damned—"

Ruiz cut him off. "Please, allow me to finish. This is very crucial. You see, the man I identified was working for the KGB."

"What?" Shocked, Knight flattened himself against the couch.

"Yes, he was a Cuban from Miami who worked for the CIA. But seven years ago, he was turned and became a double agent for the DGI, then trained in Bulgaria by the KGB. He was the man Miguel Torres was about to identify to you in 1984; but it took me nearly five years to find him after that."

Knight shifted to the edge of the couch. "So he was feeding false information back to the CIA. But you make it sound like he had another assignment. Did he?"

"That was very difficult to decipher, as you will see. We had to do it with great caution. However, with painstaking ingenuity we discovered that his real objective had been to penetrate the DLN, for the KGB. We discovered that in 1984, long before we learned his identity. We also found out that this agent, whoever he was, suspected Miguel was working for the DLN. Which is why Miguel had to be . . ." Ruiz let the sentence die when he saw the bitter expression on Knight's face.

"Then you . . . the CIA . . . Miguel . . ." He forced the words out, but his vocal cords were tied in knots.

Ruiz lowered his eyes to avoid Knight's stricken look. "Yes, David. I am sorry you had to learn it this way. Had you not developed such a close relationship with Miguel, perhaps you may have seen it more clearly. But then, how could you have known about the DLN and our working arrangement with the CIA? It had been disclosed to no one. We had no choice but to have Miguel pulled away; we could not risk having him identified by the KGB agent. And the CIA did not want to risk our relationship with them by telling you or anyone in the FBI. Of that, they were adamant."

"Damn them," Knight muttered. Another sound, a low growl, came from behind his clenched teeth. He began to shake with rage. So this is the truth about Miguel, the *whole* truth, the cancer that's been eating at me for all these years. Everything he and I did went right back to Ruiz—and to the goddamn CIA. What kind of a life have I been living? All I've been doing is chasing goddamn shadows! Dammit, if I knew where the plug was, I'd pull it right now.

Ruiz put his hand on Knight's shoulder. "I understand your anger, but you must put it aside. We must continue. You must let the past die, so that we can go forward. We have so little time."

"'So little time,' that's all I've been hearing for the last goddamn week." His eyes blazed at Ruiz and his shoulders rose with a lung-filled breath, but he held it; the faces of Tony Costas and Paul Singer suddenly burst into his mind, blocking his anger at Ruiz. He exhaled slowly and his eyelids fell. He wondered if, and how, he could continue. But he knew he had to try.

"Let's get on with it. Just tell me what you want me to do," he said softly.

"Yes, I am coming to that." Ruiz sighed and wiped his forehead with his hand. If Knight did not come through now, everything would be lost. Ruiz sent a worried glance to Monzon, standing in the kitchen doorway. Felix scowled with an intense look of urgency, but he remained silent.

"In May 1984, Miguel was to make contact with the KGB agent on Islamorada, in the Florida Keys. You were waiting with Miguel at the The Rum Barrel to surveil the meeting. But someone came in the agent's place . . . and you witnessed that contact." Ruiz paused to eye Knight closely.

"Right, because the other guy didn't show up—" Knight stopped when his voice cracked. His eyes grew wide, then snapped shut. He threw his head on the back of the couch. The room seemed to spin wildly, but a jarring realization crashed into his mind like an iron girder dropping onto a steel floor. As he fought to hold on to reason and reality, past events and emotions flooded his thoughts. Then slowly, from the midnight shadows of repressed pain, memories of the polygraph incident trickled into his consciousness, filling it with the truth.

Still dizzy, he pulled his head up and sat forward. The color in his face had drained and he stared blearily at Ruiz. His lips parted, but the words wouldn't come out. When he tried again, he spoke in a hoarse whisper.

"That man, the KGB agent . . . that was Roger Estevez," Knight said, pushing the words past his lips. Finally, he knew the answer. Estevez, the CIA, and the DLN—he had been marked for destruction because of them.

"Yes. It was Roger Estevez." Ruiz looked at him. "Are you ill? Can I get you something?" he asked, making no attempt to conceal the concern cloaking his face.

Knight shook his head and stared at his hands. His thoughts flashed back to the moment he had handed his badge and credentials to the special-agent-in-charge in Miami six months ago. But the image quickly faded, replaced by a seething rage to destroy everything around him. He clenched his jaws and bit on his lower lip, hoping Ruiz did not detect the short fuse wrapped around the ticking bomb of revenge waiting to explode. But he was still curious about Ruiz's operation, so he quickly mustered the face of a mannequin to project a calm facade.

"No, I'm all right. I'm just tired; maybe it's the vodka. Keep going, Colonel. Tell me the rest." Then I'm going to rip your head off, you son of a bitch. And then I'm going after the rest of the bastards.

Ruiz pursed his lips. "You see, David, the man Miguel met at The Rum Barrel, the man you observed, is the DGI agent who we believe is going to assassinate Fidel Castro."

Knight smiled sickly. "And you haven't identified him. Then I'm . . . you think I'm the only person who can finger the assassin? But you said you caught Estevez . . . the KGB agent. Couldn't you get him to tell you who—?"

"We tried, by every method possible, but he would not tell us all he knew. We were fortunate to get him to admit that the assassin was at the meeting with Miguel. You must understand the position we were in, with a KGB agent as our prisoner. We could not hold him indefinitely in order to wait for him to tell us what we wanted to know. Both the DGI and the Soviets were searching for him," Ruiz said excitedly.

"Then what—"

"He was executed and disposed of appropriately last week." Calm returned to his voice.

Knight nodded, pressing his lips together. He felt his back muscles constricting and wriggled his shoulders, trying to shake off the tension. Then he looked at Ruiz solemnly.

"What's your plan?"

"We have information that the assassin will be in Key West tomorrow night for the final staging. We believe he is meeting with Harrison Witham to finalize the disinformation plan that is to blame the CIA for the assassination. According to my source, the Cuban exiles who are to be caught in Cuba after Fidel is killed are scheduled to depart from Key West tomorrow night. I surmise that the assassin is too meticulous to carry out his deed unless he has personally attended to every detail." Ruiz looked down at the backs of his hands, then raised his eyes slowly.

"So you want me to go to Key West to point him out . . . if I can." Knight studied the faces watching him, wondering whether they suspected the game he was playing. "But how the hell am I supposed to find him, let alone identify him?"

"We will be there before you arrive, with several surveillance teams. My people know Key West well, David. Once we find Witham, I am certain he will lead us to the assassin, if you can identify him," Ruiz said.

"Eladio, David, I, please—" Monzon stammered as he stepped into the room.

Knight held up his hand. "Wait, Felix! My *friends*, let me tell you how it is, now that I know how you set me up," he boomed. "I have no intention of going along with your goddamn operation. I honestly don't give a good goddamn if Fidel or anyone else is blown away. The last thing I'd do now is help—"

"Stop it!" Felix shouted, rushing between Knight and Ruiz. He spoke rapidly. "I must interrupt! David, when I went to the telephone, I noticed your answering machine flashing and I took the liberty of listening to it. I think you both should hear the message before anything else is said."

The three men marched into the kitchen. Monzon and Ruiz stood on each side of Knight while he pressed the message button. Monzon raised the volume when a deep voice began to speak on the tape:

"Mr. Knight, if you wish to have Jennifer Ferrer remain alive, be in front of the federal courthouse in Key West tomorrow night at seven o'clock."

Knight fell against the refrigerator. He kept his balance, but his forehead broke out in beads of sweat. His eyes darted at Ruiz and Monzon, piercing them with a glare of uncontrolled violence. Anger rose from the pit of his stomach, heaving his chest with short breaths. He grabbed Ruiz's shoulder and squeezed it hard.

"Forget what I just said," Knight growled. "I'm going to nail that bastard. What's your plan?"

THIRTY-SIX *Key West, Florida*
December 23

The federal courthouse in Key West was just a three-block walk down Simonton, less than ten minutes from the Pier House, where Knight had taken a room. It was too early to leave to meet Ruiz's contact at the Hemingway House at four-thirty that afternoon to make the final arrangements. He glanced at his watch and decided to leave in twenty minutes.

Ruiz and Monzon had left at two the night before, after convincing Knight that their plan needed only a slight modification: They wanted him in Key West before daybreak. Knight tried to catnap, but not even a fleeting dream rose to the fringe of his mind. This time, the nightmare was real, and he knew he would not rest until it was over.

He left his apartment at four in the morning and drove to Tamiami Airport, an airfield west of Miami that was populated by private planes and a few air training schools. The pilot's monosyllabic conversational ability suited Knight's mood. Knight climbed aboard the Beech Bonanza and they lifted off in a low-hanging fog, then sped across black Everglades marshes at two thousand feet. It was still dark when they landed at Marathon Key an hour later.

From there, another taciturn driver transported Knight to the Pier House, where a desk clerk in a wicker chair yawned when Knight arrived for his predawn check-in. The usually crowded luxury resort was half-vacant in the tourist lull two days before Christmas, and the clerk had given Knight a suite overlooking the Gulf of Mexico. He had slept until noon and had been pacing since then.

Now, Knight stood in the open sliding doors of the suite, listening to lapping waves roll onto the empty handkerchief-sized beach below his balcony. Gusting breezes swept salt air against him and he looked to the west. Squinting his eyes, he watched the sun turn to bright amber as it dipped closer to the Gulf horizon. He checked his watch again. With a sinking sensation, he turned away from the scenic, postcard view and picked up his windbreaker from the bed. It was time to leave.

Knight paid his entry fee to an elderly lady sitting inside the front gate and stepped along the rough brick pathway leading to the two-story Spanish colonial mansion bought by Ernest Hemingway in 1931. Descendants of the author's fifty cats lolled on the porch, oblivious to the tourists crowding into the front hallway. In the living room to the right, more people browsed among souvenirs—tables of books in hardcover and paperback, T-shirts and sweatshirts with Hemingway's likeness, and 8×10 black and white photos taken during his Key West residency.

Knight eased past a female guide gathering her tour group together and glanced into the living room. He looked closer, then stared at the profile of a man paging through a book. The man turned and walked toward Knight. It was Gus Suarez.

"How nice to see you again, my friend," Gus said. "I am from Colonel Ruiz." He glanced over his shoulder and saw the tour group moving to another room. "We must stay with them."

Knight followed him closely. When the tour guide took the group to the second floor, Suarez led Knight to the rear second-floor balcony. Palm fronds swayed against the railing as he edged around a corner.

Suarez turned his head to peek through a window at the group. Suddenly, Knight's latent anger burst forth. He grabbed Gus by the neck and spun him around, slamming him into a wooden shutter.

"What's going on, Gus? Where're you taking me?" Knight whispered loudly.

Suarez held his hands up in surrender. "Easy, amigo, I am your friend. I told you I'm working with Ruiz." His nervous grin changed to a grimace when Knight squeezed his throat, and his words came out in a gaggle. "I was also working for Tony Costas."

"Tony?" Knight cocked his head, trying to grasp the meaning of Gus's statement. He loosened his grip, but he didn't let go. "You're still with the Agency? Talk fast!"

Gus stretched his neck to clear his throat. "Tony had me trying to find out what Harrison Witham has been doing for the last five years. The Agency thought Witham might have gone over to the other side, so I stayed close to him so I could tell Tony what he was up to."

Knight took his hand away. He stared at Gus, bewildered, but Suarez kept talking.

"*Es verdad*. It's true. Witham went psycho in seventy-six. The CIA got rid of him with a psychological disability. Something like posttraumatic stress syndrome from Nam, I think. It was kept very quiet. But Tony had me stay tight with him anyway, to make sure the Agency knew if he decided to turn. I never caught him dirty, but he did a few things that made me suspect he was.

"Whenever I talked to him, he tried to make it sound like he had never broken from the past—it was like he kept living in the early sixties, the Mongoose days. Sometimes he'd come to me with a plan to send us to Cuba for an operation, but I usually talked him out of it. At least I thought I did, until I found out he was behind some actions when the guys didn't come back. Tony had me feed him disinformation so we could trace it and see what he did with it. Then this Fidel thing came up and Tony wanted to play closer to the line—give Witham the real stuff, you know how that's done. It was me who told him about Torres in Spain. And that was only three days before the reunion dinner.

"But I cleared it with Tony first. We figured Witham would really grab that if he had gone bad. He did, and that's what got Tony killed. I'm sure of it now." Gus stared down and scuffed his foot on the wood decking. "But when Witham came to me with *his* plan to kill Fidel, he really threw me. I wasn't sure what to think. But by then—"

"By then I was in the picture," Knight said sharply. "But why did Tony—"

"Please, we're losing time. I can't answer all your questions. You must talk to someone else." Gus turned as the tour group tramped down the staircase. "Come with me," he said, falling in step with the last tourist.

The guide led them through the kitchen and out the back door, toward the two-story carriage house and servants' quarters Hemingway had converted into a second-floor writing studio. When the group stopped to listen to the guide explain the history of a cement-embedded penny by the swimming pool, Knight noticed a man standing under the metal exterior staircase leading to the studio. He looked closer at the face under a weathered crush hat: It was Eric Steiner.

Gus met Knight's glare with a shrug and an easy smile. They moved with the group but stayed behind when the guide took the others up the stairs.

Steiner frowned and tugged at his chin when Knight stood in front of him. "What can I say, David? We had to use you to get to the assassin. We figured he'd try to get to you to find out the message Milian was supposed to deliver to you, but we didn't know how he'd do it. Then Felix mentioned Mexico, and Jennifer said she . . . believe me, we never asked her, never wanted her to go to Mexico with you. She pushed herself into it because of Witham. She really wants him bad." Steiner sighed. "Knight, she's one hell of a woman. I'm sorry it worked out like this."

"You're sorry! You son of a bitch! You played all your deception games and now it comes down to this." Knight took a deep breath to keep his voice low. "Dammit, Steiner, why the hell didn't you just come to me? Why couldn't you be up-front? Why didn't you just get the message from Ruiz and give it to me?"

Steiner looked at Gus, then at Knight. "I wish it could have been that easy, but we knew there was a leak somewhere in Washington. Ruiz said he wouldn't even give it to headquarters; he didn't want it to go anywhere north of Miami. Tony went along with that, but more because he thought you'd tell us to eat shit and get fucked if the Agency asked you to help us . . . because of the polygraph."

Knight smiled wanly. "He was goddamn right."

"I know; I guess I wouldn't have blamed you, either. But I was the only one Tony told, and that wasn't until after that last meeting he had with you."

So Tony was in on it, too. Knight tilted his head back and gazed at the darkening sky. He knew as well as Steiner that this was the way the intelligence community operated. It didn't matter who got caught in the web: Using and manipulating people was simply the method of doing business in the clandestine world of secrets, with deceit and deception both the ways and means and the ultimate objective. And, he remembered, it hadn't been any different when he had been weaving his own looms.

Now, though, he realized he was back in the business, playing for higher stakes than ever before. But he looked back at the CIA men broodingly.

"I've got a lot of questions—"

Steiner cut him off. "Right, but later. Our time's getting short and we've got to move fast."

Steiner's urgency spun Knight's thought to Jennifer, and he wondered where she was being held. Panic crept into his voice.

"What's next, Eric? Where do we go from here?"

Steiner smiled, relieved. "Gus and I will be your closest cover. It's not a good spot—the courthouse—because you'll have to be standing in front of it by yourself. We think we can set up just around the corner and still keep you in view."

"Wait," Knight interrupted. "You know the guy won't have Jennifer with him. And he'll probably send someone to pick me up and take me somewhere else. You've got to have mobile surveillance."

"I know," Steiner said. "That's what makes it tough for us to set up a decent surveillance—not enough street space to park cars, and on those narrow streets we can't let our people just keep walking and driving around the block if the guy doesn't show on time. Even when you're picked up, it's going to be damn hard to stay with you," Steiner said, scowling. Then he continued.

"Look, I'll have Gus stay near you on foot, in the shadows of the building, and put my cars a block away on all four sides of the courthouse block. When you get in the car, I'll radio the description and the direction. One of the cars ought to be on your tail right away, and the others'll fall in close behind."

Knight nodded, but he had a queasy feeling when he brought up the last and most important detail of the plan.

"When I get where he's taking me, then what? What are you going to do? What about Jennifer?"

"We've got that covered, don't worry. We figure he's got her in a house or some kind of building. When you get in, just make sure you make the identification. We'll wait three minutes, then we're going to bombard the house or whatever it is with the loudest rendition of 'La Bamba' that you've ever heard. When you hear that song blasting, grab Jennifer and duck."

"Music?" Knight looked incredulous. "What the hell is rock music supposed to do?"

Steiner grinned. "We got the idea when the marines set up their ghetto blasters around the Papal Nunciate in Panama, where General Noriega was hiding out. It drove him crazy. The priests didn't like it much, either. We've tested it since then; believe me, it works."

"Anything else?" Knight asked, shaking his head glumly.

"Flash grenades," Steiner said. "That's why I told you to get down. After you hear that first guitar, all hell's going to break loose."

THIRTY-SEVEN

Damn, it's darker than I thought it would be, Knight thought. Across the street, an antique lamppost dropped a twelve-foot-diameter pool of yellow light on the corner. But the modern arc light in front of the courthouse was out, and he wondered whether it was just a bad bulb—or the act of his adversary.

He zipped up his jacket and leaned against a granite pillar by the locked glass doors, shielding himself from an upstart gale blowing sheets of cold air from the north. The wind stung his ears when he poked his head around the pillar and noticed the faint outline of Suarez's shadow at the southeast corner of the courthouse. He stretched his wrist toward the lamppost and checked his watch: four minutes to seven. Chilled and shivering from both the wind and his nerves, Knight walked down

356

the courthouse steps to the sidewalk. He stopped four feet from the curb and locked his eyes on the headlights of a car coming toward him.

Gus, Gus! I told you not to back out. Now look at what's going to happen because you turned out to be an informant. And such poor tradecraft, Gus, hiding so close to a target. I'm ashamed of you, with all your experience; I really thought you were better than that. How could you be so careless? It must be your age, Gus. You're making it so easy for me, Harrison Witham mused, glimpsing Suarez pressed to the side of the courthouse wall. He listened, then looked farther and watched a battered Ford rumble past David Knight.

Witham knelt behind a four-foot hibiscus hedge between the courthouse and the house next to it. Straining to see through the branches, he noticed the glowing red power light on the hand radio Suarez held at his side. Witham crept slowly to the hedge opening he had located earlier, then eased through to the courthouse side, less than ten yards behind Suarez. Stepping gently on the grass to avoid crunching twigs and leaves, he crossed to the narrow walkway abutting the courthouse. Then he moved forward in measured paces, crouching, deathly quiet in his rubber-soled shoes. Three yards from Suarez, he raised the silencer threaded onto his Beretta .380 and leveled it at the base of Gus's skull. At one yard, he lowered his left hand, positioning it to catch the hand-held radio before it clattered to the ground.

Suarez's head started to turn, but he never heard the *phfft* from Witham's weapon. Witham grabbed the Cuban's collar with his gun-holding hand and caught the radio with his left when it fell from the dead man's grasp. A trickle of blood began dripping from the small hole in Suarez's neck.

Witham braced the body against his right leg and put the radio into his left jacket pocket. Then he slumped Suarez over his shoulder—to prevent the sound of dragging—and carried him to the rear of the building. He laid the body carefully next to the parking compound's chain-link fence and returned to the spot Steiner had occupied.

"Knight! Quick, get over here!" Witham whispered loudly, confident Knight would not distinguish the low tone of his voice. He backed up six feet, deeper into the shadows, and bent his knees so his shape resembled Suarez's.

Knight edged around the corner, peering down the black corridor. "Gus! What's wrong?"

"C'mere," Witham rasped, backing a few feet farther.

When Knight was enveloped by the darkness, Witham stood to his full height. He held the Beretta so Knight could see it but kept it close to his hip. His teeth were visible when he smiled broadly.

"What? Who are . . ." Shock slipped over Knight's face when he recognized Witham.

"Keep coming, David. We're going for a little ride," Witham said.

"Where . . . where's Gus?"

Witham motioned toward the fence with his pistol. "He's no help to you now, David. And neither is anyone else. Now move it!" he said harshly. He cupped Knight's arm and pushed him through the hedge opening.

"Over there," Witham said, pointing to a black Pontiac parked two houses away, partially hidden by thick gumbo-limbo trees lining an overgrown driveway. When they reached the car, Witham took a roll of silver duct tape from the glove compartment. He pulled Knight's arms behind his back and wrapped his wrists with the tape, sat him in the front seat, and then entered the car on the driver's side, resting the Beretta in his lap.

Witham drove slowly toward the street, craning his neck from side to side. When the car neared the sidewalk, he grabbed Knight's neck and shoved his prisoner down into the leg space.

"Raise your fuckin' head and I'll blow it off," Witham warned. He pulled out of the driveway and turned right, heading west on

Elizabeth Street. When he had gone a block farther, the radio in his pocket crackled with static. He took it out and placed it on the seat near Knight's head.

"Hey, Knight, listen to your buddies. They just figured something went wrong," he said, laughing.

Knight turned his ear to the radio and listened to the excited voices.

"Dolphin, this is Sailfish. Where's our subject?"

"I don't know! He went to the side—"

"Do you see Marlin? He was at the southeast corner—"

"Sailfish, this is Tarpon. It's been too long. I'm closest, I'm moving in."

Knight recognized Tarpon's voice; it was Eric Steiner.

"Roger, Tarpon. We're coming in behind you."

The radio went silent. Knight glanced up at Witham and saw the grin spreading across his face. Knight looked over his shoulder and saw a traffic light overhead and the top of a 7-Eleven convenience store. When Witham turned left, he knew they were going north on Truman Avenue.

"Listen, Knight. This is going to be good," Witham said with obvious glee.

Within seconds, the radio crackled with voices again. The first belonged to Steiner.

"Goddamnit! Marlin's dead! He's been shot!"

"Oh, Jesus, no! . . . Is the subject—"

"No, he's not here. He's gone!"

"Shit, now what—"

"Call Ruiz, get him here. Immediately!" Steiner ordered, breaking the radio code.

Witham turned the volume down. "That's it. They'll never find us now," he said, with smug satisfaction. The humor was gone from his voice and he pushed Knight's head down again.

Knight hunched against the kick panel. He felt his stomach turning and closed his eyes, trying to hold down the wave of nausea rising to his throat, but he couldn't do it. When he retched and gagged, the bitter taste of bile flooded his mouth and yellow spittle dripped from his lips.

"Knight, for Chrissake, take it easy. Don't worry, everything'll be over soon," Witham said with mocking concern. "A few more minutes, that's all."

The Pontiac idled at a red light, then made another left turn. Bright lights suddenly lit up the interior of the car. Looking beyond Witham's head, Knight recognized the tops of tuna towers, the high aluminum lookout structures mounted on charter fishing boats.

We must be passing the Garrison Bight Marina, heading southwest . . . but I'm the only one who knows it, he thought. His mind suddenly shifted to Jennifer and he felt a sharp pain running to every nerve ending of his body. He knew they must be only minutes away, and then . . .

Damn, damn, damn! I've got to do something! But what? How? Think, dammit!

His panic began to give way to a numbing sensation of fear, dulling any thoughts of action. For now, all he could do was stare hopelessly at the radio resting against Witham's thigh.

Witham turned left and shut off the car's lights. The Pontiac bounced on a rutted dirt road, jarring Knight into the dashboard. A minute later, the wheels spun onto pavement and Witham cruised in the dark until he turned off the concrete again. Knight heard the rustle of high weeds brushing the undercarriage and the sides of the vehicle. When it finally rocked to a stop, he strained to see out the windows: Everything around the car was black.

"Welcome to the beginning of your end, David Knight," Witham announced. He exited the Pontiac, walked around the rear, and pulled his passenger out. Knight's arms and shoulders ached from being bound behind his back. His legs buckled, but Witham grabbed his elbow to hold him up, then shoved him forward.

Knight trembled when a chilling blast of wind penetrated his nylon jacket, but he saw a dark shanty looming fifty yards ahead.

Witham prodded him and he stumbled through knee-high weeds, looking up at moaning tall pines whipping in the same scolding wind. But a wafting aroma of brine and drying seaweed filled his nostrils: He knew seawater was somewhere behind the shanty.

The rotted wooden porch creaked as Knight and Witham stepped across it. Witham looked back at the Pontiac, scanning the area, then reached for the white porcelain knob and turned it slowly. He eased the door open and nudged Knight into a large dark room, illuminated only by the distant lights of the Garrison Bight Marina speckling through two broken windows. Inside, the putrid stench of nearby fish carcasses hung thickly in the stale air.

Knight's eyes roamed the room, trying to focus on dark shadows. His heart pounded when he saw a female shape slumped on a chair. He started to move toward it, but a blinding flashlight beam suddenly splashed in his face. As he ducked his head to shield his eyes, he heard a deep voice rumble across the room from the far wall.

"Well! So this is the elusive David Knight!" Jorge said. "You have been a most challenging quarry. But finally, you are in my snare."

THIRTY-EIGHT

Jorge doused the flashlight and stepped forward swiftly and silently, like a jungle cat approaching its prey for the kill. He wore a black sweatshirt, sleeves pushed to his elbows, black pants, and black sneakers. A Heckler & Koch 9mm P7 was dwarfed in his right hand, but he held it down at his side. He stopped less than two feet in front of Knight and drew back his shoulders, expanding his barrel chest.

"Harrison, please," he said, motioning Witham away from Knight.

"*Permiso*, Mr. Knight. I believe a formal introduction is necessary: I am Colonel Jorge Posada, of the Cuban Intelligence General Directorate—the DGI, as you so well know." He slipped the P7 into his belt behind his back, then pointed at the woman in the chair. In the dim light, Knight noticed the circular scar around Posada's extended forearm. It was the same scar he had seen on the forearm of the man Miguel Torres met in The Rum Barrel in 1984.

Jorge continued, "I am certain you have been worried about Miss Ferrer. Do not be concerned; I treated her quite gently. She is merely drowsy from a mild sedative I administered." He walked to the south window, then turned back to Knight.

"Of course, I must assume that you are aware of my mission. In less than forty-eight hours, Fidel Castro will be dead . . . and the entire world will be in turmoil. Actually, what you—we—will see is another revolution, an overthrow of the attempt by misguided Soviets to impose glasnost on the socialist countries. Already, we have seen food shortages, strikes and rioting, and massive unrest rip the fabric of our society. Communism must be resurrected; only then will stability be restored. The assassination of Fidel will begin that restoration," Jorge said, returning to gaze out of the window.

"David!" Jennifer cried out. She stood up quickly, panic in her eyes.

Startled, Knight turned sharply and saw Witham fondling her hair and neck. When Knight took a step toward them, Witham looked at him menacingly.

"Harrison, move away from the girl," Jorge ordered.

Witham obeyed the command and Knight hurried to Jennifer. As she grabbed his arm, he turned so she could see the duct tape around his wrists.

"Are you all right?" Knight asked.

"Yes . . . he didn't hurt me. But my head," she said, twisting her neck from left to right. "Are you—"

"I'm fine," he lied, glowering at Witham for putting his hands on Jennifer. Anger suddenly consumed him when he thought of his obvious impotence. He kept staring at the tall Texan, trying to think of a tactic to get the pistol away from him. If Knight had a weapon, anything, he could . . .

The radio! The goddamn radio! he thought. It was still in Witham's pocket. He had stared at it when he was in the car with

Witham, examining every knob, switch, and dial. It was the same model used by the Miami Police Department.

Knight remembered the day at the FBI office when a visiting police sergeant's radio had gone off, startling the sergeant and the agents around him. The sergeant explained that their radios contained a transponder chip, enabling the police dispatcher to pinpoint the exact location of the radio. It was designed for officer safety, the sergeant had said, but he also had joked that it kept the cops from engaging in personal pleasures while they were on duty.

Now, glancing again at Witham's jacket, Knight felt cold determination charge through his body. Somehow, he had to stall; it was the only chance. With enough time, Ruiz and Steiner—if they knew about the transponder chip—might locate them before it was too late.

Knight finally found a weapon: his words. He looked at Jorge Posada and grinned.

"Colonel, I hate to disillusion you, but you're so far out in left field, it's laughable. A revolution because Fidel is assassinated? You are absolutely *crazy* if you think anyone in the world will even give a damn. If you and your cowboy friend here kill him, it won't make a goddamn bit of difference. No one gives a shit about Fidel anymore; he's an anachronistic pain in everyone's ass."

Witham raised his pistol and started toward Knight, but Jorge held up his hand.

"Let him speak, Harrison. These will be his last words. He is entitled to them," Jorge said icily.

Knight and Jennifer exchanged worried glances, but Knight knew he had to keep talking. He raised his voice and continued.

"Look, do you honestly think Fidel going down is going to stop President Bush from selling wheat to the Russians? Will McDonald's stop selling Big Macs in Moscow? Will Pepsi-Cola shut down its bottling plants in Kiev, Murmansk, or wherever they are? Forget it, Colonel. Even if your little act makes the front page of *The New York Times* and *The Washington Post*, the next day that paper wraps garbage. No one will care if Fidel is gone, don't you see that? You missed the boat; it left a long time ago and now it's sinking so fast, neither you, Witham, nor anyone else involved in your stupid scheme can swim fast enough to catch up." He forced a small laugh, then said, "If you ask me, your plan stinks worse than this fish house. I think you're both nuts."

Witham moved forward in a blur and jammed the heavy silencer into Knight's groin. Knight went down on one knee, pain piercing through to his spine, shaking his head. Jennifer jumped from the chair and held his shoulders for an instant, then stood up and spat on Witham's chest.

"You little shit!" Witham roared. He slapped her face and she tumbled over the chair. "I'm gonna hang you on one of those hooks and beat the hell out of you." He pointed to a long row of six-inch fish-drying prongs protruding from the wall just three feet behind Jennifer.

"Enough!" Jorge barked. Then he lowered his voice, directing it at Witham. "The helicopter is coming soon for our rendezvous in the Gulf. I have the coordinates, but I must ready the boat."

Knight stood up, and Jennifer clung to him tightly. Jorge turned to them and spoke calmly.

"Your point is not without a grain of validity, Mr. Knight. Obviously, however, I must disagree with you. And unfortunately, I have no time to debate those issues with a man of such cunning intelligence. I have a job to do." Jorge paced to the window again and gazed into the sky. Havana was just ninety miles south of the cloud cover breaking high above. When he turned, a sardonic smile curled his lips.

"Perhaps you are correct, my friend. Who knows? But we both know our respective tasks are but a small part of a grand game. Sometimes we win, sometimes we lose. Yet the game always goes on. You were a most formidable opponent, Mr. Knight, one of the best I ever played against. For that, I give you my respect and admiration," Jorge said, bowing his head to Knight. He started to walk to the back door, but stopped abruptly and looked back curiously at David.

"One final question, Mr. Knight: the message from Victor Milian? You may as well tell me, now that it is of no consequence. What was it?"

"You haven't figured that out? It took me a while, too, but I'm disappointed in you, Colonel." Knight smiled wryly. "There never *was* a 'message' . . . at least not verbal or written . . . *I* was the message."

Jorge stared at Knight with a puzzled look. "I don't understand—"

"It was a plant, a goddamn deception. Ruiz made it up to get you to think Milian had something to tell me about the plot to kill Fidel. But the message never existed. He wanted the assassin—he didn't know your identity then—to believe that I knew something that could blow your operation. It was just a ploy, designed to draw you into coming after me. Ruiz figured that when you did, he'd catch the assassin—you, Colonel."

Jorge's eyes flared at Knight and his lips drew tight. He nodded, but said nothing until he looked at Witham.

"Finish the job, Harrison," he snapped. "I will be waiting." Frigid air blew into the room as Jorge slipped into the cold, black night, leaving the back door. As it creaked on one hinge, light from the marina splayed into the room.

"Well, folks, I guess this is it. Time to say good-bye," Witham said, but he focused on Jennifer. "Oh, before I go, I wanted to apologize to you, little lady. About your mother, I mean. It was just one of those things I had to do. Knight, you know how that goes." Witham bared his teeth with an evil smile.

"You bastard," Jennifer muttered.

Knight felt her push tighter against his chest as Witham stepped forward, pointing the silencer where their bodies pressed together. With her arm behind his back, she dug her fingernails furiously into the tape around his wrists. He felt it loosening, but he knew it was too late.

Suddenly, the room's walls erupted with the blaring sounds of a thousand Mexican guitars. Witham's eyes widened with surprise. He whirled around, disoriented from the song's rollicking voices, and tripped on the chair Jennifer had knocked over. As he fought to maintain his balance, the Beretta slipped from his hand and clattered on the wooden planks. Witham bent down, frantically searching for the pistol.

Knight spread his elbows and flexed his shoulders, trying to tear the duct tape apart before Witham found the gun. He turned to Jennifer for help, but she was creeping toward Witham, whose attention was still directed at the floor. She crouched low and crept in front of him. Suddenly, she was under his torso. Pulling her arms back, she shot up and forward, driving her fists into the soft tissue beneath the clavicle on each side of his neck. The blow lifted Witham off his heels and shot him backward, arms spread-eagled, slamming his head and shoulders into the wall.

Suddenly, the blinding light of flash grenades painted the room in brilliant white streaks, cascading like fireworks on the Fourth of July. Knight spotted the Beretta and grabbed it off the floor, raising it at Witham. He started to squeeze the trigger but stopped, stunned by the image of the KGB double agent. Witham was cast in a ghostly glow, eyes bulging, mouth agape, chin drooping, leaning lifeless against the wall—Jennifer's jolting blow had impaled Witham on a six-inch fish-hanging hook between his shoulder blades.

The music outside abruptly ceased, and the room became eerily silent as it faded to dark again.

Knight looked at Jennifer and put the pistol in his waistband. She was kneeling on the floor, with her hands on her thighs, breathing deeply. When he reached for her, she raised one arm and pointed to the back door. He turned toward it before she spoke.

"Get Posada, David. Stop him," she gasped.

A helicopter thudded overhead, crisscrossing the shanty with its powerful spotlight. As it blared a loudspeaker message of "Federal agents!" footsteps trampled on the front porch amid voices shouting orders. The front door flew off its hinges when Eladio Ruiz and Eric Steiner crashed into the room and ran to Jennifer. But David Knight was gone.

Knight heard the government chopper when he was thirty yards from the shanty, but the guttural beating of twin outboard engines sputtering to life kept him running. Guided by the sound, he thrashed through the thick weeds until his lungs screamed for oxygen. He stopped when he saw the water, chest heaving, one hand holding his side against the pain ripping through it.

A broad channel flowed west a quarter of a mile, expanding where it joined the open water of the Gulf of Mexico. Knight saw smoke plumes from the twin engines billowing into the black sky, and he jogged ahead twenty yards. Kneeling behind a scrub palmetto bush, he watched Jorge Posada unwinding the stern line of a sleek ocean-racing Cigarette from a cleat on a narrow forty-foot dock.

Knight rose and started toward the dock, but a sudden wave of vertigo blurred his eyes. As he blinked, the boat and dock seemed to spin. Sweat poured from his face, neck, and back. His legs trembled and he felt as if heavy roots were wrapping around his ankles, tying him to this spot of terror. He lifted one foot and stumbled, falling on his stomach, gasping for breath, clutching handfuls of saw grass to keep the ground from whirling. His aquaphobia had struck viciously.

No! No! Go away, not now! he cried silently. Get up, Knight! You have to get up! You can't stop now!

Still holding the saw grass, Knight pushed his shoulders up and shook his head. He focused on Posada, trying to clear his double vision, and saw the colonel bending over the bowline cleat. Once that was free, Posada would be gone.

Knight dragged his knees under himself for balance, then

brought each foot flat on the ground. The pounce position gave him a fragile and momentary sense of stability. But that instant was all Knight needed. He filled his lungs and sprang forward, racing for the dock.

Posada had cleared the bowline and had the rope in his hand when Knight thundered on the dock's wooden planks. He turned, shocked, and tried to hunch his body into a fighter's crouch, but Knight drove his shoulder into Posada's thighs with a tackle that slammed him on his back.

Face-to-face on top of the Cuban, Knight raised his fist, but Posada grabbed his arm and twisted it away. Grappling with flailing arms and legs, they stood and fell again, rolling near the edge of the dock until Posada straddled Knight, pinning his arms with his knees. Knight's head hung off the dock, bent backward to the water. With one hand squeezing Knight's throat, Posada reached for the loose bowline and furiously circled it around Knight's neck.

Knight tried to push Posada's legs away, but he felt his strength ebbing as Posada yanked the rope tighter. His consciousness was fading from the constricting pressure on his throat. He gagged, fighting to keep life-sustaining oxygen flowing to his brain. His eyes opened and closed as he weakened, but he looked into the sky and saw the clouds parting. Just as everything began to go black, he noticed three stars in a line. That's Orion's belt, he thought. The last thing I'll ever see.

Suddenly, blood and tissue spattered Knight's face and the tightness around his neck slackened. He looked up at Posada and saw the Cuban agent's black eyes bulge wide and freeze in a death mask. Then Posada keeled to the side, rolling off Knight. Knight edged back on the dock, gasping and coughing, and stared at the back of Posada's head. Nearly half of his skull was gone, exposing shredded brain tissue. Blood pooled beneath his ear and spread across the wood, dripping between the planks.

Knight was still sitting, looking at the dead assassin, when Ruiz and Steiner came up behind him. He turned when he felt a hand touch his shoulder, and he noticed Steiner holding an M16 with a night-vision scope. Ruiz took Knight's elbow and helped him to his feet.

"It's over, David," Ruiz said, almost whispering. "You've done your job."

THIRTY-NINE

A clean, gentle breeze swayed the drapes at the sides of the wide-open sliding glass door in the Pier House suite. Muted voices drifted from two sailboats, cabins lit, moored fifty yards off the beach below. At the poolside bar, a guitar player sent the sounds of a soft samba into the night air.

Knight sat in a cushioned wicker chair, feet propped up on a round low table, holding a vodka and tonic, eyes focused on a star-sparkled sky. Ruiz and Steiner shared a bottle of Johnnie Walker Black at a larger table, talking in low voices. The three men looked up when Jennifer came out of the bathroom and sat on the couch near Knight's chair.

"Posada said this was a game, a goddamn game that never ends." Knight said, rising to stand in the open door. "He was right, wasn't he? You guys never stop; you never miss a pitch."

He flung his glass as far as he could, watching it arc and then plummet into the water near a sailboat.

Steiner glanced at Jennifer, then looked at Knight's back. "Sure, some people call it a game; some call it a job. Jorge was a consummate professional, a major leaguer. He knew how to do his job, but it was our job to strike him out. And, with your help, we did. What's wrong with that?" He paused for a breath, not waiting for Knight to answer.

"Christ, David, you were in the business long enough, maybe you've got your own name for it. Whatever you want to call it, I guess we do play—with people, groups, leaders, countries—hell, the world's our fucking playground. That's the way it is, you know that. We try to keep what we do in the shadows, but when we screw up, someone always shoves it down our throats. When we do some good—like tonight—no one knows. They're not supposed to. So what's the goddamn problem? Why're you so pissed off?"

Knight turned, anger in his tired eyes. "You don't know? Dammit, this time I was just one of your toys! Jesus, it was my life, Eric—"

Steiner cut him off. "Not a toy, Knight, not even a goddamn pawn. Maybe you don't see it, but you were a player the whole time. Sure we used you, but think about it this way: You could've walked away from the playing field anytime. You didn't; you stayed in even when you had the chance to quit. That was your decision, friend." He sipped his drink and set the glass on the table.

Steiner lowered his voice when he continued. "We knew we couldn't persuade you or force you to get involved with the Agency—after the polygraph setup. Hell, Tony never really wanted to use you at all. He thought we could keep you out on the fringe, safe and away from the action. But after Witham had him killed, we knew we'd have to bring you into it. So we manufactured situations that would make you want to keep on going. And we figured that you might—probably would—want to call it quits if you knew the CIA was involved. That's why we put Jennifer in your office, before Tony was murdered, just to see how you'd react if we had to bring you in. But she never knew the real reason, believe me.

"Look, we *had* to play it till the last inning. That was my call. You know I won't apologize to you now or in ten years. It worked . . . and we both know that's all that counts in this game." He stepped closer when he saw Knight's face droop with fatigue.

"But why *me*?" Knight said without looking up. "Why did you front *me* out for your goddamn operation?"

"Why?" Steiner sighed. "Because you were the link between Estevez and Torres. They were your informants; you knew more about them than anyone else. Think, David: If you were KGB, wouldn't you figure that David Knight knew something about the DLN, just because of your relationship with Miguel? That made you the logical target; you fit the profile. All we had to do was drop a hint to the KGB that you knew something about the assassination plot. Once they sniffed that, they had to go after you to find out what it was."

Knight met Steiner's eyes. "It was all so simple for you, wasn't it? When the Bureau tapped me to bring Estevez back from Cuba, you already knew he was a double. But you were afraid he'd come to me with information about Miguel and the DLN, and you didn't want the FBI to know about your sacred arrangement with Fidel's secret crew. You were afraid the Bureau would raise holy hell if they found out, so you used the polygraph to nail me to the cross, to get me out of it and to keep your goddamn secret safe." Clenching his hands, Knight turned his back to Steiner and shook his head.

"Right. You were the sacrificial lamb, David," Steiner said, then raised his voice. "But that was part of their plan, dammit, getting Estevez to tell you that the Agency never told the Bureau about the DLN and that Miguel Torres, one of *your* assets, was a member of the DLN. If the KGB got the Bureau and the Agency ripping at each other's throats about the DLN, then they'd have an open field to run their assassination plan. They would have run circles around us while we were fighting with each other. We couldn't let that happen, not with a bigger fish—Posada—to catch.

"Look, you had your own reasons, whatever they were, to keep playing." Steiner touched his arm. "But the honchos at CIA headquarters made a decision to throw you out of the game because they thought Estevez would screw up our operation with the DLN. They thought you might be a liability, so they got rid of you. Bad decision? Who knows? They always pull that shit and someone always pays the price. So what else is new?" Steiner shrugged his shoulders and squinted at Knight.

"But let me ask you this, David: Can you tell me that you never used people, that you never made a bad decision, that you never got someone to do something he didn't want to do, that no one ever got hurt, I mean *really* hurt—like killed—because of something you did?"

Steiner walked back to the table and poured another drink. Knight stared at the floor; three sets of eyes stared at him. He thought of Paul Singer and felt Steiner's words like a blow crushing his neck and shoulders. He went to the couch and sat next to Jennifer, resting his elbows on his knees, head in his hands. Jennifer shot a glare at Ruiz.

The colonel spoke from his chair. "Eric was telling the truth about Jennifer, I assure you. We had no choice but to spin the web around her, also. The risk was too great to leave anything to chance. But to merely say I am sorry for the terrible experiences you went through is a gross understatement of my deepest feelings." He nodded sympathetically to Jennifer but directed his words to Knight.

"This is a very difficult business for a man of ideals, for a romantic who tries to maintain his strong belief in right against wrong, good versus evil, saints fighting devils. You try to live with secrets, hoping you can trust others but wondering when you will be betrayed. Yet at times, you find it expedient and necessary to betray those who trusted you. You often believe you are fighting for the truth, only to find you are battling against it. If you achieve your objective, you receive no credit; if you fail, you get no help—or worse." He glanced at Steiner, then continued.

"If it is a game, my friends, it is played in an arena of mirrors. And unless you are willing to watch cynicism invade your soul, working in the shadows is a trying, wrenching experience. I know men of deep conscience suffer greatly; I have seen it happen to such men before." Ruiz stood and paced to the open window, hands clasped behind his back. He spoke without turning around.

"But even in this looking-glass world, strange ironies often make me wonder if some aspects of our lives are not in fact predetermined. The older I become, the more I find myself looking at past experiences with what might be called a fatalistic viewpoint." He reached in his pocket, unfolded a piece of paper, and looked at Knight.

"Miguel gave us the idea for our code name for you: El Lanza, The Lance. But the night before we met in your apartment, I was quite apprehensive, concerned about your reaction, questioning whether you would agree to go on with us. I stayed up late, reading, and came across this." He held up the paper. "It is a copy of a letter Ché Guevara wrote to his parents in 1965, just before he left to begin organizing the DLN. I found this passage most interesting: 'Once again I feel beneath my heels the ribs of Rosinante. I return to the road with *my lance* under my arm.'" Ruiz looked up. "Rosinante, of course, was the horse of Don Quixote. But it is the word *lance* that I find a most unusual coincidence. Or is it?"

Knight glanced up, puzzled. He rose and walked to Ruiz, took the paper from the colonel's outstretched hand, and read it slowly, then handed it back. When he returned to Jennifer, his face was solemn, but he didn't sit down.

Steiner stepped to Knight and draped his arm around David's shoulder. "Maybe it won't turn out so badly, old buddy. The people at our headquarters—yours and mine—are willing to take you back . . . either agency. I pushed that through after we talked at the Hemingway House. Full reinstatement and back pay, and a promotion. You'd probably be able to name your slot, any position you want, you name it, that's what they told me. Shit, Knight, you'd be back in the game, but right at the top. Not bad, huh?" He tapped Knight's bicep with his fist.

"And remember, Ruiz is going to need someone at the top he can trust when he starts his own operation to get rid of Fidel. That could be any day, the way things are going. Hell, David, you'd be a natural for that if—"

Knight wheeled around, pulling away from Steiner. "Eric, give it up. Get serious. Don't shove that patronizing bullshit at me. Even if I wanted to, do you think I could still operate without looking over my shoulder every other minute, waiting for some jackass bureaucrat to pull my chain? How the hell could I ever live down everything your people and the Bureau said about me? Do you honestly believe I could get their trust back? Or that I should trust them? Do you really think I'd even want to try?" Knight wiped his brow, breathing heavily. The breeze and the guitar player had stopped. No one else spoke. Knight broke the silence, but his voice was calmer.

"Nice try, Eric, but not very smooth. Tell the boys I won't play. Tell them I'm not going to crawl into their cage where they can keep a lid and a leash on me. But tell them not to worry. I'm finished; I've had enough. I won't make any problems. You stay in the game—you're made for it. I'm not . . . not in Miami, not in Washington, not anywhere." Knight walked to Jennifer and smiled, then turned back to Ruiz and Steiner.

"Now, gentlemen, if you'll excuse me, Jennifer and I would like to be alone," Knight said, pointing to the door. Steiner looked puzzled and shook his head, but Ruiz motioned him to start walking. Ruiz opened the door to let Steiner pass through, then looked at Knight.

"Remember, David, about the game. It is never over. Never," Ruiz said. He tipped his head at Jennifer, then stepped into the hallway to catch up to Steiner.

Knight shut the door and leaned against it, closing his eyes. He took a deep breath and exhaled slowly. When he looked up, Jennifer was standing at the open window. He walked to her and wrapped his arms around her waist from behind, nuzzling her neck. The night air dampened her skin.

Jennifer gazed at the two sailboats. "I still don't understand, David. Steiner was right when he said you kept on going, even when you could have backed out. No one made you stay involved, but you did. Why? Do *you* even know that answer?"

He knew it all too well, and that was why he wouldn't respond to her question. He couldn't admit to her that deep within himself he knew he was addicted to the games men like Steiner played, and that he wasn't certain that even she could pull him away from that craving. And now, though he desperately yearned to leave his scarred past behind, he wondered whether he could ever make a final break with it. He knew the last statement Ruiz had made was bitterly true: The game never ends.

Knight kissed Jennifer's cheek and tightened his arms around her waist. He raised his face to the stars, searching. Ruiz's comment lingered for an instant, then faded from his mind.

"See those three stars in a line? They're the belt of Orion, the biggest constellation in this hemisphere. Orion is the hunter. Some people think of him as a protector. Those other stars make up his bow and arrow, and they're pointed at—"

"I don't think I want to hear about Orion now. He'll be around for a long time. And so will we." She turned and slid her arms around his neck. Then she kissed him long and softly, pushing him into the room.

He stopped, holding her shoulders, and looked deeply into her green eyes. "Remember when you told me the only things you wanted from life were sunsets and paydays? Tomorrow night, we'll go down to Mallory Square and watch the most beautiful sunset you've ever seen. And then we'll think about paydays."